AF823941

Select praise for internationally bestselling author Rachel Reid

"Reid's hockey-themed Game Changers series continues on its red-hot winning streak with this excellent fourth installment. . . . With this irresistible mix of sports, sex, and romance, Reid has scored another hat trick."

—*Publishers Weekly*, starred review

"It's a gorgeous May/December romance between a silver-fox goalie close to retirement, and a bartender sixteen years his junior; it's tender, funny, emotional and hot as hell."

—All About Romance

"I straight up loved it. Sexy and smart, it features a May-December, opposites attract pairing that kept me glued to the pages the first, second, and third time I read it. . . . The Game Changers series is a game changer in sports romance (wink!), and firmly ensconced in my top five sports series of all time."

—*All About Romance*, Best Books of 2020

"*Common Goal* is a fervent, tender, seductive treat by Reid that is another wonderful addition to what is ultimately turning out to be an absolutely fantastic Game Changers series."

—What's Better Than Books

Also available from Rachel Reid

Time to Shine

The Shots You Take

The Game Changers Series

Game Changer

Heated Rivalry

Tough Guy

Common Goal

Role Model

The Long Game

Unrivaled

COMMON GOAL

RACHEL REID

HARLEQUIN

Recycling programs
for this product may
not exist in your area.

ISBN-13: 978-1-335-00411-6

Common Goal

First published in 2020. This edition published in 2026.

Copyright © 2020 by Rachelle Goguen

Stock Images: © pyty/stock.adobe.com (Map); © Міша Герба/stock.adobe.com (Hockey sticks)
Illustrations by Monika Roe (Beer glass).

All rights reserved. No part of this book may be used or reproduced in any manner whatsoever without written permission.

Without limiting the exclusive rights of any author, contributor or the publisher of this publication, any unauthorized use of this publication to train generative artificial intelligence (AI) technologies is expressly prohibited. Harlequin also exercises their rights under Article 4(3) of the Digital Single Market Directive 2019/790 and expressly reserves this publication from the text and data mining exception.

This is a work of fiction. Names, characters, places and incidents are either the product of the author's imagination or are used fictitiously. Any resemblance to actual persons, living or dead, businesses, companies, events or locales is entirely coincidental.

For questions and comments about the quality of this book, please contact us at CustomerService@Harlequin.com.

® is a trademark of Harlequin Enterprises ULC.

Harlequin Enterprises ULC
22 Adelaide St. West, 41st Floor
Toronto, Ontario M5H 4E3, Canada
www.Harlequin.com

HarperCollins Publishers
Macken House, 39/40 Mayor Street Upper,
Dublin 1, D01 C9W8, Ireland
www.HarperCollins.com

Printed in the United Kingdom

26 27 28 29 CPI 10 9 8 7 6 5 4 3

This book is for Matt, Mitchell and Trevor.
Thank you for giving me the space to write this book, and I'm sorry it took so long!

Dear Reader,

My only hope when *Game Changer* was first published in October 2018 was for at least one person to read my book and love my characters.

It was the very beginning of what would become an amazing adventure. With each book that was published in the Game Changers series, I received more love from readers. When the *Heated Rivalry* television series based on those books debuted in November 2025, my characters received more love than I could have ever thought possible. I am truly, enormously blessed and grateful for that love and for my readers.

I wrote these books as a lifelong hockey fan, and as someone who wants the culture of the sport I love to be better. The series is based on an idea: that the bravery of one person could create a ripple effect that benefits others and eventually leads to real change. Each book focuses on at least one hockey player, and the man who makes him braver. Stoic New York captain Scott Hunter is charmed by cute and clever history student Kip Grady. Weary Toronto defenseman Ryan Price reunites with bold and beautiful musician Fabian Salah. Distinguished New York goaltender Eric Bennett falls for witty young bartender Kyle Swift. Miserable Ottawa forward Troy Barrett learns how to smile with adorable social media manager Harris Drover. And, of course, despite their best efforts, Shane Hollander and Ilya Rozanov couldn't stop themselves from falling in love with each other.

I love each and every one of these characters, and as I write this letter in February 2026, it feels like the whole world loves them too. It's an incredible feeling, and I'm very aware that none of what I'm experiencing now would have happened without the enthusiastic support from the early fans of my books. The success of the Game Changers series was largely driven simply by readers recommending the books to their friends and online followers. It was driven by booksellers and librarians, by reviewers and bloggers, and by BookTokers and Bookstagrammers. I will always remember and appreciate that support.

Thank you for the love, and I hope you enjoy having these beautiful special editions on your shelves.

Love,
Rachel

COMMON GOAL

CHAPTER ONE

"I'm going to be thinking about that all night," Eric Bennett confessed. "Should've had that one."

His goal posts, as always, didn't reply.

Eric grabbed his bottle off the top of the net, then squirted some water into his mouth before glancing up at the scoreboard screen, where they were showing the goal that had just sailed past him. It looked even worse in slow motion.

"We'll get the next one, right, guys?" Eric tapped each of the goal posts with his stick, then shook out his shoulders. It was now 3–1 for the opposing team and still only the first period. This game was a disaster. Eric could imagine what the commentators were saying on television about him right now. That Eric Bennett couldn't keep up with the pace of the NHL these days. That he was past his prime, and ready for retirement.

Fuck them. They'd been saying that about Eric for almost ten years now. Every time he had an off game, or a minor injury, it was time to put him out to pasture. As if Eric hadn't had off games when he'd been twenty-six and winning every goaltending award. As if he hadn't, at the tender age of thirty-eight, played a major part in winning the Stanley Cup with the New York Admirals three seasons ago.

The Admirals' captain, Scott Hunter, skated up to him and tapped his pads. "Tough one, Benny. You good?"

"I'm good. I'm shutting the door now. Think you've got a couple of goals in you?"

"Absolutely."

Eric crouched forward, ready for play to resume. "Nothing else is getting past me tonight," he promised himself.

The promise lasted exactly one minute and forty-three seconds. That was when Shane Hollander, the stupid goddamned superstar forward for Montreal, fired a textbook perfect shot that flew over Eric's left shoulder.

Fuck.

Eric glanced at the bench and was not at all surprised to see Coach Murdock gesturing at him to come to the bench. He could also see New York's other goaltender, Tommy Andersson, putting on his mask.

Fuck!

"Sorry, guys," Eric told his posts. "I guess I'm watching the rest of this one. Be nice to Tommy."

He skated toward the bench with his head down. He could hear the crowd's weak applause, which was maybe a showing of support for Eric, or maybe relief that he was being replaced.

Tommy tapped Eric's pads as he passed him. "Don't worry about it, Benny."

Eric didn't reply, because of course he was going to worry about it. Not just this game, but the whole rest of this season.

Which could very well be the whole rest of Eric's career. Eric's teammates greeted him with cautious words of support as he plopped down on the bench. He hauled his mask off and gave it to the equipment manager, who handed Eric an Admirals ball cap to wear instead. Eric hated wearing ball caps. They looked weird on his head.

Play resumed, and Tommy, barely warmed up, had to stop two quick shots. He stopped both, which earned him a roar of approval from the crowd. Tommy was a good goalie. Too good to be Eric's backup, and everyone knew it. Eric was sure Tommy had only stuck with the Admirals this long because he was waiting for Eric to retire. Maybe this entire team was waiting for Eric to retire.

His wife hadn't waited.

Eric frowned. It wasn't a fair thing to say or even think. Holly had had plenty of reasons for ending their marriage, and he understood all of them. He had known for years that their marriage hadn't been working; the spark that had been there in their youth had died a long time ago. Eric had told himself that his schedule was to blame, and that he and Holly would have a chance to fall back in love once he retired. Maybe she had hoped for that too for a while, but the truth they both eventually acknowledged was that they probably never were going to fall back in love. Their best years as a couple were behind them, and it was time to move on. Eric knew their divorce was the best thing for them both. Knowing it didn't make him feel any less lonely, though.

His teammates didn't talk to him much for the rest of the game, even during the intermissions in the locker room. They knew he preferred to be left alone for now. Tommy played a hell of a game, stopping all but one of Montreal's shots on goal, but the Admirals still lost by two goals in the end.

Long after the game had ended, and after Coach Murdock had talked to the team—which included praising Tommy for his efforts—Eric was sitting in his stall wearing half of his navy Ted Baker suit. The shirt collar was unbuttoned, and his tie hung loose and open around his bent neck. He absently rotated his wedding ring, which he couldn't quite bring himself to stop wearing.

"Hey."

Eric didn't need to raise his head to know that Scott Hunter had sat himself next to him. "Hi."

"You doing okay? I mean, besides the game tonight. Anything bothering you?"

Nope. Being freshly divorced and staring down the barrel of my forty-first birthday is awesome. "No. Just an off game."

Scott clapped him on the shoulder. "You'll be back on top in the next game."

Eric nodded. He would make sure of it.

"You're coming tomorrow night, right?" Scott asked.

As much as Eric did not feel like going to an engagement party for Scott and his fiancé, Kip, he forced a smile and said, "Definitely. Of course. Can't wait."

Scott beamed at him. Scott had been doing a lot of smiling in the past couple of years since he'd fallen in love with Kip Grady. It had been a lonely, closeted life for Scott before he'd decided to risk it all for a chance at happiness with the man he'd met in a smoothie shop. Eric was one of the first people that Scott had come out to, and Eric didn't take that lightly. He was thrilled for Scott, even if the institution of marriage hadn't been Eric's favorite thing lately.

"Good," Scott said, still smiling. "Let's put this game behind us, all right? And we'll all have fun tomorrow night."

Eric gave him a wry smile. "Even me?"

Scott laughed. "Even you, Benny. I'll make sure of it."

Kyle Swift glanced across the table for the millionth time that morning. He couldn't help it. These study dates with Kip were always completely unproductive for him. He spent far more time studying Kip's face than his own notes.

Kip was engrossed in something on his laptop, his hazel eyes darting back and forth as he read. He had dark stubble on his cheeks and jaw today, which Kyle liked, even though it made Kip's dimples less noticeable. And, oof. Kyle had spent too much of the past couple of years contemplating those dimples.

Kip's face turned up, and Kyle quickly dropped his gaze to his own laptop screen.

Kyle wasn't sure why he tortured himself like this. Just because he and Kip were both working on their MA degrees in history didn't mean they needed to have these ridiculous study dates. They weren't even going to the same university. Kyle would spend most of their first hour together stealing glances at Kip, and then Kip would get bored and start asking Kyle questions that had nothing to do with their academic pursuits. It was the conversations that always did Kyle in. The easy way they talked to each other and laughed together, because they had so many things in common. Because Kip was funny and warm and a total sweetheart. Because he was absolutely perfect for Kyle in all the ways the men Kyle usually dated weren't.

Too bad Kip was engaged.

"Kyle?"

Kyle glanced up and was attacked by one of Kip's cute, dimply smiles.

"Hey, there you are. I'm going to get a refill." Kip waved his empty coffee mug in the air. "You want one?"

"Actually," Kyle said slowly, "I need to get going."

"Oh." Kip frowned.

"But I'll see you at the party tonight."

Kip's smile returned. "I can't believe I'm engaged!"

"I don't know what you see in that guy," Kyle said dryly.

Kip sighed dramatically. "I know. But a man reaches a certain age, sometimes he has to settle, y'know?"

"Twenty-eight. Is that the age you mean?"

"I don't want to be a spinster."

"It's kind of you to marry that gorgeous millionaire athlete."

"I know," Kip said solemnly. "I'm very brave."

They both laughed, and Kyle did his best to ignore the ache in his heart.

"Maybe you'll meet *your* future husband tonight," Kip suggested playfully.

"Uh-huh. I'll see you later." Kyle shoved his laptop into his backpack and slung the bag over his shoulder.

"Your dream man might be there! Keep an open mind."

My dream man will definitely *be there. That's kind of the problem.* Which, of course, Kyle did not say. Instead he said, "I'll wear something nice just in case."

"You always look nice."

Kyle's heart clenched. "Don't make Scott jealous."

Kip snorted like that was the most absurd idea in the world. Kyle supposed it was. Anyone—Scott included—could see that Kip only had eyes for his husband-to-be.

Kyle flipped the hood of his sweatshirt up to protect his hair and glasses from the drizzle outside. He supposed he could use the party tonight as inspiration to finally, and firmly, close the door on this pointless crush on Kip Grady. Kyle had volunteered to work the bar tonight, mostly because it would give him something to do other than listen to his heart shrivel and die while Kip and Scott smooshed their perfect faces together.

This would be it, Kyle decided as he hurried down the stairs to the subway. Tonight he would stop pining for Kip and maybe have fun making straight hockey players uncomfortable by flirting with them. And then he would focus his efforts on finding a nice, available, and, most importantly, *appropriate* man to live happily ever after with.

Or a cute guy with a tight ass. Whichever.

CHAPTER TWO

Kyle had never been so disappointed by a gay bar full of hot men.

He had spent a lot of time in gay bars. A lot of time in *this* bar in particular. The Kingfisher had been his main source of income for years, and he'd flirted with a vast array of hot men in this very room during that time. He'd gone home with a decent percentage of them. Tonight the Kingfisher was celebrating the engagement of two gay men, yet was packed with straight dudes. Hockey players, mostly.

Extremely attractive hockey players. And their wives.

Water, water everywhere . . .

Kyle sighed and poured a lager for the zillionth time that evening. The hockey players were not adventurous in their choice of alcoholic beverages. He set the pint glass on the bar and offered a smile to the tall, scruffy millionaire athlete who took the beer without even a glance at Kyle.

Straight men. God.

There was a time when meeting even one NHL star would have been exciting, but since Scott Hunter had become a regular at the Kingfisher, and since Kyle had become friends with

Kip, New York Admirals players had become commonplace in Kyle's life. Boring, even.

"Having fun?" Kyle's co-worker, Aram, playfully bumped his hip as he reached for a pint glass.

"Could be having more fun if any of these boys knew how to flirt," Kyle grumbled.

"I know. What a waste, right? This place is full of tens, and they're all worthless."

"Counterfeit tens," Kyle agreed.

Aram rested both of his massive arms on the bar and leaned forward, grinning at the rowdy and attractive crowd. "Still, though. Fun to look at. Have you *seen* Matti Jalo up close?"

"Not as close as I'd like to."

Aram laughed as a man who was *not* the New York Admirals' gorgeous Finnish defenseman ambled up to the bar and asked them for a couple of pints of beer. Aram got to work pouring them while pointlessly flirting with the man. Kyle let his eyes roam the room.

Ooh. Eric Bennett.

The Admirals' star goaltender was leaning against the bar, seemingly taking in the party. Kyle didn't really know him, but he'd seen him in here before with Scott and Kip and he was kind of exactly Kyle's type. Or, rather, he was exactly the type of man Kyle wouldn't allow himself to fall for anymore. But it didn't hurt to *look*. Kyle had always loved Eric's dark, curly hair and well-groomed stubble, both of which were flecked with gray. He was tall and lean and always seemed so mature and elegant compared to the other Admirals players.

Eric was alone now, and he was *technically* at the bar, so Kyle could *technically* ask if he wanted to order anything. What if he'd been waiting patiently this whole time to order a drink? With his back to the bar . . .

"Can I get you anything?" Kyle leaned on the bar, angling his face so that Eric could see him in his periphery.

Eric turned his head immediately. "I'm fine," he said with a polite smile.

He certainly was. He was wearing a blue-and-white checked shirt, the sleeves rolled up to reveal his strong forearms. His dark eyes fixed on Kyle's, his gaze confident and unwavering.

Oof. If Kyle had one weakness—and he didn't; he had many—it was confident, attractive older men. Also, confident, attractive younger men. Also, men.

"Kyle, right?" Eric asked. "You're friends with Kip."

"That's me."

"I'm Eric." He extended his hand, and Kyle shook it.

"I know who you are." Kyle's tone was teasing and flirty, because it was pretty much always teasing and flirty. "You're the one who hides that handsome face behind a mask all the time."

He expected Eric the heterosexual goaltender to lean away and make an excuse to leave. Or maybe just leave. But instead, his lips quirked up and he said, "That's how it stays so handsome."

Kyle let himself enjoy the playful sparkle in Eric's eyes for a moment.

"Hey, Kyle! I need to get a fresh keg of the lager. You good here for a minute?"

Kyle turned to Aram. "Of course. Go use those muscles."

Aram blew him a kiss, then left for the back room.

"It was nice of Scott to book this party at Kip's place of work," Eric said dryly.

Kyle laughed. "I was thinking the exact same thing. Who does that, right?"

Eric shook his head. "Scott Hunter, that's who. He likes this place, and he's comfortable here. I'm sure that's all he was focused on."

Kyle spotted Scott in the crowd—it wasn't hard because he was six-four and looked exactly how Kyle had always imagined Achilles. Scott was laughing with some friends, and Kyle couldn't help but smile. Two years ago, Scott had been firmly in the closet, lonely, and would have been terrified to enter a gay bar like the Kingfisher. Now he was a regular here—the bar had even named a drink after him—and hosting his big gay engagement party. Kyle was happy for him. He was happy for Kip too, even if his feelings on that front were a little more complicated.

"Are you sure I can't get you anything?" Kyle asked. "I've been pouring pints all night and I would love to show off my cocktail skills."

"I don't drink."

"Oh. Oh god, sorry. I shouldn't tempt you."

Eric waved a hand. "It's not like that. I'm not tempted."

"Ah." Kyle folded his arms on the bar and leaned forward. "You're just a very good boy, then?"

Eric smirked. "Most of the time."

Wait. *Was* Eric flirting with him? The conversation seemed flirtatious, but Kyle had a long history of clocking desire when there absolutely was none on the part of the other man.

Straight men. Another weakness of his.

"You're in luck because I happen to make the most amazing mocktails in the world."

Amusement sparkled in Eric's eyes. "Do you now?"

Kyle winked. "You'll swear there's booze in them. They're that good."

"I can't really compare."

"Has it really been that long since you've had a drink?"

Before Eric could answer—if he was going to answer—they were interrupted by an excited Kip Grady.

"Eric!" Kip draped an arm over Eric's shoulders, then drunkenly lurched forward, pulling both men closer to where Kyle was standing behind the bar. Eric's nose almost brushed Kyle's cheek. "You're here!"

"I am," Eric said, calmly sliding out from under Kip's arm. He straightened and took a step back, but his face was still relaxed and quietly amused. "Are you having a good time?"

"I'm getting married!" Kip's cheeks were flushed, and his eyes glowed with drunken ecstasy and love. Kyle looked away.

"Congratulations," Eric said. He leaned on the bar, then brought his left hand up to clasp his wrist. That's when Kyle noticed the gold band on his ring finger.

Married. Right. Of course.

He blinked when he realized that Kip was trying to get his attention. He dragged his gaze away from the wedding ring and up to Kip's beaming face.

"This is Eric!" Kip said sloppily. "He's, like, the best goalie ever!"

"I've heard."

"He's smart too! He collects art." Kip's eyes widened in an expression of sudden realization. "Eric! Kyle is *studying art*!"

"Really?" Eric asked Kyle.

"Art *history*," Kyle clarified. "Ancient art, mostly. If your collection includes three-thousand-year-old mosaics, I'm your expert."

Eric's face split into a wide smile that nearly knocked Kyle on his ass. This man was *gorgeous*.

While Kyle was losing himself in Eric's handsome face, Kip darted behind the bar, bumping up against Kyle. He grabbed a pint glass and started pouring himself a beer, but Kyle stopped him. "Get out of here. You're drunk."

Kip rolled his eyes dramatically. "Fine. You pour it."

When Kyle handed him the beer that he absolutely did not need, Kip leaned in and kissed his cheek. "Love you."

Kyle's shoulders stiffened. "Love you too," he said quietly. His gaze followed Kip helplessly as he walked away with his drink.

"Where are you studying ancient art?" Eric asked, snapping Kyle's attention back to him.

Kyle managed a small smile. *See, Kyle? There's no reason to be sad. You have a beautiful, married straight man to keep you company.* "Columbia. I'm working on my master's degree."

"Impressive."

"Well, before you get too dazzled by me, I'll clarify that I am very *slowly* working on my master's degree. I'm only taking one class right now."

"Still impressive. I don't think I've ever met anyone who was studying ancient art before. What made you choose that field?"

Eric's eyes were warm and attentive. Kyle believed that he was truly interested in his answer. "I've always been interested in it, since I was a kid. I had this illustrated children's book of Greek myths that I read a zillion times." He laughed. "When I got older I learned that the *real* versions of those myths were a lot more violent. And horny."

"More bestiality than you were expecting?"

Kyle waved a hand. "That's the least of it. Anyway, obviously the R-rated versions only made me *more* interested in mythology. Which grew into an interest in the people who created and believed those myths. The storytellers, y'know?"

Eric nodded thoughtfully. "Is your undergraduate degree in art history as well?"

"I majored in ancient history and Latin, and then I decided on ancient art and architecture for my master's degree."

"That sounds like a fascinating thing to study."

Kyle shrugged. "I have no idea what I'm going to do with it, but I like learning."

"Me too."

Kyle leaned on the bar. "Oh yeah? Are you a reader?" Maybe Eric was one of those well-rounded athletes who took online college classes or listened to a lot of educational podcasts.

"I like to read. I majored in English literature."

Kyle was momentarily surprised, but when he considered the man in front of him, he decided that being a student of literature suited him more than being a hockey player. "Where did you study?"

Eric's lips twisted in a way that suggested he was embarrassed by what he was about to say. "Harvard."

Kyle blinked. "You have a Harvard degree?"

"Yes."

Kyle laughed. He couldn't help it. He quickly covered his mouth, cringing at how rude that reaction had been. "Sorry! I just wasn't expecting that."

Eric, thankfully, wasn't offended. "You're not the first person to be surprised by it. But you can check my Wikipedia page if you don't believe me."

"I believe you." What Kyle couldn't believe was how cruel the universe was for placing this absurdly perfect, absolutely forbidden man in front of him. An older, athletic, confident man with a Harvard degree in English? Come the fuck on. Kyle was so tempted to say something very flirtatious right now, just to see if he could shake Eric's calm veneer. Just to see if his dark eyes would show discomfort, or desire.

A stunning woman with blond hair and impeccable timing saved Kyle from conducting any inappropriate experiments. Regardless, Kyle felt Eric's gaze on him the entire time he made the customer her vodka soda.

"You're working at your friend's engagement party," Eric said after the woman left with her drink.

"Yeah. You noticed that, huh?"

Eric seemed to consider Kyle for a moment, as if he was trying to puzzle him out. There was something about the way Eric looked at him that had Kyle feeling very exposed. He nearly shivered.

"I'm not *working* working. It's a private event and everyone who works here is also on the invite list because that's how Kip rolls, but I don't really know most of the guests, so I'm happy to help out behind the bar."

"Better than making small talk with hockey players." Eric's lips curved up slightly as he said it.

Kyle leaned in. "Most of the time."

For a moment, Eric didn't say anything. He just stared intently at Kyle, as if he was unlocking all his secrets with his eyes. His lips were still twisted into that amused little smile, and Kyle had no idea what was happening right now. His dick was into it, though. His dick was always into unavailable men, so it could fuck off.

"So. Mocktails," Kyle said, breaking the tension probably only he felt. He clapped his hands together. "Do you have any allergies?"

"Cats," Eric said.

Kyle frowned. "Oh. I'll have to change the recipe then."

Eric laughed at that. His laugh warm and wonderful. Kyle wanted to wrap himself up in it like a blanket. *Straight. Married*, Kyle repeated to himself. *Straight, married, and a professional hockey player. Also, probably fifteen years older than you.*

"You don't have to make me anything. Really," Eric said. "I need to leave soon anyway."

Kyle shouldn't have felt as disappointed as he did by that. "You sure?"

"Yeah, I—" Eric lowered his voice. "Between you and me, I love Scott. And Kip. But I feel like I've been celebrating their relationship for going on three years now."

Kyle grinned in delight. "I *know*, right? Like, *we get it*. You're perfect and in love."

"Disgusting," Eric agreed. They both laughed.

"Seriously, though," Eric said, looking a little ashamed of what he'd said about his friends, "I'm thrilled for them. Especially Scott. I've known him a long time, and he . . . well, he's definitely earned his happiness."

Kyle spotted Kip and Scott in the crowd. Scott had his arm wrapped firmly around Kip's shoulders, and both men were beaming. "He got a good man," Kyle said wistfully. When his gaze returned to Eric, he found sympathy in the other man's eyes. It was startling.

"He did," Eric agreed.

Kyle rolled his eyes, which was the immature thing he did when he didn't want to deal with feelings. "Anyway. I should gather up some of the empties." He grabbed a tray and gave Eric a parting wink before entering the drunken fray.

Eric watched Kyle maneuver his way through the crowded bar. He watched his slim hips sliding this way and that, avoiding tables and people. He watched his long fingers plucking bottles and empty glasses from tables. He watched the way Kyle's lips would stretch into a playful smile whenever anyone spoke to him.

He watched him for probably far too long. Until a hand on Eric's shoulder broke him out of his trance.

"Who do you have your eye on?" Eric's teammate and friend, Carter Vaughan, had managed to sneak up on him, which wasn't easy. "There aren't a lot of single women here tonight, but I wouldn't rule Matti out as a possibility."

"What are you *ever* talking about?"

"Like, I'm straight. A thousand percent. And I'm committed to Gloria a million percent, but I'll admit it: Matti Jalo turns my head sometimes."

"I'm not looking at anyone," Eric lied. "I just zoned out for a minute."

"Well, that I believe. As long as you're not thinking about last night's game. This is a party, Benny!"

"I'm not."

Carter raised both eyebrows, then took a sip of his beer.

"I'm *not*," Eric insisted.

"Okay. You having fun at all?"

Eric shrugged. "Sure. I'm glad they're finally getting married, y'know?"

"It should have happened a year ago."

"I think it's smart to wait. You should know for sure it's the person you want to spend the rest of your life with."

"I'm pretty sure Scotty knew within a week."

Eric couldn't argue with that. His own marriage had taught him that rushing into a commitment to someone was a bad idea, but even *he* saw the hearts in Scott's and Kip's eyes when they looked at each other.

"How are you holding up?" Carter asked. The playful glint in his eyes softened to something more like concern. "Is this hard for you?"

Eric took a moment to consider his question. He liked to consider every question before answering. "A little. Maybe. Not that I'm not happy for Scott, but I've been thinking about my own wedding, I guess."

The teasing sparkle was back in Carter's eyes. "You can remember back that far?"

"Shut it."

"I forget. Was Holly a war bride? Was she your nurse after the Germans shot you?"

"All right, I'm going home."

Carter nudged him. "Seriously, though. I'm sorry if this is rough for you."

"It's been a year, almost. I'm over it. Really. I don't miss Holly, but I do miss . . ." Eric shook his head.

"Regular sex?" Carter guessed.

"Companionship," Eric finished with a glare at Carter. "Holly and I didn't spend much quality time together the last few years, but it was still nice to have someone to talk to at night. When we were both home."

"I'll bet we can find someone who wouldn't mind being your *companion*," Carter said, making the word sound dirty.

Eric's gaze found Kyle again, his tray now heaving under the weight of empty beer bottles and pint glasses. Eric could see the bulge of his bicep straining the fabric of his white T-shirt. He had an athletic figure—not jacked like the other bartender, but slim and toned. Eric wondered if he played any sports, or if he just worked out a lot.

"I think I'll head home," Eric said, because checking out the very young man tending bar was definitely a sign that it was time to leave.

"Gotta rest those old bones," Carter joked.

"Yeah, yeah." Eric retrieved his long, black wool coat and olive-green cashmere scarf from the back of a barstool.

As he was wrapping the scarf around his neck, Kyle returned and plunked the heavy tray down on the bar. He brushed the strands of blond hair that had fallen over one eye back into place with his fingers. "You're leaving?"

"Yes." Eric glanced at his watch, as if the time was any kind of justification for leaving a party right now. It wasn't even eleven o'clock yet.

"Past your bedtime?" Kyle's voice had dropped into a sultry, husky timbre, which Eric knew was meant to be teasing, but it sent a surprising jolt through him.

"I'm not really a party guy."

The thing Kyle was doing right then, leaning against the bar with his arms crossed, one shoulder raised just enough to make the hem of his T-shirt ride up to reveal the barest half inch of his flat stomach, probably worked on a lot of men. It was undeniably alluring. Eric tore his gaze away from the strip of pale skin, shaking his head as he buttoned his coat.

"I remember when you used to be fun, Benny," Carter said.

"No you don't," Eric said flatly.

Carter laughed. "No. I really don't."

"Goodnight, Carter." Then, Eric turned to Kyle. "It was nice talking to you, Kyle."

"Likewise." The word slid out of Kyle's mouth, rich and bordering on ridiculous. Eric was embarrassed by the heat that bloomed low in his belly in response. He turned and strode toward the exit before anyone noticed how flustered he was getting. He didn't like to ever appear anything less than steady and unshakable at all times.

He stepped outside into a cold November drizzle and wished he'd worn something water-resistant instead of his wool Burberry coat. The frigid rain worked like an ice bath, though, easing the sparks that had been racing through Eric's veins since he'd first laid eyes on Kyle tonight. The truth was, he'd been . . . *aware* of Kyle for some time. Eric had gone to the Kingfisher a handful of times over the past couple of years. He'd go if Kip was working, ostensibly keeping Scott company but in reality just sitting there while Scott watched his boyfriend serve people drinks.

The second time he'd agreed to go, Kyle had been working with Kip, and Eric had been drawn to him for reasons he still couldn't explain.

Well. He *could* at least partially explain it. Certainly it had something to do with Kyle's winter-blue eyes, and his easy, seductive smiles. He seemed confident and fun in a completely different way from Eric's teammates. It was alluring.

Eric noticed people. He always had. His ability to observe everything and everyone around him was an integral part of his goaltending career. Despite this, he wasn't often *attracted* to other people. But he was definitely attracted to Kyle.

Even though it had been over a year since he'd last had sex, Eric hadn't been missing it. His sexual needs, such as they were, had always been satisfied one way or another. But now a few flirtatious words and smiles from a beautiful young bartender and suddenly Eric's libido was demanding attention.

There was a time when the fact that the bartender in question was a *man* would have terrified Eric. For most of his life, he had chosen to ignore the part of him that was attracted to men. He'd been married to Holly, after all, so there'd been no reason to think about it. That was what he had told himself.

But since Scott Hunter had come out as gay, things had changed. Eric was lucky enough to have had a front-row seat to witness Scott's happiness as he finally allowed himself to live and love the way he'd always been afraid to. He wasn't like Scott. He had loved Holly once, and he'd never been forced to hide who he really was. Not in the same way. He'd just chosen not to reveal all of himself, because he'd never needed to.

But since his divorce, and now living in a brave new world where being attracted to men wasn't an unthinkable thing for a hockey player, Eric had allowed himself to examine this thing that he'd buried so long ago. To poke it a little. It was something that he thought he might like to explore, now that he was able. But *how*? Where on earth did one start with that sort of thing?

With a flirty bartender?

No. Absolutely not. Kyle was much too young—barely older than the rookies on the team—so it was completely inappropriate. More than that, it would be humiliating. How much of a midlife crisis stereotype did Eric want to be? Dating a man who was almost half his age was not happening. There had to be a safer and more sensible option.

For the first time in Eric's life, safe and sensible didn't seem particularly appealing.

CHAPTER THREE

The smell of coffee lured Kyle out of bed late the next morning. He'd been awake for about twenty minutes, contemplating the benefits of staying in bed forever. But then he'd smelled the coffee.

His roommate, Maria Villanueva, made great coffee. She'd been a barista at Starbucks for the past two years—part-time for the past year since she'd gone back to school—and Kyle was happy to benefit from her expert training.

"Sit," Maria instructed, looking less than intimidating in her fluffy purple housecoat and panda bear slippers. Kyle obeyed her anyway. She plunked a steaming mug of coffee on their kitchen table and waited for him to take exactly one sip before she said, "How's your heart holding up?"

He pushed fingers under his glasses to rub at his eyes. "I have no idea what you're talking about."

"Bullshit. You know exactly what I'm talking about. Do you want a bagel?"

"Only if they aren't—"

"They aren't the jalapeno kind, you baby. Are sesame seeds too spicy for you?"

"I like spicy food. Just not first thing in the morning. Do we have cinnamon raisin?"

"No, because those are disgusting. Do you want yours toasted?" She held up a sesame seed bagel.

"Are they fresh?"

She glared at him, then gestured at her outfit. "Do I look like I've left the apartment this morning?"

"Toast it, please." He watched Maria as she prepared their breakfasts the same way she did everything: in quick, efficient movements, treating their tiny kitchen like a Starbucks at rush hour.

"So you're fine?" she asked. "Because between the two of us, I'm the one who was drunk last night, but you're the one who looks like shit."

"Thanks."

Maria placed a neatly plated bagel with cream cheese in front of him, then sat down with her own bagel. "What do you have planned for today?"

"I think I'll lay low."

Maria eyed him suspiciously, waiting for Kyle to admit he needed a friend right now.

"God," Kyle sighed. "All right. Last night took a lot out of me. Is that what you want to hear?"

"If you need to talk about it, then yes, I want to hear."

Kyle picked at the sesame seeds on his bagel. "It's stupid. I don't know. It was fine."

"Watching the man you are basically in love with celebrating his engagement to another man was fine?"

"I'm not in love with him," Kyle grumbled. "It's just a crush. And he's never been a possibility, so it's not a useful crush anyway."

"I wish I could tell you otherwise, but no. It isn't. You need someone new to obsess over."

"I'm not obsessed with Kip. I just . . . like the idea of Kip. And me. Together." He pushed his bagel aside and folded his arms on the table, then buried his face in them.

Maria reached across the table and patted his arm. "I know. But you know what I have to say next, right?"

Kyle shook his head, face still buried. "You don't have to say it."

"I'm saying it. You and Kip are not going to be together. Not ever. Okay?"

"I know."

"If he and Scott were into threesomes, or opening their relationship up in any way—"

"Oh my god."

"Then I would say you'd have a shot. But those two are *committed*. Like, my parents have renewed their vows *twice* and I don't think they're as committed to each other as Scott and Kip are."

Kyle laughed into his arms. "Okay, I get it."

Maria always made him laugh. They'd become friends through Kip, who used to work with her at the smoothie shop where he'd first met Scott. Kip invited Kyle out for drinks with some of his friends one night more than two years ago, and Kyle had instantly adored Maria. A few months after that, Kyle had learned that she needed to find a new place to live, and he'd offered his second bedroom to her. The arrangement was supposed to be temporary, but they got along so well that Kyle insisted she stay.

"Can you imagine?" Maria mused. "Getting in the middle of that sandwich?"

"I could probably write a thesis about it, I've imagined it so much."

"I'll bet Scott is such a generous lover."

"Stop." Kyle groaned. "How is this helping?"

"I guess it isn't. Hey, speaking of impossible crushes, I totally talked to Matti Jalo last night for like six whole minutes."

"Alone?" Kyle gasped. "You're compromised! He'll have to offer to marry you now!"

"I wish. Oh my god. Like, I understand that he is several leagues above me, but damn. A girl can dream, can't she?"

"He's not out of your league! You are completely awesome and beautiful. He's just a big ol' hockey player."

"With perfect genes and millions of dollars."

"Yeah, well. He'd be lucky to have you."

"Speaking of hockey players . . ." Maria sucked a gob of cream cheese off her finger, releasing it with a pop. "I saw you talking to Eric 'Dream Daddy' Bennett last night."

"Oh, you mean the straight man with a wedding ring on his finger? Yes, it was very promising. I expect him to call on me any moment now."

"Straight, old, and married. Isn't that exactly your type?"

Kyle flicked a sesame seed at her. "I also like them gay, young, and engaged. I'm very open-minded."

"Why don't you go for Aram? He's a sweetheart and he's smoking hot."

"Because he's one of my best friends and he works with me."

"You just exactly described Kip."

"Yeah, but—" Kyle wasn't sure how to elegantly finish that sentence, so instead he sputtered out some nonsense. "Kip was a crush *first*. Like, I saw him one night at the Kingfisher with his friends and I was *smitten*. We flirted a bit, and I really thought I'd be taking him home that night. But then he left. The next time he came back, you were there. I think it was his birthday."

"Oh yeah. I was super drunk that night."

"You all were. And once again, I thought I'd be leaving with him at the end of the night. Turns out, of course, he was secretly dating Scott at the time."

"And then there was that time you kissed him."

Kyle dropped his head back on his folded arms. "And then there was that time I kissed him." He raised his head. "But in my defense, he *really* led me to believe that he wanted it. He showed up alone, sat at the bar and flirted with me all night."

"Getting drunk alone. Always a sign of emotional stability."

"I *know*. I should have realized something was wrong. Honestly, I probably did, but I chose to ignore it because it was my *chance*. He left with *me*. And then I kissed him and . . ." He squeezed his eyes shut as if he could erase the memory. "I'm just glad we're friends now."

"I am too. But mostly I'm glad that *we're* friends now."

"Totally. It was worth all this heartache and embarrassment to have you making coffee for me in the mornings."

"It's the least I could do."

It was true that Kyle had offered Maria a pretty sweet deal. Because the apartment had been paid for by his wealthy parents, Kyle didn't even charge Maria rent. She just helped with the groceries and bills. Kyle had thought he'd prefer to live alone, but mostly he'd felt guilty about having so much space to himself. Plus, he'd been lonely.

"What are you up to today?" Kyle asked.

"I have to meet with my group for a school project this afternoon." A year and a half ago, Maria had completed the entrance exam for the police academy and passed with flying colors. Then she'd swiftly decided that she wanted, in her words, to actually help people. Immigrants, like her own parents, in particular. So she was now studying Human Services at a local college. "How about you?"

"I might wrap myself in a blanket and binge that Alyssa Edwards Netflix series."

Maria stood and patted him on the shoulder as she took her dishes to the sink. "You earned it, buddy."

★ ★ ★

Eric fought the tremble that crept up his body from where he was balancing on his forearms. He took deep, controlled breaths and commanded his body to settle. His body, as always, obeyed.

Eric loved that feeling, when his body accepted the pain and pushed through it. He'd started practicing yoga fifteen years ago to increase his strength and flexibility on the ice, but now he considered his daily practice a gift he gave himself. He loved being perfectly attuned to everything his body was doing. Everything it gave him when he asked, and everything it asked of him. Some days he could easily hold a vertical pose like this one for well over a minute. Today his body was fighting him.

Three more breaths, he told his body. His left shoulder—the one he'd had two operations on during his career—had been tight lately but seemed all right now. His body had taken a lot of abuse over his decades of stopping pucks, and he knew he wouldn't walk away from this game without some permanent souvenirs, but he could try to keep them to a minimum. He could treat his body with the respect it deserved, and control what went into it, and what he did with it between games.

One more deep inhale and exhale, and Eric slowly curled his extended legs back toward his torso and came out of the handstand. He finished his practice, going easier on his body with the final poses, and taking care to listen to what his body was telling him.

Eric knew what his body needed. It was grumbling about it now, but at night it practically screamed. It had been far too long since he'd last had sex.

As he headed downstairs to his kitchen, his thoughts involuntarily turned to Kyle. He was sure that Kyle flirted with lots of men—it was practically his job to do so—but Eric couldn't help the fact that Kyle had captured the seldom-used lurid part of his imagination.

It was absurd. Kyle was young and, flirting aside, probably had no real interest in an old man like him. In fact, Eric was very sure that Kyle was hopelessly in love with Kip, based on the way he'd gazed longingly at Kip at the party. Scott and Kip's happiness seemed to pierce Kyle like a blade. If Kip was Kyle's type, then Eric definitely had no chance.

No chance. Jesus. No chance of *what?* What did Eric even want?

Eric filled a glass with water and drank it down quickly. He refilled the glass, then returned his water pitcher to the fridge and grabbed a jar of overnight breakfast quinoa. He stood at the window in his kitchen and watched the morning traffic on 36th Street as he ate. The large house he'd shared with Holly had been on Long Island with a spectacular view of the water. But Eric preferred this: a front-row seat to the bustle of Manhattan. This Murray Hill townhouse suited him better in every way.

It was, in all honesty, ridiculous for Eric to have an entire four-story townhouse to himself. He had considered an apartment—maybe a penthouse like Scott's—but this house had been for sale at the right time and Eric hadn't been able to resist it. He'd worked with a designer to create a home that exuded serenity and comfort, while also providing a complementary backdrop for his art collection. The final result was, Eric had to admit, stunning. But he hadn't been prepared for how lonely it would feel to only have art and designer furniture for company.

His phone lit up where it rested on his kitchen counter. Eric set his empty quinoa jar next to the sink and picked up the phone. It was a message from Jeanette, his friend and art dealer. She had a collection of paintings by a new artist that she thought he would be interested in.

Well. Maybe *this* would be the painting that would make his life feel whole.

ERIC:
When can I see them?

They planned for Eric to come to the gallery on Tuesday—his day off. As always, Jeanette didn't send a photo of any of the paintings. She insisted his first impression of the art be the one he got when he viewed it in person. She was never wrong about what Eric would like, though, so he was excited to see what she had.

Kyle was studying art history, which was something that Eric couldn't stop thinking about. He had made the fatal mistake of *learning* about the man. He wished he could go back to the time that he didn't know Kyle was studying ancient history and art, or that he loved mythology and was just generally brilliant and fascinating.

It was one thing to be flirted with by a cute bartender, but when it was a cute bartender who was smart and shared Eric's interests . . .

Well. It had been a nice surprise.

He could, he thought, attempt to flirt with Kyle the next time he happened to see him. Kyle seemed naturally flirtatious and would probably be able to provide Eric with some much-needed practice. It would be harmless, and Eric could use whatever he learned from it whenever he attempted in earnest to date again.

Practice was all he needed, he decided as he jogged up the two flights of stairs to his bedroom. It was something that he understood, as an athlete. Practicing something over and over would eventually yield results. He could improve his ability to flirt the same way he had improved his rebound control on the ice. He would practice flirting, practice dating, practice being intimate with another person.

With a man.

Maybe.

But first, flirting.

CHAPTER FOUR

If Ilya Rozanov didn't get his ass out of Eric's face right fucking now, Eric was going to chop his legs off.

Eric pushed him hard in the back with his blocker pad. "Fuck off, Rozanov."

But Rozanov—an all-star center who had been a thorn in the side of Eric and every other NHL goaltender for nearly a decade—held his ground.

"I swear to fuck, Rozanov," Eric growled as he stretched his neck to try to see over Rozanov's shoulder.

"I heard Hunter's getting married," Rozanov said conversationally, as if they were having lunch together and not in the middle of a 1–1 hockey game.

"Looking for an invite?" Eric asked, shoving him again.

"To the most boring event of the century? No."

Rozanov was a big guy, not easy to move. But Matti Jalo was bigger, and he finally came to Eric's rescue.

"Took you long enough," Eric grumbled, but Jalo was already gone, chasing after Rozanov. A few seconds later, Rozanov was racing toward the net with the puck. Instead of sinking back into the net, Eric moved to the top of the crease, fearless and challenging. *Try me, motherfucker.*

Rozanov let off a lightning-quick wrist shot that sailed toward the top corner of the net. The puck was fast, but Eric was faster, gloving it down with probably a little more flourish than was necessary. He only had so many chances left to make a highlight reel.

"Nice save," Rozanov said calmly as he skated by.

"Plenty more where that came from."

Rozanov turned back and grinned. "I doubt it. You are a hundred years old. I could hear your bones creak."

"That's not what your girlfriend said." Eric was instantly embarrassed by his immature comeback. But Rozanov was laughing.

"I'll have to ask her about it," he said, then skated away, still laughing. Eric's brow furrowed. He didn't even know if Rozanov *had* a girlfriend.

The game ended with the Admirals beating Ottawa 3–1. Normally beating a team as low in the standings as Ottawa wouldn't make Eric feel this good, but after his abysmal performance in the last game, winning felt incredible. When the siren sounded to end the game, he raised both arms over his head as first Jalo, and then the other defenseman on the ice, Brisebois, engulfed him in jubilant hugs.

Carter skated down the ice and butted the front of his helmet against the forehead of Eric's mask. "You put on a fucking *clinic* tonight, Benny. Send them crying back to Ottawa."

"They actually stay in town for a couple of nights," Eric pointed out, because he couldn't be cool and let things go. "They're playing Brooklyn on Saturday."

Carter looped an arm around Eric's massive, padded shoulders. "Maybe I'll recommend a bar they can drown their sorrows in."

The locker room was boisterous and celebratory after the game. It was always a relief to win the last home game before a road trip; the confidence boost would hopefully carry into their game in Nashville in two nights' time.

Eric sat to Scott's left, as always, and listened to him happily telling Carter about his plans to visit Kip at work that night. Scott truly did love hanging out at the Kingfisher. Maybe after nearly thirty years of hiding, he was making up for lost time by openly hanging out in gay bars. Kip had done that for him. Or rather, the love Scott felt for Kip had done that. It had been strong enough to push Scott out of his comfort zone and into a better life.

Eric wondered what that felt like, to love a person so deeply that you become braver for it. Become better. Scott laughed all the time now, where before he had always been quiet, guarded and stoic. He'd rarely been social, always offering excuses to avoid going out. Never dating anyone, obviously. Never sharing his life.

How different was it from how Eric was living now? Eric had ostensibly shared his life with Holly for two decades, but looking back, he realized they hadn't shared much with each other at all. A house. A bank account. A bed sometimes.

And he had liked Holly a lot. She'd come from money, but Eric had found her remarkably down-to-earth and funny. They'd been friends first, and then it became more when she'd playfully asked him if he was ever going to kiss her. He'd been considering it for a long time, so he'd accepted her invitation, kissing her and forming a partnership that lasted twenty years. Her parents hadn't been thrilled with her choice of boyfriend—a charity case hockey player from Canada—but they had changed their tune about him when Eric signed his first NHL contract.

Eric wasn't sure, even now, if he'd ever truly been in love with Holly. It was entirely possible he didn't have the ability to love at all. Not the way Scott loved Kip, or Carter loved Gloria. The love his friends felt for their partners shone out of them, lighting up their faces when they talked about them. Maybe that kind of love was rare, and all Eric should hope for was a spark of attraction with someone, and some enjoyable conversation.

Scott's chatter about the Kingfisher had Eric wondering if a certain other bartender would be working that night. And that maybe going out for a while would do Eric some good.

"Are you heading to the bar right from here?" Eric asked.

"Yeah. It's closer to the arena than to my place."

Eric considered this. He would be wearing a suit when he left the arena, but so would Scott. He supposed he could remove the jacket and tie before entering the bar.

"Maybe I'll go with you," Eric said. "If that's okay."

Scott looked surprised, then grinned broadly, his blue eyes sparkling. "That would be awesome!"

It was probably a terrible idea. Kyle had pretty clearly rejected Eric last week and probably wouldn't be excited to see him at his place of work. But Eric wasn't going to bother Kyle; he wasn't that stupid. He would enjoy an evening hanging out with Scott, and if he stole a few furtive glances at Kyle, no harm done.

Eric and Scott shared a car from the chauffeur service they both liked. As soon as the car started moving, Scott began removing clothing. First his jacket, then his tie, and Eric did the same. But as Eric began rolling up his shirtsleeves, Scott pulled his entire dress shirt off, revealing a tight charcoal T-shirt underneath. It was then that Eric noticed that Scott's "suit pants" were actually a pair of sleek black jeans.

When he raised an eyebrow at him, Scott grinned sheepishly. "The dress code is a stupid rule anyway."

Eric shook his head, smiling. "When did you turn into such a rebel?"

"Probably when Kip ranted for twenty minutes once about

how professional athletes are only required to wear traditional men's suits as a way of repressing creativity and of enforcing gender norms."

"Right." Eric kept his shirt on, but he unfastened a couple of the top buttons. "Funny how we never talk about stuff like that in the locker room."

"We're getting there." Scott said confidently. Eric knew that Scott truly believed there was a not-too-distant future where hockey would be every bit as inclusive and welcoming as the bars that Scott now frequented. Eric wasn't sure if the future of their sport was quite that rosy, but if hockey culture changed at all, it would be largely due to this man sitting beside him.

Eric was proud to be his friend. He would be prouder still to stand beside him on Scott's wedding day. But tonight, Eric was nervous because he was secretly hoping that Kyle was working, and he wasn't sure what that meant. Or what exactly he was hoping for. For right now, all Eric knew for sure was that he wanted to look at Kyle. To enjoy the way his blood fizzed a little when Kyle smiled at him. Maybe it was sad that Eric's sex life had gotten so dire that he was surviving on flirtatious winks from a man who had no actual interest in him, but at least it was *something*.

"So, um . . ." The unease in Scott's voice got Eric's attention. "I think someone else might be joining us tonight."

"Oh? Who?"

"Rozanov. He texted me after the game. Asked what I was doing tonight, and I told him."

Eric was stunned. "Ilya Rozanov wants to hang out with you tonight? At a gay bar?"

Scott shrugged. "Apparently."

"That guy is so weird."

Scott laughed. "He's mysterious, for sure. But I think he's maybe a decent guy. Remember when he showed up at that gay club in Vegas to hang out with us?"

Eric did remember. A nightclub had been holding a Scott Hunter Night to celebrate Scott publicly coming out. The party had been the same night as the NHL Awards, after the ceremony. Scott had extended the invitation to the entire audience at the awards, but other than the handful of Scott's teammates who had been in town, Rozanov was the only one who'd shown up. Eric had been as surprised as Scott had been to see Rozanov—a man who had gleefully taunted Scott as often as possible for years, who had a well-earned reputation as a ladies man, who was a famous hockey player from *Russia*, for fuck's sake—calmly approaching them in a gay nightclub. To this day Eric couldn't wrap his head around it.

"So he's in New York City, home of some of the best nightlife in the world, and he wants to hang out with you?"

"Yeah. Because I'm very cool and fun now. Haven't you heard?" Scott nudged him playfully. Eric forced a smile, but having Rozanov there would . . . complicate things. Eric wasn't quite ready to tell *Scott* his true reason for joining him tonight, let alone Ilya Rozanov. Eric wanted to come out to Scott—he thought he might want to come out to *everyone*—but he didn't like to do anything until he had all of his ducks in a row. For whatever reason, it made sense to Eric to try out flirting with a man first. Maybe going on a date or two, or kissing a man; anything that might make his bisexuality seem *real.* If he did that, he might be able to tell his best friend, with confidence, that he was bisexual.

The ridiculous thing was that he could hear Scott's voice in his head, scolding him for believing he needed to prove his own sexuality to himself. But still, Eric wanted to be sure, and he didn't want Scott to guess that Eric was at the bar to ogle Kyle. Unfortunately, Rozanov seemed a lot more observant. A lot more into giving people shit too.

The car pulled in front of the bar, and Scott and Eric thanked the driver as they slid out of luxurious leather seats and into the bracing cold of late November. They hurried inside, with backpacks crammed full of their discarded clothing slung over their shoulders.

The Kingfisher was, as always, warm and lively, despite being noticeably rough around the edges. Most of the chairs and tables had patches where the wood stain had worn off. The wallpaper was torn and peeling in places. The speakers in the corners that pumped pop music into the bar were in desperate need of dusting. The large television in one corner showing a West Coast NBA game was an older model. It was a bit of a dump, but there was something comforting and inviting about the place.

Most of the tables were full, but Kip dashed over as soon as he spotted Scott and gestured to an empty table near the bar. It had a little reserved sign on it, which Eric was sure was only ever used for Scott's visits.

Kip greeted Scott with a kiss, which went on long enough that Eric had to look away.

"You were amazing tonight, sweetheart," Kip said, his arms still looped around Scott's neck. "We had the game on in here. You were awesome too, Eric."

"Thanks." Eric scanned the room and spotted a familiar trim body in faded jeans and a form-fitting white T-shirt. He was at a table across the room, standing with his back to Eric, but Eric had no problem recognizing him.

"Have a seat," Kip said cheerfully. "I'll bring you boys a lager and a soda water with lime?" He glanced at Eric with raised eyebrows, silently checking to make sure he'd remembered Eric's usual correctly.

"Soda with lime, yes. Thank you."

Kip left to get their drinks, and Scott never took his eyes off him. Eric carefully turned his gaze on Kyle, letting his eyes linger for a few seconds, and then looking away. Kyle was smiling at an attractive young man who was standing at the bar in the same space Eric had been standing the other night. The wicked glint in Kyle's eyes as he talked to the man now was the same glint that had been there when he'd been flirting with Eric that night.

A hot stab of jealousy bloomed absurdly in Eric's chest. This was Kyle's *job*. He flirted with countless men like this all the time. Eric had just been one of them. He wasn't special.

But then Kyle's gaze met Eric's, and Kyle's eyes went wide as the smile fell from his lips. It was only for a second, and then Kyle snapped out of it and turned his attention back to his customer, lips turned up in a seductive smile once again.

Oh no. What was *he* doing here again?

Kyle could accept that Eric Bennett was here at the Kingfisher to keep his friend company. It probably had nothing to do with Kyle. But that would mean ignoring the way Eric's gaze kept landing on Kyle as he worked. The way he frowned when Kyle flirted with other customers, even as Eric fiddled with his fucking wedding ring.

Kyle was all too familiar with men like Eric. Men who liked to spend their evenings away from their wives so they could scratch an itch they would never dare speak a word about to any of the people in their lives who actually mattered to them. Men who were happy to get off with Kyle, men who maybe even claimed to want more than secret hookups with him, someday. But those men were all the same. As soon as there was even a chance the secret might get out, that their desire for men might be known by anyone important to them, they bolted.

Fuck men like that. Kyle had wasted too much of his life—of his heart—on them. Eric could ogle him all he liked with those gorgeous dark eyes. Kyle wasn't biting.

"I hate it when Scott comes here," Aram grumbled as he filled a couple of pint glasses. "All eyes are on him until he leaves."

"Aw," Kyle said. "I think at least one pair of eyes is on you, babe." He nodded at a tall, muscular man who was definitely trying to get Aram's attention for reasons beyond wanting to order a drink.

Aram perked up. "Well, hello. Let me go see what he's thirsty for." Kyle laughed. Aram finished loading his tray with full pints, then winked at him. "Hey, I see Scott brought his hot dad tonight."

Kyle followed Aram's gaze to where Eric was sitting. As soon as Kyle's eyes landed on him, Eric turned his head quickly away. Busted. "Oh, you mean Husband of the Year over there? No thank you."

Aram wrinkled his nose. "Right. I forgot. Ick."

He left with his tray of drinks, and Kyle took a cute, chubby bearded guy's order.

"That's Scott Hunter, right?" the man asked as Kyle prepared his gin and tonic.

"The one and only."

"He's even more gorgeous in person. Damn."

"Oh I know."

"The guy who's sitting with him is hot too, in a sexy professor kind of way."

Kyle had to fight to keep himself from rolling his eyes. "Mm."

When the bearded guy left with his drink, he was immediately replaced by Kip. "You should come over to the table to say hi."

"I'm *busy*."

"Busy with that handsome lumberjack?"

Kyle narrowed his eyes at him. "The handsome lumberjack who has a giant crush on *your* fiancé?"

For a moment, Kip looked outraged, but then he grinned and said, "Well, I can't blame him. I mean, just *look* at Scott. Sometimes I can't believe he's really mine."

Ugh. "Lucky you."

"You're in a mood tonight."

"I'm *fine.* I'm just . . . hungry. And I probably need to get laid."

"Good thing you work in a bar that has both food and horny men."

Kyle couldn't help but laugh at that, which made Kip beam. His horrible dimples arrived on the scene to torment Kyle. "Let me check on my tables," Kyle said, "and then I'll go say hi to Scott. And Eric. And . . . wait. Who's that guy?"

Kip turned to glance at Scott's table and his eyes went wide. "Holy shit."

"Is that . . ."

"Ilya Rozanov." Kip blew out a breath. "This night just got a lot more interesting."

"Why? Is he your third or something?"

"Hell no. Rozanov is definitely into women. And he kind of hates Scott."

"Is he in a committed relationship?"

"Not that I know of."

"Then maybe I'll see if any part of him might be into men." Kyle smiled coyly at Kip, then zipped away with an empty tray.

Kyle was definitely avoiding their table. Whether that was because of Eric or because he didn't like being around Scott and Kip as a couple, Eric couldn't say. Maybe he was just busy and Eric was being paranoid. He wished Kyle would stop by for at least a moment, if for no other reason than to save Eric from having to choose between looking at Kip snuggled into Scott's lap, or at Ilya frigging Rozanov.

Rozanov was sitting calmly, observing the room with the same bemused little smile that infuriated his opponents on the ice. It *had* to be practiced, because it was a masterpiece. A smile that simultaneously said *I am figuring out exactly how to torture you* and *I don't care about you at all.*

"So," Eric said. "*You're* here."

"Yes," Ilya agreed.

"Is there a reason for that, or . . ."

"This place is cozy." The way Ilya said it—the way he said *everything*—made it hard to tell if he was making fun of Eric.

"It's nice," Eric said carefully.

"You are here a lot?"

"Not a lot. I come with Scott sometimes."

"Your wife left you, yes?"

Jesus, he was blunt. "We *separated*."

Ilya smirked. "Okay. But she divorced you?"

"It was mutual."

"Yes. And now you hang out here?"

Eric almost never blushed, but he came dangerously close just then. "To keep Scott company, like I said."

Ilya nodded in the direction of Kyle, who was now behind the bar. "Lots to look at."

Eric clenched his jaw. How the fuck was Rozanov so perceptive? He really seemed like he didn't give a shit about anyone around him, but his powers of observation were sharper even than Eric's. "I guess."

Unfortunately, Kyle chose *that* moment to finally visit their table. "Good evening, boys. Kip, when you've finished the lap dance, your booth in the corner needs another round."

Kip slid out of Scott's lap, cheeks pink. "It wasn't a lap dance!"

"Hunter probably thought it was," Ilya quipped.

Scott glared at him. "Fuck off, Rozanov. I know what a lap dance is."

Kip hurried away to check on his table, and Kyle turned his attention to Rozanov. "I don't believe I've had the pleasure." Eric didn't like the glimmer in Kyle's eyes as he drank in Ilya's admittedly attractive face and body.

"Kyle," Scott said, "this is Ilya Rozanov. Ilya, this is my friend Kyle."

Ilya reached across the table and shook Kyle's hand. "Kyle." He held his hand for, Eric felt, longer than necessary.

"What can I get you, sexy?" Kyle asked in that effortlessly flirtatious tone of his.

Ilya pointed at a chalkboard beside the bar that advertised the drink special that hadn't changed in over two years. "I would like a Scott Hunter. Please."

Scott groaned. "Just bring him a beer, Kyle. He's being an asshole."

"Have you had it?" Ilya asked Eric.

"No."

"I want to try it. And bring one for Bennett."

Eric caught Kyle's gaze and shook his head. "I don't—"

"I can make one without alcohol," Kyle offered.

Ilya looked delighted. "Yes! A virgin Scott Hunter."

"Jesus fucking Christ," Scott grumbled.

"You don't have to," Eric said. "I'm fine."

"I never got to make you that mocktail the other night." Kyle placed a hand on Eric's shoulder. "I was watching you show off on television earlier. Let me show you what *I'm* good at."

Eric swallowed so hard the rest of the table must have heard it. There was that fizzy feeling he'd been chasing. "Okay."

Kyle grabbed their empty glasses, then left with a wink at Ilya. Eric hated how jealous he was of that wink. Ilya didn't even react beyond his usual infuriating half smile.

Scott stood up. "I'm gonna hit the men's room."

He lingered a moment before leaving, which left him vulnerable for a Rozanov attack. "Are you hoping for company?"

Scott scowled. "No." He turned and left, and Eric had to bite his cheek to keep from laughing. His amusement didn't last, because as soon as Scott was gone, Ilya started on Eric.

"Kyle seems nice."

Eric kept his expression as neutral as possible. "He is."

For a long moment, Ilya didn't say anything. He just quietly studied Eric, as if searching for a weak spot. "He is attractive."

"I suppose."

"He looks like Hunter a bit. But younger." He paused, and grinned. "*Much* younger."

Eric's expression got a whole lot less neutral. He didn't reply, so Ilya kept going. "Is like if Scott Hunter had a younger brother. And that brother had a son."

Eric did not like *anything* that Ilya was implying. "He seems to like *you*," he volleyed back, hating that it was true.

Ilya shook his head. "This table is a mess."

"What do you mean?"

Ilya leaned forward, uncomfortably close to Eric. "You want to fuck Kyle. Kyle wants to fuck Hunter's boyfriend, but maybe also you, since Hunter and his boyfriend do not see anyone but each other."

"I do not!" Eric sputtered, even though he was pretty sure everything Rozanov had just said was true. Jesus this asshole was perceptive. "I barely even know him. And I'm not—I'm just here with Scott."

"Yes." Ilya's eyes darted to where Eric's left hand rested on the table. "Also, you are wearing a wedding ring but have no wife."

Eric covered his left hand protectively with his right "I like wearing it. I've worn it my entire NHL career, and it doesn't feel right to take it off. Not when I only—" He stopped himself just in time. Or at least, he'd thought he had.

"Not when you only have this season left," Ilya finished for him. God, Eric hadn't told *anyone* that yet. He was planning to announce it after the Christmas break, maybe.

"Don't say a word to anyone, Rozanov."

Ilya leaned back in his chair. "Is not going to shock people, Bennett. You are very old."

"Thanks."

"Tommy Andersson will be happy."

Eric spotted Scott coming back from the bathroom. "Shush. I mean it."

Ilya pressed his lips together, but his eyes danced and Eric really wasn't sure if he was going to keep quiet or not. His stomach clenched at the possibility of having his two biggest secrets revealed right now by Ilya goddamned Rozanov.

But Ilya didn't say a word, and shortly after Scott sat down, Kyle returned with their drinks. "One naughty Scott Hunter," he said as he placed a blue cocktail in front of Ilya. "And one *nice* Scott Hunter." He placed an identical drink in front of Eric, then darted away before Eric could even thank him.

Ilya lifted his glass. "Should we drink to Scott Hunter and his future husband?"

"I think we drank enough to that last week," Scott said sheepishly.

"To love, then. And—" he glanced at Eric "—to being brave."

They all clinked their glasses, and Ilya winked at him in a gesture that Eric translated as *your secret is safe with me.*

Ilya took a sip of his drink, and his face scrunched up. "Ugh. Tastes like Scott Hunter. Too sweet."

Eric thought the drink was remarkably well balanced, but his obviously had different ingredients.

"Kyle!" Ilya called out. "Help!"

Eric saw Kyle pause on his way from the bar to a table. He

was carrying a tray loaded with drinks. "Leave him alone. He's working."

"I am a customer," Ilya argued. "And I need a beer or something to get this taste out of my mouth."

"I once watched you drink three Cherry Cokes at an All-Star weekend lunch, so don't pretend you don't like sweet drinks."

Ilya looked a little stunned by Eric's snark. Then he grinned. "I did not know you were so interested in me."

"I'm not. At all. It was a shocking amount of Cherry Coke for a pro athlete to consume. It was memorable."

"You know," Ilya said with a weird little smile. "You were not the only one to think so that day." He took another sip of his drink, and made a disgusted face. "Where is Kyle? Or the other one, Hunter's guy."

Eric sighed. "Stay here. I'll get you a beer."

Ilya's smirk was far too knowing. "Yes. You go talk to Kyle. Would you like me to hold your wedding ring?"

Eric didn't answer him. He turned and strode toward the bar before Ilya could see his cheeks darken.

Kyle was just returning to the bar when Eric got there. "Oh, hey," Kyle said. It definitely wasn't warm.

"Ilya wants a beer, and I wanted to stretch my legs," Eric said.

"Uh-huh. What kind of beer?"

This conversation wasn't going at all the way Eric wanted it to. He tried for flirtatious. He leaned forward a bit, resting an elbow on the bar top. "I might need to rely on your expert opinion for that."

Kyle stared at him, his expression so unfriendly that Eric slid his elbow off the bar and let his arm hang at his side. Then Kyle said, with a huff of irritation, "I like the red ale."

"Okay. I'll go with that, then."

Kyle grabbed a glass and wordlessly filled it with ale. Eric awkwardly accepted it, but didn't move to return to the table.

He *should* leave, he knew that, but he also desperately wanted Kyle's attention, if only for a moment.

Why is he still here?

Kyle was starting to wish Eric would outright proposition him so he could turn him down and be done with it.

Maybe he doesn't want to proposition you.

It was definitely a possibility. Kip had said that Eric could use a friend—someone to talk about art and history and other non-hockey things with. In fact, it was *extremely* possible that Kyle was being an asshole because he was projecting his past heartbreak onto a perfectly innocent attractive older man.

An attractive older man who looked completely lost right now, holding someone else's beer and seemingly trying to think of something to say that would make Kyle be nice to him.

Kyle decided to throw him a bone. "Do you have the day off tomorrow?"

Eric's face lit up, and Kyle flooded with shame. "I do."

Kyle pretended to be busy wiping down the bar. "And how does Eric Bennett spend his days off?"

Eric seemed to think about it for a moment. "I do a more intensive yoga practice at home on days when I don't have a game or practice."

"Wow." Kyle laughed. "Is that how you kick back and unwind? Intensive yoga?"

"Yes." There was nothing playful in Eric's tone, so Kyle let it drop. Maybe the yoga was enjoyable for Eric. Maybe intensive yoga turned into intensive, flexible morning sex with his wife.

"I'm also going to visit my friend's gallery," Eric said. "She's preparing a new exhibit and wants to show me the paintings in advance. I'll be on the road for the opening."

"Oh, that's right! You're a patron of the arts." Kyle said it as if he'd completely forgotten that Eric collected art. It was one of many enchanting things about Eric Bennett that Kyle was trying not to think about.

"I buy art that I like," Eric corrected. "It's mostly selfish."

"Is that something a lot of hockey players do? Collect art?" Kyle already guessed that it wasn't.

"Not many that I've met. Nothing against my teammates—some of them are my best friends—but they aren't the most cultured bunch."

The way he said it suggested to Kyle that when Eric went to galleries and openings, it was probably alone. "Where's the gallery?"

"In Chelsea. It's the Saint-Georges Gallery."

"I know it!" Kyle exclaimed. "I mean, I haven't been in it, but I am very familiar with the empanada shop next door."

Eric's face split into another broad, devastating smile. "Córdoba Bakery! I love that place."

Why couldn't he stop being perfect? "I'm a regular there. I live a block away from it. The spicy beef empanadas are like sex, oh my god."

"I'll have to take your word for it."

Kyle couldn't help himself. "About sex?"

Eric chuckled. "About beef. I'm a vegetarian."

Of course he was. "That's great! I mean, great for . . . the environment. And for you! And, um, animals. I've been trying to cut back myself."

Eric's face settled into the same calm amusement Kyle had found so bewitching at the engagement party. "I'm not offended that you eat meat. Most of my friends do."

"Oh." Eric's crisp white dress shirt was open at the collar, giving Kyle an excellent view of his throat, which was sexier than it had any right to be. A few curls of dark chest hair were visible just above the first closed shirt button. Kyle loved chest hair. He bet Eric had the perfect amount of it, and maybe some of it was silver. God, that would be hot.

"If you want, I mean," Eric said, and Kyle realized he'd completely missed whatever had preceded it.

"Sorry. Want to what?"

"Come with me. To the gallery tomorrow. Jeanette, the owner, is very excited about these paintings and I thought you might like to see them."

It would be so easy for Kyle to say yes to this. It was a normal thing that two people who shared an interest might do. It didn't have to mean more than that. It could be . . . safe.

But Kyle knew himself. Eric, he couldn't be sure of, but he knew himself. Spending cozy one-on-one time together would lead to Kyle falling back on bad habits. So instead of saying yes, he said, "I can't tomorrow. Maybe I'll try to make the opening, though. What night is it?"

Eric told him the details, disappointment written all over his face, and Kyle pretended to commit them to memory.

Kip came up behind Eric, grinning from ear to ear. "I knew you guys would get along. What are you two talking about?"

"Art," Kyle said, taking a step back from the bar, and from Eric.

"See? Best friends," Kip said. "But also, Rozanov is looking for his beer."

"Shit, I forgot about him," Eric said. He picked up the beer. "I guess I'd better deliver this."

"Doing my job for me?" Kyle teased.

"Terribly, clearly."

He turned to leave, and Kyle blurted out. "Hey, um." Eric turned back, his expression all interest. "If you're hungry, you should know that we do great cauliflower wings here. One hundred percent meat-free."

Eric smiled like Kyle had just offered to grant him his greatest wish. "Thank you. For letting me know."

Oh god. Kyle really did want to take this man apart. He was the perfect blend of distinguished and shy. Confident about who he was, but timid about what he wanted. Whether he wanted Kyle's friendship or he wanted Kyle to fulfill every secret gay fantasy he'd ever had, it was clear that Eric had no idea how to ask for it. He needed someone to take charge, and Kyle very much wanted to be that person.

But he couldn't. Obviously. Eric was married, probably closeted, and probably self-loathing. Everything Kyle absolutely did not need in his life.

CHAPTER FIVE

Eric couldn't decide what was more humiliating when played back in his head: the fact that he'd basically asked Kyle out, or the efficient way Kyle had shut him down completely. Because of course he had; Eric was far too old and far too dull.

Even *if* the attraction was mutual, it wouldn't be enough to make Kyle do something as ridiculous as date a man who had probably been in high school when he had been born.

Date. Jesus.

If Kyle was looking for anything from Eric—and he almost certainly wasn't—it would be a hookup. A one-night thing. That wasn't normally Eric's style, but he had been out of the dating game for so long he couldn't honestly say what his style was, really. Maybe he would love hookups. His teammates certainly seemed to enjoy them.

And if Eric didn't want a one-night stand with Kyle, then what *did* he want? A boyfriend? No, of course not. But maybe . . . a friend. Eric couldn't deny how lonely he'd been, beyond the time he spent with his teammates, especially these past few months.

He put these thoughts away as he entered Jeanette's gallery. He wanted a clear head when he viewed the paintings.

Jeanette was on her phone when Eric walked in. She waved at him, then held up a finger. He nodded and used the time to remove his gloves and shake off the cold. A minute later she was walking briskly over to him.

"Eric!" She embraced him quickly, then stood back to inspect him. "You get more handsome every time I see you. Tell me you're seeing someone."

"No one."

She clucked her tongue. "What a waste. Have you made any new prints lately? I think the last ones I saw were from Wales."

"No, I don't have much time for photography during the hockey season." Eric had been dabbling in photography for years. He'd splurged on a professional-quality camera and had spent much of his off-season traveling and taking photos. He was hardly an artist, but he believed he had a good eye, benefiting from the same attention to detail that helped him on the ice.

"Your talents are being wasted," Jeanette sighed.

Eric chuckled at that. "Some people think my greater talent is goaltending."

"Fools." Jeanette flipped her hand in a gesture that invited him to follow her. "Come. The paintings are in the other room."

"Young artist?" Eric asked as he followed her.

"Actually, no. The artist is in his fifties, but he's new to the art world." She nudged him. "You can become an artist at any age, Eric."

"Noted."

"He was a power line technician, if you can believe it."

"That would give you a different perspective of the world, I guess. Is he American?"

"Swedish." They entered the second room, which had some

canvases tilted against walls, waiting to be hung. But Jeanette led him to the far wall, which had four smaller paintings installed. "He does abstract landscapes, and I know you're going to see right away how special his work is."

Eric studied the four paintings. They were stunning, mostly dark tones with pops of lighter colors like yellow and green. They were almost purely abstract, but with enough structure to suggest a landscape. "They're beautiful," he said.

"Aren't they? But *this* is the one I really want you to see." She placed her hands on his shoulders and turned him to face the wall behind him. It had a larger canvas with a cloth draped over it. "Prepare to fall in love," she said, then removed the cloth.

Eric nearly gasped. This painting was an intense surge of blue and black that seemed determined to pull him into its depths. "Wow."

"Breathtaking, isn't it?"

"I can't look away."

She touched his arm. "I'll leave you alone with it for a bit. I need to make a call. I'll warn you, though, that I have another interested—"

"I'm buying it," Eric said, his gaze still locked on the painting. "I know exactly where to hang it. It's perfect."

"Wonderful. The exhibit will run until January, but after that it's yours."

Eric couldn't help but wonder, as he stood alone in the gallery, what Kyle would have thought of the paintings. He barely knew the man, and had never much cared about getting a second opinion on the art he'd purchased in the past, but he found himself wishing Kyle were here now. Would Kyle have gasped when the painting had been revealed? Would he be standing close enough to Eric that their arms might accidentally brush together? Would he say something flirty and playful that would make Eric's blood fizz?

God, why was Eric so enchanted by him? Maybe it *was* a midlife crisis thing. He was turning forty-one next week, which was basically a hundred in hockey years. It had felt weird, last year, turning forty right after he and Holly had split up. Forty was a milestone, but he hadn't felt much like partying. His friends had made an effort, but when a buddy is depressed about a break-up and doesn't drink, hockey players generally aren't sure what to do with him. So Scott and Carter had suffered through what must have been a very boring and sad birthday dinner with Eric at his favorite Indian restaurant.

He didn't expect his forty-first birthday to be much better. He wasn't miserable about the divorce anymore, but he was lonely, and anxious about the impending curtain drop on his career.

Also, it had been over a year of celibacy. Even with his relatively quiet libido, he was feeling the ache. The need for human touch—a kiss, a caress, anything. Someone to travel with or, hell, watch a movie with.

Someone to visit galleries and museums with. Someone with a bewitching smile and faded denim eyes.

Eric spent a few more minutes with his painting, pleased that he'd been able to obtain at least one beautiful thing he'd desired this week.

Kyle was on the couch watching *Guy's Grocery Games* when Maria emerged from her bedroom on Thanksgiving morning.

"Uh oh. A Triple G emergency," she said. "Did your parents call or something?"

Kyle shrugged and pretended to be engrossed in someone trying to make a Thanksgiving dinner using just items from the cereal aisle. The only reason he was out of bed right now was because he'd been jolted awake by his mother calling him. The obligatory Thanksgiving phone call. As usual, it had been stiff and awkward, with Mom asking basic questions about school and the weather, and Kyle answering them without any enthusiasm. He used to be desperate to hear from his parents, hope blooming in his chest each time they called that this would be the time they would . . . forgive him? Apologize? Listen? And then Kyle had just stopped caring.

But the phone calls still unearthed all sorts of unpleasant feelings.

Maria joined him on the couch. "Sorry," she said.

"Thanks." He didn't need to say more. Maria had heard it all before.

"Good thing you get to go to the best Thanksgiving ever today," she said cheerfully.

Kyle's lips curved up at that. The Villanuevas really did host the best Thanksgiving dinners. "I'm going to eat until I explode."

"That's the spirit!"

He snuggled into her and they watched the rest of the show together. When it was over, Kyle said, "I want to change my whole life."

"Wow. I know *Guy's Grocery Games* is inspiring, but—"

"I'm serious. What even is my life? I'm working on a degree I don't even want. I have a crush on my unavailable best friend. I haven't been in a good relationship . . . ever?"

"Okay, but let's look at the positives."

"Like what? I work in a bar?"

"I mean, sure. You have a job you don't hate. That's a big deal!"

"I kind of hate it. Sometimes." He actually loved his job. It was easily his favorite thing about his life. He just got so frustrated at how the Kingfisher was run sometimes.

"Still better than most people. And you have great friends, including a dream roommate."

Kyle smiled. "True. Continue."

"You hang out with NHL players."

"Sure. Okay."

"You may be relying on your parents' generosity, but you have a two-bedroom apartment in Chelsea, dude. That's pretty sweet."

"I know. Fuck, I know. I'm really fucking privileged and it's horrible for me to complain." God, it was gross for Kyle to whine about his life to someone who was in school to learn how to help some of the most disadvantaged people in New York. Maria was a better person than he'd ever be.

"It's okay to complain, but we're being positive right now. Which brings me to my next point: you're totally hot. You just need to focus that hotness on the right man."

"Great. If someone wants to tell me who the right man is, I will happily ensnare him."

She put both hands on his shoulders and stared hard into his eyes. "Not. Kip."

"I'm trying, okay? I'm . . . almost over him."

"You know what would help? A man who isn't Kip."

"I *know*."

She poked his arm. "You know, Rafael is going to be at my parents' today. I think he's still single."

"Uh huh. Is he still exclusively into bears?"

Her brows pinched. "Raf is into bears?"

"*Yes*. Remember the last time you tried to set me up with him? Was it your dad's birthday party? He let me down easy, but I am *not* going to be trying that again." It was too bad. Maria's cousin was hot.

"Okay. So not Raf. But maybe Raf has a friend who—"

"Stop. Please. Thanksgiving is not a time for seduction anyway. It's a time to eat a ridiculous amount of food and then collapse on the couch."

Maria snapped her waistband. "I've got my stretchiest pants on. I'm ready."

"Hot."

A new episode of *Guy's Grocery Games* had started. They watched in silence for a moment, and then Maria said, "Oh no."

"What?"

"I watched a minute of this episode."

Kyle grinned, realizing the problem. "Well, we're invested now."

"Yep. Gotta watch the whole thing." She leaned against him, curling her legs on the couch.

"Should I get snacks?"

"No! It's Thanksgiving. You can't pregame Thanksgiving!"

Kyle laughed, and decided to be thankful for the family he'd found in New York, rather than dwell on the shame and anger he felt whenever he talked to his parents. "I don't know what I was thinking."

"I'm having a party."

Eric's announcement was met by stunned silence. He had expected as much, so he hurried to explain. "It's my birthday on Thursday, we have Friday off and I want to have a party. At my house. On Thursday night."

The idea had struck him when he'd woken up that morning. He, Eric Bennett, would celebrate his forty-first birthday—his final birthday as an NHL player—with a big, fun party. Because if not now, when? He had a house to himself, he had friends who he loved like family, and he had, frankly, a bit of a crush on someone. Someone who might enjoy a fun party.

The Admirals locker room remained silent for another few seconds, and then Carter clapped his hands and said, "Party at Benny's! Come on, boys, it's his ninetieth birthday. Let's go hard."

The room erupted into laughter, cheering, and teasing.

"All right, Benny!"

"You still going to be alive next week?"

"What time is the party? Five until seven?"

"BYO chocolate milk?"

Eric pretended to be annoyed, but he couldn't hide his smile. "Regular party time, you assholes. And I'll have a fully stocked bar. Bring your partner, bring your friends." Then, for whatever ridiculous reason, he added, "Bring your partner's friends."

There was whooping and hollering. This team loved a good party.

"So what's this all about?" Scott asked in a low voice as he removed his skates.

"What do you mean?"

"I've known you a long time, and I don't think you've ever hosted a party. You barely even *go* to parties."

Eric unfastened the straps on his chest protector. "Maybe I want to try something new." It was an absurd thing to say, given that almost every fucking thing in Eric's life lately had been new. His house was new, living alone was new, being single was new, facing retirement was new.

Allowing himself to fantasize about men was new.

Wanting to maybe do something about it was definitely new.

"Well, Kip and I will be there for sure. And maybe Kip can invite Maria. She's fun. Oh, and Kyle. She lives with him, so if he's not working, maybe—"

"Sure. That would be cool," Eric interrupted, far too eagerly. "If he's not busy. He can definitely come. I'd like that. I mean . . . the more the merrier, right?" He cringed inwardly. *The more the merrier?* God, he sounded like his mother.

"We have to be up sort of early on Friday," Scott said. "Kip and I, I mean. We're doing an interview for a documentary about queer athletes. There's going to be hair and makeup and the whole deal. Kip is excited about it."

"That sounds great." Eric meant it. Scott and Kip had done a lot of interviews, events, and photoshoots since their relationship had become public. It was basically a second job for

Scott, taking up most of his free time. But Scott had told Eric once that, in the past, that time might have been spent doing paid work for his sponsors, and representing and boosting the LGBTQ community was far more rewarding than endorsing razor blades and sports drinks. "I won't be offended if you need to leave the party early. I've left plenty of parties early for no reason at all, so . . ."

Scott smiled. "I wasn't exactly a party animal myself before I met Kip. I mean, I'm still not, but at least I go out without feeling terrified that I'll let the mask slip, y'know?"

Oh, Eric knew. His situation wasn't the same as Scott's, but he understood how it felt to live with a secret. To love playing hockey, but hate having to endure the endless homophobic slurs. To have to pretend you didn't take them personally. At least Eric had been with Holly for most of his career. He hadn't denied himself love or companionship out of fear, he just hadn't been completely honest about who he was.

Scott had never had that luxury. By the time Scott had finally come out to his friends, Eric had already suspected that Scott might be gay. It wasn't just that he'd never shown any interest in dating or hooking up with women—it was the unease that Scott always carried with him into social situations. Into locker room conversations about women. It was the sadness that had always lurked under his steady, heroic exterior. Most of the guys probably hadn't noticed, but Eric had seen it for years.

He'd never asked Scott about it beyond a perfunctory "are you all right?", which probably made Eric a bad friend. Or maybe it just made him a hockey player, conditioned to only be interested in feelings that came from, or affected, the game. Either way, Eric had done nothing to help.

It almost felt selfish to come out to Scott now. After Scott had done all the hard work on his own. It had been two and a half years since Scott had publicly come out as the first gay NHL player, and now, after watching his friend shoulder that burden alone, Eric wanted what? Some advice? Some dating tips?

He needed to figure out a way to tell Scott that didn't make him feel like an asshole.

"I like you better with the mask off," is what he said now.

Scott beamed at him. "Me too." He clapped Eric on the shoulder. "I'm excited about this party, Benny! This is going to be great."

Eric nodded. Maybe he could be a little more adventurous. The kind of guy who hosted fun parties and who maybe opened the door, just a crack, to let a little chaos into his life.

CHAPTER SIX

Going to the gym with Aram was like going to karaoke night with Jennifer Hudson. Kyle felt absolutely outclassed and ridiculous every time he agreed to work out with his Atlas-like co-worker. Aram was maybe three inches taller than Kyle, but he had to have at least thirty or forty extra pounds of muscle on him. His arms were like balloon arches.

Kyle watched as Aram added more weight to the barbell before stepping into the rack. "Why don't we just go outside and you can lift a bus?" Kyle suggested. "It would be free."

"Because there are less hot boys in tank tops out there," Aram said.

Kyle positioned himself near Aram, ostensibly to spot him as he did his squats, but if Aram actually did lose control of the barbell, it would go right through Kyle, the floor, and probably end up near the center of the earth.

Aram was definitely one of the *hottest* boys in a tank top at the gym. Tall, muscular, and arrestingly handsome with his long, dark hair and trim beard, rich brown eyes, and a killer smile. It was kind of shocking that he and Kyle had never hooked up, but

Kyle figured if it hadn't happened by now, it wasn't going to. And despite Aram's good looks, Kyle didn't think of him that way.

Kyle's gaze had mostly been drifting toward one of the treadmills where an older, distinguished-looking man had been running for the past half hour. His hair was silver, but he was probably only in his forties. He looked like an executive; a man who was used to getting what he wanted. Kyle allowed himself a moment to fantasize about having that man underneath him, begging for Kyle's cock.

Oof. Anyway.

Aram finished his set and led Kyle to some mats where they could do some stretching before hitting the locker room.

"Is Kip really going to keep working at the Kingfisher?" Aram asked as he settled himself on his back. "It's not like he needs the money now that he's locking Scott down."

Kyle lay down beside him, and they both turned toward each other to do identical thoracic rotation stretches. "I don't know," Kyle said honestly. "Maybe not."

"If I was marrying a millionaire I sure as fuck wouldn't be working there anymore," Aram said.

"He's proud, y'know? He doesn't want to be a kept man."

"God, *I* do. I would be very happy spending my husband's money for a living, I think."

Kyle shook his head. He had a taste of what it was like to spend money that wasn't his own. His parents had given him a lot of money over the years—money he knew they could easily afford, but still. He definitely appreciated how lucky he was, but he couldn't be proud of it either. In a lot of ways, it made him feel like he'd never truly grown up.

"Someday your prince will come, Aram."

"Well, he can take his time," Aram said with a grin. "I'm having fun enjoying all the city has to offer for now."

As if on cue, a young, fit man with a full sleeve of tattoos strolled by their mats, causing Aram to sit up and smile at him.

"Maybe *he's* a millionaire," Kyle teased.

"I should probably go find out." Aram wrapped one sweaty, beefy arm around Kyle's shoulders and squeezed. "See you later, all right?"

"Good luck." Kyle headed to the fountain to refill his water bottle. As he walked he pulled his phone out of his pocket. There was a text from Kip.

KIP:

Eric Bennett is having a party on Thursday. You should come.

Oh, absolutely the fuck not. The last thing Kyle needed to be doing was going to a party hosted by the unavailable man he'd been lusting after as the guest of the unavailable man he'd been low-key in love with for two years. That sounded like torture.

KYLE:

I'm busy.

KIP:

Doing what? I know you're not working.

Kyle frowned at his phone. What excuse would work? Not that he even owed Kip one.

KYLE:

I have a date.

Well, that was a giant lie. But it felt good. Which was probably not healthy.

KIP:

OMG really?! That's awesome!

KIP:

Impress him by bringing him to an NHL player's house party!

Kyle shoved his phone back in his pocket.

By the time Kyle returned home, there were four more texts from Kip.

KIP:

Who is your date with? Do I know him?

KIP:

Did you meet him at work?

KIP:

Maybe if the date doesn't go well you can bail and come to the party?

KIP:

Maria is going. I think Eric would really like you to go too.

Kyle sighed and wrote back: **Maybe next time.**

One minute later, his phone rang.

"There isn't going to be a next time," Kip said. "Do you know how often Eric throws a party? It's basically never happened before. That's what Scott said, anyway."

"Then I guess I'll have to miss the event of the century. Sorry."

"He has an amazing art collection. You should see it. Scott and I were at his new house like a month ago. Holy shit, Kyle. His house is incredible. It's so . . . *fancy*. But not, like, gross? It's very minimal and beautiful. It really suits his personality. I only went to his old house once, and it was, like, a mansion on Long Island. It was so wrong for him." He paused, probably because he needed oxygen, then said, "I guess his wife was wrong for him too."

"His wife?"

"Yeah. They split up a year or so ago. He's divorced now. That's why I think this party is so important. He's probably lonely."

Eric was divorced. Huh. Well, that was something.

"And," Kip continued, "I'm not kidding about him wanting you there. I think he really likes you. You guys have some things in common."

"Right." Eric was *divorced*.

"I know he's, like, old. But he mostly hangs out with twenty-something-year-old hockey players. He's cool."

"He's divorced?" Kyle asked, to make sure.

"Totally. It wasn't even messy. I think they just grew apart. But Eric is a great guy. Not the life of the party, but a good person for sure."

"He still wears his wedding ring."

"Huh? He does?"

"Yes. He was wearing it at the bar the other night. And at your engagement party."

"Really? That's weird. Maybe Scott knows why."

"Don't ask him."

"Why?"

"Because it's none of my business." Kyle sighed. "Why am I even invited to this? Is it going to be all hockey players?"

"No! I mean . . . mostly, yeah. But Maria is going!"

"So she can look at Matti Jalo."

"Look, we're *all* going to be looking at Matti Jalo. Let's get real here."

"I'm not because I'm not going."

"Oh right. So who's your date with?"

"Just a guy. You don't know him. Whatever. He probably won't even show up."

There was silence, and then Kip said, "You don't have a date, do you?"

"Of course I do. Why is that so hard to believe? I'm a catch."

Kip laughed. "I know. Honestly, I hope you do have a date. And that it's with the most amazing man on earth."

"Thanks."

"But if you *don't* have a date . . ."

"God, would you stop? Put Scott on the phone. I'd rather talk to him."

"I can't. He's in St. Louis."

"Oh."

"Hey, do you want to come over? I'm super bored and totally alone and we could watch a movie or something."

Holy shit no.

"Aw, I can't. Sorry."

"Another date?"

"Yeah. I'm on his dick right now, actually. So I should probably go."

"That's awkward," Kip agreed. "Especially since we were just talking about your next date."

Kyle snorted, then pretended to whisper to his nonexistent sex partner, "Sorry if I was being rude earlier." Then he pitched his voice comically low and said, "I didn't even notice you were on the phone, baby, because you're so good at riding me."

Kip howled. "Why is his voice so much deeper than yours?"

Kyle cracked up too, then pulled himself together enough to say, in the same deep voice, "Because I'm a fucking beast."

"He sounds like *Groot!*" After that, neither of them could speak for a full minute. In the middle of that minute, Maria returned home.

"Jesus, what's so funny?" she asked.

"Is that Maria?" Kip asked, still laughing. "Holy shit, has she been in your bedroom this whole time?"

"Hey, I put on a great show."

"I'll bet you do." Kip was joking, but his words made Kyle's dick twitch. "Give the phone to Maria. I want to talk to her."

"No. You're just going to tell her to convince me to go to the party."

"Eric's party?" Maria asked as she pulled her boots off. "You're totally going."

"Tell her about your date," Kip said.

"No."

"Come on. I want to hear you tell Maria to her face that you have an actual for real date on Thursday night."

"Bye, Kip."

Kip was still laughing when Kyle ended the call. He turned to Maria, who was holding up her phone.

"Text from Kip," she said. "He says to ask you why you can't go to the party."

Kyle gave an exaggerated sigh. "I told him I have a date. I *don't*," he clarified before Maria could start asking questions. "I just sort of blurted it out. I was probably trying to make him jealous, which is so sad I'm going to eat a whole bag of frozen perogies right now." He headed for the kitchen, and Maria followed him.

"First of all," she said, "you're only going to eat half of those perogies because I'm starving. Secondly, why don't you want to go to the party?"

"I don't know. Because I don't want to watch Kip make heart eyes at his fiancé. And I don't want to be around Eric."

"Why not? Wait. Is he actively trying to cheat on his wife with you? What a fucking scumbag. I'll fucking—"

"He's not. Married, I mean. Or actively trying to do anything with me. But . . . I know myself, and if I have a few drinks and he says anything even slightly flirtatious to me I will do something regrettable."

"Oh come on. You're not that easy."

"With men like that? Oh yes I am."

"What's so bad about liking older men? I know you had a bad experience."

"Or three."

"Yeah, but you know the one I mean. That guy in Vermont was a fucking trash bag. It doesn't mean it's wrong to be attracted to older men. I like tall men, and I've been with four of them who fucking sucked. Doesn't mean I'm not gonna keep trying to find that perfect, tall, probably Finnish prince who may or may not play for the New York Admirals."

Kyle smiled at that. "Ian *was* a trash bag, but I made my own choices. And those choices are always bad when it comes to a certain type of man."

Maria gave him a hard look. "Kyle. You were eighteen. Cut yourself some slack."

"Why? No one else did." Fuck, he shouldn't have said that. He put on a smile that probably didn't look any more real than it felt. "Anyway. It all worked out for the best, right? We get this sweet, free Manhattan apartment and I get to live my best gay life away from the gossip mill of Shaw, Vermont."

Maria had heard the story shortly after she'd moved in with

him. During Kyle's senior year of high school, his dad had gotten him a job in the offices of the Shaw Area Business and Tourism Association. The director of the association, Ian, was in his midthirties at the time, married with two kids, and was a very well-liked and respected member of the community. He was also, in virginal teenage Kyle's eyes, extremely hot.

Kyle had been working with him for about a month when Ian had asked him to stay late and help him brainstorm new festival ideas. He'd kept moving his chair closer to Kyle's, and he'd kept finding innocent ways to touch him. And then the touches had turned less innocent.

Kyle had known it was wrong, but he'd never had any kind of sex with anyone, and he'd been too horny and too flattered to care. He'd allowed their secret relationship to continue into the summer because he'd believed everything Ian told him: that he was unhappy in his marriage. That he was in love with Kyle. That he would leave his family for him. That it would be the best for everyone because Ian was living a lie.

Kyle, young and naive as he was, believed that this was a fairytale romance. That their love was so strong it would endure anything. The secrecy only made their relationship seem more important, like no one else got to know because no one else would understand how perfect they were together. Ian had let him believe that Kyle was the one in control. That Ian was helpless around him, and Kyle had loved that. He'd wanted to be irresistible. He'd wanted to be Helen of Troy, and have important men fall over themselves to win his favor.

It had all come crumbling down when Ian's wife had found out. She had hired a private investigator, because of course she had suspected; being the director of the business association of a tiny town was not a job that demanded a lot of late nights. The investigator had set up a hidden camera in Ian's office, and Kyle and Ian had given it plenty to record.

Ian had been confronted with the most explicit stills from the recordings, along with the news that his wife had left with the kids. The gossip spread around town like wildfire. It was the most interesting thing to happen in Shaw in forever: a gay affair. With a teenager.

And that was how Kyle had been outed as gay. To the town, to his friends, and, most devastatingly, to his family.

His parents had assured him repeatedly that they had no problem with him being gay. But he had embarrassed them by causing a scandal, and they'd felt it was best that he leave town. Kyle had always been an exceptional student, and he had been accepted to a few prestigious universities. He decided to go to Columbia because New York City seemed like the quintessential place to reinvent yourself, or to just get swallowed up. Both sounded good to Kyle at the time. His parents found and paid for an apartment in Chelsea, and Kyle found a part-time job as a server at a Chelsea restaurant to cover his expenses. He never saw or heard from Ian again, and he only saw his parents the rare times they visited him in New York.

"I want to fuck that guy up so bad," Maria said, bringing Kyle back to the present. "He should be in jail for what he did to you."

"I was legal," Kyle argued, for some reason.

"Barely. I mean there should be a law against that kind of . . . manipulation, y'know? Plus he was your boss. That's not okay."

"I know."

She hugged him suddenly, which was an unusual gesture from Maria. "You deserved better."

Kyle hugged her back. "I just think," he said carefully, "that heartache and temptation are a dangerous mix. If I go to that party I know what might happen."

Maria pulled back to look at him. "What exactly is the worst that can happen, though? If Eric isn't interested in you, you're not going to, like, trick him into making out with you."

"I'm more worried about the scenario where he *is* interested in me."

She stood back and started counting on her fingers. "He isn't married. He's a sweetheart by all accounts. And he's bonkers hot. I don't see how making a move on him would be bad in your worst-case scenario."

"Because it's always great *at first* with these guys. Then they get scared or whatever and flee. And then I'm scooping up the pieces of my heart *again*. No thanks."

"Well, if you change your mind . . ."

"I'm not changing my mind," Kyle said firmly. "For once in my life I'm going to make a good decision."

CHAPTER SEVEN

On Thursday night, Kyle followed Maria up the front steps of Eric's townhouse. Because of course he'd decided to go to the party.

Here was the thing: by trying to make the right choices, Kyle realized he was actually making terrible choices that alienated him from his friends. And prevented him from making new friends. He reminded himself that not everything needed to be about sex. Kip was a wonderful friend, and Eric seemed like a very nice guy who was intelligent and lovely to talk to. There was absolutely no reason to avoid any of that.

And Kyle had totally convinced himself of all of that right up until the moment Eric answered the door. Because holy hot damn. Eric, who, as far as Kyle could tell, never wore anything less formal than tailored slacks and a dress shirt, was wearing dark jeans and a charcoal T-shirt that clung to his broad, muscular chest and fluttered over his flat stomach. When Kyle's gaze made its way back up to Eric's face, he found him studying him before his eyes widened in recognition. "Kyle?"

"Surprise," Kyle said weakly. It looked like Eric was letting his beard fill in a bit, which was definitely a good look on him.

"I almost didn't recognize you."

Kyle grinned. "I know. I look different when I'm not at work."

"You do. It took me a moment." Eric tapped his own eyebrow. "Glasses."

"Yeah, I um, I never wear them when I'm at the bar, but this is basically what I look like most of the time."

Eric was staring at his face as if he couldn't quite believe Kyle was the same person who served him sodas with lime. "You look good," he finally said. "In glasses, I mean."

Kyle enjoyed Eric's brief and bashful smile. "Thank you."

"I can take that bag for you," Eric said. "And your coat."

Kyle set the heavy bag he'd been carrying on the floor and removed his jacket. "Nice try, but the bag has a surprise in it." He'd vowed to be playful, pleasant, and not overtly flirtatious tonight.

"I don't normally like surprises, but I'll admit I'm intrigued." He held Kyle's gaze as he took his coat and draped it over his arm. His eyes danced, even as the rest of his face stayed neutral. It was unfairly sexy.

"Hi," Maria said. "Maria is here."

That made Eric's cheeks turn pink. "I'm sorry. Nice to see you again, Maria. Let me take your coat."

Maria removed her coat, and Kyle stifled a laugh when Eric's eyes widened at the sight of her outfit. Maria had come to *play* tonight. Her breasts were pushed up to show maximum cleavage over the deep-V neckline of her black sweater dress. She looked fantastic, with the dress hugging her curves and her flawless hair and makeup. She may have only been five-foot-one in a house full of tall, athletic men, but Kyle fully expected her to stand out tonight.

For his own part, Kyle had kept it casual in a way that announced that he was not here to seduce anyone. He wore his most comfortable faded jeans with a long-sleeve blue T-shirt, had a scarf bunched around his neck, and finished the look with his second-favorite glasses. He was dressed to fade into the background and be a temptation to no one.

Kyle looked incredible. Eric's heart had started skipping in his chest the moment he recognized the man behind the glasses. He loved this version of him: the sweet, artistic grad student. He was pretty into all versions of Kyle, if he was being honest, but he was so damn cute in those glasses.

And he'd brought Eric a surprise.

He watched as Kyle retrieved the mystery bag from the floor, unable to take his eyes off him. "Where's the kitchen?" Kyle asked.

"I'll show you." He gestured for Kyle to follow him. Maria, who looked like a bombshell tonight, had already headed to the basement, where most of the party guests were. The kitchen was one story above them, so Eric led Kyle to the staircase. When Eric turned on the lights in the stairway, Kyle gasped.

"These are stunning!" Eric had three paintings displayed on the wall leading up to the next floor. They were abstracts, all by the same artist from the same series.

"Aren't they?" Eric agreed. "These were the first paintings Jeanette ever showed me. I knew I'd found my dealer after that."

Kyle leaned against the opposite wall with his feet planted at different heights on two different steps. He was smiling at the art, his face lit up the same way Eric's had been when he'd first seen the paintings himself. The way Eric's face was probably lit up right now watching Kyle.

"I love the orange in this one," Kyle said, pointing to the one Eric had hung in the middle.

"That one's my favorite." Eric realized they were both speaking in hushed tones. Everyone was either on the first or basement floors, so the floor above them was completely empty. The situation suddenly seemed very intimate.

Kyle turned to face him, and his face changed. It was like the light had suddenly gone out, the corners of his mouth turned down and his eyes looked almost scared. Eric shifted so he wasn't leaning quite so close.

"So," Kyle said. It wasn't the husky whisper he'd been using a moment ago. This was bright and loud and jarring. "Where's the kitchen?" Without waiting for an answer, he turned and headed up the rest of the stairs.

Of course. Eric's attraction to Kyle was probably written all over his face. His old, divorced, boring face. Kyle couldn't be blamed for being uncomfortable.

Be cool, Eric instructed himself. *You are in control of your feelings, your body, and your libido.* He took a centering breath, then followed Kyle up the stairs. Kyle had found the kitchen, which made sense since it took up most of this floor. He set the bag on one of the counters and looked around.

"You're having a party and your kitchen is *this* spotless?"

"The food is catered. I ordered from a barbecue restaurant the guys like."

"Uh huh. And what are *you* going to eat?"

"They have a kale salad I like."

Kyle smiled but didn't say anything about that as he began pulling bottles out of the bag and setting them on the counter. The last thing he pulled out was a cocktail shaker. "I wasn't sure you'd own one yourself," he said, holding it up.

"I do. But what is all this?"

"A birthday present. Just wait."

Eric got a hit of that fizzing sensation in his blood when Kyle winked at him then. "Do you need ice?"

"Yes, please." Kyle set everything up on the kitchen island

like it was a bar, so Eric filled a bowl with ice and then sat himself at one of the stools on the other side.

"I have a friend who makes incredible fermented juices and sodas," Kyle said as he cracked open a tall glass bottle full of vibrant, yellow liquid. "Here, smell this." He held out the bottle and Eric sniffed. It was warm and spicy and familiar.

"Ginger?" He asked.

Kyle nodded. "It's a fermented ginger and turmeric tonic. Delicious, healthy and the main component of your birthday mocktail."

"Birthday mocktail?" Eric was touched. He'd planned on drinking soda water tonight.

"I figured you might like fermented juice. You seem, y'know . . ."

"Like a health nut?"

"Like someone who takes care of himself," Kyle said with another wink. Eric watched as he carefully measured out ingredients and added them to the shaker. It was weird, having bartender Kyle and daytime Kyle blend into this single person in Eric's kitchen. Eric missed the short sleeves of the tight, white T-shirts that Kyle normally wore at work. He'd be able to see the slight bulge of Kyle's biceps right now as he shook the cocktail shaker.

Kyle held up a finger and went to Eric's cupboards, opening doors until he found what he wanted. He came back to the island with a tall glass, then tossed some ice cubes into it. "I hope you like this. I made a test one for myself earlier today."

"You didn't have to go to so much trouble."

"It's not trouble. I love inventing cocktails, with or without alcohol. I'm trying to convince my boss, Gus, to introduce an artisanal cocktail menu at the Kingfisher. He's pretty happy just serving beer and basic bitch mixed drinks, though."

"What about the Scott Hunter cocktail?"

Kyle smiled as he strained the contents of the shaker into the glass. "That was my creation. I put it on the chalkboard one night and it's been there ever since. Gus is terrible at marketing, but even *he* had to see the value of promoting the bar's connection to New York's favorite gay hockey star."

"Did Kip know about the cocktail? Before you put it on the board, I mean?"

"I ran it by him. He was pretty thrilled about the idea. He suggested making it with blueberry juice. I think it's an inside thing with those two." He poured some of the fancy tonic on top, then slid the glass toward Eric. "Maybe we can call this one the Eric Bennett."

Eric lifted the glass and admired the cloudy, yellow color of the liquid inside. He took a sip and tasted the sharp bite of the ginger, the warmth of the turmeric, and something sweet that balanced it all out. It was delicious.

"That's incredible," Eric said. "Is there something sweet in there, or is that the tonic?"

"It's a pineapple syrup that I made. You like it?"

Eric took another sip, closing his eyes this time and savoring the perfect blend of flavors. He swallowed and said, "I really do. Thank you."

Kyle beamed. "I can make a few more with the supplies I brought. I'll keep you plied with them all night, if you like."

"You don't have to. But if one finds its way into my hand, I'll definitely drink it." He tilted his head toward the stairs. "There's a bar downstairs. And a stocked beer fridge."

Kyle followed him to the stairs. "Why do you have a bar and a beer fridge if you don't drink?"

"Because all of my friends are hockey players."

"Except the ones who are art dealers?"

"The non-hockey friends are a small and very separate group. Tonight it's just hockey and hockey-adjacent, I'm afraid."

"Is that me? Hockey-adjacent?"

Eric paused at the landing in the middle of the stairs and turned back toward Kyle. "Technically I met you through hockey, but . . ." He stopped himself because there was no non-intense way to finish that sentence. If he was answering as honestly as possible, the sentence would have ended with something like *I think I might be able to be my whole self with you.*

"But?" Kyle asked. His pale blue eyes sparkled under his glasses.

Eric shook his head, trying to appear calm and collected even as his heart rate accelerated. "Nothing. Let's get you a drink. Do you like barbecue?"

"Only if there's kale salad."

Eric laughed. He loved the way Kyle teased him. It was playful and almost fond, as if they were old friends. "I'm sure there's plenty of salad left over."

Kyle really had no idea what he was doing at this party, but the stolen time alone with Eric in the kitchen was . . . nice. He'd felt sort of warm and buzzy since they'd joined the party in the basement, even though Eric had been pulled away from him immediately by a couple of women, who were probably wives or girlfriends of his teammates.

Kyle was now sitting on a sectional sofa with Scott, Kip, Carter, and an attractive Swedish hockey player whose name Kyle kept forgetting. He looked about Kyle's age.

Kyle knew Carter Vaughan because he often accompanied Scott when he'd visit Kip at the Kingfisher. Carter and Eric were Scott's best friends on the team, but the two men couldn't be more different. Carter was loud and fun, always the life of the party. He loved food and top shelf spirits, often giving Kyle shit about the subpar whiskey selection at the Kingfisher.

Carter, like most of the party guests, was closer to Kyle's age than Eric's. He was movie-star handsome, with dark skin and a strong jaw that was usually clean shaven. Eric was gorgeous, but in a more distinguished way with his salt-and-pepper beard and thick, curly hair that was begging to be rumpled.

What they had in common was that Carter and Eric were both good people, and they fully supported and loved Scott. Kyle liked them both.

"When are you and Gloria getting engaged, Carter?" Kip asked.

"Whenever she wants," Carter said, which made everyone laugh. "I'm serious. She knows I'm ready when she is. It's just hectic right now. We're both traveling constantly."

Carter was dating a very famous actress, Gloria Grey. She wasn't here tonight, but she'd come to the Kingfisher a few times and she was super cool.

"Where is she tonight?" Kyle asked.

"Atlanta. She's filming an action movie with Rose Landry where Gloria is an assassin and Rose is the special agent trying to stop her. Then they end up working together."

"Boo. Spoilers," Kip complained jokingly.

"It sounds badass," Carter said.

"Do they fall in love?" Kyle asked. "The assassin and the special agent?"

"Not officially." Carter grinned mischievously. "But Gloria said she and Rose are gonna play it like they're totally hot for each other. See if anyone notices."

"I love it," Kip said.

Carter stood. "I'm hitting the bar. Anyone need anything?" He turned to Kyle. "Can I get *you* a beer for a change?"

Kyle laughed. "I'm okay." It was probably silly, but knowing Eric didn't drink made Kyle not want to drink either. "I might try to get a peek at some more of Eric's art collection."

"It's nice, right? I need to get that classy son of a bitch to teach me about that shit someday."

"It won't help," joked the mystery Swedish guy.

"Fuck you, Tommy."

Tommy. Right. Kip and Scott were clearly lost in each other's eyes at the moment, so Kyle turned his attention to Tommy. "I don't think we've met. I'm Kyle." He held out his hand, and Tommy shook it.

"Tommy. Andersson."

"Right! You're the other goalie. Sorry I didn't recognize you."

Tommy smiled. He was really goddamned handsome. He looked like a Skarsgaard. "Don't worry about it."

There was nothing flirtatious about the way Tommy spoke to or looked at Kyle, but it occurred to Kyle that it was pretty cool that this probably-straight hockey player was calmly sharing a sectional sofa with three gay men. Like, he shouldn't get a trophy for it or anything, but from what Kyle knew about team sports, especially hockey, it wasn't an insignificant gesture. He wondered how big an impact Scott had made on the way his teammates viewed queer people.

"So you like getting hit by pucks too, huh?"

"Most of the time, yes." He was so much younger than Eric. Kyle wondered if he was Eric's competition, or if Eric was more like his mentor. Maybe it was a bit of both.

"Do you like New York?" Kyle asked. It was maybe the most boring question he could ask, but at least it filled the silence.

Tommy, thankfully, seemed enthusiastic when he answered. "Yes, I am very lucky. Not only because it's New York, but because I get to play with Benny. Eric, I mean. He was my hero, growing up."

"Whoa, really? That's nuts!" Kyle couldn't imagine what that was like for Eric. It must make him feel old.

"Yes," Tommy said seriously. "He is one of the best ever. He has been a great teacher."

Kyle knew that Eric was considered to be one of the greatest goaltenders to ever play the game, but he kind of forgot about it when he was talking to him. He couldn't quite reconcile the man behind the mask and the quietly intense man who collected art.

At that moment Maria dropped on the couch next to Kyle, and a very tall and beautiful blond woman snuggled up to Tommy. They began speaking to each other in Swedish, so Kyle assumed this was Tommy's girlfriend or wife.

"How's it going?" Kyle asked Maria. "How's Operation Finland?"

Maria exhaled with enough force to blow the tendrils of hair that fell in her face straight out. "Terrible. Have you seen the women at this party?" She subtly nodded in the direction of the woman Tommy was now kissing. "How am I supposed to have a chance?"

Kyle's gaze dropped to her chest. "You could try more cleavage."

Instead of telling him to fuck off, like he'd expected, she laughed and then curled into him. "God, I look ridiculous. And desperate."

Kyle kissed the top of her head. "You look gorgeous. So was Jalo a dick to you? I can beat him up. It might take a few days of punching him, but eventually he would feel it. I think."

"I haven't even tried to talk to him," Maria said into his shoulder. "I don't know what I was expecting to happen."

"Well, what *should* have happened was that he spotted you across the room, and then parted the crowd with his massive shoulders and thighs so he could get to you. Then he should have swept you off your feet and carried you back to his place for six days and seven nights of lovemaking."

"Like, would that have been so hard? Men. Honestly." She sighed. "I'm going to die alone."

"You're not. You're going to die during a threesome with Oscar Isaac and Michael B. Jordan."

"That's really nice of you to say."

"Do you want to look at art with me?"

She lifted her head. "I think I'd rather look at that bar over there."

"Pace yourself, girl."

"Fuck yourself, boy." She playfully punched his arm before standing and heading for the bar. He turned his attention to Kip, who was actually for real booping Scott on the nose, so Kyle stood up and got the fuck out of there.

He headed out of the crowded basement and upstairs to the front entrance area. He'd noticed some paintings and sculptures on display there that he hadn't had a chance to inspect earlier. He figured he could poke around a bit, maybe mix Eric another drink, and then hit the road. He wasn't in much of a party mood tonight.

Eric's house was undeniably beautiful, but Kyle wondered what it looked like when it wasn't full of lively party guests. The stark white walls and modern, minimal furniture were ideal for displaying art, but Kyle imagined it might be a cold place to live alone.

There was a canvas hanging by itself on one wall that had caught Kyle's eye earlier. It was hard to miss, really: an enormous abstract oil painting that was full of frantic angular scrapes of dark brown, indigo, black and stark white. Scattered in a few places were dots of eye-catching fuchsia. Kyle lost himself in it for several minutes.

"Powerful, isn't it?" Eric's hushed voice rumbled behind

him. Kyle hadn't heard him approach, so he turned quickly, startled. Eric held up his hands. "Sorry. I didn't mean to scare you."

"It's okay." He turned back to the painting. "This is really beautiful."

"It's called *Guardian*. I fell in love with it the moment I saw it, but the name really sold me."

It took Kyle a moment. "Because that's your job. Guarding the net."

"Right." Eric was standing so close that Kyle would only have to lean back slightly to feel Eric's chest against his back. He had to close his eyes for a moment to fight the longing to have Eric wrap his arms around him from behind. For him to kiss Kyle's neck and nibble his ear. For Kyle to press his ass against Eric's crotch, and feel him grow hard against him.

These were all bad thoughts. Kyle took a step forward under the guise of wanting a closer look at the painting. "I love the energy of it. You can feel the artist's urgency."

"Urgency?"

"In creating the guardian. Blocking out whatever it is they feared or hated."

"So the guardian is good, you think?"

Kyle turned to him. "You don't?"

Eric frowned at the painting. "I'm not sure. I thought maybe the guardian was an obstacle to something better. The pink spots—" he pointed to a couple of them "—might be the good trying to break through."

"Huh." Kyle considered this perspective. It did make sense. "Then that makes you the bad guy."

"In a way, I am. I keep people from scoring goals. From winning. I stand between them and victory."

"Or you protect your own teammates from defeat."

"Perspective is important," Eric agreed with wry smile. "I'm glad you like the piece. When I showed it to Carter, he said it should be called *Rectangles*."

Kyle laughed. "At least he knows his shapes."

"It's a start."

The smile faded from Eric's lips at the same moment Kyle felt his own heart seize in his chest. He couldn't miss the way Eric's gaze had landed on Kyle's mouth.

What would happen if Kyle leaned in, just slightly? Would Eric kiss him? Would he back away? Was Kyle misreading the desire he was sure was darkening Eric's eyes?

Footsteps pounded up the stairs, and Eric turned quickly away from Kyle. Kip, followed closely by Scott, came into view, pausing in surprise when they saw Eric and Kyle.

"Oh, hey guys," Kip said. "We have to head out."

"Early morning tomorrow," Scott said apologetically.

"Right," Eric said. His calm voice didn't suggest that he'd almost been caught kissing Kyle, so maybe Kyle had been imagining things. "I remember. Thank you for coming. Let me get your coats."

"Already on it," Kip said, holding up a finger before returning to the basement. Scott crossed his giant arms in front of his massive chest and smiled at Kyle and Eric.

"What?" Eric asked.

"Kip and I have been trying to get you two together for months."

"*What?*" Kyle sputtered.

"Together? Why?" Eric asked, much more smoothly.

"We thought you guys could be friends. Y'know. About art and stuff." He nodded at the painting.

So maybe Kyle's sputtering was unwarranted. He turned back to the painting to hide his embarrassment while Eric said, "It *is* nice to talk about something other than video games and fantasy football."

Kip emerged from the basement wearing his coat and carrying Scott's. "There are at least three guys playing *Fortnight* on their phones down there. I'm going to write a tell-all about how uncool pro hockey players are."

"You'd better not," Scott teased.

"Oh, I'm going to have a whole chapter about your love of word search puzzles."

"They're relaxing!"

Kip threw his arms around Eric. "Happy birthday, buddy."

"Thanks."

Kyle was hugged next, which was always an exercise in not nuzzling Kip's neck. It was easier to resist with Kip's fiancé looking on. "Goodnight, Kip."

"I'm glad you came out tonight. Have fun, all right?" He gave Kyle an extra squeeze, then released him. Kyle could still feel Kip's arms around him as he watched Kip take Scott's hand and lead him out the front door.

When Kyle turned back to Eric, he saw that same sympathetic look on his face that he'd seen the night of Kip and Scott's engagement party. He hated it.

"So," Kyle said brightly, refusing to acknowledge the fact that his feelings for Kip were so fucking obvious that even this near-stranger noticed them. "Can I get you another drink?"

Eric's face shifted into the quietly amused expression that Kyle greatly preferred. "Sure."

CHAPTER EIGHT

The party went on for hours. Long past Eric's usual bedtime. He tried to mingle with everyone, drifting between the basement and the living room upstairs, but like magnets he and Kyle kept being drawn together.

He wasn't sure if Kyle was doing it on purpose, or if he didn't know enough people at the party, but almost every time Eric spotted him, he was standing alone. Sometimes he would be admiring a piece of art, sometimes just watching the party. A couple of times he'd had his phone out. Eric had been unable to resist checking in on him every time.

The guests were finally starting to clear out, and Eric thought maybe Kyle had left while he'd been upstairs, but when Eric returned to the basement he found him collecting empty beer bottles.

"You don't have to do that," Eric said.

Kyle glanced up from where he was bent over a side table and grinned. "Habit. And *someone* needs to do this. Your friends are animals." Kyle had removed his scarf, and now Eric could admire the long lines of his neck.

"They're not the most considerate bunch," Eric agreed as he helped Kyle gather up the bottles.

He heard the front door open and close a couple of times above them as they worked, and soon he couldn't hear evidence of anyone else in the house besides the two of them.

"Where's Maria?" Eric asked.

"She left over an hour ago. One of the couples offered to drop her off at home. I can't remember their names, but the wife is pregnant."

"That's Breezy and Martine."

"Decent, non-murderous people, I assume?"

"They're great. And they're from Montreal, so they have no problem driving in Manhattan."

"Good to know. Should these go to the kitchen?" Kyle had his arms full of about a dozen empty bottles. He was obviously well practiced in the art of carrying large numbers of glass containers.

"Yeah. We can rinse them out up there. Or I can. You can go home." Eric laughed nervously. "You are under no obligation to help me clean up."

"I really don't mind." Kyle headed for the stairs, then paused and looked back over his shoulder. "You're the birthday boy. You shouldn't have to clean." He winked, and Eric *really* wished he'd stop doing that.

"I have cleaners coming tomorrow," Eric said as he followed him up the stairs, trying but failing to not admire Kyle's ass as it swayed in front of his face.

"So you were just planning to go to bed with this mess of bottles everywhere?" It was a question, but it sounded like Kyle already knew the answer.

"No," Eric admitted. He would have at least rinsed out the empties like Kyle was doing. He hated mess. It was something his teammates had been teasing him about for years, but Eric wondered why Kyle had been able to guess it so quickly about him. Probably from seeing his kitchen. Or maybe Eric obviously presented as the fussy neat freak he was.

"By the way," Kyle said as they entered the kitchen, "if I haven't mentioned it already, your house is incredible."

"Thank you. I'm very happy with it."

"Is there a rooftop terrace?"

"Yes."

"Goddamn you."

Eric laughed. "Sorry. You're welcome to use it any time." He mentally kicked himself for saying something so weird, but Kyle smiled.

"Maybe I'll wait until spring."

"Right. Yeah."

Kyle pushed up his sleeves and began rinsing the bottles out in Eric's sink, which Eric could not allow. "Really," he said, placing a hand on Kyle's arm. "I can do this later."

Kyle looked at Eric's hand, and then met Eric's eyes. "Later when? It's almost two in the morning."

"Exactly. You should go home to bed."

"I'm at work past two most nights," Kyle said. "This is nothing. Let me help."

Eric surrendered and stood there awkwardly, watching Kyle work with his head full of thoughts that he knew he shouldn't say out loud. He chose one of the safest ones. "It was nice spending time with you tonight. I'm glad you came."

Kyle didn't look up from the sink. "I almost didn't."

"Why?"

He saw Kyle's shoulders tense, and he thought he wouldn't answer, but he said, "I think you know why."

Eric did have some idea, though he was surprised Kyle was bringing it up. "Because of Kip. And Scott."

"I'm pretty fucking obvious, I know. And pathetic." He set

the last of the bottles on the counter and turned, bracing himself with both hands on the edge of the sink behind his back. "Anyway. I need to get over it. I mean, I *am* getting over it."

"I'm sorry."

Kyle laughed without any humor. "You know what the most ridiculous part is? Kip was supposed to be the end of me having crushes on inappropriate men. He was supposed to be a *good choice*."

"Inappropriate men?"

He shook his head. "I shouldn't be talking about this with you. Or anyone. It's fine. Forget I said anything."

"No, I—" Eric's hand found itself back on Kyle's arm. "I want to listen. If you want to talk."

"I'm way too sober for that."

Eric studied his face. "You *are* sober, aren't you? You didn't drink tonight?"

Kyle shrugged. "Didn't feel like it."

The possibility that Kyle had abstained because Eric didn't drink warmed him. But maybe Kyle truly hadn't felt like it and Eric shouldn't read any more into it. "Why don't I get us both some water, and we can sit in the living room for a bit?"

"Okay."

A few minutes later, Kyle was wedged into the corner of a sectional sofa, and Eric was sitting a safe, platonic distance away. Kyle took a sip of his water and said, "So what do you want to know?"

There were a lot of careful, easy questions Eric could have asked. Ones that wouldn't have been completely selfish. But what he asked was, "Is Kip not the type of man you're normally attracted to?"

Kyle's eyebrows raised over the frames of his glasses, and his lips quirked up. "No. Not usually. I mean, I don't have a strict type, but . . ."

Eric shifted to the edge of his sofa cushion. "But?"

"I have a bit of a weakness for . . . older men."

He swallowed. "How much older?"

"Oh, I don't know. Maybe forty. Or—" Kyle smiled mischievously at him "—forty-one."

Eric's dick arrived to the party at that moment. Late, but very keen to celebrate his birthday. He knew he should reply to Kyle, but his head had gone fuzzy.

Kyle waved a hand. "Don't take me too seriously when I flirt. It's basically a defense mechanism for me."

"Defense," Eric repeated thickly. "Right." He shook away some of the haze of lust. "Of course. I know you're not serious."

"Good. But let me know if I ever make you uncomfortable, please. I really don't want to do that."

"I'll tell you." Uncomfortable was one way of putting it. Although, whether he was uncomfortable from being unsure of how to respond to Kyle's suggestive remarks, or if it was from the sudden tightness of his jeans, it was hard to say. Did Kyle *know* that Eric was attracted to men? Was it as obvious to him as Eric's inability to leave his basement a mess?

"You are gorgeous, though," Kyle said easily. "If you didn't know that."

"Thank you." *Return the compliment, Eric!* Or should he? Would that only make things more weird? It was probably safer if the flirting was only one sided. But he had to say something, so he said, "I like your glasses."

Kyle laughed. "As in you want to buy a pair for yourself, or as in you want to see me wearing nothing but them?" Before Eric could respond, Kyle quickly said, "Sorry. That was too much."

Eric crossed his legs as casually as possible as he fought to banish the mental image of Kyle wearing only his glasses. Maybe he would be stretched elegantly across Eric's bed, his back arching as Eric trailed kisses up the inside of his thigh . . .

"I'm trying to be anyway," Kyle said.

Trying to be? Trying to be what? Oh god, Eric had completely missed everything that Kyle had just said.

"Trying to be, um . . . pardon?" Eric said elegantly.

Kyle grinned. "Good. Or smart. Trying not to date creeps."

"Creeps?" Anger flared inside of Eric at the thought of a man hurting Kyle. "How do you mean?"

"Oh, you know. Secretly married. Closeted and staying there. Manipulative and selfish. Any combination of those things. That's my type, apparently."

That didn't sound like the sort of man Kyle should be with at all. Kyle should be with someone who cherished every one of his playful smiles and devilish winks. Who appreciated how smart Kyle was, and how easy he was to talk to. "Those guys sound like assholes."

"Yeah, well." Kyle pulled his knees up and rested his tilted head on them. "You wanna hear something funny? I thought you were going to be one of them."

"One of them? What do you mean?"

"I thought you were married. Because of the ring. And I thought you were . . . well. It doesn't matter."

"Thought I was what?" Dammit. The ring. Carter was right. He should have taken it off ages ago.

"I probably project it on every handsome older man now, but I thought you were another closeted married man who was looking to have a little secret fun with the gay boy."

Eric's stomach clenched at the thought. "I would never—that's—"

"I know. I was wrong. I get it. Like I said, I project. But you really do seem like a great guy, and I'd like to be friends."

Friends. "I'd like that too." It wasn't a lie. Eric did like talking to Kyle, and he'd love to go to some galleries with him. Maybe share some meals. Maybe—

Kyle yawned then, and Eric was reminded of the late hour. And of the fact that Kyle lived all the way in Chelsea.

"You should stay here tonight," Eric said. It was an obvious offer and he should have made it before now.

"Oh no. I can get a cab."

"Stay. I have two guest rooms. I'll even make coffee in the morning."

Kyle lifted his head off his knees. "That is very tempting."

"I've got extra toothbrushes and everything. I have nowhere to be in the morning. You can sleep as late as you like."

Kyle yawned again, then laughed. "All right. You win."

Eric beamed, far too happy about this development. He stood and offered Kyle his hand, a natural gesture that he would offer one of his teammates on the ice or at the gym. But when Kyle took his hand, suddenly nothing about it seemed natural or familiar. Kyle's fingers were cold, probably from rinsing out the beer bottles, and his skin was rougher than Eric had been expecting. He pulled Kyle to his feet, and then Kyle's face was inches away from Eric's own. Their chests were almost brushing against each other as Kyle gazed at him with sleepy blue eyes.

Eric was still holding his hand.

"I'll, um. I'll show you your room. I can lend you some pajama pants, if you like."

Kyle brushed his thumb over Eric's knuckles, then released his hand. "Thanks."

Eric turned away before he did something unforgivable, like invite Kyle to share his own bed. He led Kyle to the bedroom that was on the same floor as the kitchen. It was Eric's favorite of the two guest rooms.

"Oh wow," Kyle said when Eric turned on the bedside lamp. The room was at the front of the house, and there was a large window that looked to the street. The wall with the window was exposed brick, which Eric loved, and the rest of the walls were stark white, as was the bedding, the armchair in the corner, and the rug. Above the bed's light-stained maple headboard hung a large framed black-and-white photograph of a fog-laden rocky beach.

"There's a white noise machine," Eric said, gesturing to the small device that sat beside the lamp. "If you need it."

"I might," Kyle said. "I've been in the city for over six years and I still can't quite block out the noise at night."

"Where's home?"

"Vermont. Or, it was home, anyway."

Eric didn't like the sound of that, but he also knew that three in the morning wasn't the time to be getting into sad stories. So he just said, "I love Vermont."

"Me too. This photograph is beautiful. Do you know where this is?"

"Wales." Eric hesitated a moment, then said, "I took it."

Kyle's head whipped around, his eyes wide under his glasses. "*You* took that?"

"I dabble. I'm not a professional by any stretch."

"You could be. Holy shit." He winked. "What other talents are you hiding?"

Heat crept up Eric's neck. Kyle was not making it easy to think pure thoughts.

"Sorry," Kyle said. "That was the last one. I promise. I'm just sleepy and silly. And I haven't had sex in forever."

"Right. No problem," Eric said stiffly. "I'll go get you those pajamas. And a toothbrush. Do you need anything else?"

"Can't think of anything."

Eric left quickly. He did not like how easily flustered he got in Kyle's company. In his bedroom, he took a moment to compose himself, then he grabbed his softest pair of pajama pants and a T-shirt before going to the bathroom to find a new toothbrush and some toothpaste. When he returned to Kyle's room, he nearly dropped everything he was carrying.

Kyle was sprawled out on the bed, shirtless with the button of his jeans unfastened. His body was lean and toned—the body of an athlete who was built for speed.

Kyle propped himself up on his elbows, his abs flexing as he curled up to face Eric. "Is this duvet cover *linen*?"

"Yes," Eric said weakly. "The sheets are too."

Kyle fell back on the bed and let out a long, guttural moan of pleasure that made Eric lower the bundle in his hands so it covered his crotch. "Fuuuuck. And these pillows," Kyle continued, oblivious to the alarming spike in Eric's arousal. "I am so fucking horny for this bed."

Oh, come on, universe. Not fair.

"I have pajamas. And a toothbrush. I'll just . . ." Well, Eric couldn't *hand* them to him. Not with his erection trying to bust through his pants. "I'll leave them here." He set them on the chair in the corner and turned quickly toward the door. "Goodnight."

"Hey," Kyle said.

Eric paused, but he kept his back to Kyle. "Yes?"

"It was a good party. Everyone had fun."

"You think?" Eric turned his head to the side so he wasn't completely shutting Kyle out.

"Definitely. I watch people drinking and having fun several times a week at work. I'm an expert on who's having a good time and who isn't. The party was a hit."

"That's good to hear." He stood for another moment, waiting to see if Kyle had anything more to say, then said, "Sleep well."

"I am going to sleep *so hard* in this bed."

Eric smiled to himself and pulled the door closed behind him. When it was almost shut, he heard Kyle say, "Happy birthday."

* * *

Eric had his jeans unfastened before he'd even reached his bedroom on the top floor. He couldn't remember the last time he'd been this desperate to jerk off.

The moment he closed his bedroom door behind him, his jeans hit the floor with the loud clatter of his belt. He shoved his hand into his briefs and groaned so loudly when he gripped his cock that he shoved the knuckles of his free hand into his mouth to muffle the noise. He fell on his bed and slid his briefs down to his ankles, kicking them away as he yanked his shirt off and threw it to the floor.

Eric had never directly—or indirectly—compared his masturbation techniques to another man's, but he assumed he was in the top percentile for efficiency. Eric was efficient in all things; efficient, disciplined, and practiced. He had jerking off down to a science.

He wondered if Kyle was stroking himself too. If at this moment he was naked and writhing on Eric's linen bed sheets, his long, work-rough fingers working a cock that Eric could only imagine. And god, could he imagine it. Long and beautiful and jutting out from pubic hair that was the same dark blond as the hair that had trailed into the waistband of his jeans. Kyle's abs clenching and flexing as he got closer to the edge. As he got himself to where Eric was right now, teetering on the brink.

If Kyle was jerking off too, was he thinking about Eric? Was he about to come with Eric's name on his lips like Eric was about to—

"Fuck. Kyle. Please." Eric whispered the words as he arched and came all over his stomach.

When it was over, when the last rush of pleasure had left his body and Eric was left holding his softening dick with semen drying on his skin, shame set in. What the fuck was he doing? He was a dirty old man jerking off to thoughts of the lovely young man who'd been kind enough to help him clean up after his party. Barely more than an acquaintance. A possible new friend.

Eric was pathetic.

But he was definitely attracted to men. His bisexuality felt a whole lot less theoretical, even just allowing himself to fantasize about another man. A specific other man. A man who was sleeping two floors below Eric right now. Wearing Eric's pajamas.

Unless he was sleeping naked.

Oh god.

Eric took a few long, slow breaths and then began to reason this thing out. No one was getting hurt here. And Kyle had to know that his flirtations would have an effect on Eric. Assuming that Kyle knew Eric was attracted to him—attracted to *men*.

Was it a problem if he did know? Eric had always assumed it was something that people wouldn't guess about him, but he'd never been faced with a man he'd wanted as much as Kyle. Maybe his desire was plain as day when he was talking to him. It was something to think about, for sure.

Eric dragged himself into the bathroom and cleaned himself quickly. He went to his walk-in closet and found his second-softest pajama pants, enjoying the caress of bamboo as he pulled them on. The slick fabric felt cool against his heated skin.

When he got into bed, he realized how exhausted he was. As he drifted off to sleep, he thought of winter-blue eyes dancing behind glasses, calloused hands, and disheveled corn silk hair.

CHAPTER NINE

Kyle woke up late.

He stretched languidly, sliding his limbs inside the butter-soft layers of Eric's expensive bedding. The sheets felt so wonderful he had left the pajamas Eric had brought him on the chair and slept in his underwear. The luxurious caress of the fabric had done nothing to quell Kyle's raging arousal, but he'd resisted jerking off last night. It seemed wrong to do that in Eric's house. Kyle didn't want to be rude.

But now his dick was screaming for attention. Kyle did his best to ignore it, flipping to his stomach and burying his face in a perfectly soft pillow.

Eric had been ogling him last night, Kyle was sure of it. He'd been ogled quite a lot in his life, and the heat in Eric's eyes when he'd taken in Kyle's bare chest had been unmistakable. And the way he'd hurried out of the room, flustered and adorable.

Eric wanted him.

But that didn't mean Eric was going to do anything about it. And it didn't mean Kyle should *want* him to do anything about it. Eric, Kyle reminded himself, was off limits.

His dark eyes were off limits. His muscular forearms and broad chest were off limits. His silver-flecked beard and gorgeous thick hair were off limits.

Kyle wasn't sure how long he'd been humping the mattress, but he needed to stop. He didn't even see a box of tissues in the room.

He forced himself to leave the bed, adjusting his erection in his briefs and hoping it would fade soon. He normally indulged in a leisurely jerk-off session when he woke up, so his dick was confused and angry about his refusal to acknowledge it today.

He put his glasses on and ran a hand through his hair. He pulled on the pajama pants and T-shirt Eric had given him—both exquisitely soft—grabbed the toothbrush and toothpaste, quietly opened the bedroom door and slipped into the hallway to the bathroom. He wasn't sure if Eric would be awake yet. He seemed like he'd be an early riser, but it had been a very late night.

Kyle got freshened up in the bathroom and considered taking a shower. His dick was very into that idea, but Kyle wasn't going let that idiot call the shots. He wasn't sure where Eric kept the towels, or if it would be presumptuous to use the shower.

The house was very quiet. Kyle wandered into the kitchen, hoping to find the coffee Eric had promised, but found it empty. The bottles Kyle had rinsed last night had been put away somewhere, so Eric must be awake.

Kyle stood at the bottom of the stairs that led to the top two floors, but he couldn't see anything past the point where they turned a corner. He slowly ascended the stairs, hoping Eric would make his presence known before Kyle looked too much like a stalker. When the room at the top came into view, his jaw dropped.

The whole floor seemed to be a studio space. The front wall was entirely windows, and the other walls were white, reflecting the midday sun. The floor was a light-colored wood, and the room was sparsely decorated with lush green plants and quiet pieces of art. It was a gorgeous space, but the most stunning feature was the man in the middle of the room balancing, shirtless, on his elbows with his legs stretched high above his head in a perfectly straight line.

Kyle stared for a moment at the tension in Eric's muscular forearms and biceps. At the elegant lines of his bare feet. At the defined muscles of his back. He was physical perfection.

"Holy shit," Kyle whispered, which made Eric open his eyes. His brow furrowed when he saw Kyle, then he calmly bent his knees, tucking his legs into his body before slowly shifting to a kneeling position on the mat.

"Good morning," Eric said.

"Is it still morning?"

"Barely." Eric stood and sauntered over to Kyle, his chest glistening with sweat. He had dark hair covering his pecs, which was exactly what Kyle had pictured. When he'd allowed himself to picture. Which was more often than he should have allowed it.

"Sorry to interrupt."

"It's okay. Are you hungry?"

"Always."

"Let me grab my shirt."

"Is that necessary?" Kyle groaned at himself. "Sorry."

Eric chuckled as he snatched his shirt off the floor. "You didn't even last five minutes."

"Well, can you blame me?" Kyle waved his hands in the direction of Eric's bare chest. "I had no warning at all."

"I'll be sure to text you before I remove my shirt in the future."

They both kind of froze after Eric said that. Then Kyle laughed, mostly to break the tension. "I would appreciate that."

"I'll make some coffee. What do you like to eat in the mornings?" Eric headed down the stairs and Kyle followed.

"Lucky Charms. Coco Puffs. That sort of thing."

Eric frowned. "Oh, uh. I don't really—"

"I'm kidding. I know we don't know each other well, but I am pretty sure you don't eat a lot of garbage sugar cereal."

"No." His smile was sweet and a little embarrassed. "I don't."

"Did you eat already? You don't have to feed me."

"I haven't eaten. I like to work out first. I'm hungry." They reached the kitchen and Eric got started on the coffee. Kyle, unsure of what to do, sat himself on one of the stools at the island.

"Did you sleep well?" Eric asked.

"Like the dead. You?"

"Same. I don't usually stay up so late. I was exhausted. Do you like Greek yogurt?"

"Sure."

"I have berries and granola. And honey."

"Fancy."

The coffeemaker gurgled as Kyle watched Eric assemble two bowls of yogurt with fresh berries and what looked to be locally made granola sprinkled on top.

"Thanks again for your help last night," Eric said. With a shy smile he added, "Do you really think everyone had a good time?"

"Definitely. They love you, I can tell."

"They *respect* me," Eric clarified, setting a beautifully put together bowl in front of Kyle.

"Scott loves you. And Carter."

Eric swallowed a spoonful of yogurt with a thoughtful expression on his face. "You know, for years I was basically a loner on the team. Being a goalie creates a natural separation between you and the rest of the team anyway, but because I don't drink and I'm not the most social guy . . . well. I never really felt like part of the gang."

"What changed?"

Eric smiled. "Scott Hunter joined the team."

Kyle ignored the way his heart clenched like it was in a vise. "Oh yeah?"

"Scotty's not the life of the party either, but he has this quality that I have always envied. He earns the respect of everyone around him instantly. Right from his rookie season. There was no question he was going to be team captain someday."

"Right."

"The other guys are always seeking his approval. They want him to like them. They want his respect. And Scott probably noticed that I wasn't being invited out after the games, and that no one was really talking to me in the locker room. So he made a point of talking to me. Of inviting me out."

Kyle sighed. "He really is perfect, isn't he?"

"I'm afraid so. Sorry."

Kyle smiled to himself as he took a bite of yogurt and blackberries. It was kind of nice to be talking about this with someone other than Maria. "I need to get out there. Actually go on some dates."

"That makes two of us."

"Oh yeah?" Kyle perked up. Here was an interesting conversation topic. "You haven't been dating since . . . I mean, since . . ."

"My divorce?" Eric offered helpfully. "Nope. Not a single date. Or hookup, or whatever people are calling it now."

"Wait. You haven't had *sex* since, um . . ."

"My wife left me? No."

Kyle knew it was none of his business, but he couldn't help himself. "And that was . . ."

"Over a year ago."

"Wow. That's, um . . . are you okay?"

Eric chuckled. "I'm okay."

"How are you not, like, vibrating with pent-up arousal?"

Eric stared at him with that sexy bemused smile on his face. "Vibrating with pent-up arousal?"

"Yeah! I'd be . . . I mean, it's been a couple of weeks for me and I basically want to fuck this yogurt."

"Please don't. And I've never had an overwhelming need to . . ."

"Bone down all day every day?"

"Right. That."

Kyle took another bite of yogurt to prove he was kidding about wanting to fuck it. "You don't like sex?"

"I do. Sometimes. Sometimes I like it a lot. It just doesn't . . . consume me. Usually."

Kyle lifted his brow. "Usually?"

"I can be . . . distracted. By sexual thoughts. Sometimes." God, Eric was blushing a little and Kyle was in heaven.

"Maybe next time you're distracted by sexual thoughts about someone you should see if they're interested."

Eric froze, spoon halfway to his mouth. Kyle mentally kicked himself.

"Is the coffee ready?" Kyle asked as he practically leaped off his seat to put some distance between himself and Eric.

"Yes. I think. Probably," Eric stammered, lurched forward in the direction of the coffee maker, then stopped when he realized that's where Kyle was headed. "You can, um. Check."

"It looks done. The light is—"

"Green. Yes. The green light means done."

"Okay." Kyle almost laughed at how ridiculous they both sounded. "How do you take it? Black, right? Just a guess."

"Black. Yes."

Kyle promised himself to stop being flirty with poor Eric. It wasn't doing either of them any good. He found two clear glass coffee mugs—all of Eric's drinkware seemed to be clear glass—and filled them both with coffee. "Another guess: you don't have cream."

"I have oat milk."

"Holy hell. All right. Where's the oat milk?"

"In the fridge. It's an unmarked glass bottle, but it's the only thing that looks like milk. It's beside the green juice."

Kyle opened the fridge and stared for probably a full minute. It looked like a cold storage unit at a lab more than a fridge. It was immaculate, for one thing. One shelf held an array of unmarked glass bottles containing various colors of very healthy-looking liquids. Another shelf held jars full of what looked like some sort of oatmeal or wet grains. There were eggs, yogurt, berries, and a few condiments, all neatly organized. The crisper drawers appeared to be full of fresh produce.

Kyle thought of the fridge in the apartment he shared with Maria. It was crammed full of god knows what. Definitely cheese, beer, and leftover takeout. There might be a vegetable in there.

"This looks like a magazine advertisement for refrigerators," Kyle said. "This is what I imagine Gwyneth Paltrow's fridge looking like."

"There are no jokes you can make about my diet that my teammates haven't made a million times."

"You're so *healthy*. How do you do that?"

"It's important. I can't perform at my best if I don't take care of my body. Especially at my age."

"Right. Such an old man at forty-one."

"In hockey years I'm ancient."

"Well, you look all right to me." *Oops.* He handed Eric a mug of black coffee, meeting his gaze and finding the same interest he'd seen last night. Kyle pulled his hand back quickly, not trusting himself not to brush Eric's fingers with his own. *Stupid sexy Eric.*

Kyle took a sip of perfectly brewed coffee that was only slightly hindered by the oat milk, and tried to think of a way to throw a bucket of ice water on the conversation. He definitely needed to steer things away from sex.

But Eric ruined everything by saying, "I've been thinking about sex a lot lately."

"Oh?" Kyle asked, a little squeakily. "Any reason?"

"Yeah. I'm, um. I'm . . . bisexual." Eric blew out a breath after he said it. "I've never said that out loud before. Wow."

Wait. What the fuck? "You've never told *anyone* that before?"

"No. Not yet, anyway. I want to. I just . . . haven't. Yet."

"But you're telling me?"

Eric's brow furrowed. "Should I not have?"

Oh god. Kyle was being a douche. "No! No, I'm glad you told me. I'm . . . flattered. That you felt you could trust me. You can, you know. Trust me. I won't tell anyone."

"I appreciate that. I want to tell everyone soon. But for now . . . I just wanted to tell *someone*. If that makes sense."

"It does! Totally. And I'm honored. But it doesn't really answer my question about why you're thinking about sex a lot lately."

"Right. That wasn't what I meant." Eric laughed uneasily. "It's more that I've been thinking about maybe, you know, dating. Men, I mean. But I don't really know how."

"How? Like . . . you don't know how to have sexy times with a man?"

"I don't even know how to find a man to have sexy times with."

Kyle grinned broadly. "I'm no expert—actually, that's a lie. I totally am—but I think you could probably walk into a gay bar and walk out with, like, five very willing men. You've seen yourself, right?"

Eric shook his head, but he was smiling. "Do I whistle or something to announce my presence?"

"Yes. Or, if you can do one of those hog calls?"

"Oh god," Eric said, laughing. "Yuck."

"I mean, you asked how to pick up men. Don't blame me if you don't like how it works."

"If," Eric said, still laughing, "you think of any actually useful advice for the forty-one-year-old divorcé who is looking to meet a nice man, please let me know."

"Are you looking for someone to date or just, like, trade blowjobs?"

Eric's whole face turned pink, which was incredible to witness. "I don't know. Date, I guess. Trading, um—that sounds so . . . transactional."

"It is, I suppose. But it also kinda rules."

"I don't think I could do that. I've never been one for hookups. I like to know the person first."

"That's cool. You're not alone there. I'm sure we could find you a nice man to have dinner with."

"We?"

"Yeah. Sure. I want to help you." This was a terrible idea, but Kyle was going all in. "We should go out together. See what your type is, and then take it from there."

"Um."

"It doesn't have to be, like, a *club*. It could be a bar like the Kingfisher—but *not* the Kingfisher, please god—and we'll get a drink and have a little look around."

He watched Eric's face carefully. Eric didn't look repulsed by this idea, so that was a win. "When you say *take it from there* . . ."

Kyle held up his hands. "No pressure to do anything. I'm just suggesting a super casual outing where we do some low-key ogling. It's an easy, safe first step."

Eric seemed to consider this. "Okay."

"Awesome!" Kyle was getting excited about this now. "This is great for me too, because I need to get myself out there."

"So, when do you want to do this?"

Kyle drummed his fingers against his lips. "I'm working tomorrow night. I could do Sunday . . ."

"I've got a game on Sunday. I'm free Monday."

"I'm working that night. Tuesday?"

"I'm in Boston on Tuesday. Then Toronto."

Damn. This was not working out.

"Well," Eric said slowly, "what about tonight?"

"Really?"

"Sure. No time like the present, right?"

"I know the perfect place. There's a great bar called Fortune that is totally chill, but it's busy on Fridays, so we'll have lots to look at. I know the bar manager there and he's a sweetheart. He'll take care of us."

"Okay." Eric chewed his lip. "What should I wear?"

Kyle clapped his hands together. "I love you in a dress shirt, but you looked hot as hell last night in a T-shirt and jeans."

Eric ducked his head adorably. "Hot as hell?"

"*Yes*. You should go that route. Dress down, look like you're not trying too hard because you don't *have to*. You'll have your pick of the men."

"I thought we were just going to look."

"We are. I'm just kidding. Why don't you come by my place? I live a couple blocks away from Fortune. Here, give me your phone."

Eric retrieved his phone from where it had been charging on the kitchen counter and handed it to Kyle. Kyle entered his contact info, including his address, texted himself, then handed the phone back to Eric.

"I should get going," Kyle said. "I have a pile of reading to do for school."

"Right. Okay."

Kyle went to the guest room and quickly changed back into his clothes from last night. "I'll miss you most of all, perfect bed," he said as he slipped out of the room.

Eric walked him to the front door, and they shared an oddly awkward moment where Kyle felt the urge to kiss him goodbye.

He settled for a quick hug, which seemed normal enough. Kyle hugged everyone.

"I'll see you tonight," he said, wrapping his arms around Eric's back.

"Tonight," Eric agreed, encircling Kyle with his muscular arms. He smelled wonderful—a spicy, manly shampoo, maybe—and Kyle just barely stopped himself from nuzzling his neck. Then he felt the soft brush of Eric sighing against his ear, and Kyle suddenly found it very hard to let go.

The hug lasted a moment too long to be considered quick and friendly, but Kyle tried to pretend it hadn't. Eric looked like he was doing the same as he shoved one hand into his sweatpants pocket and held up the other hand to wave awkwardly. Kyle nodded at him, stepping backward until he hit the door. He turned quickly, opened the door, and practically jumped down the steps to safety.

CHAPTER TEN

Knowing that Kyle was a bartender and part-time student living in Manhattan, Eric assumed his apartment would be small and rundown. When he stepped over the threshold, though, he was shocked to see a bright, spacious living room that was connected to a modern, well-equipped kitchen. The entire apartment had clearly been recently built; everything from the appliances to the floors looked new.

"Nice place," Eric commented as he drifted toward the windows. He glanced down at 19th Street, four stories below.

"Thanks. Just give me a sec." Kyle disappeared into what Eric presumed was his bedroom, so Eric poked around the living room a bit. He was immediately drawn to a shelf full of books on a wall next to a flat-screen television. Eric had gotten rid of most of his own book collection when he'd embraced minimalism and ebooks a couple of years ago. He'd found himself regretting his decision lately, wishing he had made room in his new house for a library. He loved looking at books, holding them. He missed the smell of paper.

Kyle's collection was eclectic, and horrifically disorganized. On one shelf there were graphic novels, history books about ancient Rome, South America, and World War I, celebrity autobiographies, cookbooks, and novels in English, Spanish and French. Eric pulled one well-worn hardcover that was missing its dustjacket off the shelf and flipped it open. It was in Italian, which made him smile.

He slid the book back where he'd gotten it—between a cocktail manual and a paperback copy of *The Iliad*. His fingers itched to reorganize the shelf, but instead he turned his attention to the top of the bookshelf, which was lined with framed photographs and knickknacks. There was a photo of Kyle and Maria, both laughing with elaborate cocktails in front of them. Next to it sat a snow globe with little ski hills inside that said *Vermont* on the base. Eric picked it up and turned it over, watching the snow fall over the little plastic skiers inside.

"Almost like being there, huh?" Kyle's voice startled Eric, and he nearly dropped the snow globe. It was rare that someone was able to sneak up on him.

"Sorry. I didn't mean to snoop." He placed the snow globe back on the shelf. When he turned to face Kyle, he noticed that Kyle looked extremely hot in a V-neck, purple T-shirt and dark, slim-cut jeans.

"It's okay," Kyle said easily. "You already know about my top secret Vermont origins."

"Do you go back there at all?" Eric couldn't stop himself from asking.

The smile fell from Kyle's lips. "Haven't been back in years."

"Oh."

"Mom and Dad send money. They paid for this place." He swept a hand around. "But, no. I haven't been invited home."

Eric couldn't understand why Kyle's parents wouldn't be eager to see him as much as possible. He was brilliant and lovely, and working on a master's degree from Columbia. Surely his parents were proud of him?

He opened his mouth to say . . . something, but Kyle cut him off. "Are you ready to go?"

Eric decided not to push it for right now. At least the mystery of the very nice apartment had been solved. "Sure."

Kyle grabbed his jacket and scarf from where he'd tossed them over a chair. His smile was back, and he winked at Eric as he said, "Let's go turn some heads."

They didn't speak until they reached the street, and then Eric thought of a question that had nothing to do with Kyle's family. "How many languages do you speak?"

"How do you know I speak more than one?"

"The books on your shelf. I saw a few different languages there." Something occurred to him. "Or maybe those were Maria's."

"You *were* snooping," Kyle teased. "They're mine. Maria speaks Spanish too, but I also speak Italian and French. One of my undergrad majors was Latin, so I can read that. Some ancient Greek as well. I'm working on modern Greek."

"Holy shit."

Kyle shrugged as if he'd just rattled off a list of movies he liked. "I'm a quick study when it comes to languages. Always have been."

"You're lucky. I know enough French to get by, but languages definitely don't come easily to me."

"We all have talents. I'm not much of a goaltender."

Eric laughed. "Have you ever tried?"

"God no. What kind of maniac lets people shoot pucks at them?"

"Someone whose cousin had goalie gear they didn't need anymore."

"Is that where it started?"

Eric nodded. "We were poor. I was lucky to get that hand-me-down gear." He still remembered how thrilled he'd been the first time he'd strapped those heavy pads to his legs. He'd loved being a goalie from the very first puck he'd stopped. He'd taken the game seriously, because he took everything seriously, even as a child, and by the time he was a teenager he saw it as a way of solving his family's financial struggles. Of maybe having a chance to go to university.

"Where are your parents now?" Kyle asked.

Eric smiled. "Living very comfortably on the shores of Lake Ontario. I bought them their dream house when I signed my first NHL contract."

"That must have been one hell of a contract."

"Their dream house isn't anything extravagant. Just a nice little Cape Cod outside Hamilton, Ontario. That's where I grew up. Hamilton, I mean."

"Are you their only child?"

"I have a younger brother and an older sister. They both still live in Hamilton. I'm glad for it because I rarely make it home. I'm a bad son."

"Bad sons don't buy their parents houses."

"It was the least I could do. They sacrificed a lot so I could stay in hockey. Dad was working days at a Mr. Lube and sometimes nights unloading trucks at a grocery store. Mom worked at Walmart for most of my teen years. My sister worked there too, when she was old enough. We were always struggling to pay the bills."

"And now you take care of them all."

It wasn't quite true. Eric's sister was a school principal and his brother was a contractor. But he certainly helped them as much as their pride would allow. "I do what I can."

Kyle stuffed his hands in his jacket pockets and hunched his shoulders against the cold. "I used to ski competitively. It was a lot of time and money for my parents." He huffed. "Money wasted, I guess."

Eric could see it. Kyle's lean, toned frame was definitely a skier's body. "I doubt they see it that way."

"Yeah, well." Kyle went quiet again.

"I've always been nervous on skis," Eric said, trying to lighten things. "I can't imagine flying down a mountain at top speed."

Kyle laughed. "So having pucks fired at you is fine, but skiing is scary?"

"Rinks are flat."

"But skiing has the most incredible views. I went glacier skiing in Switzerland last winter and, man. I feel bad for anyone who doesn't get to experience that. I can't even describe it."

"I'll definitely take your word for it," Eric said, though he could suddenly see the appeal of learning how to ski. He lost himself, for a moment, imagining Kyle teaching him. He wondered if Kyle had ever worked as an instructor.

He didn't get a chance to ask, because they had reached the bar.

Eric had spent time in gay bars before, obviously, but only when accompanying his openly gay friend. He'd never been uncomfortable going out with Scott to gay bars, but this felt different. This time he was at a gay bar for himself, for the purpose of openly checking out men. And being checked out by men.

He took a slow, centering breath, which Kyle noticed. "You all right?"

"Yeah. I don't know why I'm so nervous."

"Nothing to worry about. Besides, they'll all be looking at *me*." Kyle batted his eyelashes cartoonishly at him, which made Eric laugh.

"Good point."

Kyle held the door open and Eric stepped into the bar. It looked . . . like a bar. Dark, crowded, and lively. Pop music was playing, but not overly loud. The patrons were men and, mostly, Eric noticed right away, attractive. And younger than Eric.

This was a mistake.

"I'm too old for this," Eric muttered.

"You are absolutely not. I see a table we can grab. You sit, and I'll get us some drinks. You want a soda and lime?"

"Sure. Thanks."

Eric kind of wished he was the one going to the bar because at least that would give him something to do other than sit alone and vulnerable in a pick-up bar. He removed his coat and draped it over the back of his chair, then tugged at his T-shirt a bit. He'd chosen a light gray one that was tighter than he normally wore, and he'd paired it with jeans that were identical to the ones he'd worn last night. When Eric found something that fit him well, he tended to buy multiples.

He ran a hand over his hair and beard as he sat down, then picked up a drink special card so he'd have something to look at. He was terrified that if he glanced up he'd inadvertently lock eyes with someone and give them the wrong idea.

Kyle returned after what seemed like a very long time carrying two drinks. "Sorry," he said. "Calvin was chatty."

"Is that the bar manager?"

"Yeah. We used to work together at a shitty restaurant. Nice guy. Great kisser."

Eric gave a startled laugh. "Do you kiss all of your friends?"

Kyle narrowed his eyes as if he was thinking hard about it. "Most of them, I think."

Eric took a sip of his soda instead of replying.

"What? Hockey players kiss each other all the time. I've seen it," Kyle teased.

"Not on the mouths usually."

"Shame."

Eric shook his head, smiling. "What are you drinking?"

"It's something autumny and spicy that Calvin came up with. I'll switch to soda after this, though."

Eric was touched that Kyle was willing to abstain for his benefit, but it really wasn't necessary. "You don't have to."

Kyle waved a hand. "I don't mind. Besides, we're here on a mission. I need to keep a clear head." He leaned in. "So. Who do you like?"

Eric was caught off guard by the question. And by the answer that immediately popped into his head: he liked Kyle. He liked his clear, blue eyes and his carefully styled hair. He liked the peek of collarbone that jutted from the wide V of Kyle's neckline.

"I don't know," Eric lied. "Everyone here is very attractive."

Kyle turned to the side and observed the crowd for a moment before returning his gaze to Eric. "It's a good bar for that. What about him?" He nodded at someone over Eric's shoulder, which meant Eric would have to turn around to see him.

"Who?" Eric asked, without turning.

"Tall, beard, muscles."

Eric turned, as subtly as possible, and easily spotted the man Kyle had described. He was definitely handsome, but more in the way Eric's teammates were handsome, which didn't do it for Eric.

"Attractive," Eric agreed, turning back to Kyle. "But not for me."

Kyle's eyebrows shot up as he sipped his drink. "Too big? Too hairy? What's the issue?"

"I think . . ." God, this was torture. "Too . . . hockey player."

Kyle laughed like this was the funniest thing he'd ever heard.

Eric buried his face in his hands. "I can't do this," he groaned.

"You can. I get it. So we'll look for someone less macho and athletic."

"I didn't say not athletic," Eric argued. "Just not . . . that guy. I don't know."

"How about him?" Kyle blatantly pointed a finger at the table next to theirs, and Eric batted it down.

"Don't *point*!"

Kyle crossed his arms. "Sweetheart. We're all here for the same thing."

Eric glanced in the direction Kyle had been pointing and found three men drinking cocktails. One of them was smiling at Eric.

Eric quickly turned back to Kyle. "He looks nineteen!"

"Is that a no?"

"That's an absolute no."

"Good to know."

Eric glared at him. "Was that a test?"

"Not at all. First of all, he's older than nineteen. And secondly, I dated men about your age when I was younger than him."

Eric did *not* like thinking about that. "Well, I'm not interested in anyone that young."

Kyle looked down at the table, frowning. "What would be an appropriate age, do you think?"

"I don't know. Thirty at least?" Eric had picked the number because it felt right. It *was* right, wasn't it?

"Got it," Kyle said. It sounded a little icy. "Let's see . . ." He glanced around the room. "Okay. What about the cute accountant-type over there?"

Eric found the man Kyle was looking at. He looked to be in his thirties, slim, blond, and clean cut with glasses and a V-neck sweater over a checked shirt. He was, indeed, cute.

"Oh," Eric said. He looked back to Kyle, who was smiling from ear to ear.

"Did I nail it this time?"

Almost. "He's very . . . yes. I like him."

"He looks smart, but not pretentious," Kyle mused. "Let's guess his name."

Eric scoffed. "You can't guess someone's name by looking at them."

"You can have fun trying," Kyle insisted. "I'll bet it's . . . Alex."

"This is ridiculous," Eric said. "And besides, it's Justin."

Kyle laughed. "See? Fun. So Justin the accountant . . ."

"Did we agree that he's an accountant?"

"Yes. And he's from . . . Wisconsin."

"Wisconsin?"

"Little Justin left the farm for New York City to follow his big accounting dreams."

"And here he is."

"And here he is. About to take an NHL superstar to bed."

Eric nearly choked on his soda. "He is *not*."

Kyle reached across the table and placed a hand on his forearm. "I'm kidding."

Eric's skin prickled under Kyle's fingertips. "You'd better be."

Kyle leaned back in his chair, removing his hand. "You look hot, by the way. I like the shirt."

"Oh." Eric resisted the urge to pick at it. "Thanks. You look good too."

"On a scale of one to kill me, how uncomfortable are you right now?"

He smiled. "Hovering near kill me."

"Relax. We're not going to do anything that you're not comfortable with. I promise. We're just talking, and enjoying the scenery."

"How does it compare to glacier skiing in the Alps?"

Kyle grinned as his gaze followed a handsome dark-haired man who walked past their table. "Reasonably close."

Eric chuckled and took a sip of his drink, but his heart clenched with something that felt embarrassingly close to jealousy.

"So you haven't told Scott that you're bi?" Kyle asked, pulling Eric's attention away from his confusing feelings.

"No, not yet. I want to."

"Do you think he'll be surprised?"

It was more likely, he thought, that Scott would be hurt when Eric finally told him. "I don't know. Probably."

"Were you surprised when he came out?"

Eric thought about his answer before he spoke. "I was surprised that he came out, but less surprised that he was gay."

"I lost my mind when I saw him kissing Kip on television. It was on the big screen at work and I nearly dropped a whole tray of glasses."

"I knew they were a couple and I was still shocked."

"It was brave as fuck. It meant a lot, y'know? The vibe in the bar that night, after he did that? It was like we *all* won the Stanley Cup. It was a party for sure." Kyle snorted. "And, it made me feel pretty stupid for thinking I had a chance with Kip."

Poor Kyle. Eric wanted to say something comforting, but no. Kyle truly did not have a chance with Kip. "You weren't stupid. Scott and Kip did a good job of keeping their relationship a secret. No one knew."

"Yeah. Well."

"So how about you?" Eric asked, changing the subject. "Who's catching your eye in here tonight?"

Kyle pressed his lips together and looked oddly shy. For a wild second, Eric thought he was about to say that *he* was the one Kyle had his eye on. But then Kyle said, "Your four o'clock. In the dark blue shirt."

Eric turned, trying to appear as if he was fishing something out of his coat pocket, then glanced up to spot a tall man with silver-flecked hair wearing a crisp blue dress shirt unbuttoned at the collar. Eric turned back to Kyle, surprised. "He looks . . . mature. For you."

"That's how I like 'em."

"But I thought you avoided men like that." *Like me.*

"I *try* to. But I can't help who I'm attracted to. I know it's a bad idea to involve myself with them."

Eric fidgeted with his glass. "Why do you like older men?"

Kyle blew out a breath. "That's a big question."

"You don't have to tell me," Eric said, even though he itched with the need to know why someone like Kyle might be attracted to someone like him.

"I can try. I guess it has something to with the way I feel when I'm with them. I like men my own age, don't get me wrong. I've slept with plenty of them and I've had a great time doing it, but older men . . ." Kyle bit his lip. "They make me feel *powerful*. Like I'm irresistible and they would do anything to please me." He grinned, his gaze turning dreamy. "It's a rush."

Eric exhaled shakily as blood rushed to his cock. Kyle had just described the vague fantasies that had been overwhelming Eric for months, and especially for the past couple of weeks. He wanted to please Kyle. He wanted to spoil him rotten and have Kyle reward him for it however he chose to. He wanted this stunning young man to conquer him and leave Eric gasping for more.

"But they've hurt you?" Eric asked, because he needed to hear the other side right now. The darkness on the edge of this fantasy.

"Not physically. But it's never ended well with any of them. Too many lies or . . ." Kyle waved a hand around. "Anyway. Whatever."

Eric wanted to hear more, but he didn't want to push. What tumbled out of his mouth instead was, "They didn't deserve you."

Kyle's smile was sad and all wrong. "That's nice of you to say."

It was true, was what it was. If Eric were lucky enough to take Kyle to bed, he would treat him like a prince. A vivid image of Kyle reclining, naked, on a mountain of pillows popped into Eric's head. Eric would be between his spread legs, using his hands and mouth to pleasure Kyle however he was instructed to.

He took a long sip of his drink, and gave a silent thanks to the universe that his lap was safely hidden by the table right now.

"I would also be very okay with taking Justin the accountant home, though," Kyle said with a sly smile. "Or the twink, to be honest. Or any combination of the three."

Eric was in way over his head. Threesomes? *Foursomes?* He just wanted to find a nice man to have dinner with. Maybe a goodnight kiss. "You're not particular, then?"

"I have high standards, but I like to sample from every aisle of the supermarket."

Eric laughed shakily. His brain was a mess. "Okay."

Kyle's eyebrows lifted. "Ooh. I think Justin is coming over. I wonder which one of us caught his eye?"

"You for sure," Eric said. "Wait. He's coming—?"

"Hi," said a voice behind Eric's shoulder. "I just wanted to tell you that your eyes are the most gorgeous color."

He glanced up at the man who had easily said the words Eric had been thinking privately for days. It was, indeed, the cute accountant-type guy. Possibly cuter this close up.

"Well, thank you," Kyle said playfully. "You came all this way just to tell me that?"

"That depends," the man said with a questioning glance at Eric. "Are you available to hear more?"

Eric started to push his chair back. He would make an excuse, go to the bar or to the bathroom. Maybe go home. He should let Kyle have this.

Before he had a chance to make his exit, Kyle spoke. "We're actually celebrating our anniversary tonight." He reached across the table and took Eric's hand. Eric's mouth fell open. "Well, *month*iversary, right, love?"

Kyle's eyes were full of mischief. Eric's must have shown his confusion, but he managed to say, "Right."

"I figured." The man sighed. "I had to try, though."

"You're cute," Kyle said, still holding Eric's hand. "What's your name?"

"Alex."

Kyle shot Eric a quick, victorious smile, then said, "I'm Kyle, and this is Eric. My boyfriend."

Alex nodded. "Well, happy monthiversary."

"Thank you," Kyle said, "*Alex*."

Eric fought to keep himself from rolling his eyes. When Alex left, Kyle released Eric's hand and leaned back in his chair. He folded his arms over his chest, looking smug as hell.

"Fine," Eric said. "You guessed his name. Congratulations."

"I'm a genius."

"You're lucky."

"I could have been," Kyle said wistfully, gazing in the direction Alex had gone.

"Why did you tell him we were a couple?"

"Because I'm not going to *abandon* you tonight. I'm here to support you."

"I could have gone home. It's fine. I have a practice in the morning anyway."

"Do you *want* to go home?"

No. Eric wanted to have this view of Kyle for as long as possible. "I can stay a bit longer."

Kyle was having a great time.

Okay, yes, he wouldn't have minded leaving with cute Alex, and, yes, it was weird that he had spontaneously lied about being Eric's boyfriend, but still. He definitely wasn't *bored*.

Eric had gone to the bar to get their second round, Kyle

insisting that he wanted a soda and not another cocktail, which was the second lie he'd told that evening.

He really did want to help Eric. He was probably more invested in the idea of guiding Eric to his first sexual encounter with a man than he should be. He wanted to make sure Eric's first time would be enjoyable. That it would be with someone patient and sweet and *good*. Someone who understood how important this was.

Normally Kyle wouldn't think of this sort of thing as important. Hookups had been a way of life for him for so many years that he had a hard time thinking of sex as an event. Part of him wanted to gently push Eric into the arms of the first man who caught his eye, but he knew that wasn't what Eric wanted.

Eric was looking for *more.* A date. A . . . boyfriend, Kyle supposed. Someone to share meals and conversations with. Someone to share his life with. As much as Kyle wanted to help him, he was extremely aware that he hadn't been able to successfully find that for himself, let alone another person.

So maybe they both needed a little practice.

"It's busy up there," Eric said when he returned. He set two identical glasses of soda on the table and sat down. "I think the bartender was flirting with me."

"We do that," Kyle said. "But sometimes we mean it. Was he cute?"

Eric shrugged. "I've seen cuter."

Oh, Eric. You are not helping. "Did you flirt back?"

"I honestly have no idea. I guess I tried. I have absolutely no game when it comes to that sort of thing."

"I think you're selling yourself short. But—" Kyle gave an exaggerated sigh "—I suppose I *am* here to coach you."

Eric's dark eyes twinkled. "What would you be doing right now, in this bar, if you weren't here with your *boyfriend*?"

"Well, I'd probably be rounding third base with our friend Alex right now."

Eric nearly spat out his drink. "*Third base?* How old are you?"

"Twenty-five." Eric had been teasing, but Kyle realized he'd never told Eric how old he was before. The laughter left Eric's eyes as soon as he heard the number.

"Oh."

"Is that older or younger than you were expecting?"

"I guess it's what I'd assumed. You look like you could be younger." Eric cringed. "I mean . . . we have some young guys on the team—around twenty—who look about your age."

"Oh yeah? Are they hot?"

Eric's cheeks flushed. "I would never look at a teammate that way. Especially not one of the kids. Jesus."

Kids. "Right," Kyle said stiffly. "Thirty and over. I forgot."

They were silent a moment, and it felt oddly tense. Kyle was annoyed and he wasn't sure why. He sucked it up and said, "So, if I were here to pick up, instead of celebrating my one month anniversary with my lovely boyfriend, I would probably be standing by the bar. If I saw someone I liked, I'd send them some obvious signals, and wait for them to come to me. Once mutual interest is established, the rest is easy."

"Easy?"

"Yeah. Decide where you're going to go, maybe what you're going to do when you get there, and then . . . go do it." Kyle shrugged. "Like I said, almost everyone in here is hoping to have sex tonight. There's no guessing about that. The trick is finding the right person."

"And if someone is looking to maybe just talk to someone? Maybe exchange numbers?"

Kyle considered it. He imagined being that man, the one

who Eric approached in a bar because he thought he might be nice to talk to. Would Eric be shy when he initiated conversation, or calm and confident with that quiet amusement in his eyes that made Kyle want to kiss him?

"I think it would be a refreshing change," Kyle said. "I haven't been on a real first date in a long time."

"Probably not as long as me. Twenty years, give or take."

Twenty years ago, Kyle was five years old. But that didn't seem like the right thing to mention.

Eric held up his wrist to check his expensive-looking watch, and that's when Kyle noticed something.

"You took your wedding ring off."

Eric glanced at his fingers as if he had no idea what Kyle was talking about. "Yeah. I thought it might be time." He said it like it wasn't a big deal, but Kyle guessed it hadn't been an easy thing to do.

"My first tip for getting lucky was going to be: always remove your wedding ring before trying to pick up."

Eric laughed. "I probably should have figured that one out sooner. I said I was wearing it for superstitious reasons, but maybe I was wearing it like a shield."

"You weren't ready before," Kyle said gently.

"No," Eric agreed. "And as weird as it feels to not be wearing it now, I think I'm ready to get back out there."

"Shields down."

Eric nodded. "Shields down." He flexed his fingers, then rested the hand on the table. "This is going to sound silly to you, but I'm nervous about playing without it."

"Without the ring?" That didn't make any sense to Kyle.

"Yeah. We head out on a road trip the day after tomorrow, and it will be the first time I've played a game without wearing the ring since my second season."

Kyle thought he understood now. "You're superstitious."

"Very. I know the ring doesn't actually make me a better goalie, but still. It'll be weird."

"You'll have to find a new good luck charm." Kyle's imagination went off on another adventure, thinking up a scenario where Eric would be wearing something Kyle had given him under his hockey gear. Maybe a thin leather bracelet . . .

"I have plenty of superstitions. I don't need a new one."

"Oh yeah? Like what?"

Eric crossed his arms. "No way. You'll make fun of me."

"I won't. I can't picture you doing anything too wacky. So what is it? Lucky socks?"

"I put my gear on, and take it off, in exactly the same order. Every time."

"Okay. And what happens if you don't?"

"I don't know. It's never happened."

"But you've done it and played a bad game."

"Of course."

"So . . ."

Eric huffed. "I know. It doesn't make sense. Just forget it."

"No! I'm not making fun of you, I promise. I'm just . . . interested."

"Interested in how nuts I am." Eric smiled. "It gets worse. Would you believe that I talk to my goalposts?"

Kyle's eyes went wide with delight. "Seriously?"

"Dead serious."

"That seems so . . . out of character? What do you tell your goalposts?"

"I thank them when they stop a puck that got by me. I complain about other players to them." Eric shrugged. "It's a lonely job sometimes, being a goalie."

"That is extremely adorable. I love it."

Eric smiled, and then he covered his mouth with one hand as his face stretched into a yawn.

"Do you need to get to bed?" Kyle asked.

"I do. I try to be in bed before eleven most nights. This is two late nights in a row."

"I'm a terrible influence."

"Maybe I need one."

That hung in the air for a charged moment. Then Eric stood and grabbed his coat, throwing it on as he turned toward the door. He certainly seemed to be in a hurry.

Kyle surreptitiously adjusted himself under the table, then grabbed his much-too-short jacket and slid it on as he followed Eric out of the bar.

"I'll walk you home," Eric said when they were both on the sidewalk.

He didn't have to, but Kyle wasn't going to turn him down. They walked half a block and Eric said, "Thank you, for tonight."

"Do you think it helped?"

"I do. I know it didn't seem like much, but this was all new for me. I think it's a little less scary now. So thanks."

"I'm glad."

They walked another minute in silence, then Eric huffed out a laugh.

"What?" Kyle asked.

"Nothing. I mean, nothing funny. Is it awful if I admit that a big part of me wants to stick to dating women because at least I have some familiarity with what to do there?"

"It's not awful. That actually makes a lot of sense. But sex with a man isn't that different."

Eric scoffed, and Kyle admitted, "Okay. It *is* different. I assume. I've only been with men. But it doesn't have to be scary."

Eric seemed to consider this. "I want to see what it's like, being with a man. I know it's probably ridiculous to say, but I feel like something will click into place when I do it."

Kyle understood what Eric was trying to say, but he wanted

to make something clear. "You know you're not any less bisexual if you never hook up with a man, right? Your sexuality is still completely valid and real, whether you have sex with one gender, multiple genders, or no one at all."

Eric was silent a long time before answering, "I know. But it still feels . . . theoretical."

"It's not. You know who you are and who you're attracted to. You don't have to act on it to make it real." He glanced over to see Eric's furrowed brow, and decided to add, "But wanting to act on it is valid too. If doing this is important to you, then you should do it."

"Thank you," Eric said quietly. "That was nice to hear. All of it."

"It's all true."

They reached Kyle's building. He rocked up on his toes, then back on his heels, his hands stuffed firmly in his jacket pockets to keep from reaching out for Eric.

"Well," Eric said. He was facing Kyle, leaving maybe a foot of space between their chests. They were close in height—Eric an inch or so taller—and it would be so easy for Kyle to lean in a bit and help Eric check that *Kiss a Man* box.

But he didn't. Because he had no right to steal that first time from him. Even if Eric's eyes were a shade darker than they had been a moment ago.

"We could do this again, if you want," Kyle said. "Maybe go to a club. Dancing. Sometimes it's easier when you can just . . . let go."

Eric held his gaze. "I'm not good at letting go."

Kyle's lips quirked up. "I've noticed." But god, he wanted to help him. He wanted to absolutely unravel this man, and have him desperate and uninhibited. It would be a challenge to get him there, but Kyle felt up to the task. Which is *not* what he should be thinking.

"I'm going to be busy for a while, but maybe after that we can—"

"Initiate phase two of Operation: Get Eric a Man?"

Eric snorted. "Yeah. But let's not call it that."

"I might call it that. So, we hit a club next week?"

Eric nodded at the sidewalk, then lifted his gaze. "Maybe."

Kyle did lean in then, because he couldn't help it. He kissed Eric on the cheek. It was chaste, but his lips lingered greedily on Eric's skin. He pulled back enough to meet Eric's gaze. There was a question there, a silent request for permission. Kyle knew he should step away, but he could feel Eric's breath against his lips, and he just wanted this so much. So instead of doing the right thing, Kyle tilted his head and waited for Eric to close the distance.

For a terrifying moment, Eric didn't react at all, and Kyle thought he'd misread the situation. Then, finally, Eric's lips touched his own, perfectly gentle and sweet. Kyle forced himself to stay still, to let Eric explore his lips with careful, tentative brushes that sent sparks shooting throughout Kyle's body.

He pulled back, just to make sure Eric was okay with this. Eric helplessly chased his mouth, which made Kyle laugh and kiss him properly. He placed a gentle hand on the side of Eric's face, caressing his soft beard, and parted his lips, inviting Eric in. When the tips of their tongues touched, Kyle groaned and opened for him, needing more. He was charmed by how innocent this kiss was, but he was dying for Eric to truly take him.

This time Eric broke the kiss, pulling back enough to look at him with wide eyes and mouth hanging open, as if he was surprised to see Kyle there. Kyle was ready to make a joke to relieve the tension and let Eric know this didn't have to be a big deal, but before he could say a word, Eric was on him again. His arms wrapped around Kyle's back, pulling him tight against his body as he bent Kyle back slightly and kissed him hungrily.

Kyle's stomach swooped with the overwhelming rightness of it as he kissed him back, swallowing the little moans Eric was making.

Finally they broke apart, and Eric leaned his forehead against Kyle's, the white clouds of their breath mingling as they both panted.

"Wow," Kyle said. "We just did that."

"Yeah," Eric agreed.

"Was that okay?"

Eric was still for a moment, and Kyle's stomach dropped. What if it hadn't been okay? What if Kyle had stolen Eric's first kiss with a man, something that was supposed to have been special?

But then Eric nodded against Kyle's forehead. "It was way more than okay."

Kyle smiled, relieved. He was tempted to kiss Eric again, but he knew he needed to put up some walls before things got out of hand.

Kyle took a step back. "So you got that over with."

Eric frowned. "Over with?"

"Your first kiss with a man. You can check that box off."

"That wasn't what I—"

"You did good, by the way," Kyle said, before Eric could say anything that might make Kyle invite him upstairs. "A-plus kissing."

"Thanks." Eric touched his fingers to his lips. He looked bewildered, and Kyle realized he was probably being heartless. He reached for Eric's other hand.

"Hey," he said gently. "I had fun tonight."

"Me too." God, he looked so lost. He looked like he would follow him anywhere, and Kyle found that hard to resist. He wanted this man, wanted to bring him upstairs and teach him everything he knew about sex. He wanted to keep talking to him, and kissing him. But Eric wasn't into hookups, and he'd made it clear that Kyle was too young for him to date. But maybe there was a third option.

He decided to float Eric a casual offer. "I'm going to put this out there: if you want me to help you with any other . . . firsts . . . I'd be happy to. Anytime. No strings attached."

Eric's eyebrows shot up. "Um, thank you. That's . . ."

Kyle held up his hands. "It's an offer. You don't have to take it. And you don't have to decide now. But I could teach you a few things in a safe, nonjudgmental way. It might make you feel more confident about dating."

Eric looked stunned, but he nodded. "I'll think about it."

Kyle bit his lip, then leaned forward and gave him a quick kiss on the mouth. "You have my number."

Eric's gaze was still on Kyle's mouth. "I do. Goodnight, Kyle."

"Happy anniversary, darling."

CHAPTER ELEVEN

Obviously Eric shouldn't have kissed Kyle. Not that it hadn't been nice.

Nice. Jesus, it had been earth shaking. It had been . . . affirming. He hadn't been kissed in over a year, and he'd never been kissed like *that.* He hadn't been able to stop smiling or touching his own lips for the entire cab ride home.

But just because it had been a hell of a kiss it didn't mean—

Ow!

Eric shook his blocker off and then removed his mask. "Hey, you want to fuck off with those head shots?" he yelled to everyone on the ice at once. "That fucking hurt."

"Sorry, Benny," Matti said, skating up to him with a concerned expression. "That one got away from me."

Eric sighed as he rubbed his forehead. In truth, he should have been paying closer attention. He hated how distracted he'd been all practice. "Just be careful," he grumbled as he put his mask back on.

He was exhausted. Not only had he stayed out later than usual last night, he'd also been completely unable to sleep after he'd gotten home. His body had buzzed with adrenaline after that kiss. His mind had raced with the possibilities of what Kyle had so casually offered him.

No strings attached.

Eric knew that was a thing. Friends with benefits, or whatever. He'd just never had that before and he wasn't sure he *could* have that. He might not be built that way.

But he also couldn't ask Kyle for more. Sex with an older man was one thing, a relationship with someone fifteen years older than you was another. So last night he'd convinced himself that he would not take Kyle up on his generous offer. Then he'd gotten himself off in his usual, efficient manner. Even that relief hadn't been enough to lull him to sleep, though, and he'd been left tossing and turning for hours.

Eric needed to focus. His team was fourth in their division and they were heading out on a road trip tomorrow morning against some tough opponents. His personal goals against average was far from his best, but it wasn't abysmal either. He was still on track to finish this season—finish his career—with dignity.

He'd like to keep some dignity in his personal life too. Dating a much younger man would pretty much make him a walking midlife crisis, and Eric really didn't want that kind of attention. He couldn't stomach the idea of being a recently divorced man rebounding with a pretty young thing. And then there was the fact that Kyle was a man.

Coach Murdock blew his whistle. "Let's bring those nets in. Farmer, Woody," he barked at two of the rookies. "Grab a net. Push them to the edges of the circle here." He pointed his stick at the circle in the corner to Eric's left.

Eric skated over to Carter, just to get out of Woody's way. Carter fist-bumped Eric's blocker and said, "Tiny rink!"

"You love tiny rink."

"Because I'm the best at it."

Eric snatched a puck with his goalie stick and started batting it back and forth on the ice. "I've been shit this practice."

"Did someone keep you up last night?"

The puck got away from Eric. "No," he lied.

"In the locker room you looked a little . . ." Carter waved a hand around in a manner that suggested absolutely nothing Eric could decipher. "Dreamy."

"You're making shit up."

Carter pointed at his own eyes. "These don't lie."

"Apparently they do because—"

"Okay, gentlemen," Coach bellowed. "Get to the circle. One goalie in each net, and we're doing one-on-one drills until I tell you to stop."

Eric skated off to the far net. When he passed Tommy, he nudged him and said, "Give 'em hell."

"You know it."

The players gathered to one side of the circle, and Coach sent two players in to battle each other for the puck and to try to take shots on one of the nets. Eric usually enjoyed these drills, but the small ice surface meant he could never relax. He had to stay focused on the action because it never moved more than a few meters away from him. Today it felt exhausting.

Eric didn't like being scored on during practice any more than he liked it during games. But his ability to stop pucks was far more dependent on his mental state than his physical state, and today his mental state was a shitshow. Even the rookies were scoring on him.

When the drill was finally over, the goalie coach, Quinn Cameron, gestured Eric over to the bench. "What's going on, Eric?"

Eric flipped his mask up. "I didn't sleep well last night."

"Explains why you look like shit." Quinn studied him, frowning. "Not sleeping. That's not like you."

"I know."

"Is that all it is?"

Eric shrugged one massive, padded shoulder. "I think so."

"How's your head? That shot from Matti looked like it stung."

"It wasn't that bad. I'm just cranky today."

Quinn smirked. "Comes with getting older."

"Yeah yeah."

Quinn only had ten years on Eric, but he looked much older. He walked with a noticeable limp thanks to a slap shot that had shattered his ankle when he'd played in the NHL himself. He'd had a hip replacement when he was about Eric's age, and, thanks to years of taking shots to the head like the one Eric had just downplayed, he was prone to dizzy spells. Eric had had his share of injuries himself over the years; his left shoulder was a frequent source of grief but had been relatively fine since the last operation he'd had. He did as much as he could off the ice to balance the punishment his body endured on the ice. He was teased by his teammates for being a health nut, but Eric didn't want to end up like Quinn. If yoga, sleep, and eating clean even gave him a chance of avoiding that, he would keep it up.

This was the fourth practice in a row that Eric had planned to tell his coaches that he would be retiring after this season. It would be so easy to ask Quinn, right now, to assemble the coaches so Eric could tell them. But he couldn't bring himself to form the words. The truth was, he was scared. Once he announced it, it would be real. No matter how sure he was in his heart that this was the right decision, he wasn't ready for it to be real.

His brain was so cluttered today. His fear of walking away from hockey warred with his fear of his desire for Kyle. These thoughts swirled with the stress of his poor performance in today's practice, the exhilaration of finally exploring his sexuality, and the terrifying uncertainty his future held.

He really needed a nap.

He decided, after he'd showered and dressed, to walk from the arena to his house. He hoped the fresh air and the additional exercise would help to clear his head. As he walked, he tried to think reasonably about what Kyle had suggested. He unpacked the facts and laid them out neatly in his mind.

The first was that he liked Kyle, was attracted to him, and it seemed that the attraction was mutual. The second fact was that Kyle seemed to have a very uncomplicated relationship with sex and had offered to have sex with Eric. The third fact was that Eric was nervous about having sex with a man. Or with anyone, really. It had only been Holly since he'd been a teenager, and it hadn't been very often during their last few years together. The fourth fact was he couldn't really imagine hooking up with a stranger. It just didn't appeal to him. In fact, it kind of repulsed him.

Fact number five: the idea of sex with Kyle did *not* repulse him. At all.

Eric sorted through these facts for his entire walk home. He examined each one, shuffling them around like cards and hoping a clear course of action would appear. The thing he kept getting stuck on was that he wasn't sure what it meant, that he wanted to have sex with Kyle. He knew it was a simple logic problem: Eric Bennett only likes having sex with people he has feelings for. Eric Bennett wants to have sex with Kyle. Therefore . . .

And that right there was why he *couldn't* have sex with Kyle.

Unless he could.

Fucking hell.

When Eric got home, he ran straight up to his room and collapsed on his bed. It was so soft and wonderful.

And lonely.

Eventually, when he felt like moving again, he slipped out of his clothes and settled himself under the blankets. When he closed his eyes he remembered every detail of kissing Kyle last night. The heat of Kyle's tongue, and the cool press of his fingers where they'd touched Eric's jaw. The sweet way he'd laughed when Eric had greedily leaned in for more.

Eric blushed. Was Kyle thinking about that kiss as much as he was? Probably not.

His skin felt hot everywhere, and he kicked off the blankets. Normally, jerking off was not a daily event for him, but his hand found its way to his cock and started his usual routine of quick, hard pumps. He came quickly, as always, catching his release in his hand.

As he was washing up in the bathroom a few minutes later, he wondered what it might be like for sex to be something that he wasn't just trying to get over with. For sexual release to not merely be maintenance he provided to his body, like getting a massage, or stretching. He'd never been adventurous in bed, and he'd never deliberately drawn out his jerk-off sessions. He focused on achieving orgasm, and the way his body responded to the release of tension.

He had no doubts that Kyle could teach him exactly how good sex could feel. His imagination had been shocking him lately with detailed fantasies of Kyle teasing and slowly drawing orgasms out of him. That morning, when he'd been making breakfast, he'd become thoroughly distracted by a daydream that was so vivid he could practically feel Kyle's caresses. And that was after the memories of last night's kiss had compelled him to bring himself off in the shower. He'd imagined filthy, coaxing words in Kyle's light, playful voice as he'd stroked himself, then gasped Kyle's name as Eric's release splattered his dark shower tile.

He wanted it to be real. All of it. He wanted Kyle to remove his anxiety about being intimate with a man, and he wanted to reward Kyle for his efforts. He wanted to be *good* at pleasuring a man. At pleasuring Kyle.

And he wanted to stop thinking about this. He was losing control of himself and he hated that feeling. Maybe the only way to extinguish the thoughts was by doing something about them. And what Kyle had offered him wasn't a hookup, and it wasn't a relationship. It was instruction, and patience, and it might be exactly what Eric needed.

He wished he had someone else he could talk to about this. He rarely sought a second opinion on anything, but on this particular matter he could use some advice.

Scott, of course, was the obvious choice. He had never been one to talk about sex—in fact, Scott tended to blush and stammer at the very mention of it—but he certainly knew about finding the courage to be your true self. He knew how important this would be to Eric.

And it was well past time Eric came out to his best friend.

Four days later, Eric knocked on Scott's hotel room door. He could hear him talking to someone, and thought about leaving, but the door opened before he could retreat. Scott smiled when he saw him, then held the door wide open with the hand that wasn't holding his phone to his ear.

"It's Benny," Scott said to his phone as Eric brushed past him into the room. Then, to Eric, "Kip says hi."

"Hi, Kip."

At least they weren't having phone sex. Carter had once stolen one of Scott's room keys in an attempt to prank him. When he'd opened the door, thinking Scott was out, he'd gotten an eyeful. Whenever Carter told the story, he looked haunted.

Scott ended the call after three *I love you*s, then turned to Eric, his eyes bright and his cheeks touched with pink. He really was absurdly handsome.

"What's up?" Scott asked.

Scott's expression turned serious when Eric sat on the bed. He wheeled a desk chair over and sat facing him. "Everything okay?"

"Yeah. Fine. Just, um . . . there's just something I've been wanting to tell you."

Scott's brow furrowed. "Okay. I'm listening."

Eric took a breath. This was his moment. It shouldn't be hard to come out as bisexual to your openly gay best friend, but. Well.

"I just wanted to tell you . . ." Eric huffed and shook his head. "It's not even a big deal. I don't know why I'm—"

"Eric." Scott placed a hand on Eric's wrist. He hardly ever called Eric by his first name. He didn't say anything else, just calmly waited for Eric to be ready to speak.

Eric remembered when Scott had come out to him. It had been in a hotel room like this one, but Carter and their former teammate, Greg Huff, had also been there. Eric had thought about inviting Carter this time, but he decided this was less about Eric coming out to his friends, and more about getting advice from Scott, specifically. He would tell Carter soon.

How had Scott managed to say the words at the time? Eric felt like they were lodged in his throat, thick and impossible to budge. He took a slow breath, jiggled the words loose, and said, "I'm not . . . straight."

Scott's eyebrows shot up. "You're gay?"

"No. I'm bisexual, I guess. I've always assumed that's what I am, anyway."

"Always?" Scott looked gobsmacked, and Eric didn't blame him. If Eric had known all this time that he was bisexual, why had he waited so long to tell Scott? Why had he let Scott break down that wall alone?

"I *knew*," Eric said carefully, "but I wouldn't acknowledge it. I've always *known*."

Scott clasped his hands together and looked at the floor. Eric felt like shit. He'd been such a coward.

Then Scott looked up. His eyes were glistening and he was smiling. It was confusing.

"Scott?"

"Jesus, Benny. Come here." Scott stood and opened his arms. Eric, still bewildered, stood and stepped into them. Scott wrapped him in a tight hug that Eric tried to reciprocate, but his arms were mostly pinned to his sides. He tapped the sides of Scott's waist with his fingertips in what he hoped was a show of affection.

When Scott pulled back, he was beaming, and his eyes were still wet. "Thank you for telling me."

"I just . . . needed to say it, you know?"

"Oh, believe me, I know." Scott scrubbed a hand over his face. "Have you told anyone else? Wait." His eyes went wide. "Are you *seeing* someone?"

"No," Eric said quickly. "I mean, yes. I've told one other person. But, no. Not because I'm dating him. Or anyone. I'm not dating anyone."

Scott looked disappointed, then smiled sheepishly. "Sorry. I got a little excited there. So you have told someone else?"

Eric sat back on the bed. For some reason the idea of telling Scott that he had confided in Kyle felt more terrifying than announcing his sexuality. So instead, he asked, "When you and Kip . . ." He paused, unsure how to phrase this. "Was Kip the first man you'd . . ."

God, why was this so hard? They were both adults.

But Scott, predictably, blushed when he realized what Eric was asking. "No, um. He wasn't my first." He smiled shyly. "I wish he had been, but there were a few quick hookups before him. Why?"

Eric traced a fingertip over the hotel comforter. "I've been thinking that I'd like to try it. Being with a man, I mean." Scott's eyes went wide, and Eric realized suddenly how this might be misinterpreted. "Not with you! That's not why I'm here."

Scott let out a shaky laugh. "Oh. Good. Jesus, I was nervous there for a second."

Eric shook his head. "With someone else, I promise."

"The person you came out to already, maybe?"

Eric averted his gaze, realizing too late that Scott would interpret it as the *yes* that it was. He had only planned to tell Scott that he was bisexual, and maybe ask some vague questions about dating men. But now, with Scott grinning at him expectantly, Eric decided he wanted to share at least part of this with his best friend. "It's going to sound weird, but I actually told Kyle."

"Kyle? Like, Kyle who we wanted you to be friends with?"

"Yes."

"Kyle who I *said* you'd get along really well with?"

"The same. Congratulations."

Scott fist pumped, and Eric bit his lip to keep from smiling.

"Are you guys, like . . . I mean, did you, um . . ." Scott stammered.

"We are *friends*. He's half my age."

"He's not *half* your age, for fuck's sake. But, yes. He's young."

"Too young for me," Eric said. If he said it enough times, maybe his brain would start to listen. "But he's been helping me navigate this thing."

Scott's expression turned thoughtful and he said, "He'd be good at that. The last two years haven't been easy on Kip, and Kyle's been a good friend to him."

"Haven't been easy?" Eric asked. As far as he could tell, Kip had found Prince Charming and was going to ride into the sunset with him.

"He's suddenly in the spotlight. I know he's happy with me, but the rest hasn't been easy. He's lost friends, and had to deal with being one half of a very public couple. We get tons of support, and that's awesome, but we also get . . . the other stuff."

Eric knew this, of course. He'd seen the comments posted at the end of articles online, and he'd heard the ignorant things yelled from the crowds when the team was on the road. Hell, he'd heard them yelled by people—he refused to call them fans—at their home games in New York. It always infuriated him. Oddly, he realized now, he had only ever felt outrage on Scott's behalf when he'd heard the slurs. Never for himself.

"I'm sorry," he said, now.

Scott waved a hand. "I spent my whole life worried about what *they* think. I'm done."

Eric smiled at that.

"So," Scott said. "You're getting yourself out there, then? Dating?"

"I mean, not yet. But I'd like to."

"Men, huh?"

"Maybe. I'm curious I guess." Eric scoffed. "That sounds so cliché."

"It's exciting is what it is! You should come out with us sometime. There's a fundraiser at a club next week that we're helping out at. It's a drag show—a Christmas thing—and there will be dancing after, of course. I'm going to be on stage for part of the show, so you can at least watch me being roasted by some drag queens."

"That is very tempting." It actually did sound ideal. It would be low pressure, because Eric could just be there to support his friend. And he could leave before the dancing started. Maybe this could be the night out Kyle had suggested. He would like it if Kyle was there. For support.

"Seriously," Scott said gently as he sat back in the chair in front of Eric, "it would be great to have you there. And I'm glad

Kyle is advising you on the actual, um, dating side of things. Honestly, I am terrible with that stuff."

"He's very enthusiastic," Eric said. He bit his cheek to suppress a smile he was sure would give away the fact that Kyle had offered to have sex with him.

Scott beamed. "I can't believe I've had a queer teammate this whole time!"

The words were said cheerfully, but Eric couldn't stop the guilt from creeping in again. "I'm sorry I didn't tell you sooner, and that I wasn't brave enough to come out when you did. I should have been standing beside you."

"You were," Scott said simply. "You've been supporting me since the moment I came out to you. And after I went public, you've always been right there with me: going to LGBTQ events, going to the Kingfisher with me. You think I don't know how much you hate going to bars?"

That made Eric smile. "I like the Kingfisher."

"Me too. And it's always nice having teammates join me there. Hell, it was nice having *Rozanov* there."

"Why *was* Rozanov there, anyway? I never really figured it out."

"Oh, he wanted to talk to me about his charity. You know, the one he started with Shane Hollander?"

"I still can't believe that's a real thing, but yes."

"They have these summer hockey camps and he asked if I might like to be a coach at one." Scott laughed. "I could tell it killed him to ask me."

"Why you? I mean, I know why someone would want you to be a coach at a hockey camp, but why would *Rozanov* want you there?"

"I'm not sure, exactly. But he mentioned that the camps are inclusive. He actually used the words *safe space*, which almost knocked me off my chair. How many hockey players do you know who use that term?"

"You mean in a non-mocking way? Very few."

"Right. So they want the staff to be diverse. I wouldn't even be the only gay guy, because they have Ryan Price helping out."

"I keep forgetting he's gay."

"I heard he has a great boyfriend. A musician. I'm happy for him."

"That's good to hear."

"Anyway, I told Rozanov I'd like to help, but this summer will be busy with the wedding and the honeymoon, and the other obligations I already have."

"Maybe next year."

"That's what I said. I'm sure Kip would enjoy a week or two in Montreal. That's where one of the camps is."

"It seems like a good charity," Eric said. "I was reading that they already provided the funds for a huge renovation of a youth home in Montreal."

"It's impressive," Scott agreed. "I've been thinking about starting my own charity, but maybe I should talk to Rozanov and Hollander about joining forces with them."

Rozanov and Hollander. The two rivals' names still sounded weird next to each other. "Who knew Rozanov had such a big heart?" Eric said.

Scott smiled. "I had a hunch. I think he might secretly be a big softy."

"He does a damn good job of hiding it."

"He sure does. Anyway, why are we talking about Ilya Rozanov? I'd rather talk about you."

Eric held up a hand. "No thanks. I said everything I need to."

Scott glanced at the clock on his nightstand. "I guess it's getting late. And I'll be damned if I'm not in top form against Toronto tomorrow night."

"Yeah. But thanks, for listening to me." Eric huffed. "Sorry if it was a shock."

"Are you kidding? I'm thrilled." Scott pulled him into one of his signature hugs. "Your secret is safe with me. I promise."

Eric sighed against his shoulder. He'd miss these hugs after he retired. "I know. But I don't know if it needs to be a secret. If people find out, they find out. But I'm not going to make a big public announcement."

"That's fair."

They broke apart, and Eric ran a hand through his own hair, needing to make one more request of Scott and not sure of how to say it. "Hey, um, could you maybe not tell Kip? About Kyle, I mean. Not that there's anything to tell, really, but still."

Scott mimed pulling a zipper across his lips. "I won't say a word. But Benny?"

"Yeah?"

"For what it's worth, I think he'd be good for you. Even if it's just for . . ." Scott palmed the back of his own neck nervously. "Instruction. Or whatever."

Eric felt his own cheeks heat up. "Got it."

Scott squeezed Eric's shoulder and said, "I'm proud of you, Benny."

"Thanks."

Eric left Scott's room feeling a million pounds lighter.

CHAPTER TWELVE

Eric loved playing against Toronto because he hated Dallas Kent.

Toronto's star forward had loads of talent but was one of the biggest assholes Eric had ever met. He was obnoxious like Ilya Rozanov, but without any of the charm. Because for all of the talk about what a bad boy Rozanov was, he'd never, to Eric's knowledge, used slurs on or off the ice, or posted sexist or homophobic jokes on Twitter. Rozanov had a reputation as a ladies man, but he always seemed to treat women—and talk about them—with respect.

Basically the opposite of Dallas fucking Kent.

Eric had a lot of career achievements to be proud of, but his secret favorite might be that he'd never let Kent score on him. Not once. And that wasn't changing tonight.

Eric noticed that Kent seemed a little quieter tonight than he had been last season. Probably because he didn't have his protector anymore—Ryan Price had quit hockey in the middle of last season. Frankly, Eric couldn't blame him; he'd rather drink poison than have to defend Dallas Kent for a living.

Kent might also be quieter tonight because he knew slurs weren't going to fly with Scott Hunter's team. If he dared utter anything even remotely homophobic, the New York Admirals entire roster would come crashing down on him. It hadn't been a completely smooth road for the team since Scott came out—a few players had felt blindsided and uncomfortable by Scott's very public announcement—but now, over two years later, there wasn't a single man on the team who wouldn't defend their captain.

Eric didn't miss the way Kent glared at Scott on the ice, though. The sneers. Kent was a piece of shit.

And he probably wasn't a fan of all the rainbow flags.

Since Scott came out, every arena the Admirals played in would have at least a couple of rainbow flags in the crowd. Sometimes there would be homemade signs thanking Scott, or proposing marriage to him. The flags might be for Scott, but Eric was heartened by them too. It was nice to feel supported, even if the fans didn't know they were showing support for him, specifically.

He wondered how many other players secretly felt that way. Maybe some of homophobic Dallas Kent's unfortunate teammates. He remembered, again, that Ryan Price was gay, and it had been his job to *protect* Kent. How was Kent even still alive?

Eric narrowed his eyes at Kent as the asshole waited to take the face-off. "You see that guy? He doesn't get a thing past us tonight, all right?" His goalposts were silent, but Eric was pretty sure they understood their orders.

Fortunately, Scott won the face-off and the puck was carried quickly to the opposite end of the ice. Eric stood up straight and shook out his shoulders, which had been tight for the past couple of days.

"Pass it to Carter, he's all alone over there," Eric muttered. But instead Scott took a shot that was deflected, and now Kent was racing toward Eric with the puck. "Okay, fellas. Remember what I said. He gets nothing by us."

Matti caught up with Kent, so Kent dropped the puck back to his linemate, Troy Barrett, who Eric had always secretly thought of as "Dallas Kent-light." He was almost as talented, and almost as gross. At least, Eric assumed he was because he was known to be tight with Kent, and Eric didn't think someone could be friends with Kent unless they were a shitty person too.

So Troy Barrett wasn't allowed to score on him either.

Barrett was forced to turn back to the blue line with the puck so the Toronto forwards could regroup.

"Watch Aucoin!" Eric yelled, because the only Toronto forward who wasn't a superstar was being left wide open. "Get on him!"

Matti heard him and went to cover him, but not before Barrett got the puck to Aucoin. Eric went to the corner of the net and waited. He was known for his patience, for being excellent at waiting the opponent out and forcing them to move first. He did this now, and was rewarded with a flick of Aucoin's gaze that told Eric exactly where he planned to shoot it. If Aucoin had been a more intelligent player, like Ilya Rozanov or Shane Hollander or, hell, Dallas fucking Kent, Eric would have to decide if that shift in his gaze was a bluff. But Aucoin was more predictable, and he shot the puck exactly where Eric expected him to: high on the glove side. An easy save.

Kent bumped into him right after Eric caught the puck, knocking Eric back so his shoulders slammed against the crossbar of the net. It fucking hurt.

Eric shoved him back, hard. "Real fucking nice, shithead."

Matti and Scott were both there too. "Get the fuck off of him!" Scott yelled, grabbing Kent.

Kent shook him off, then shoved him, "Don't fucking touch me, Hunter." He made a disgusted face, as if Scott were a pile of rotting meat, and tried to knock Scott's hand away. Scott held tight and pulled him closer. Kent looked horrified, as if Scott was going to kiss him or something.

"Let go of me, you—" Kent cut himself off just in time.

"You what?" Scott yelled in his face. "You *what*? Finish your fucking sentence."

"All right, that's enough." One of the refs arrived to separate them. "Go to your benches now or you both get penalties."

"Finish your sentence!" Scott yelled again, over the ref's shoulder at Kent's retreating back.

"Hey." Eric shook his glove off and put a hand on Scott's arm. "Forget about him."

Scott was a sweetheart most of the time, but he could turn violent on the ice if someone got to him enough. He was a big guy—over six feet tall and made of muscle—so he could do a lot of damage when wanted to.

"I hate that fucking guy," Scott said. His voice was calmer now, so the ref released him.

"We all hate him," Eric said.

"No comment," the ref muttered, then skated away.

Eric noticed, then, that Troy Barrett was standing a couple of meters away, watching them. He didn't look menacing at all. In fact he looked . . . embarrassed? Certainly uncomfortable.

Eric flipped his mask up and shot him a questioning glance. Troy opened his mouth, closed it, then skated away.

Toronto was a team of weirdos.

Eric drank some water and got ready for the face-off that would be happening right in front of him. "And that," he told his goal posts, "is why we don't let Kent score on us."

It was too bad that Kent was such a shithead homophobe, because Toronto had a large and vibrant queer community. It would be nice if their star hockey player was a better role model.

Kyle had suggested that Eric go out while he was in Toronto. Check out one of the many gay bars and find, in Kyle's words, some sexy Canadian sweetheart to keep him warm. Eric was definitely not going to do that, and he tried not to think about the possibility that Kyle was looking for his own bed warmer tonight back in New York. Eric would much rather replay their kiss in his head. And fantasize about Kyle's offer to do more.

More. There was no way that was a good idea.

Also not a good idea: daydreaming about sex with Kyle while in the middle of a hockey game.

The play had been at the other end, but Toronto was charging back toward Eric with the puck now.

"Here we go, fellas," Eric told his posts. "I'll do my job, you do yours."

The shot came from an unexpected angle. Eric had positioned himself to block a low shot from his right-hand side, but the puck was passed at the last second. Eric tried to slide over to stop it, but the shot was high and sailed over his blocker.

Ping!

That sound, that glorious sound, was Eric's favorite in the whole universe. The crisp chime of a puck hitting the post and deflecting away from the net was a chorus of angels to a goaltender. If Eric made it to old age, he wanted that sound playing on a loop next to his deathbed as he passed.

The disappointed groan of the Toronto crowd that followed the ping was also a pretty excellent sound.

"Thanks, pal," Eric said, once the play had moved out of his end of the ice. He gave the post a loving pat.

Okay. Focus, Eric. He couldn't count on the posts to save his ass a second time, so he needed to clear his head.

Win this game, he told himself, *and you can think about Kyle all you like when you're back in your hotel room.*

He didn't feel good about using something that pathetic as motivation, but it worked. Toronto didn't score again, and New York won the game.

KYLE:
I found someone for you.

Eric squinted at the message on his phone screen. Normally he'd be asleep at this hour, especially after a game, but he'd been restless tonight. He wondered if Kyle was at work right now. He wondered what made him text.

Oh. Right. He found someone. As in, someone for Eric to date who wasn't Kyle. Eric ignored the way his stomach clenched at that idea.

ERIC:
Who?

KYLE:
I don't know his name yet. But he's perfect for you.

Eric laughed into the dark hotel room and pulled himself up a bit so he could lean on his elbow.

ERIC:
Sounds amazing.

He hoped his sarcasm was clear.

KYLE:
He's definitely in his thirties, cute as hell, and I overheard him say he's a vegetarian.

Right. Because dietary preferences were the number one thing Eric was attracted to.

ERIC:
He's a customer?

KYLE:
Yes. I think he was on a date tonight but it didn't go well. Now he's sitting by himself.

ERIC:
You were spying on a customer while he was on a date?

KYLE:
I just bring the drinks! I can't control what I hear!

There was a long pause, and then Kyle wrote, I also took a pic of him.

Eric groaned. It was week one of being a bisexual man on the prowl and this was already getting way out of hand.

ERIC:
That's creepy.

Kyle didn't reply. Eric sighed and wrote, Send it.

A few seconds later Eric was looking at a dark and slightly blurry photo of a man sitting at a table, turned so he was in profile. It was hard to tell, but he did look like he might be handsome. Tidy, brown hair, nice clothes, and, yes, he appeared to be reasonably close to Eric's age.

ERIC:
Shouldn't you be working?

KYLE:
I'm on my break!

Oh. Eric couldn't help but be touched that Kyle was spending his break talking to him. And spending his evening trying to find Eric a date.

ERIC:
He does look nice.

KYLE:
I wish you were in town. You could slide into that empty chair and ask him his name.

The back of Eric's neck heated just thinking about that.

ERIC:
And then what would I say?

KYLE:
Normal stuff?

Eric had no idea what normal stuff was when it came to flirting.

KYLE:
Let's practice. I'll be him. You be you.

ERIC:
That's not necessary.

KYLE:
So you don't need the practice?

Eric grimaced. He definitely needed the practice. He sighed and wrote, Fine. So I sit down and say, "Hi. I'm Eric."

KYLE:
Solid start. Ok. I'm shaking your hand and saying "I'm Neil. Nice to meet you, Eric."

ERIC:
Neil? Really?

KYLE:
Yes. Why are you making fun of my name, dickbag?

Eric laughed, then wrote, Sorry, Neil. It's a lovely name.

KYLE:
I'm named after my grandfather.

Wow. Kyle was going deep on this character.

ERIC:
Oh. That's . . . neat.

KYLE:
He was the first man to walk on the moon.

Eric threw his head back on the pillow and barked out a loud laugh. He was relieved that Kyle wasn't taking this little exercise too seriously.

ERIC:
Wow. That's amazing.

KYLE:
ANYWAY. What do you do, Eric? You look familiar for some reason.

ERIC:
I play hockey for the New York Admirals.

KYLE:
Holy shit! Do you know Scott Hunter?

ERIC:
I'm afraid so.

KYLE:
He's really hot.

ERIC:

Yes. He's wonderful. And engaged.

If this was supposed to be helping Eric learn how to flirt, it wasn't working. He decided to take control.

ERIC:

Are you here alone?

KYLE:

Not anymore.

He punctuated it with a winky face emoji.

Eric had no idea what to say next. It was hard to flirt with an imaginary person. Maybe if he called the imaginary person Kyle in his head . . .

ERIC:

You have beautiful eyes.

Hey, there was nothing wrong with stealing lines from that Alex guy. Besides, Kyle *did* have beautiful eyes.

KYLE:

I'll bet you say that to all the boys.

ERIC:

I really don't.

KYLE:

I like your eyes too. And the way you're looking at me right now.

Eric wasn't actually looking at anyone right now, but he still felt the urge to avert his gaze. He wrote, I've been looking at you all night.

KYLE:

I've been looking at you too. I was hoping you might notice me.

ERIC:

Oh yeah? Why's that?

KYLE:

Because I think you might be a good kisser. I want to test that theory.

Eric absently brushed a thumb over his lips as he considered his reply.

ERIC:

I can help you with that.

In this imagined scenario, there would be a table between himself and, um, Neil. Not conducive to kissing. He was trying to figure out a smooth way to suggest leaving the table when Kyle wrote, I only live a couple of blocks away.

Oh. Okay. Well, this is where things would get awkward. It was where things *were* getting awkward, right now.

ERIC:

I'm not really into hookups.

Kyle's reply seemed to take forever.

KYLE:

That's cool. Is there anything you might be into with me?

ERIC:

Can I buy you another drink? Maybe we could talk for a bit?

KYLE:

I'd love that.

Eric grinned at his phone, wondering if "Neil" would actually be this easygoing. He also wondered if Kyle was playing a part, or just playing himself. Is that how he would truly react if a man suggested they have another drink instead of rushing off to have sex?

Except now Eric wasn't sure what to write. Was he supposed to go to the bar and buy "Neil" a drink, or just keep talking? This was weird.

ERIC:

So then what happens?

KYLE:

Are you asking me, or Neil?

ERIC:

You.

KYLE:

You buy Neil a drink, and then you lose track of time talking to each other. It goes really well. You definitely want to see him again.

ERIC:

OK. So should I ask him to have dinner with me sometime?

KYLE:

You can try.

Eric snorted, and wrote, I'd love to see you again. Would you like to have dinner sometime?

KYLE:

Definitely. Let me give you my number.

Well, that wasn't so hard. Eric found himself staring at those last two lines, and how much it looked like he had just successfully asked Kyle on a date.

KYLE:

You still there?

ERIC:

Yes. Sorry. Wasn't sure what to say.

KYLE:

You must be awesome at sexting.

Eric laughed and wrote, I have never even tried.

KYLE:
Well, if you ever want to practice . . .

Practice. There was that offer again.

ERIC:
I came out to Scott.

KYLE:
Yay! How'd it go?

ERIC:
Great. He was very supportive, of course.

KYLE:
Of course.

Eric steeled himself. It was time to bring up the thing he'd been obsessing over for days.

ERIC:
I've been thinking about your offer.

KYLE:
Oh?

ERIC:
I'm back in town on Wednesday night. I have Thursday off.

He held his breath as he waited for a response.

KYLE:
Oh yeah?

ERIC:
Come over for dinner?

KYLE:
Dinner or "dinner"?

Eric's stomach fluttered. He wanted to be bold and confirm the latter, but he still wasn't sure he was ready.

ERIC:
Let's start with dinner.

KYLE:
And if we're still hungry after . . .

Eric bit his lip and wrote, I'll text you when I'm back in town. Goodnight.

Kyle sent a kissy face emoji. Eric didn't send anything back because emojis always felt silly to him.

So Eric had a possible date with Kyle. Or rather, a possible scheduled platonic sex session. Ugh, that was a depressing way of thinking about it.

He was maybe going to have sex with Kyle. Possibly *anal* sex, which was both thrilling and scary to think about. It was something he had never done with Holly—giving or receiving—but he'd done a bit of experimenting with his own fingers. Enough to know that he wanted more. Eric wished Scott *were* the type of friend he could talk about sex with, because he'd like someone to relieve his anxiety about having sex with a man. Eric wondered if Scott's shyness about sex carried to the bedroom, or if he was secretly a sex god.

Okay. That right there was proof that Eric needed this

scheduled platonic sex session. He should definitely not be thinking about his best friend, and captain's, sexual personality.

He let his thoughts drift back to Kyle, which wasn't difficult. His imagination supplied a vision of Kyle gazing down at him, his eyes hooded and his pink lips shiny and slack with desire as Eric took his cock into his mouth. Eric had never done that, but god, he wanted to.

He jerked himself off quickly, as usual, and felt a lot more ready for sleep after he finished. He cleaned up in the bathroom, and when he returned to the bed he saw his phone had a new message.

KYLE:

His name is Sebastian. I wasn't even close.

CHAPTER THIRTEEN

At six o'clock on Thursday evening, Kyle was at Eric's front door with a backpack and a serious appetite for both food and sex.

Eric opened the door looking absurdly gorgeous. His white dress shirt was open at the collar and had the sleeves rolled up, and suddenly Kyle couldn't care less about food.

"Hey," Eric said, stepping aside to let Kyle in. "Thanks for coming."

"I was probably going to be watching *Guy's Grocery Games* or something, so I appreciate the invitation." He kissed Eric's cheek as he walked past him into the house.

Eric took his coat and gestured to the bag Kyle was holding. "What did you bring this time?"

"Ingredients for another mocktail."

Eric smiled warmly, as if he was immensely touched by this. "That's very thoughtful. I do have some wine, if you'd—"

"Nope. I'm good." No way was Kyle going to be even slightly tipsy tonight if things turned to Eric trusting Kyle to take him to bed.

"I hope you don't mind vegetarian food," Eric said as they went up the stairs to the kitchen.

"Of course not." Kyle also didn't mind this view of Eric's ass and thighs as he followed him up the stairs. Even covered in denim, his thighs looked like they could crush cars.

"I'm not a chef by any stretch, but I can make a few things. Do you like eggs?"

"Love them."

"Good. I made shakshuka. It's—"

"Eggs cooked in a tomato sauce. I love that stuff!"

"Me too. I bought some good bread and I thought we could eat it at the island in the kitchen, since you need to eat it out of the skillet."

Kyle loved this idea. It was fun and intimate. The perfect date meal. Maybe Eric had more game than he let on.

He followed Eric to the kitchen. You couldn't tell that anyone had been preparing food in there, except for the cast iron skillet full of bubbling tomato sauce. Other than that, the room was immaculate. Eric went to the fridge and pulled out a carton of eggs. Kyle decided to get to work on the drinks.

"What are you making?" Eric asked.

"It's going to be kind of a zero proof version of a mojito." Kyle waved a bunch of fresh mint in the air.

"I've never had a mojito."

"Since you like soda and lime so much, I thought it might appeal to you." Kyle went to the cupboard and pulled out two tall glasses. "It's lime and mint muddled with some syrup or sugar, and then topped with soda water. Obviously there's normally rum as well, but I made a spiced syrup to stand in for that missing flavor."

"Impressive." Eric cracked a fourth egg into the skillet. "You'll have to teach me how to make some of these drinks."

"You can help me make these, if you want." Kyle began plucking leaves from a mint stem. "So you've really never been a drinker?"

"Never. Not even in college."

"I know it's none of my business, but is there a reason?"

"I like control." Eric picked up a stem and joined Kyle in removing the leaves. "I need to be in charge of my mind and body. And I like to keep my body as clean as possible."

"You've never felt the urge to cut loose? Relax that control?"

"Not often. But when I do, there are . . . other ways to do that."

Kyle tore a leaf in half, his fingers suddenly clumsy. "I might know a couple of ways."

Eric gazed at him with dark, smoldering eyes. Kyle held his gaze, letting him know that he was comfortable discussing this. Or, hell, just doing it, shakshuka be damned.

Eric went to check on the eggs. "Another couple of minutes and they'll be perfect, I think."

"Come help me muddle."

Kyle showed Eric how to gently mash the mint leaves into the bottom of the glasses with a muddler Kyle had brought along. He explained how he'd made the syrup, and the importance of flavor balance in a cocktail. Eric was a keen student, listening closely and asking questions. When they were done, there were two tall glasses of non-alcoholic mojitos that were worthy of Instagram.

"You should be a bartender," Eric joked.

"I *wish* I could make stuff like this at work." Kyle sighed. "Someday."

"Someday?"

Kyle could guess how Eric, with his Harvard degree and impressive NHL career, might react to this. "I think it's what I want to do. Bartending. Hospitality. Maybe have my own bar someday."

Eric's brow furrowed. "What about your studies? I thought you might want to be a professor. Or maybe work for a museum."

Sorry to disappoint you, buddy. "I like what I'm studying, but I think my real passion is taking care of people. Making sure they're having a good time. I think providing an inviting space where people can relax and have fun is an important service." Good god, Kyle was overselling the hell out of this. It was uncomfortably similar to conversations he'd had with his parents. He waited for Eric's admonishment.

"You're good at it," Eric said. "I think you'd be great at running a bar or restaurant."

Kyle was so thrown by Eric's encouraging words that for a moment he just stared at him, stunned. Then he finally nodded and said, "Thanks. It's just a dream for now."

"Dreams are important." Eric brought the skillet over and set it on a folded towel in the middle of the island. "I wouldn't be in the NHL without dreams."

Kyle wasn't sure why Eric's kind words were so jarring. His friends said encouraging things to him all the time. Was it because Eric was older? Or maybe because he was one of the most impressive people Kyle had ever met? Or was there another reason that Kyle was so thrilled by his approval?

Kyle spotted the bread in a paper bag and grabbed it. "God, this all looks amazing." He sat in one of the stools opposite where Eric was standing. "This bread smells incredible."

"Bread is my weakness," Eric said sheepishly. "I've tried to give it up, but . . ."

"You've got to have *some* fun."

"Yeah. I can't quit bread."

Kyle lifted his glass. "To bread."

Eric smiled and clinked his own glass against Kyle's. "To bread." He took a sip, and smiled. "This is delicious."

"Refreshing, right?"

"Very. We just need a beach instead of Manhattan in December." Eric stayed on the other side of the island, standing with one elbow resting on the countertop. They ate the first few bites in silence, ripping chunks off the loaf of bread and dragging them through the rich tomato sauce.

"This is a good move, by the way," Kyle said. "The shakshuka. It would be a smart thing to serve if you have a real date over. I'm totally charmed by this."

For a moment, Eric looked confused. Then he smiled in a way that didn't look entirely natural and said, "I'll keep that in mind."

They hadn't even made it through dinner and Eric already felt vulnerable and stupid. Of course he knew that Kyle wasn't his boyfriend or anything, but the reminder that this wasn't a real date still felt like a slap shot to the stomach.

He needed to get over himself. Kyle was here to help, not fall in love.

"I've been considering the best way to approach this," Eric said. It sounded like he was conducting a job interview. He tried again. "I mean . . . I've been thinking about what we might do. Tonight."

Kyle's blue eyes sparkled. Eric was glad he'd worn his glasses tonight. They made him seem . . . softer. "Oh yeah? What have you been thinking about?"

Eric pushed a chunk of bread around the skillet, trying to gather courage. "I don't know if I'm ready for, um, penetration."

He glanced up to find Kyle shrugging easily. "Fine with me. I have about a million ideas for things we could do that don't involve anal. I assume that's what you mean."

"Yeah. That."

Kyle walked around the island until he was standing beside Eric. "We can do whatever you're comfortable with. Even if that's me thanking you for a lovely meal and saying goodnight."

"You came over here for more than that."

"Doesn't matter." Kyle grabbed his hand. "Lesson one, Eric: you are never under any obligation to do anything. If you invite someone over for sex and then change your mind, you can do that. Always."

Eric stared at their joined hands, fascinated by the long, slender fingers that tangled with his own meatier ones. "Seems rude, though."

"Again, that doesn't matter. You are never obligated. Although, if someone gets you off and they aren't a complete fucking jerk, it *is* considered bad manners to leave them hanging. But it's still your choice. And if they *are* a complete fucking jerk, then let them walk out of here with aching balls, I say."

"Noted." Kyle was so close, and all Eric could think about was kissing him. "But if they aren't a complete jerk, and if I'm still . . . interested?"

"Then," Kyle said huskily, "you should let them know. Just so they're sure."

Finally Eric gathered up his courage and asked, "Can I kiss you?"

Kyle tilted his chin up. "Please."

He stayed perfectly still, letting Eric come to him. A jolt shot through Eric when their lips met—excitement mingled with relief that he finally had what he'd been obsessing over for days. Kyle's lips were so soft and warm, and he was kissing him back so sweetly, not pushing. When Eric opened his mouth, and their tongues brushed against each other, he tasted the spices from the tomato sauce, and the mint from the mojitos.

Kyle tangled his fingers into Eric's hair, tugging gently, and why was that so fucking hot? When Eric groaned into his mouth, Kyle took control of the kiss, walking Eric backward until he bumped up against the refrigerator.

That small change—the sudden feeling of being trapped between the stainless steel and Kyle's firm, warm body—flipped a switch inside him. He had a very rare lapse of control, kissing Kyle wildly, desperately trying to pull him even closer. When had he last been this turned on? Had he ever been?

"Let's go upstairs," Kyle murmured against his lips.

As turned on as he was, Eric still couldn't help glancing around the kitchen. He knew he'd get teased for this, but he had to say it. "Okay. But first, do you mind if I clean up?"

Kyle stepped back, grinning. "It would kill you to leave this mess here, wouldn't it?"

Eric picked up the skillet and stepped around him. "I wouldn't be able to focus. No joke."

"I believe you." There was no judgment in Kyle's tone. He just went to the island and gathered their dirty dishes. It only took about ten minutes, with the two of them working together, and the shift in activities gave Eric a chance to cool off a bit. He needed to approach this thing with a clearer head otherwise he was going to, a) jump Kyle like a horny teenager, and b) come immediately.

When they finished, Kyle looped his arms around Eric's neck. "Now then. Where were we?"

Eric chuckled. "That was cheesy."

"It's eager," Kyle corrected. "I've been thinking about taking you apart for days."

Eric froze. "Have you really?"

"Of course," Kyle said easily. "I have so many plans for you."

God, he was stunning. So confident and sexy and, well, *young*. Eric couldn't believe he was really in his arms. About to be in his bed. Even if it was just in the interest of being a helpful friend. He kissed him again, because he could do that, for now.

"Let's go," Eric murmured, hoping his desire masked his nerves. He led Kyle up the two flights of stairs to the master bedroom, taking deep, calming breaths as he tried to slow his racing heart.

"Wow. This is . . . wow," Kyle said when they reached the top of the stairs.

The bedroom and en suite bathroom took up the entire top floor of the house. Eric loved this room, with its large windows and exposed brick wall. One of his favorite paintings hung on the wall opposite the bed—a large abstract oceanscape he found both calming and overwhelming. The floors and the sturdy frame and headboard of his king-size bed were made from reclaimed wood. It was a very peaceful space, and one that, right now, with the dramatic lighting he had set earlier and the beautiful man standing in the middle of the floor, he could also describe as sexy.

Kyle sat on the end of the bed, still gazing around the room. "So what's on the menu?" he asked. "I want to ask now before we start making out again. What do you want to do tonight?"

"I . . ." Eric *should* have an answer ready for this question, but he was coming up blank. He thought about Kyle's mouth and how it felt against his own. How it would feel other places. And also how it would feel to be on his knees for Kyle, using his mouth to earn words of praise and moans of pleasure. "I'd like to try . . . oral."

Kyle crossed his arms and grinned. "You want to suck my cock, Eric?" His tone was playful and seductive at the same time, and, god, those words. Eric's erection had flagged a bit when they'd journeyed upstairs, but now he shifted his stance so his arousal wasn't quite so obvious.

"I can't promise to be great at it," he said honestly. "But I'd like to try."

Kyle slid off the bed, chewing his lip as he walked toward him. "I don't mind being your test subject." His gaze darted to the obvious bulge that had formed in Eric's pants. "I also wouldn't mind giving you a demonstration first."

"Oh—"

Kyle crushed their mouths together, kissing Eric fervently. Eric's brain was sluggish with lust—a sensation he wasn't used to—but he did his best to keep up with the kiss. He wanted Kyle to take charge and do whatever he liked, but he didn't know how to ask. He didn't *want* to ask. For once in his life, Eric didn't want to be the one in control.

Kyle dropped his hand to Eric's crotch and began caressing his rigid cock through his pants. "Nice," Kyle murmured appreciatively. He kissed Eric's jaw, and then nipped his earlobe. Eric's head tipped back and he let out a completely involuntary moan. "You're so hard for me already. Been too long, hasn't it, baby?"

The pet name should have sounded weird—they barely knew each other—but Eric found it thrilling. "Too long," he agreed breathlessly.

"We'll fix that," Kyle promised. "I'm going to wring you out tonight."

God, that sounded wonderful. Eric kissed him again, which he hoped showed his approval of Kyle's plans. He stilled, his whole body buzzing with anticipation, as Kyle unfastened Eric's pants and slipped his hand inside. His fingers wrapped around Eric's cock, making Eric whimper into Kyle's mouth. He knew he'd wanted this, but now that he had this beautiful man's hand wrapped around him, and his slick tongue stroking his own, Eric didn't know how he'd ever lived without it.

Kyle's grip was loose, his fingertips lightly brushing against Eric's shaft. Eric thrust his hips a couple of times, needing more.

Kyle laughed and took his hand away. "You're desperate for it. Why don't you get undressed and meet me on the bed?"

Eric had never gotten his clothes off faster. He'd been naked in front of other men so many times in his life that he wasn't a bit bashful about being on full display now. He gazed at Kyle, wanting his reaction. Wanting his approval.

"Jesus." Kyle sounded horrified. It wasn't encouraging. But then Kyle lightly touched Eric's chest, over a bruise that had formed after Eric had taken a slap shot there during the game in Toronto.

"It's nothing," Eric said, not wanting any distractions.

"There are so many," Kyle said quietly. He trailed his fingers over to another bruise. And another one.

"Part of the job. I barely feel them anymore."

Then Kyle was tracing the lines of his surgery scars on his shoulder. "I'll bet you felt this one."

"Just some repairs. Everything is in working order now."

Kyle kissed the scar tissue, which was shockingly sensual, and made Eric's eyes flutter closed and his mouth go slack. Kyle's lips lingered, gently tracing the thin line of the scar while Eric struggled to breathe. It was just a scar—it didn't even have an interesting story—but what Kyle was doing felt so intimate and adoring that Eric lost himself in it.

Then, Kyle's lips were gone, and when Eric opened his eyes he saw that he had stepped back to pull his own T-shirt off. Kyle's body wasn't bruised and blemished, it was exactly as Eric had remembered it from seeing him half undressed in his guest bedroom: perfect. His flat stomach and toned pecs with that trail of hair Eric hadn't been able to stop thinking about were on full display, and this time Eric could admire as much as he liked.

He sat on the end of the bed and watched as Kyle opened his jeans and slid them down over his slim hips. He looked like a model as he stood in front of Eric in nothing but his royal-blue boxer briefs.

A model with a very obvious erection straining the fabric of his underwear.

Kyle stood between Eric's legs and tipped his chin up. "Take them off," he instructed.

In the hockey world, Eric was known for his steady hands, and for generally remaining calm in the face of pressure. But he couldn't stop his hands from trembling a bit as he reached for Kyle now. He placed his palms on Kyle's waist and slid them down over his warm, smooth skin, to the waistband of his briefs. He glanced up, and Kyle nodded his approval, so Eric hooked his thumbs into the waistband and tugged the briefs down an inch or so. Then he paused and leaned in so he could press his lips to Kyle's stomach. He kissed across his abdomen and then down to where the trail of dark blond hair started.

"That's good," Kyle murmured. "Take your time."

Eric flicked his gaze back up and found Kyle watching him intently. "You're beautiful," Eric said, because he'd never told Kyle that before and he thought he should know. He kissed his bellybutton.

Kyle combed his fingers through Eric's hair. "Thank you."

Eric pulled the briefs down until the tip of Kyle's cock was visible. He pinned it there, against Kyle's belly, with the waistband. For a few seconds he just stared at it, mesmerized. He was really about to touch another man's cock.

"Having second thoughts?" Kyle asked. His tone was playful, but Eric suspected he was concerned.

"No," Eric said. He met Kyle's eyes. "I just can't believe how lucky I am."

They both smiled, and then Eric pulled Kyle's underwear down over his thighs and let it fall to the floor. Kyle's cock bobbed in front of his face, long and narrow with a distinct curve upward, like a ski jump. It was perfect, but Eric wasn't exactly sure what to do with it.

"Anything you want, gorgeous," Kyle said, likely noticing the uncertainty on Eric's face.

Heat crept up the back of Eric's neck. "Could you . . . *tell* me what to do? I like it when, um . . ."

Kyle's smile was wicked. "You want me to be in charge?"

Eric nodded.

"We can play that way. I'll even go easy on you. Why don't you put your hands on my thighs and go back to kissing my stomach? I liked that."

Eric placed his palms above Kyle's knees and stroked, slowly, up toward his hips. He relished the feeling of soft hair and muscular flesh beneath his hands, and the firmness of Kyle's belly against his lips.

"Fuck, I love how your beard feels against my skin," Kyle said, so Eric rubbed his cheek against his stomach, and then down toward the base of his cock. He could feel Kyle's abs flexing in response. Eric kept rubbing his palms up and down, and his thumbs stretched out to press into the crease of Kyle's thighs.

"Play with my balls," Kyle instructed. "However you want. I fucking love that."

There was something about being told what to do that made all of this easier. Eric carefully cupped Kyle's balls in one hand, rubbing a thumb over the tight, wrinkled skin that, he noticed, seemed to be meticulously waxed or shaved or something. Should Eric be waxing his own balls? It wasn't something he had considered doing before.

"That's perfect," Kyle said as Eric gently rolled and tugged at his heavy sac. "Love having my balls played with. I could spend hours fondling and sucking your balls, never even touch your cock. You'd love it."

It sounded like torture, but it also sounded extremely hot. Kyle had to be exaggerating about taking *hours*, though, right? "I think I'd like that," Eric said.

"I'd make sure you did."

The head of Kyle's cock was still bobbing close to Eric's lips. Eric's gaze was locked on the slit, and without meaning to, he licked his lips.

Kyle noticed. "Go ahead, baby. Whenever you're ready."

Eric parted his lips and leaned in. He kissed the tip, letting his tongue flick against the smooth, hot skin. When he heard Kyle's sharp intake of breath, he continued kissing around the head, and then down the underside of his shaft. He opened his mouth wider as he went, using more tongue, and Kyle moaned his approval.

Eric kissed his way back up to the tip, then wrapped his lips around the head and silently prayed to anyone who was listening that he wasn't about to give Kyle the worst blowjob in history.

He closed his eyes, trying to shut off the very loud part of his brain that insisted he be perfect at anything he attempted. He'd wanted this for so long, and now he was here with this wonderful, patient young man. He wouldn't ruin it by second-guessing himself. He would just feel his way through it.

He slid his lips down as far as he could, brushing his tongue over the velvety skin of Kyle's shaft and moaning at the relief of finally knowing what it felt like to take a man into his mouth.

"That's good, baby," Kyle said. He gently brushed Eric's hair with his fingers. "I know I don't have a beginner's cock. It's got a wicked curve to it."

Eric loved the curve in Kyle's cock. As silly as it would probably sound to say, he thought that it suited him. Everything else about Kyle had been a delightful surprise; why not his cock?

Kyle's encouraging words helped Eric relax, and he began

to do whatever felt right, licking and sucking the shaft and head, and flicking his tongue over the slit. Then he remembered Kyle's favorite thing, and brought a hand up to play with Kyle's balls again. Kyle groaned and jerked his hips, thrusting once into Eric's mouth before stilling.

"Sorry," Kyle said hoarsely. "Didn't mean to."

Eric really liked the idea of Kyle thrusting into his mouth, but maybe not tonight. First, Eric needed to practice taking him—or someone, anyway—deeper. Tonight he would enjoy the sensation of having his mouth filled with warm, hard flesh, and the weight of Kyle's full balls in his hands. The first taste of tangy precum touched Eric's tongue and he lapped at the slit, wanting more.

"So sweet," Kyle panted. "You're so fucking eager. I love it. God, you're a natural."

There was no way this was a good blowjob, as much as Eric was enjoying it, but he still appreciated the praise. He kept going, his efforts earning him more salty drops of precum, which he lapped up greedily. He wondered if he'd be able to tell when Kyle was close. He wanted to try to swallow Kyle's release, but wasn't sure if he'd be able to.

Suddenly, Kyle was stepping back, and Eric nearly fell off the bed trying to chase him. Trying to get his lips back around him.

"That's enough, gorgeous." Kyle was half panting and half laughing. Eric must have looked ridiculous, naked and stretching forward for Kyle's cock like a baby bird. "Don't want to come yet. Why don't you get yourself comfortable?"

Eric took that as an invitation to lie back on the bed, so he did. He piled pillows behind his head and stretched out on top of the duvet. He was, he realized, in the exact position he had always arranged Kyle in his fantasies: naked, sprawled on his back with his legs apart, his cock hard and flat against his stomach.

"Jesus, look at you." Kyle grinned, then moved onto the bed until he was kneeling between Eric's calves. "Better than I even imagined."

"You imagined?"

"Fuck yeah. Don't pretend you haven't been thinking about me."

Eric's heart raced with embarrassment and excitement. "I thought about you. Imagined you when—" He cut himself off, embarrassment winning the battle inside him.

"When you were jerking off?"

Eric nodded.

"That's hot. What did you imagine?"

Eric closed his eyes. He couldn't look at Kyle and say this at the same time. "You telling me how to . . . please you." He swallowed. "Commanding me."

Kyle sucked in a breath. "Fuck, Eric."

Eric opened his eyes and found Kyle gripping the base of his own cock with an awestruck expression on his face.

"You're something else," Kyle said. "This is going to be even funner than I thought. How about you stroke that beautiful, thick cock of yours for me? Show me what you did when you thought of me."

Exhibitionism was way out of Eric's usual comfort zone, but he didn't hesitate a second to comply with Kyle's command. His hand wrapped around his cock and gave it his usual firm, quick strokes. With Kyle watching, and the visual of Kyle's naked body combined with the lingering taste of his precum in Eric's mouth, Eric was close to coming in only a few tugs. He grunted and lifted his hips off the bed, bringing his other hand close to catch the impending mess.

"Stop," Kyle said sternly. Eric did. He breathed through the shock to his system that came from the sudden loss of sensation. He'd never just *stopped* before. It was . . . exhilarating.

Like catching a slap shot in his glove: awful pain mingled with a heady rush of power.

"You were about to come, weren't you?" Kyle leaned down, stretching himself over Eric's body, and kissed his mouth. "That's incredible. Why the hurry?"

"It's . . . it's how I always do it."

Kyle seemed to consider this. "Hard? Fast? *Punishing?*"

"Efficient," Eric corrected. "Not punishing, just . . . not leisurely."

"Well," Kyle said, kissing his chin, and then his neck, and then his right shoulder, "let's try another way."

He sat back on his heels, returning to his place between Eric's widespread legs. "Start again," he instructed. "Slowly, this time."

Any embarrassment Eric had felt at performing for Kyle was pushed out by an overwhelming desire to follow his instructions. When he took his cock in hand, he didn't hold back his moan of pleasure at the contact. He knew Kyle wanted to hear it, and Eric was determined to give Kyle whatever he wanted.

"That's right," Kyle said huskily, watching as Eric moved his hand slowly over his shaft. "Nice and easy."

Warmth bloomed in Eric's stomach at Kyle's praise. He dragged a hand lazily over his own chest, rubbing lightly at skin that felt as raw and sensitive as his cock. Like every inch of him was an erogenous zone, like Kyle could touch him anywhere and he would come instantly.

But that wasn't what Kyle wanted, so Eric kept up the achingly slow strokes on his cock, as he brushed his fingers over his torso. He was desperate for more. He wanted to go faster, harder. He wanted Kyle's hand or his mouth. He wanted Kyle to tell him he could come.

"See how good that is?" Kyle said.

Eric nodded thickly, not even sure if it *was* good or if it was torture.

"You want more, baby?"

Eric nodded again, more certain of that one. "Please."

Kyle leaned down and pressed a soft kiss to Eric's chest. The contact was barely anything, but it made Eric's back arch. Kyle laughed against his skin, then kissed down to Eric's bellybutton, each graze of his lips making Eric squirm and gasp. Finally, he hovered his mouth above Eric's straining cock. Eric exhaled raggedly, commanding himself not to come the moment Kyle's lips touched his dick.

If they ever *were* going to touch his dick. Kyle began kissing along the jut of Eric's pelvic bone, then down the crease of his right thigh. When he reached the inside of Eric's thigh, Kyle nuzzled Eric's balls, parting his lips only to tickle them with warm puffs of breath. Eric wanted his tongue, his fingers, anything, but Kyle switched to the left side and began kissing back up to Eric's stomach.

"Bend your knees," Kyle ordered. "Feet flat on the bed. I want a good look at you."

Eric assumed he meant he wanted a view of his . . . well. His asshole. Or at least the area it lived. He complied, trying not to be embarrassed about it.

"You can say no to anything I do or ask, okay?" Kyle said seriously. "You can say stop. You can shut this whole thing down at any time. Do you understand?"

"Yes?"

"Try it without the question mark. This is important."

"Yes," Eric said, more steadily this time. "I'll tell you if I'm uncomfortable. With anything."

"Good. I'm going to suck your cock now, and, if you don't mind, I'd like to play with your hole a bit while I'm doing it. Would you like that?"

"I don't know," Eric said honestly. He'd liked it when he'd

done it to himself, but would it be uncomfortable to have another person touch him there?

"I'll go slow, and I'll be gentle. And you can tell me to stop. Remember that."

"I will."

"Okay." Kyle grinned. "Then let's have fun, gorgeous."

He licked up Eric's shaft, slow and hard, and Eric's hips flew off the bed. Holy *fuck*. It wasn't like Eric had never been blown before, but it had been a damn long time. And Kyle *really* knew what he was doing. He suckled the head until Eric thought he might die, and then swallowed him down like pro.

"Wow," he gasped. "That's . . . wow." He was pretty sure the head of his cock was in Kyle's throat, which was an overwhelming and excellent sensation.

Kyle pulled off. "Just getting started, champ. Relax and let me give you your reward for that win in Toronto."

Those words ignited something in Eric. He liked the idea of being rewarded for his accomplishments. He liked feeling like he had earned this pleasure.

He propped himself on his elbows so he could watch Kyle take him deep again. Kyle glanced up at him through his lashes, his lips stretched wide around Eric's cock, and if he could smirk right now, Eric was sure that he would. Kyle didn't seem at all self-conscious about being watched; he seemed to enjoy it, actually, working Eric's cock while moaning happily as if it was the best thing he'd ever tasted.

Kyle's fingers trailed over Eric's balls, and then down to the sensitive skin below them. He pressed there, and the pressure sent a jolt through Eric. Kyle chuckled around Eric's cock and kept massaging him, rubbing slow, firm circles that felt incredible.

Eric tensed when Kyle touched a fingertip to his hole. It was a gentle touch, brushing the puckered skin, but it was so unusual and exciting that suddenly he was right on the edge of coming again.

He closed his eyes and breathed through the intense desire to come. He commanded himself not to, wanting more of Kyle's mouth and his fingers. He wasn't ready for this to be over.

Mercifully, Kyle pulled off then, giving Eric a moment to retreat from the brink. Eric watched as Kyle sucked two of his own fingers into his mouth, soaking them in saliva, then grinning as he held them up for Eric to see. Before Eric could react, Kyle was taking his cock into his mouth again. A second later, his slick fingers were pressing against Eric's hole.

Distantly, Eric had the thought that he should have set a bottle of lube on his nightstand so Kyle could have easy access, but he didn't want to interrupt what was happening now. Even without proper lube, the circles Kyle was tracing on Eric's entrance were electric.

"Good?" Kyle asked, checking in.

"Yeah," Eric said hoarsely. "Feels amazing."

"This?" Kyle asked, pressing slightly at his hole. Eric gasped, shocked at how good that felt. He had told Kyle he wasn't ready for penetration, but suddenly he was desperate for *something*.

"Do that again," he panted. "Please."

Kyle grinned knowingly as he pushed again, slightly harder this time. Eric's groan was so loud he instinctively covered his mouth with his arm.

"Uh uh," Kyle said, wrapping a hand firmly around Eric's wrist and pulling his arm away. He held it in the air above Eric's head, which was an entirely new intense sensation. "Don't hide those beautiful noises from me. I earned those."

Eric's mouth spread into a wide, probably goofy smile as he gazed up at Kyle. One hand still held his wrist high in the air, and the other was rubbing careful fingers against his hole. In that moment, Eric felt perfectly happy and relaxed and he enjoyed the view of the beautiful man who was taking care of him. Kyle's erection jutted out, dark and still shiny with Eric's spit. Without even realizing he was doing it, Eric reached for it, wrapping his free hand around the shaft and stroking it slowly and gently like he'd been instructed to do to his own cock before.

Kyle dropped his wrist, which felt like a loss until Kyle moved that hand to Eric's cock. They locked eyes as they stroked each other, and Eric was shocked by how dark Kyle's normally pale eyes were. His lips were red and swollen from sucking Eric's cock, and his skin was flushed across his chest and up his neck. He looked absolutely stunning, like a fallen angel who was only on this planet to teach mortals how to fuck. The whimsical fantasy made Eric groan, which made Kyle smile wickedly.

He let go of Eric's cock, and shifted down the bed, forcing Eric to release Kyle's cock as well. He licked a stripe up Eric's shaft, then said, "You want me to finish you like this?"

Every part of Eric screamed yes, even though he knew he'd be sorry when it was over. He nodded, then bravely said, "I want you to push inside me. A little."

Kyle looked thrilled by this request. "I'll go slow," he promised. "Tell me if you want me to stop."

"Okay."

Kyle took Eric's cock in his mouth, and for a minute or so his fingers just continued their gentle circles around Eric's entrance. The anticipation, mixed with the ecstasy of having his cock expertly sucked, sent him soaring. His toes curled and his fingers flexed against the blankets as he willed himself not to come before Kyle could press inside him.

Finally, he felt the thrilling pressure of Kyle's fingertip breeching him. He tried to relax, wanting to invite him in. Kyle kept working his cock with his talented mouth, but his gaze flitted up to Eric's face, watching his reaction.

Eric couldn't say anything. He could only grit his teeth, as the inevitability of his orgasm set in. He tried to fight it, but Kyle was bobbing his head and doing complicated things with his tongue in exactly the right spot, all while his finger created a perfect, burning pressure inside him, and Eric couldn't stop his orgasm from triggering.

"I'm coming. Fuck, Kyle, I'm—"

He was cut off by the force of his climax, his release rocketing out of him while his mind went blissfully quiet. Every part of him was consumed by pure pleasure, and Kyle stayed right where he was, sucking and swallowing until Eric was drained.

When it was over, Eric dropped his head to the pillows, panting. "Sorry. I tried to last."

Kyle was kissing the insides of Eric's thighs. "You were perfect." He slid his finger out of Eric's ass, and Eric felt a surprising sensation of emptiness.

"That was . . ." Eric searched for words. "Incredible."

"Mm." Then Kyle sat up and walked on his knees until he was straddling Eric's waist. He took his own cock in his hand and started stroking quickly. "I'll make sure it lasts next time. I want to edge you for ages, until you're begging for release. You ever done that?"

"Done what?" Eric's brain wasn't functioning well after that orgasm, or with a front-row seat to Kyle jerking himself off. Or with Kyle's casual mention of *next time*.

"Edging. Seeing how long you can last. Bringing yourself right to the brink and then backing off. Over and over again." His voice was strained as he described it. "I want to do that to you. Make you absolutely lose control. I think you need that."

"Yeah," Eric said hoarsely. Suddenly he absolutely needed

the thing that he'd barely heard of until now. He wanted Kyle to pull him apart like that.

Kyle reached behind himself and Eric realized he was probably playing with his own hole. Should Eric be offering to help here? Probably. But Kyle wasn't telling him to and he looked so fucking hot doing this to himself that Eric couldn't move. He was mesmerized, watching the blur of Kyle's hand as it flew over his cock, and the beautiful blissed-out expression on his face. His lips were slack and swollen, and his eyes were closed.

"Aw, fuck. I'm gonna come."

"Yeah, do it," Eric said, then added, boldly, "All over me. Come on."

Kyle opened his eyes. "Fuck. *Fuck*."

They both watched as his release jetted out of him, striping Eric's chest. Kyle's face was gorgeous when he came, dreamy and flushed as sweet little whimpers of ecstasy tumbled out of him. Eric steadied him with firm hands on his hips, and for a moment they just stared at each other, wide-eyed and, for Eric's part at least, thunderstruck by how strongly he wanted more of this man.

He pulled him down into a long, slow kiss that he hoped expressed gratitude more than the adoration he actually felt. When they broke apart, Kyle collapsed on the bed beside him and said, "I'll clean that up. Just give me a second."

"No rush."

Kyle laughed. "So this mess you don't mind?"

Eric gazed down at the glistening, sticky streaks on his chest as Kyle's beautiful moans from a moment ago echoed in his ears. "It doesn't bother me at all, actually."

They stayed like that for a while, beside each other, but not speaking or looking at each other. Eric was grappling with the enormity of this moment. He knew that this sort of thing meant almost nothing to Kyle, but Eric had never had sex outside of a romantic relationship before, let alone with a man. And his heart was screaming, absurdly, for him to wrap his arms around Kyle and never let him go. It was a lot to process.

Eventually, Kyle pulled himself up to a sitting position and patted Eric on the shoulder. "I'll get a cloth. Is there one in the bathroom?"

"Yeah, there's a shelf with some."

"Okay."

Eric stretched his arms out in a T-shape, and blew out a long breath. This was the same bed he'd woken up in. Did he feel different now? Was he ending his day a changed man?

Well, he had another man's cum drying on his chest. That was different.

He started to laugh. Kyle emerged from the bathroom and paused when he heard Eric's uncharacteristic giggling. "Uh oh. I broke you."

"No." Eric scrubbed a hand over his face, trying to compose himself. "No. I'm just . . . overwhelmed."

Kyle sat on the bed beside him. "Good or bad?"

"Good," Eric said quickly. "Really good."

"It seemed like you enjoyed yourself," Kyle teased. Eric grinned lazily in response.

The cloth felt warm and soothing as Kyle washed away all traces of himself from Eric's skin and chest hair. Again, it occurred to Eric that he should be helping, or just take the cloth and do it himself, but this was nice, and Kyle didn't seem to mind.

"I love your chest hair," Kyle said. He dragged the fingers of his free hand through the damp curls. "So fucking sexy."

"Thanks." Eric grabbed his hand and tangled their fingers together. He kissed the top of Kyle's hand, then pulled him on top of him so he could kiss him again. It was another slow and lazy exploration, and Eric thought it might be even better than their urgent, hungry kisses. He would happily kiss Kyle like this forever, especially if he kept making those happy little sighs.

Kyle stacked his fists on Eric's sternum, then rested his chin playfully on top. "So. Sex with men: what's the verdict?"

A million thoughts flew through Eric's brain, but all he managed to say was, "I liked it."

Kyle's eyes went wide, then he rolled off of Eric. "Wow," he said flatly. "*Wow.*"

Eric laughed and tried to grab him, but Kyle scooted away. "I loved it," Eric clarified. "That was great."

"Too late. You just described sex with me the same way people describe a new flavor of M&M's."

"Kyle." Eric rolled to his side and shuffled over until he was gazing down at Kyle. "That was incredible. Life changing. I never lived until today."

Kyle's eyes narrowed. "It's a start."

Eric kissed his forehead and then rolled off the bed and onto his feet. He went to the bathroom, feeling giddy.

"Ooh. I haven't gotten a good look at your ass yet," Kyle called from the bed. "Holy hell, dude."

Eric wiggled it a bit, which earned him a whistle. He knew he had a great ass. It was one of many things that he was in danger of losing once he retired.

When Eric returned from the bathroom, Kyle was already dressed.

"You're leaving?"

"Yeah. I thought . . . I mean, it's still pretty early. I can go home."

Eric tried not to let his disappointment show. "Sure. That makes sense."

"Although I'm sure I would sleep like a log in that bed. Or your guest bed again," Kyle added quickly. "I'm not going to assume that—"

Eric grabbed a fresh pair of underwear from his dresser. "If you stayed the night, you'd be welcome to share my bed. Or sleep in the guest room. Your choice."

"Maybe next time."

Eric froze for a second, then resumed stepping into his briefs. Kyle had mentioned a next time before, but that had been when he was on the brink of orgasm. Did he really want to do this again? Did he actually want to do that edging thing?

"Next time?" Eric asked, hoping his tone didn't betray how eager he was.

"If you want. I mean, I know your mind is blown right now, but we barely scratched the surface tonight. I have much to teach you."

Eric huffed. "Okay, professor. Maybe we can schedule something next week."

"Sounds hot. I'll send you an appointment reminder."

Eric pulled on some sweatpants. "Or you can be a brat about it."

Kyle crossed the room and wrapped his arms around Eric's waist. "I just remembered I'm busy for the next six years."

"That's too bad. I'll probably be dead after that."

Kyle kissed him. "You'll be even sexier in six years, I'll bet."

Eric walked Kyle down to the front door and got him his jacket. Kyle fished his phone out of the pocket and laughed. "Kip's inviting me to your Saturday afternoon game."

Eric loved the idea of Kyle watching him play. He wanted to show off for him. "Can't get enough of me, huh?"

"I want to see how flexible you are." Kyle waggled his eyebrows, which made Eric laugh.

"Thank you," Eric said awkwardly before opening the door. "This really was . . . well, it was more than I'd ever hoped for. It was perfect. Thanks."

Kyle's eyes were soft. "I had fun. Keep in touch, all right?"

"I will."

"And," Kyle added cheerfully. "I'll keep an eye out for any potential suitors for you."

That threw Eric for a moment, which was silly because he knew *Kyle* wasn't going to date him. He forced a smile. "Sounds good. I'll wave to you at the game."

"I'll be the one in the *I kissed Eric Bennett* T-shirt." Kyle winked at him, and then he was gone.

CHAPTER FOURTEEN

"Do you ever get used to that?" Kyle asked over the roar of twenty thousand people cheering as Scott's goal was announced.

Kip grinned, his eyes fixed on Scott's face on the enormous scoreboard screen. "Nope."

"Like, that's your boyfriend. Your *fiancé*." It was suddenly a lot easier to tease Kip about Scott. He no longer felt a stab of jealousy or longing when reminded that Kip was spoken for, and Kyle didn't want to think too hard about why that was.

"I know," Kip said. "We argued about coffeemaker settings this morning."

Kyle laughed, imagining it. He'd felt a surprising lurch in his own chest when Eric was announced at the beginning of the game as the starting goaltender. Eric wasn't his boyfriend, but their night together had been incredible, and Kyle had been obsessing over it ever since. And it wasn't just the sex that he couldn't stop thinking about. It was all of it: the dinner, the conversation, the way Eric hadn't dismissed him when Kyle had confessed that he was more passionate about bartending than academia. In fact, every moment they had spent together had been wonderful, starting with their brief conversations at

Scott and Kip's engagement party. Eric had Kyle thoroughly smitten.

And now he was on the ice in full hockey gear, looking like a gladiator as an arena full of fans cheered him on. It was hard to believe he was the same man who'd shyly asked Kyle to boss him around a bit in the bedroom.

It was an afternoon game against New Jersey, so the building was rowdy. The score was now 2–0 for New York in the third period, thanks to some amazing saves by Eric.

"I want him to get a shutout," Kyle said.

Kip nudged him hard. "Don't say it out loud! You'll jinx him!"

"Wow, Scott has really rubbed off on you." Kyle regretted saying it immediately because he knew what was coming.

"All the fucking time," Kip drawled.

Kyle looked at the clock. Six and a half minutes left.

Come on, Eric. You've got this.

He hadn't gone to a game with Kip in a while, and he'd never been this on edge watching one. His stomach twisted with nerves, not just because he wanted the Admirals to win, but because he didn't want Eric to get hurt. How did Kip deal with all this stress?

"We picked a venue," Kip said, casually stealing a handful of Kyle's popcorn. "For the wedding."

"Really? Where?"

"We found an inn near Bay Shore—more of a resort, with a main building and cottages around it. We booked the whole thing."

"That sounds . . ." *Expensive* was the first word to pop into Kyle's head, but he finished with, "awesome."

Kip smiled. "I know. It's a total dream wedding. We wanted to do it out of the city, but not too far. And we wanted somewhere private. We're hoping we can do the ceremony outdoors, near the water."

"So no center-ice wedding?"

"Fuck no. Scott loves the fans, but this is for us."

Kip gazed dreamily at the circle where Scott was now bending to take a face-off. Kyle's eyes locked on Eric, crouching at the top of his crease. Kyle indulged in a brief fantasy of dancing with Eric at the wedding. It could happen, even as friends.

The crowd started yelling angrily, and his attention turned back to the game. One of the Admirals players had gotten a penalty.

"Total bullshit," Kip grumbled. "That wasn't even close to slashing."

Kyle hadn't seen it, but he agreed. "Fucking ridiculous."

Now the Admirals would be short one player, and the face-off was happening in their zone, close to Eric. Kyle wondered if Eric was stressed about that. Or maybe this was fun for him. Maybe this was the hockey goalie equivalent of a skier standing on the rim of a headwall. Kyle had lived for that feeling once, and still loved it whenever he got the chance.

New Jersey won the face off and, for the next fifty seconds or so, unleashed a barrage of hard shots at the Admirals' net. Eric was unbelievable, shutting down a scoring chance at one side of the net, then quickly sliding to the opposite side to stop the rebound shot. A slap shot came from the blue line that hit Eric so hard in the chest that *Kyle* could feel it. The crowd roared their approval. When the play finally stopped, they chanted *Ben-ny, Ben-ny* and the DJ started playing Elton John's "Benny and the Jets."

"He's so fucking good!" Kyle said, beaming with pride like he was somehow responsible for Eric's talent.

"He's amazing," Kip said. "I'll bet he could play another five seasons at least."

Kyle wondered. Eric seemed healthy and, based on his impressive upside-down yoga abilities, very fit, but how much longer could a body endure this level of punishment?

On the ice, Eric seemed to be shaking off that last save. As if being hit with a hundred-mile-an-hour slap shot was the same as stubbing your toe. The jumbo screens showed a close-up of Eric's face as he flipped his mask up. He looked remarkably calm as he squirted water into his mouth, like he was hanging out at the park instead of throwing himself in front of rocket-fast hockey pucks.

There were now less than four minutes left in the game, and one minute left in the penalty. Kyle handed Kip the rest of his popcorn because he was too nervous to eat anyway. Besides, he needed to clasp his hands together even though he didn't believe in prayer. It just felt right.

He wanted Eric to get this shutout.

He wanted Eric to invite him over to celebrate tonight.

The possibility that Kyle might get to again have this man—the same man who was right now being loudly adored by an arena full of excited fans—was exhilarating. He wanted nothing more than the chance to take him over, and then completely take him apart.

He suddenly understood why Kip had been sexually obsessed with Scott for almost three years now. This was heady fucking stuff.

The last minute of play was announced. The penalty was over, but New Jersey had pulled their goaltender for the extra attacker. Kyle resented them for it. It was so unlikely that they would score *two* goals in the next minute to tie the game that Kyle wished they wouldn't bother trying. Why ruin Eric's shutout for no reason?

They had several good scoring chances during that final minute, but Eric stopped any pucks that made it through the defensemen. When the final ten seconds were being counted down, Kyle was yelling out the numbers louder than anyone. Finally, the siren sounded to end the game, and Kyle leaped out of his seat. "Yeah! Fuck yeah, Eric!"

Kip laughed as he bent to gather his coat from his seat. "Looks like Benny's got a new number-one fan."

"I'm happy for him," Kyle said, though what he was actually thinking was *I want to fuck him*. He watched as the Admirals hugged on the ice, then saluted the crowd with their sticks before leaving the ice.

"This is the boring part," Kip said. "The post-game stuff takes forever. Especially after a win. You wanna go to Shake Shack?"

Kyle blinked at him. "You ate for pretty much this entire game."

"There's always room for Shake Shack. Come on. My treat."

"No way. You provided the tickets. The least I can do is buy you a burger."

Kip waved a hand. "The tickets were free. Come on."

"Scott told me about Eric."

Kyle froze, dangling the ShackMeister fry he'd been about to pop into his mouth in the air. Did Scott know Kyle and Eric had hooked up? "What about Eric?"

"That he's bi. Scott told me Eric told you first, which is *interesting*."

Kyle tried to play it cool. "Were you surprised that he's bi?"

"Yes! I had no idea. Scott didn't even suspect, and he's one of his best friends." Kip laughed. "Scott's not really the best at clocking people, though. So why did Eric tell you?"

Kyle dropped his fry back into the container. "I don't know. We've been hanging out a bit. I guess he just wanted to tell someone who wasn't that close to him."

"What, like he practiced coming out? With you?"

Kyle bit his cheek to keep from grinning. Eric had practiced a lot of things with Kyle. "Yeah. Something like that."

Kip studied him, frowning. "What's going on with you two?"

"Nothing."

"Because I did the secret dating thing with an NHL star and it wasn't—"

"I'm not dating him," Kyle said truthfully, though he wished it were a lie. "We're just friends. Like you *wanted us to be*."

Kip smiled at that. "That's cool. Scott told me Eric was in a great mood at practice yesterday. Maybe you're a good influence on him. He needs to have some fun."

Kyle looked down at his fries so Kip wouldn't see the flush that was creeping up his neck. Had Eric been in a good mood because of Kyle? Had he also been unable to stop thinking about their night together?

Kip was looking at his phone, so Kyle pulled his own phone out. There was a message from two minutes ago.

ERIC:

Are you free tonight?

Kyle grinned at his phone, then quickly wrote, I am. Feel like celebrating?

ERIC:

I really do. Can you come to my place? Maybe in an hour?

KYLE:

I'll be there.

"What are you smiling about?" Kip asked.

"Uh, just a guy wants to meet up with me."

"Oh yeah?"

"Someone I met at work." Kyle realized as he said it that it wasn't actually a lie. "So . . ." He stood up, grabbing what was left of his cookies and cream milkshake because there was no reason to waste it. "I should get going. Gotta freshen up a bit first, y'know?"

Kip grinned at him. "Have fun. Scott's going to meet me here."

Kyle quickly dipped and kissed him on the cheek. "Thanks for inviting me today."

"Anytime. See you soon."

Kyle rushed out of the restaurant and into the nearest subway station, giddy with excitement about getting his hands on Eric Bennett tonight.

Eric felt invincible. He was always charged up after a win—especially a shutout—but tonight he felt confident and attractive and horny as fuck. This must be how his teammates felt when they talked about needing to get laid after a big win.

He tried not to let any insecurities creep in and ruin this incredible high he was riding. He ran upstairs to his bedroom to make sure nothing was out of place, which, of course, nothing was. He checked his nightstand drawer and was relieved that he had plenty of lube left in the bottle. After a moment of worrying about appearing too forward, he set the bottle on top of the nightstand. There was no reason to be shy tonight. Eric found the simplicity of this arrangement exciting. He didn't have to guess or be subtle. He could see why hookups were appealing for a lot of people, as long as it was with someone he trusted.

His doorbell rang and Eric darted down the stairs, heart hammering with anticipation. He opened the door and found Kyle, bundled into a scarf and hat, cheeks pink from the cold.

"Hey," Kyle said. He was smiling, and for a moment Eric couldn't speak because he looked so beautiful. Then he finally snapped out of it and stepped aside to let Kyle in.

Kyle set his backpack down and removed his outerwear, which Eric took from him to stow in the closet. Kyle was in bartender mode tonight: a white T-shirt, faded jeans, and no glasses. It was a look that was designed to tempt men, and it was probably what Kyle normally wore when he was meeting a hookup. Eric wasn't sure if he was disappointed that he wasn't getting the softer, grad student version of the man.

"It was fucking hot watching you get that shutout," Kyle said, stepping close.

"It was pretty hot getting that shutout," Eric said. He tilted his head, his lips hovering in front of Kyle's. "I feel like celebrating."

"Yeah, let's do that."

There was no caution in this kiss. No chaste warm-up. The moment their lips collided they were devouring each other, Kyle's fingers gripping Eric's jaw, and Eric palming the back of Kyle's head. Every nerve in Eric's body buzzed with need. He felt ravenous and ready to drink his fill of this gorgeous man.

Kyle pushed him back against a wall, Eric's back thudding next to the painting they had been admiring together at the party. Kyle grabbed Eric's wrists and pinned his arms against the wall. The sudden vulnerability sent a jolt through him, and he gasped as Kyle kissed his throat.

"You like that?" Kyle said against his skin. "Would you stay like that for me if I ask you to?"

Eric groaned in response, then managed a strangled, "Yes." He would stay like this as long as Kyle wanted, sore muscles be damned. He would fight through the discomfort, like he did when practicing yoga, and command his body to endure it. For Kyle.

He could feel the press of Kyle's teeth against the tender flesh near his Adam's apple, and he guessed that Kyle was smiling.

"You seemed to like it when I was calling the shots last time."

"I did."

"Maybe we can play with that, then. Because I meant what I said last time: I'd love to introduce you to the wonderful world of edging. I have a feeling you'd love it."

Eric nodded. "Okay. We can try that."

Kyle stroked a gentle hand over Eric's beard, then gripped his jaw and kissed him fiercely. The force of it made Eric's legs wobble. He wanted Kyle to do whatever he had planned right here, against this wall, but Kyle was the voice of reason.

"Why don't we go upstairs so we don't knock that painting to the floor?" he murmured.

Startlingly, in that moment, Eric couldn't give a fuck about the painting. But Kyle was right; they needed a bed. "Yeah. Yes. Upstairs."

Kyle stepped back. "You go up. Get naked and wait for me on the bed." He chuckled, probably amused by the dazed expression on Eric's face. "Go. Now."

Kyle played two levels of *Angry Birds Blast* on his phone, which he felt was enough time for Eric to get undressed and ready for him. He walked up to the story below the master bedroom—the yoga studio. He took his time, taking a leisurely stroll around the dark studio space, making his footsteps heavy. He hoped Eric could hear him, and that he was tense with anticipation.

When he finally ascended the stairs to Eric's bedroom, he found him stretched out on the bed, naked, with his hands folded on his chest and his ankles crossed. His cock was thick but not quite hard, and rested against one muscular thigh. Kyle gave himself a moment to drink that image in. God, there were so many things he wanted to do to this man.

Kyle dropped his backpack on the bed. He considered removing his shirt, but decided to leave it for now. He liked the imbalance of being fully dressed while Eric was naked. Up close he could admire the definition of Eric's finely honed muscles. And the numerous dark bruises all over his body. What this man put himself through every day was astonishing.

He could tell Eric was trying to appear comfortable and relaxed, but the tightness in his knuckles, and the way his abs were clenching and releasing, gave him away. Kyle wrapped a hand around Eric's ankle and squeezed, then released him and trailed the backs of his fingers up Eric's leg until he reached the top of his thigh. Eric sucked in a breath when the hand got close to his crotch, but Kyle pulled it away.

"You are absolutely stunning," he said. "Look at all that muscle."

"I exercise."

"How much tension do you carry in those muscles?" Kyle asked, squeezing one of Eric's biceps. "How much pressure is on these shoulders?"

In response, Eric closed his eyes and sighed out a long breath. Kyle played with his hair, gently combing through the thick curls. He wanted to soothe him and pamper him, and then he wanted to wring him out.

"You can let it all go," Kyle said softly. "Your only job tonight is to feel good. And it's my job to make sure you do."

"Yes," Eric whispered, keeping his eyes closed.

Kyle bent down to kiss him. Eric opened eagerly, pulling himself up to get a better angle to deepen the kiss. He slipped a hand under the hem of Kyle's T-shirt, sliding his palm up Kyle's stomach to lift the shirt.

Kyle covered the hand with his own, stopping it. "Nice try," he said. "I think I'll keep my clothes on for a bit."

"Seems unfair."

"I never promised to be fair. Lie down."

Eric's eyes went wide, and Kyle pressed him back into the mattress with a firm hand on his chest. Having even this much control over this powerful, beautiful man was intoxicating. Kyle wanted a weekend alone with him. A week. A year.

When Eric was settled, Kyle began to warm up his body with the lightest brush of his fingertips. There were fresh bruises from the game that day, and Kyle avoided them as he traveled across Eric's chest, down to his chiseled stomach, then dipped into the deep grooves under his obliques. He watched Eric's dick twitch and thicken in response, but he didn't touch it. Instead he walked to the end of the bed and opened his backpack.

"What's in there?" Eric asked.

"You'll see."

Kyle decided that he'd better get started; otherwise they were still going to be here at midnight, and he had no intention of sleeping here. He considered blowing Eric first, but he knew from last time that it would get Eric too close too fast. He would save that for a later round. The first one would be relaxing and slow, with lots of talking.

Eric was fully hard now and Kyle hadn't even touched his dick. This was going to be fun. He'd noticed the lube Eric had set on the nightstand, but Kyle pulled a bottle of his personal favorite lube out of his backpack.

"Did you jerk off today?" Kyle asked as he drizzled some lube into his palm.

"No."

"Good. Yesterday?"

Eric furrowed his brow, as if he needed to think about it. "No."

Kyle wrapped his slick hand around Eric's cock, which made Eric hiss and clench his abs. "You must be dying to come then."

"I can go . . . a while," Eric said hoarsely.

"Really?" Kyle asked conversationally as he slowly pumped Eric's cock. "Not me. I need to come at least once a day, usually."

"You're young."

"And you're not old." Kyle kept stroking him, closely watching Eric's face. He was grimacing and his brow was still furrowed. Far too tense. "I think you're going to like this."

"You say that to everyone you torture?"

"I don't do this for just *anyone*. This is premium service you're getting here." He added a twist on the down strokes as he continued to stroke Eric, keeping his grip loose. "This is going to be the best orgasm you've ever had. I promise."

Eric grunted in response. Kyle picked up the pace a bit.

"I love edging myself," he continued. "This morning I got myself close three or four times before I let myself come."

Eric swore quietly, and Kyle knew he was picturing it. Good. He wanted Eric to imagine it, the way he'd been sprawled out naked on his bed, cock swollen and glistening and his skin flushed and slick with sweat. God, Kyle had never taken a dirty photo of himself—not after what had happened with Ian—but maybe he would, if Eric wanted one. If Eric wanted to see what Kyle looked like when he was fantasizing about him. When Kyle was worn out and desperate to come.

Kyle gripped a little harder and kept talking, wanting to make it clear. "You know what I was thinking about when I was doing that?"

"What?"

"I was imagining this. You laid out for me to play with for as long as I wanted." It wasn't a lie at all. Kyle had been fantasizing about exactly this when he'd brought himself to the brink repeatedly that morning. Well. Almost exactly this. "In my fantasy you had a vibrating butt plug in, but we can work up to that."

"Fuck."

Kyle wasn't kidding. He knew exactly which plug he wanted to fill Eric with. He could control it with an app on his phone.

"Tell me when you're close. That's my only rule."

"What happens—" Eric sucked in a breath. "What happens if I don't?"

"Then the fun will be over, and I don't think you want that. I know I don't." Kyle was no sadist, and he'd never been into mixing pain with pleasure. He had no interest in adding to the bruises that covered Eric's body. What Kyle really loved was having impressive, confident men surrender control to him, and he'd never had anyone as impressive as Eric Bennett.

Eric didn't reply, but he did open his eyes. They locked gazes as Kyle started stroking him harder, faster. He used his free hand to fondle Eric's heavy balls. Eric was racing toward climax already, Kyle could tell. He wondered if Eric would follow his instructions and tell him when he was about to come. How much did he trust Kyle?

"I'm close," Eric warned, and Kyle bit his lip to stop a delighted, goofy grin from taking over his face. He was trying to look commanding here. He gave Eric a couple more strokes, then released his cock, but kept caressing his balls.

"Fuck." Eric half groaned, half laughed the word. "You do this for fun, huh?"

"Just wait." Kyle stretched over Eric's body and kissed him slow and deep for a minute or two. He stopped when he realized that Eric was humping him. Kyle swatted his thigh. "Naughty. Do you want me to leave you like this?"

"I could handle it."

"Then I haven't worked you hard enough. Let's try again."

In one fluid move, Kyle slid down Eric's body and took his cock deep into his mouth.

"Ah! *Fuck*." It was the loudest sound Kyle had ever heard Eric make. If he hadn't had his mouth full, he would have smiled about it.

Kyle was in love with Eric's cock. It was the thickest one Kyle had ever seen in person, and it was decently long as well. Kyle usually preferred to top, but damn, he wanted to know what that monster cock would feel like inside him. He relaxed his throat, taking Eric as deep as he could. He wanted this one to be quick, so he was relentless, sucking hard and swallowing around the head.

"God, I'm close again. I'm going to—"

Kyle pulled off, and Eric punched the mattress.

"Uh oh. Are you mad at me already?"

"No," Eric grumbled.

"We've barely started." Kyle straddled his hips and smiled down at him.

"You could at least take off your shirt," Eric complained.

"I suppose you've earned that." Kyle pulled his T-shirt off and dropped it to the floor. Eric's hands were on him immediately, gliding over his flanks and then across his chest.

"You're beautiful," Eric said, then pulled him down for a kiss. Eric's kisses had quickly become Kyle's favorite thing. There was a sweetness to them that Kyle wouldn't have expected before they'd started doing all this.

When Kyle had watched him from afar, the few times he'd come into the bar with Scott over the past couple of years, he'd enjoyed brief fantasies of Eric taking him hard against the wall in the back room. Maybe after Kyle had gotten him so turned on that Eric couldn't resist him anymore. And he'd imagined Eric on his knees for him, his strong hands digging into Kyle's ass cheeks as Kyle fucked his mouth. The fantasies had been hot, but the reality was exhilarating beyond anything that Kyle could have imagined. Eric kissed him like he was important, like Kyle was something precious, and Kyle couldn't get enough of it.

It was a dangerous way to be thinking.

He forced himself to break the kiss, then rolled off Eric and walked to the end of the bed. He needed a moment of distance to clear his head, to remind himself what he was doing here. He wasn't important or precious to Eric. Kyle was just a helpful friend who knew his way around a cock.

He reached into his backpack and pulled out a new masturbation sleeve that he'd only used a couple of times but had completely blown his mind both times. "You ever use one of these?"

"I don't even know what that is."

Kyle sighed dramatically, as if he didn't love being the one to introduce Eric to new levels of pleasure. "Oh, Eric." He poured some lube inside the toy and lined it up with Eric's cock. Without further ceremony, he carefully pushed the sleeve down until it covered Eric's shaft completely.

"Holy—what the hell is that?"

"It's a sex toy," Kyle said, deliberately bratty.

Eric narrowed his eyes at him. "I've heard of sex toys. I'm not *that* ignorant."

Kyle laughed. "It's a sleeve that has fun bumps and ridges inside. Feels great, doesn't it?"

Eric let out a long groan as Kyle gave him a few slow strokes. "That's incredible."

"I know. I used it last week on myself, and I came like a fucking volcano."

Eric groaned again, possibly at the vision of Kyle using the toy on himself, and possibly because he was envious of Kyle's orgasm. Maybe both.

Kyle gave him another long, slow stroke watching as the toy swallowed Eric's dark, swollen cock. "Let's see how long you can last with this guy."

It turned out to not be long at all. About two minutes until Eric's toes started curling.

"Something you wanna tell me?" Kyle asked mildly.

Eric pressed his lips tight together.

"Because it looks like you're about to shoot your load."

Eric was breathing hard, and Kyle let him believe he'd won for a second, then pulled the toy away. Eric whimpered as his cock jerked angrily against his stomach, red and shiny with lube.

"Were you not going to tell me that time?" Kyle teased. "Because maybe you don't even need to. Maybe I can just. Tell." To prove it, he counted to ten in his head, then started stroking Eric with his hand. In under a minute Eric's abs were clenching and his balls were lifting, and Kyle let him go.

"Ah. God. Fuck you," Eric gasped. "I was so close that time."

"Your balls are so fucking tight," Kyle chuckled, tracing a finger over them. "I can't wait to see this load." He idly thumbed the sensitive spot just under the head of Eric's cock and watched a bead of precum escape from the slit. Kyle was sure his own cock was leaking right now. It was getting difficult to remain in control, the way Eric was unraveling for him.

Eric's chest was rising and falling rapidly as he struggled to compose himself. "Can . . . can you take off your jeans?"

Kyle smiled. "I like that you're turning this into a game of strip poker." He stood and made sure Eric was watching as he thumbed open the button on his fly. His erection was obvious, straining against the denim, so he massaged the bulge with his hand as he watched Eric's face. He looked wrecked: eyes glazed, skin flushed, and sweat dampening the curls at his temples. Kyle would bet he would do almost anything he asked right now.

"I want you to do this one," Kyle suddenly decided. "Stroke yourself. Get close, but don't come."

Eric made an irritated rumble, but he did as he was told. He wrapped his hand around his dick and started slow, careful strokes while the rest of his body trembled with the effort of not coming.

"That's right. Slowly," Kyle said. "Like last time. Remember last time?"

Eric nodded, his teeth digging into his bottom lip as his brow furrowed with concentration.

"Good," Kyle whispered as he slid a hand inside his own underwear. "You're doing great, baby. You've got me so hard."

"I want to see," Eric panted.

Kyle stepped out of his jeans, then pushed his briefs down and off. He pulled his rigid cock down and let it slap back against his stomach. "See how fucking hard I am? That's because you look so fucking gorgeous right now, stroking yourself for me. Doing what I say."

Eric whimpered, and squeezed his eyes shut for a second. When he opened them again, Kyle noticed how glazed they looked. Eric's gaze fixed on Kyle's cock, so Kyle gave it a few lazy strokes for him.

"Can I—can you—" Eric gritted out. "*Fuck.* I can't. I'm going to—"

"Let go," Kyle said firmly.

Eric did, though he looked surprised about it. He scrubbed a hand over his face and groaned in frustration. Kyle sucked in a breath, and he felt like his heart had stopped. He could tell Eric was in agony, but he was willing to endure it. For Kyle. Fuck, it was staggering. He gripped the base of his own cock, and took a steadying breath, before reaching to pick up the toy again.

"Get on your knees," he instructed, hoping the tremor in his voice wasn't obvious. Eric was up in an instant, legs wide with his knees pressing hard into the mattress. He was magnificent.

Kyle bent to drop a soft kiss to the head of Eric's weeping cock. It was an apology, and a promise. And a thank-you. He straightened, then slipped the toy over the head and held it still. "You're doing the work this time. I want you to fuck it."

Eric didn't need to be asked twice. He braced his hands on Kyle's shoulders and started thrusting into the toy with gusto. Kyle let out a whimper of his own as he watched him, imagining what it would be like to be fucked by this man.

"I wish that toy was me," he said, daringly. He didn't want to pressure Eric, but his head was full of awesome dirty thoughts and he wanted to share them. "I'd love to feel that thick cock of yours inside me. Fuck, I'll bet you'd tear me apart with that thing."

Eric grunted and thrust faster. He was so strong, and so *fit*. Kyle bet he could go for hours if he could hold off on coming. He could hold Kyle down and just pound into him.

"You picturing it?" Kyle asked. "You pretending this toy is me? That you're stretching me and filling me and—"

Eric's nostrils flared as he squeezed his eyes shut. Kyle yanked the toy away, and Eric *screamed* in frustration, humping the air uselessly.

Okay, maybe it was time.

"Lie down," Kyle said gently. "On your back."

"Please," Eric whimpered.

As soon as Eric was arranged how Kyle wanted him, Kyle settled between his spread thighs. He took a moment to admire the results of all his hard work: Eric Bennett, flushed and glistening with sweat and lube. His eyes wild and pleading, and his hair damp and tangled against the pillow. Kyle slid a hand up one of Eric's thighs, and watched Eric's desperate cock twitch. His balls looked huge, full to bursting, and Kyle wanted to open the floodgate.

He started jerking him off. There was no teasing this time; he stroked hard and fast, cupping his loaded balls with the other hand. Eric begged him with his eyes, and Kyle nodded. "Yeah, gorgeous. Let's see it."

Two more pumps and Eric erupted. He arched off the bed, howling with relief as the first spray hit his chest. Kyle moaned along with him as his own cock jerked and released precum, eager for his own release.

Kyle stroked Eric through his epic orgasm, watching in amazement as he kept spurting. He didn't let him go until he was drained, his cock managing one last dribble to join the impressive amount of come that coated Eric's stomach and chest.

"Oh my god," Eric gasped. "That was—holy shit."

"Yeah," Kyle agreed breathlessly.

"I've never come like that. Fuck."

Kyle pulled himself together, then chuckled. "Good, right?"

"Amazing. I didn't know."

"Stick with me, babe." Kyle leaned down and kissed him. "I know all sorts of stuff."

Both men rested beside each other while Eric caught his breath. He was so wrecked that it took him several minutes to notice that Kyle was calmly stroking himself. Eric rolled on his side to watch him.

"Can I help with that?"

Kyle smiled lazily at him. "I have a feeling you'd rather clean yourself up."

Eric ducked his head, embarrassed by how accurate Kyle's words were, but also touched by how well he knew him already. And by how considerate he was. "I'll just be a second," he promised.

"Take your time."

He watched Kyle for another moment—he truly looked like he was in no hurry at all to finish, despite the fact that his cock was rock hard and glistening with precum—then went quickly to the bathroom.

He figured being drunk had to feel a bit like this. His legs were like jelly, and his head was floaty. Every part of him was loose and relaxed and . . . happy. He felt so damn happy.

Eric had never experienced anything like what Kyle had just done to him. Not even close. He would definitely play with edging the next time he was jerking off. He knew it wouldn't be the same as having Kyle do it for him—of giving that control to somebody else—but it would be an exercise in discipline, and Eric was no stranger to that.

He cleaned himself off and examined himself in the mirror. His hair looked like he'd just pulled his goalie mask off, damp and unruly. His eyes were glassy and his skin was flushed and glistening with sweat. He looked, as some of his teammates might say, well-fucked.

And Kyle was in his bed right now, stroking himself and possibly thinking about Eric and the way he'd made him lose control. Eric was surprised he wasn't ashamed of how unrestrained he'd been.

He wasn't ashamed of anything they had done, he was only concerned about how much he wanted to do *more*. He wanted Kyle to show him everything he knew, and Eric wanted to give him whatever he had to give in return. That part was scary enough, but it was Eric's longing for intimacies with Kyle beyond sex that had him truly terrified. He wanted to spend time together even if they were doing nothing at all. He wanted to learn everything about him, and open himself up to him, and Eric needed to put a stop to that line of thinking before he did something stupid.

When Eric returned to the bedroom, Kyle was resting against a stack of pillows, one arm draped over his head and the other hand slowly working his cock. He was exquisite, as rare and beautiful as any piece of art in Eric's collection. His long, toned legs were stretched out in front of him, loose and relaxed. His cock, with its delightful curve, was still hard and was now glistening with lube.

"What do you want?" Eric asked. The sight of Kyle languidly pleasuring himself had sparked some energy back into Eric's exhausted body. Even his cock was making an effort to rise again.

"Come here," Kyle said. He patted the mattress next to him, and Eric went immediately. He sat up with his back against the headboard because he was worried that if he lay all the way down he might fall asleep, as drained as he was. Kyle surprised him by wedging himself between Eric's thighs, then reclined backward against Eric's chest.

Eric wrapped an arm around him, pulling him tight against him, loving the feeling of having him so close. Loving how perfectly Kyle fit against him.

"Am I hurting you?" Kyle asked.

"Hm?" The last thing Kyle was doing right now was hurting him.

"The bruise, I mean. Bruis*es*, rather."

It was adorable how concerned Kyle was about Eric's bruises. They'd been something Eric had carried on his skin for so long, he couldn't remember how it felt to be without them. He supposed he would find out, soon enough. After he retired. "It's fine. I'm used to them." He kissed Kyle's temple. "I like this."

Kyle turned his head and kissed Eric's bicep. "Yeah?"

"Mm." Eric dragged his free hand over Kyle's stomach, then wrapped his fingers around his cock, replacing Kyle's own hand. He stroked him slowly, trying to match the pace Kyle had been keeping.

"Yeah. Just like that," Kyle said dreamily. "Love being held like this while you work my cock."

Eric huffed shakily. "You don't keep much to yourself, do you?"

"Why would I? I think you like my dirty talk."

"I do," Eric admitted. There was no point in lying about it; his cock was hard again and poking Kyle in the back. He liked so much about this man, but he knew he needed to keep most of it to himself.

He watched the glistening head of Kyle's cock peek in and out of the tunnel of his hand as he stroked him faster. It was only Eric's second night being with a man, but he felt confident in what he was doing. The angle was familiar, like he was jerking himself off, but the lovely moans and sighs Kyle was making as he squirmed in Eric's arms were new and exciting.

"Good?" Eric asked, his lips brushing Kyle's ear.

"So fucking good," Kyle drawled. He shifted so he was rubbing his ass against Eric's dick, which felt incredible. Eric had been thinking a lot lately about what it might be like to fuck a man. More honestly, he'd been thinking about what it would be like to fuck *this* man. Even as spent as he was right now, he wanted to bury himself deep inside Kyle. But that was probably a lesson for another day.

The thought made him groan, and he muffled it against Kyle's shoulder.

"What are you thinking?" Kyle asked breathlessly. "Tell me."

So bossy. Eric had been conditioned by a life of playing hockey to obey orders, but obedience had never felt this thrilling before. He helplessly shared his thoughts with Kyle. "I want to fuck you."

Kyle tensed against him. "Yeah?"

"Can't right now, but soon. If you want." Kyle had said he'd wanted it, earlier. But had that been real? Or just dirty talk?

"Oh, fuck, Eric." Kyle started thrusting into his hand. "Want you in me. I'd make it so good for you."

"I know you would," Eric said gently. He kissed his hair and held Kyle tighter. He had only known Kyle a short while, but trusted that he would be patient and kind with him. That he would make it fun and relaxing, making Eric laugh as much as he made him gasp and moan. It would be wonderful, and Eric should probably make sure it never happened because he was certain there'd be no coming back from that. His heart would be gone.

Kyle's head rolled against Eric's shoulder, his mouth slack as they both watched Eric's hand blurring against his cock. Eric was focused on his goal, pushing nonsensical thoughts about losing his heart away and commanding himself to be present. He listened to Kyle's body the same way he listened to his own while practicing yoga, wondering if he should stop before Kyle came. If he could be attuned to his body enough to edge him as expertly as Kyle had done for him.

Kyle's body tightened in Eric's arms, head tipping back and toes curling. He let out a long moan, and again Eric considered stopping. Before he could make a decision, it was too late. Kyle's release jetted out of him, coating his stomach and oozing through Eric's fingers.

Eric held him close, kissing his temple, his cheek, his ear—anything he could reach. He murmured a stream of soothing endearments, unable to stop them from tumbling out of his mouth. "So beautiful. I've got you. You're so sexy."

"Oh wow," Kyle sighed, sliding bonelessly down Eric's body until his head was pillowed against Eric's thigh. "That was nice."

As much as Eric had loved holding Kyle against him, this view of the man, spent and happy in his lap, was breathtaking. "I did okay?"

"Oh yeah. Top marks." He grinned up at him, and started sleepily chanting, "Ben-ny! Ben-ny!"

Eric laughed and combed Kyle's hair back with his fingers. His heart felt huge, full of inappropriate feelings that definitely didn't belong in a no-strings-attached arrangement. If Eric wasn't careful, he'd become entangled in the strings his brain seemed determined to create.

Kyle, fortunately, was stronger. Or, probably more accurately, he was less interested. "Give me a few minutes to recover," he said, "and then I'll get out of here."

Eric wanted to invite him to stay. "No rush," he said instead.

Kyle rolled over and pulled himself up until his face was level with Eric's. "You're very sexy, Eric."

"Am I?"

Kyle kissed his cheek, his jaw, and then his mouth. "Don't pretend you don't know."

Eric didn't know, but he let Kyle believe he had at least a bit of sexual confidence. "You're very . . . inspiring."

"It's a gift." Kyle yawned, then laughed. "I'd better get cleaned up and go while I can still walk."

"You could—"

Kyle pressed a finger to Eric's lips, then moved it to kiss him sweetly. "I'm going to go home."

Please stay. "Okay." But Eric couldn't let Kyle leave without being sure of seeing him again. He took a risk. "I don't suppose you'd be interested in visiting my friend's gallery this week? With me, I mean."

Eric couldn't quite read Kyle's expression. He was either pleasantly surprised by the request and deciding if it would be a bad idea to say yes, or he was annoyed by it and about to tell Eric so.

"Is this a date?" Kyle asked, which hadn't been either of the things Eric was expecting. He did note that Kyle wasn't smiling.

"No," Eric said, though he wished he could say yes. "Just thought you'd like to see this exhibit. If you want. It's fine if you'd rather—"

"Can we get empanadas?" Kyle's lips curved up, and Eric's whole body relaxed.

"Of course."

Kyle kissed his cheek. "I'm in."

He went to the bathroom, and Eric looked at the empty space on the bed beside him, wishing things could be different.

CHAPTER FIFTEEN

As they entered the gallery together, Eric reminded himself for the hundredth time that this wasn't a date.

"Hello?" Eric called out into the empty room. He heard the clacking of stiletto heels against the concrete floor, and then Jeanette appeared from the back room.

"Eric!" She embraced him and kissed his cheek, then turned to Kyle. "And who is this?"

"Jeanette, this is my friend Kyle. He's studying art history at Columbia." He hoped he hadn't tripped over the word *friend*. Not that it was a lie. "Kyle, this is Jeanette Saint-Georges, my friend and the owner of this gallery."

"I've walked by so many times and never been in," Kyle said, shaking her hand. "It's a beautiful space."

"Thank you, and it's lovely to meet you. I don't think Eric has ever brought a *friend* here before." She shot Eric a look that held a question he had no intention of answering. God, was he really so transparent? He'd never said anything to her that would suggest he was attracted to men. Did she just *know*? Would anyone he introduced Kyle to suspect that Eric was sleeping with him?

He averted her gaze and asked, "How was the opening?"

"Wonderful. We sold everything."

"I'm not surprised."

"Neither am I. But everyone was jealous of you. Your piece was the showstopper."

"I can't wait to see it," Kyle said. "Eric has great taste."

Jeanette eyed him appraisingly, as if she was considering exhibiting Kyle in her next show. "He certainly does have an eye for beauty."

Heat raced up the back of Eric's neck. She definitely suspected. Eric felt suddenly ridiculous, like he was showing off the prize of a man he was having sex with, rather than bringing a friend to his favorite gallery.

A much younger friend.

Christ, what was Eric doing?

Jeanette led them to the second room, and Eric walked behind both of them, trying to sort out his feelings. Trying to get a grip.

He thought he might be under control right up until the moment when Kyle spotted the painting Eric had bought. Kyle's face lit up, and Eric's heart fluttered traitorously.

"Oh wow," Kyle said in a reverent whisper. "It's stunning."

"Yes," Eric said quietly. As Kyle examined the painting, Eric examined Kyle. His long fingers were curled in front of his plush lips in contemplation, and his hip was jutting slightly to one side. Why was everything about him so fascinating?

His mind wandered back to Sunday night, when those fingers had been curled around Eric's cock. Had been holding that wonderful toy steady while Eric fucked it. He remembered those same plush lips suckling the head of his cock, brushing soft kisses over his skin. Those same hips writhing in his lap as Kyle climaxed while Eric held him close.

Then he noticed that Jeanette and Kyle were both looking at him, and it was clear by their expressions that they were waiting for him to respond to something. "Pardon?"

"I asked Kyle if you've shown him any of your photography."

"I said just one piece, but I'd love to see more," Kyle said.

"Oh." Eric felt uncomfortable having his hobby discussed as if he were a great talent. Especially in the presence of such exquisite actual art. "It's more of the same. I'm a tourist with a camera. Sometimes I get lucky."

"Luck has nothing to do with it," Jeanette scoffed.

"Well," Eric said slowly, "if I have any talent at all, it's patience. I suppose that's useful, when it comes to photography."

"Patience and attention to detail," Jeanette said. She nudged Kyle. "This one doesn't miss a thing, you know."

Kyle didn't say anything, but he held Eric's gaze while his lips curved into a slow, sexy smile. Eric quickly turned his attention to the painting, because it was safer territory. After that smile, however, the colors on the canvas seemed drab.

Kyle moved to stand right next to Eric, and they both studied the painting in silence. After a minute, Eric turned and was surprised to see that Jeanette had left at some point.

"Where are you going to hang it?" Kyle asked. His voice was hushed even though they were alone.

"My living room. I want to rearrange the space so this will be the focal point."

"You're going to spoil it rotten."

"It deserves it."

Kyle laughed quietly. "Thank you for showing it to me."

Eric wanted to show him so much. Everything. He wanted to see his face light up in every gallery in the world. Every museum. Every historic site and breathtaking view. "I'm glad you came. You should look at the rest."

They spent another twenty minutes or so examining the art and discussing each piece. Finally Kyle grinned at him and said, "Is it empanada time?"

"Definitely."

They thanked Jeanette and she hugged both of them before they left. When they were outside, Kyle said, "That was nice."

"The gallery?"

"Yes, but . . . I meant the overall experience of going to a gallery with you."

Eric's heart flipped. "I liked it too. I mean, I like spending time with you."

Kyle smiled at him, and Eric considered kissing him. But Kyle stepped back and said, "Empanadas! Let's go."

Kyle smelled the delicious aroma of spiced meat and fresh-baked dough before he even opened the door of the Córdoba Bakery. He stepped into the welcome warmth of the cramped, brightly colored Argentinian bakery, holding the door for Eric. As Eric brushed past him, Kyle reminded himself, again, that this wasn't a date.

Valentina, who owned the bakery with her husband, greeted Kyle in Spanish, and they made small talk for a minute in her native tongue. He hadn't been kidding when he'd told Eric he came here all the time. He ordered his usual—four spicy beef empanadas; two to eat now, one to give to Maria, and one for later. He assumed he'd be heading home after this. He and Eric hadn't made plans to do . . . other stuff. And if Maria heard he went here and didn't bring her back an empanada, she would be furious.

"Siempre tan predecible," Valentina teased him. "Es uno para Maria?"

"Si tiene suerte."

She glanced at Eric over his shoulder, seemingly recognizing him, and switched to English. "Grilled vegetable, right?"

"Right," Eric confirmed. A grilled vegetable empanada sounded like a waste of dough to Kyle, but it was probably the least healthy thing that Eric allowed himself to eat.

"Do you know each other?" Valentina asked. "I see you both all the time, but not together."

"We're friends," Kyle said, throwing Eric a grin over his shoulder.

Valentina handed Kyle a paper bag that was stuffed with piping-hot empanadas. As always, she had "secretly" added two free dessert empanadas to his order. Kyle, as always, was pretty happy about it. Eric got his order, and they moved out of the way for the next customer. Córdoba was a popular spot.

Kyle gestured to a miraculously empty table. "Should we sit?"

Eric nodded. "Yeah, okay."

He seemed uncharacteristically nervous. Kyle had noticed it at the gallery as well. Was it because Jeanette had been subtly teasing him about Kyle? Was Eric embarrassed to be seen with him? Stressed out about people suspecting?

Kyle wanted to tell him not to worry about any of that, but a cramped bakery wasn't the place to discuss it. Especially not since four more customers had just walked in, filling most of the middle of the shop.

He wasn't sure what exactly Eric wanted. Their last time together had been hot as fuck, and Kyle was pretty sure they'd both thought so. But that wasn't what had been making Kyle's head spin for days. It was how hard it had been for Kyle to leave that night. How he'd been dying to stay in Eric's bed, not for sex, but because he wanted to be held by him. He wanted to fall asleep in his arms and wake up to his tender kisses. He wanted to talk as they ate breakfast and planned their day together.

And all of that was exactly why Kyle should be putting some distance between himself and Eric. He was in danger of falling for this man, and that was a mistake Kyle wasn't willing to make. For one thing, Eric didn't seem quite ready to be in a public relationship with a man. For another, he clearly wasn't comfortable with the age gap between them. He probably managed to convince himself that it wasn't a big deal when they were in Eric's bed, or when they were visiting a gallery together, but Kyle knew how fragile it was. Eric could decide at any time that Kyle was too young, too male, too . . . ridiculous for Eric to be in a relationship of any kind with. Kyle would rather not have his heart invested when that happened.

He watched Eric pull one of the empanadas out of his paper bag and take a bite. He closed his eyes and sighed happily around his mouthful of grilled vegetables. He had flakes of pastry clinging to his lips that Kyle couldn't look away from.

Eric swallowed and said, "God, that's good." The tip of his tongue darted out to remove the crumbs from his lips.

"Yeah," Kyle agreed, even though he hadn't even taken his empanada out of the bag yet.

"Are you going to eat?" Eric asked before taking a second bite. Kyle snapped out of it and reached into his own paper bag. He was, in fact, starving, but he was apprehensive about digging into his lunch in front of Eric. It seemed rude to cram his mouth full of beef in front of a vegetarian.

"I don't mind," Eric said, as if reading his mind. "Eat. Please."

Kyle obeyed, sinking his teeth into the warm, buttery crust and then into the spicy, cheesy deliciousness within. He groaned a little more orgasmically than he'd meant to, but fuck, those empanadas were good.

He grabbed a napkin from the dispenser on the table and dabbed delicately at his lips. "I love these empanadas," Kyle said sheepishly.

"I liked listening to you order them." Eric's eyes looked a shade darker than they'd been a moment ago. Kyle shifted in his seat.

"Yeah?"

"It was impressive. I speak very little Spanish."

"Well, you know. I was young and had dreams of marrying Diego Luna."

Eric studied him a moment with those sharp, espresso eyes, as if he wasn't sure if Kyle was kidding or not. Then his lips curved up into that sexy hint of a smile he liked to torture Kyle with, and Kyle turned his attention to the last bite of his empanada. His safe, uncomplicated empanada.

"Your semester must be almost over," Eric said.

Kyle swallowed his food. "Yeah. Next week."

"You don't seem stressed out about it."

"It's just one class. I have a term paper to hand in, but it's pretty much done. Just fine tuning it."

Eric was smiling at him again. "What?" Kyle asked.

"I'll bet you're a good writer."

Kyle shrugged. "I'm all right. Fast, usually. I enjoy the research more than the writing."

"I did too, when I was in school."

"I think you're the first Harvard grad I've met who says *school* instead of *Harvard*," Kyle teased.

Eric grabbed a napkin and wiped his fingers. "I went there for hockey, not because I'm a genius."

Kyle huffed. "Right. And did all of your teammates at Harvard graduate?"

Eric hesitated, then admitted, "No."

"And how many NHL players have Harvard degrees?"

Eric balled up his napkin and set it on his empty paper bag. "Currently?"

"Sure. Or, hell, how many have *ever* had Harvard degrees?"

Eric's lips twisted, then he said, "Just me, currently, I think. And maybe . . . I don't know. Three? Five? Ever? I'm really not sure."

"So we're agreed then? You're extraordinary."

Eric shook his head, but his eyes sparkled. "I like to read. That doesn't make me extraordinary."

Everything about Eric was extraordinary. Kyle was struck with an overwhelming sense of disbelief that the man eating empanadas with him was really Eric Bennett. How was *this* Kyle's real life?

They'd both finished eating, and Kyle found himself clamoring to come up with a reason to prolong their time together. "There's a great café on the next block," he said.

Eric gave him a warm smile that turned Kyle's heart to mush. "I could go for a coffee."

They decided to take the coffee to go and walk on the High Line. As they strolled along the trail, Kyle sipped his latte and hunched his shoulders against the cold. He'd been out of Vermont for too long, for the cold to be bothering him this much.

"So why aren't you dating Jeanette?" Kyle asked. "She seems amazing."

"She is," Eric agreed, "but her wife wouldn't like that."

"Ah." Kyle found he wasn't too sad about that. "Did your ex get some of your art collection in the divorce?"

"We split everything fairly. There were a couple of pieces that she liked more than I did, so she took those. I let her have most of the furniture from our old house. I wanted to start fresh."

"That must have been rough." Kyle had never been part of a breakup that had *stuff* involved. He couldn't imagine having that stress heaped on top of heartbreak.

"It wasn't so bad. Holly and I are both pretty low-drama. She comes from money anyway, so the financial side wasn't as big a deal as it might have been otherwise. I was pretty indifferent to splitting everything up." He huffed. "I guess I was pretty indifferent to the entire marriage, especially for the last few years. We both were."

Kyle had only been in relationships that burned white hot, then extinguished quickly and—for himself, anyway—unexpectedly. "So it wasn't a surprise? The divorce?"

"Not really. Again, I wasn't really paying attention, so if it came as a surprise it was only because of that. Holly wasn't angry with me. She sat me down one evening and gently pointed out that there was no reason for us to stay married." He smiled wistfully. "She was always so organized. She presented a very compelling argument, and when she was done I told her she was right. We hugged, and the next morning we started the process."

"Wow. I don't think that's usually how divorce goes."

"Probably not. We're still friendly, though. And she has a new boyfriend. Nice guy."

They walked in silence for a moment. "Would she be surprised if you had one?" Kyle asked. "A boyfriend?"

Eric took his time answering, as if he'd never considered the idea. "I think she would be very surprised."

"Does that matter to you?"

"I honestly don't know. I do care what other people think, typically. And I don't like that kind of attention."

"Right," Kyle said tightly.

"If I were in a relationship with a man, someone I was in love with, it might be different, I guess. Maybe I wouldn't care what other people think, if I felt that strongly about someone."

If. If Eric met someone who met his standards. Someone he could be proud to introduce as his boyfriend. Someone who wasn't Kyle.

Kyle forced himself to ignore the bitterness that had crept in. "Feel free to introduce me as your friend-slash-sex instructor," he joked.

Eric did that small, half-suppressed smile thing that Kyle loved. "I really do appreciate your . . . assistance."

"It hasn't been a chore." The truth was it had been the best thing in Kyle's life lately. He was halfheartedly finishing his final essay for a class he barely cared about, and dragging himself to a job that would be a lot more fun if his boss gave a shit about the bar or any of his staff's suggestions. On top of that, he hadn't been hooking up with anyone besides Eric for reasons he didn't want to examine, and he was facing another lonely Christmas in Manhattan.

As if reading his mind, Eric asked, "Do you have plans for Christmas?"

"Nope. Just watching movies or whatever."

Kyle could tell Eric was carefully trying to find his way to the questions he *really* wanted to ask. "Do you talk to your parents much?"

"Not really." They stopped at an overlook, and Kyle braced himself for the question he knew was coming.

"You don't have to answer if you don't want to talk about it, but . . ." Eric started. "Your family. Is it because you're gay? Is that why they've . . ."

"Cast me out?" Kyle finished for him.

Eric's eyes looked so sad. "Yes."

Kyle sighed. "Not officially, no. At least, it's not the only reason. I think it's part of the reason, no matter what they say." He ran a fingertip over the ridges of his coffee cup sleeve. "I guess I'll never really know."

Eric was quiet, his gaze fixed at the street below, and Kyle knew he was trying not to push for more information. For some reason, Kyle wanted to offer it up voluntarily. It had been a long time since he'd told anyone about the most shameful chapter of his life.

"I caused a bit of a scandal, back in little ol' Shaw, Vermont."

Kyle worked hard to keep his tone breezy, as if this wasn't killing him to admit to someone as impressive as Eric Bennett. "I was in a . . . relationship . . . with a man who was my boss at the time."

"Oh."

"He was married. To a woman, I mean. And he had two kids."

"Oh," Eric said again, this time more gravely. "I see."

One of Eric's hands gripped the railing so tightly, Kyle was sure his knuckles were white under his glove. Kyle wasn't surprised—it couldn't be pleasant to learn that the man you've been spending time with was a monster.

"And," he continued, because Eric deserved to know how bad it got, "I knew. Just to be clear, I knew he had a family, but he told me he loved me, and I believed it." He laughed darkly. "I'd never been with anyone before. I thought I was in love."

Eric's jaw was tense, as if he was gritting his teeth. "How old were you?"

"I had just turned eighteen."

"Jesus."

"His wife found out, and then the whole town. There were . . . photographs. Video."

Eric shook his head, his gaze fixed on something in the distance. Kyle took a slow, stabilizing breath. "After that, my parents felt it was best that I leave town. I know they wanted to protect me, but they also . . . couldn't stand the sight of me."

Kyle didn't want to talk about how any of it had *felt*. How his fragile, teenage heart had been crushed when Ian had abruptly shut him out completely, and then he'd had to face his parents. God, he'd been a wreck. Heartbroken, devastated, and so, so ashamed. He'd gone from being "that sweet boy, Kyle Swift" to being a depraved sexual vampire, preying on the most respectable man in town. To being the boy in *those pictures*.

Kyle waited, now, for Eric to walk away from him. For him to tear into him for being so stupid and selfish. Eric had been married. He would be able to relate to Ian's wife.

"Kyle," Eric said. His voice was soft, and Kyle wished it wasn't. It would be easier if he'd just yell at him. "You know that you're not the villain in that story, right?"

"I'm not the hero."

Eric turned to face him. "You were a kid."

"Not according to the law." Kyle realized, now that he was a bit older, that Ian's behavior had perhaps been worse than his own. Kyle should have said no to his advances, but Ian shouldn't have made them in the first place. Kyle knew, in his heart, that he would never have attempted to seduce Ian. He wouldn't have even known how to.

"You were a kid," Eric said again, more firmly. "And that guy took advantage of you."

"Well. I was certainly a willing participant."

"He was your boss. I think it's normal for younger people to develop . . . crushes . . . on older people who they admire. Authority figures, even. But it's up to the older people to not indulge it. A coach should never sleep with a player, even if the player wants to."

Damn. Eric was making a lot of sense. But Kyle still had arguments to make.

"So people should only date people their own age?"

Eric grimaced, then said, "I think it depends on the situation. But maybe, most of the time, yes. It's probably best."

Kyle turned his gaze to the ground. He already knew how Eric felt about dating a younger man, so it shouldn't sting this much to hear it now. Kyle was feeling a lot of things at once, and he preferred to feel nothing at all. It was safer.

"Anyway," he said, forcing cheerfulness as he raised his head. "It's all in the past now. I learned some lessons. Maybe he did too." Had Kyle actually learned anything, though? He still let his heart make terrible decisions. He still lusted over older men.

God, Eric should run as far as he could from Kyle.

But Eric wasn't running. In fact, he was setting his coffee cup down on a bench and approaching Kyle with open arms. Kyle set his own cup down and accepted Eric's hug. Eric's arms were strong and they tightened firmly around Kyle's shoulders and around his back. Kyle's face was pressed into the solid warmth of Eric's shoulder, and he allowed himself to close his eyes and breathe in Eric's scent for a moment.

"I'm sorry that was your first experience with, um . . ."

"Sex? Love? Men? It was. All of that."

"I'm sorry."

Kyle blinked rapidly against the burning behind his eyes. It's not like no one had been sympathetic about this before. Maria had said all of this to him and more. Kip didn't know about it, because Kyle had never been able to bring himself to tell him. He probably assumed that Kyle's parents were homophobes. Maybe they were.

"Let's keep walking." Kyle was glad his voice was so steady. He felt like he was crumbling apart inside.

"Okay."

They broke apart and Eric retrieved both of their coffees from the bench. He handed Kyle's cup to him, and Kyle wanted to take his hand. He wanted to hold it as they walked, and enjoy the comfort he often got from physical connection. He shoved his free hand in his pocket.

Eric was stiff and quiet as they walked, his jaw set and his gaze fixed on something far ahead of them. Kyle suspected that, despite the support and comfort Eric had shown him after he'd told his story, it was hard to overlook the fact that Kyle was a homewrecker. That Kyle had been selfish, and stupid, and was lucky to still be getting financial help from his parents. There was nothing impressive about him. He was a rich kid who'd taught himself languages because he'd been lonely and bored: first as a gay teenager in a very small town, then as a nervous country mouse living alone in Manhattan.

"I should get home," Eric said suddenly.

Of course. "There's a subway station near here." Kyle pointed to a stairway that would take them back down to street level. "Just down there."

He followed Eric down the stairs. They realized, when they got inside the station, that they'd be taking the E train in opposite directions. There was an awkward moment where Kyle thought about kissing Eric, but decided not to. Even a kiss on the cheek seemed like a privilege he didn't deserve right now.

Eric nodded at him. "I had a nice time, Kyle. Thank you."

"Me too." Kyle's throat felt tight, but he managed the two words without giving away his misery, he thought.

A minute later, they stood on opposite sides of the wide chasm of train tracks. Eric was looking at his phone, and Kyle was looking at Eric. He wondered, as the train pulled into the station and blocked his view of him, if he'd ever hear from Eric again.

CHAPTER SIXTEEN

Kyle's story had clinched it.

Any romantic thoughts Eric may have had about Kyle needed to be locked in a very secure box and kicked into the Hudson. If he thought he'd felt like a dirty old man *before* . . .

Kyle didn't seem to realize how horrific the older man's actions had been, but Eric saw it clear as day. That man—*Ian*—had been preying on his young employee. What if he'd just been waiting for Kyle to turn eighteen, and then as soon as that had happened he'd offered him a job? Eric would bet his contract that's what had happened.

Maybe the man had moved to a different town and had done the same thing again.

Eric *hated* this guy. He wanted to hunt him down.

"I need you to relax, Benny."

"Sorry." Eric took a breath and let his right arm fall limp in the hands of Sully, the team's massage therapist.

"That's better," Sully said cheerfully.

It was less than two hours before game time, and Eric needed to stop thinking about Kyle. His obsession had caused him to perform abysmally in practice the day before. He couldn't repeat that tonight.

Sully finished Eric's massage, and Eric went to the gym to do some deep stretching.

Eric was always the first player at the arena before games. He had a long pre-game routine that was important to his preparation, both physically and mentally. He got a massage, he stretched, he got on an exercise bike for a bit, he stretched some more, he drank water and ate a healthy plant-based meal, and then he started to put his gear on.

When Eric had just finished his first round of stretching, Coach Murdock entered the room. His jaw was set, but Eric detected an apology in his eyes.

Dammit.

"I'm on the bench tonight, aren't I?" Eric asked.

Coach nodded. "We're giving Tommy the start. Your head isn't where it needs to be. Quinn agrees."

Eric flinched, but he didn't argue. He *couldn't* argue. *Just let me finish this season as a starting goalie*, he silently begged no one in particular.

"I'll fix it," he promised.

Coach clapped his shoulder. "We all know you will, Benny."

Eric still finished his routine. By the time he was done, the locker room had filled up with his teammates. Tommy gave Eric a nod when he walked by, and Eric nodded back. He was happy for the kid, really. He'd be starting every night next season, and the coaches probably knew it.

Kid. Tommy was the same age as Kyle. The thought made Eric's stomach clench. What the fuck had he been thinking?

Kyle was too young for him. It didn't matter that he was one of the brightest and most charming people Eric had ever met.

It didn't matter that Eric's heart raced at the thought of kissing him. It didn't matter that, in the bedroom, when Kyle was the one in charge, Eric didn't feel older at all.

In fact, the age gap only seemed to exist when Eric was away from Kyle. That was when he had time to think about it, and feel uncomfortable about it. When he was with Kyle, he was barely aware of it.

But it did exist, and so did Eric's feelings for Kyle. And that was a dangerous combination.

"Hey, that thing is tomorrow night," Scott said, breaking Eric out of his vortex of confusing thoughts. "The drag show I told you about."

"Oh." Eric blinked, and focused on his friend. "Right. The charity one."

"Yeah. You still want to go?"

He wondered if Kyle would be there. He wondered if he wanted him to be.

Fuck, of course he wanted him to be there. And that was why he couldn't go.

"I don't think I can."

Scott frowned at him, and Eric knew he wanted to argue that he probably wasn't busy at all. But instead Scott just sighed and said, "No problem." It was the long-suffering sigh of a man who was friends with a wet blanket.

Eric felt bad, but he knew it was the right decision. He couldn't think clearly around Kyle, so it was best to stay away.

It had been days since Kyle had heard from Eric. They had gone longer without communicating before, but this stretch felt endless. And significant.

Kyle had handed in his term paper, and found himself with a lot of free time on his hands. He'd thrown himself into practicing Greek, and was now sitting on his couch, casually looking into study abroad programs in Greece. Manhattan was starting to feel suffocating.

The thought of traveling alone didn't appeal to him as much as it usually did. He kept getting unwanted visions of exploring ruins with Eric. He imagined long days of hiking together along the coast, and swimming in the Mediterranean. Eric probably looked spectacular in a bathing suit.

What were these thoughts? Kyle had hooked up with roughly a billion men, and none of them had him daydreaming about European getaways together.

He regretted telling Eric about Ian, but he also knew that Eric deserved to know. Eric had been nice about it, but Kyle wasn't going to kid himself about getting any more invites to his beautiful house.

His phone lit up with a message from Kip. Drag show tonight. Don't forget!

Kyle *had* forgotten. He didn't feel like going out, but he would do this because he was a good friend.

KYLE:

Right. I'll be there.

It would have been an ideal thing for Eric to go to, he thought miserably. God, that would have been fun.

Another message, which he expected was a thumbs-up from Kip. Kyle made a weird squeak of excitement when he saw that it was from Eric.

ERIC:

Are you going to the drag show thing tonight?

Kyle wasn't sure what to say. Did Eric want him to say no, so it would be safe for Eric to go? Did he want Kyle to say yes for the same reason?

KYLE:
I was planning to.

ERIC:
Scott wants me to go.

Okay. What was Kyle supposed to say to that?

KYLE:
Do you want to go?

ERIC:
Maybe.

Lord god. What the hell was this?

KYLE:
I think it could be a good intro to the gay club scene for you.

Eric's reply seemed to take forever, but Kyle's screen finally lit up with, You know there's a really good chance I'm never going to be into the gay club scene, right?

Kyle laughed into his empty living room.

KYLE:
But it's FUN!

ERIC:
I'm too old.

KYLE:
Nope.

ERIC:
I can't dance.

KYLE:
As if.

ERIC:
I can prove it.

Kyle grinned, and wrote, So you're coming tonight?

He wondered if Eric would make a dirty joke. Most of Kyle's friends wouldn't be able to resist that setup. He doubted Eric even noticed the double meaning.

ERIC:
Wow. You skipped a few steps there.

Kyle fell back against the couch, laughing. He knew he shouldn't flirt with him, but he couldn't help it.

KYLE:
Obviously you've never danced with ME.

For a long time, Eric didn't reply. There weren't even dots indicating that Eric was writing anything. Kyle cursed himself for being so stupid.

ERIC:
Can I call you?

Oh god. That sounded . . . well, Kyle wasn't sure, actually. Ominous? Exciting?

KYLE:
Sure.

A moment later, his phone rang. He bit his lip, staring at the screen, then answered. "Hi."

"Hi." Even that one simple word sent a spark racing through Kyle's body. He'd *missed* Eric. It had been *days* and Kyle had *missed* him.

"What's up?"

"I just . . . I wanted to talk about . . ." Eric exhaled into the phone. "If I go tonight, to the club, I don't think we should—"

"Got it," Kyle interrupted. He couldn't stand to hear Eric finish that sentence. "Hands off."

"Yeah. I just . . . think it's best."

"Whatever you want," Kyle managed to keep his tone light, even though his overdramatic heart ached in his chest. "It's not like there won't be plenty of men to choose from when you're there."

Eric huffed. "I'm not going to be staying late."

"Do you have a game tomorrow?"

"No. I just . . ."

"Don't worry," Kyle teased. "You can watch the show, dance for a song or two, and still be home in plenty of time to do your pre-bed Tai Chi."

"I don't do that *every* night."

"You'll have fun. I promise. And if there happens to be a hot guy there over the age of thirty . . ."

"I'm not hooking up with some random person I meet at a club."

"I wasn't talking about *you*."

That made Eric laugh, which Kyle always loved hearing. He laughed too, but his eyes began to sting. The truth was that he only wanted to dance with Eric. To feel Eric's body against his as they worked each other up until they couldn't stand it anymore. Until they had to hurry off to Eric's house—or maybe Kyle's apartment—to tear each other's clothes off. He could do that with any one of hundreds of men who would be at the club tonight, but Kyle was only interested in doing it with Eric.

Well, he'd have to get over himself. Eric didn't want him, so Kyle needed to find someone who did. Kyle was not inexperienced when it came to heartache. The best thing to do was to move on as quickly as possible.

"I'll see you tonight, then," Eric said.

"If you're lucky."

He heard Eric sigh. It sounded wistful, not annoyed. Or maybe tired.

"I'm—" Eric cut himself off. "I want to be friends, Kyle. I like you."

"We *are* friends," Kyle assured him. "We can be the kind of friends who don't have sex. I've heard some friendships work that way. Seems weird, but I'm willing to try."

Eric chuckled. "See you later."

"Later."

They ended the call, and Kyle pledged to himself that he could find a cute boy tonight who would make him forget all about Eric Bennett.

CHAPTER SEVENTEEN

Eric was worried that Carter might die from laughing so hard.

Scott Hunter was center stage, wearing a very revealing elf costume. It consisted of tight, green shorts, a red vest worn open over his bare chest, a pointy hat, and curly-toed shoes with little bells on them.

"Ho-lee shit!" Maria yelled. "That's a lotta Scott."

It was definitely more skin than Eric had ever seen Scott flash outside of a locker room. He'd done some shirtless photo shoots, but the shorts he was wearing now were obscene.

The drag queen who'd been hosting the evening's entertainment—Helen St. Mount—had just stuck a candy cane into the waistband of Scott's shorts, which made Scott blush and Carter howl.

"I heard you're getting married," Helen said.

"Yes I am."

"Well, that fucking sucks," Helen quipped. Scott laughed, and the audience cheered.

"Sorry," Scott said. The crowd was eating up the bashful sweetheart thing that Eric knew for a fact wasn't an act. Once again, he was amazed by how far Scott had come in a couple of years. From being terrified that someone would figure out that he's gay, to participating, half naked, in a drag show and making jokes about marrying his boyfriend. While Carter couldn't stop laughing, Eric felt his own throat tighten a bit.

"He really fills out those shorts nicely, doesn't he?" Kyle said into Eric's ear. Eric tried not to react to the soft flutter of breath against his skin. It wasn't easy. Just seeing Kyle again had nearly knocked Eric on his ass. He looked especially stunning tonight, dressed for the club in a tight, dark blue T-shirt with tighter black jeans, and his skin glistening a bit from the heat of the packed room.

"I have no idea what you're talking about," he replied, as evenly as possible.

"The hell you don't."

"I see that guy naked more days than not," Eric reminded him. "He's not gonna turn *my* head."

Kyle winked at him, and Eric's stupid heart did a backflip. He really did want to be just friends with Kyle, but it was hard to remember that when every part of him was aching to touch the man.

"Is your lucky fiancé here tonight?" Helen asked Scott.

"Yes. He's backstage."

Helen rolled her eyes and slumped over dramatically. "*Fine.* Bring him out, I *guess*."

Kip walked out wearing a very baggy Santa costume, complete with a fluffy white beard. The crowd whistled and cheered.

"Hey," Scott said, doing his best attempt at acting. "I think that was supposed to be *my* costume."

"Oh no," Helen said innocently. "Someone must have switched the names on the costumes." She did an exaggerated shrug. "Oops."

"You're on the naughty list now," Kip teased.

"Darling, I was born on the naughty list." She turned to the audience with a game show host smile. "Isn't it wonderful to have . . ." She glanced over her shoulder at Kip.

"Kip," he told her, laughing.

"Kip!" Her face fell into a scowl and she said, in a dark tone, "*Kip*."

Kyle laughed loudly beside Eric, and Eric smiled. He was glad he came.

"Do you mind if I take some of this costume off?" Kip asked. "It's kind of warm."

"What do we think, beautiful people? Should he take off the suit?"

A loud cheer, and then Kip grinned and pulled off the beard and hat, and then the Santa jacket. He was wearing a black tank top underneath, which the audience appreciated. He dropped the baggy pants to reveal slim-fitting jeans. Eric had always thought Kip was a good-looking guy, but tonight he looked . . . hot. Scott was a lucky man.

Eric glanced at Kyle, because if *Eric* was noticing how good Kip looked, then Kyle must be in agony. But Kyle was laughing along with everyone else, eyes shining with amusement. He must have felt Eric's eyes on him, because he turned his head, and the beauty of his smiling face knocked Eric breathless.

He turned his attention to the stage, where Scott was talking about the LGBTQ youth charity they were raising money for tonight. He was saying earnest things about the great work the organization did. Eric was proud of him. It was really thrilling to watch Scott be his true self, on and off the ice.

There were three drag performances after Scott and Kip left the stage. Eric stood and watched them with the group they'd assembled for tonight: Carter, Kyle, Maria, and Matti. Scott and Kip joined them halfway through the second act. Scott had changed into jeans and a T-shirt.

"How'd I do?"

"That was fucking hilarious," Carter said. "You're a good sport, Scotty."

Scott grinned. His eyes were bright and he was bouncing on his feet, as if he were filled with the same adrenaline that made him hyper after a big win. "It was fun. I mean, I felt ridiculous, but it was fun."

"You just like being ogled by a sea of men, admit it," Carter teased him.

"I mean, I'm not going to *deny* it."

Matti wrapped Scott in a tight hug and kissed the top of his head. He was one of the more physically affectionate straight men Eric had ever met.

"That was epic," Matti said loudly. He said everything loudly, but at least here, in this club, his volume level was appropriate. "You are a legend."

"I need a drink," Scott announced. "What can I get you guys?"

"I'm going to head out," Carter said. "I've got a Skype date with Gloria."

"I am starving," Matti said. "This place does not have food."

"There's a diner on the corner that has amazing food. Open all night," Maria said. Eric couldn't help but smile when she added. "I could eat."

Matti beamed at her and said, "Yes. Let's go."

Eric didn't miss the giddy look Maria and Kyle exchanged.

"You coming, Benny?" Matti asked.

Eric glanced at Kyle, who had his eyebrows raised as he waited for the reply. "Actually," he said slowly, knowing it was a terrible idea, "I think I'll stick around for a bit."

Kyle was glad Eric decided to stay, but he also wasn't sure what to do with him. He'd thought this event would be the perfect place for Eric to cut loose a bit and maybe try to pick someone up, but now that they were here Kyle realized that Eric was probably never going to do either of those things.

Eric was talking to Scott at the moment, sipping a soda with lime. Kyle was watching the dance floor, which had gotten very busy over the last hour.

"I'm bored," Kip complained in his ear. "Let's go dance."

"Scott won't dance with you?"

"I think I need to lure him over. Come on, I haven't danced with you in forever."

Kyle smiled at his friend. It *had* been too long. "Sure. Okay."

Kip grabbed his hand and pulled him into the throng of dancers. The music was loud and sexy, and he quickly lost himself in it. He loved dancing, and he loved Kip. And maybe his love for Kip wasn't quite what he'd thought it was.

They were close together, arms and chests and hands brushing each other, but it was firmly platonic. They didn't put their hands on each other, they didn't grind into each other. They didn't kiss. It was just . . . fun. And nice. Two young, gay men being silly and having a good time.

As Kip had predicted, it didn't take long for Scott to arrive on the dance floor. Kyle moved back so Scott could take his place. When Scott and Kip danced together, it was definitely not platonic. Scott's big hands were gripping his fiancé's hips, and Kip looped his arms around Scott's neck and pulled his head down so they could devour each other for a while. Kyle decided to find his own boy to kiss.

As he was searching the floor for a potential partner, his gaze found Eric, standing alone against a wall. Watching. Kyle jerked his head toward the dance floor in invitation. Eric shook his head, which was annoying. What was the point of all the work Kyle had been doing with him if he wasn't even going to *try*? At the absolute least he should enjoy the press of a hard, sweaty body against him on the dance floor. It didn't have to lead to a hookup.

But if Eric wanted to be stubborn and lonely, then that was his problem. Kyle had his own problems. Like whether to dance with the cute blond guy or the cute guy with blue hair.

Blue hair won when Kyle noticed he had a tongue piercing. It had been a while since Kyle had been with a guy who had one of those. The man smiled when Kyle locked eyes with him, and Kyle smiled back as he squeezed through bodies until he was standing in front of him. For the rest of the song, neither man said anything. Kyle was a good dancer—his years of racing down mountains had taught his body grace and agility. The other man was a *great* dancer. New York City was, Kyle had quickly learned, full of great dancers.

Partway through the second song, the man brought his mouth close to Kyle's ear. "I'm Jesse."

"Kyle."

Jesse grinned wickedly at him, then hooked a finger in one of Kyle's belt loops, pulling their groins together so Kyle could feel the hard bulge there.

He probably shouldn't be thinking about Eric at all right now. Not when Jesse was expertly grinding his hips into Kyle, and Kyle's cock was plumping up in response. Not when Jesse's hand slipped into the back pocket of Kyle's jeans and his breath was hot on Kyle's neck. But maybe Eric could gain something from this.

Watch and learn, gorgeous.

Eric should leave. He should not be standing alone, watching Kyle make out with another man on the dance floor like a creep. But every now and again Kyle would make eye contact with him, as if inviting him to watch. Maybe this was supposed to be another tutorial for Eric, but he wasn't learning much. Except that he was really turned on by watching Kyle dance. And jealous from watching Kyle kiss someone else. And maybe turned on by that jealousy.

Eric was a bad person. Kyle just wanted him to relax and have fun, and instead Eric was standing alone, half hard, and staring daggers at a kid with blue hair. As if he were Eric's competition or something. When Eric had *explicitly* told Kyle that he wanted to end the benefits part of their friendship.

This was ridiculous. Eric should have been in bed hours ago. He was sure Kyle wouldn't mind if he slipped out. He knew Scott would be leaving soon; there was no way he was going to stay out all night when they had a practice the next morning.

All he needed to do was leave. Just tear his gaze away from Kyle's beautiful body moving against the other man's and leave. Even though his instincts were, terrifyingly, to march onto the dance floor and yank Kyle away from Little Boy Blue. Pull Kyle's body against his own and let Kyle feel his arousal. Kiss him the way he'd been dying to for days.

Jesus. Eric was obviously way too horny to be thinking clearly. He inhaled deeply, commanding his libido to heel. This friendship with Kyle had become a bright light in Eric's life; something to offset the upheaval of his divorce and the anxiety he felt about his impending retirement. Kyle made Eric feel like his life wasn't over, that he was simply about to turn a page. For the first time in over a year, he was excited about the future.

He wouldn't ruin that.

He left as quickly as possible, barely remembering his coat. The frigid air outside would have reminded him quickly. He made it halfway down the block, not even sure where he was walking or why he hadn't looked for a cab, when he heard his name. He turned to find Kyle running toward him with his jacket clutched in his hand. "Eric! Wait!"

Kyle caught up to him, his cheeks flushed and his breath huffing out in white clouds. Eric took his jacket from his hands and held it open for him to put his arms in the sleeves. It was way too cold to be outside in a T-shirt.

"Didn't you have a scarf?" Eric asked, heart hammering against his ribs. Kyle had come after him.

"What? Oh yeah. I did. I guess it's gone now."

Eric took his own scarf off and looped it around Kyle's neck. He flipped the collar up on his coat, which was much warmer than Kyle's corduroy jacket. "Why'd you follow me out?"

"Why did you leave?"

"I'm tired. And you seemed . . . busy."

"I thought you were going to dance." Kyle's bottom lip jutted out petulantly. Eric wanted to capture it between his teeth.

"You should go back in," Eric said, arranging his scarf so it covered more of Kyle's exposed neck and chin. "You're young and I'm . . ." He sighed. "Not. You should be having fun with that guy with the blue hair. Not worrying about me."

"I'm not *worried* about you. I just . . ." Kyle's mouth pinched, like he didn't want to finish his sentence. "I wanted to dance with you. Or at least watch you dance with someone else."

"I'm not a good dancer."

"As if I'm going to believe that! I saw you do full splits like three times during that game the other night. We need to get you on a runway. You could be death dropping all over the place."

Eric smiled fondly at him. He liked how Kyle looked, all bundled into Eric's scarf. "I have no idea what that means."

"So much to learn," Kyle sighed.

"I know."

God, he was beautiful. His pale blue eyes sparkled as he worried his red, kiss-swollen bottom lip with his teeth. Eric hated that those plump lips were the result of someone else's efforts, but not enough to keep himself from wanting to kiss him. To erase all traces of that other man.

Without even realizing what he was doing, Eric bunched the ends of the scarf in his fist and tugged Kyle to him, walking backward until Eric was against a wall. He watched Kyle's face for one moment, searching for any signs of resistance. All he saw was Kyle's gaze drifting to Eric's mouth, and the tip of his tongue poking out to wet his bottom lip.

Their mouths crashed together. Eric probably should have been embarrassed about his lack of control, but he didn't care. He was frantic, needing to claim Kyle after almost losing him to some pretender with blue hair.

Not that Kyle belonged to him. At all. But right now, with Kyle matching his urgency as they kissed, Eric could pretend. Kyle pressed him hard against the brick building, wedging a thigh between Eric's legs and letting him feel his arousal. Eric inhaled sharply and moved his hips to gain some friction against his own erection. Kyle moaned into his mouth, then broke the kiss and said, "Is that from watching me make out with another guy?"

Eric didn't want to answer that. "Come home with me."

Kyle grinned, then kissed him again. "My place is closer."

"Your place has a roommate."

"We both bring people home all the time. We're used to it."

Eric shook his head, frustrated by the time they were wasting. "I won't be able to relax if I think someone is listening. My place."

"Fine."

Kyle stepped back, and Eric took his phone out so he could call his car service. When he ended the call, he noticed Kyle hugging himself, clearly freezing.

"You need a parka," Eric said.

"I have one, I just didn't wear it because I'm an idiot," Kyle said.

Eric wrapped his arms around Kyle's shivering body. Kyle relaxed against him, and Eric closed his eyes. This was nice. They stood like that for a few minutes, not speaking. Kyle turned his head and nuzzled the side of Eric's neck, which made Eric's breath hitch.

"You're warm," Kyle murmured.

"Glad to be useful." He wanted to offer to hold Kyle all night. He loved the idea of having Kyle snuggled against him while he slept.

"It might have been fun," Kyle said, tilting his head up to grin mischievously at him. "If we'd gone to my place. Seeing if you could stay quiet. We could have made a game of it."

"I don't want to be quiet." Eric was shocked by how gruff his voice was. Kyle must have been surprised too, because his eyes went wide.

"Fuck. Where's that car?"

Eric huffed and kissed him again. He couldn't believe how much he wanted this, how shamelessly he was behaving. Had he ever been so overcome with lust? He might go down on Kyle in the car.

A black SUV stopped on the street in front of them, and Eric reluctantly released Kyle.

"Oh," Kyle said faintly. He stepped back and turned toward the car. Eric followed him, dizzy with desire.

He kept the middle seat between them. He didn't trust himself to behave without the barrier. The partition was up between the back seat and the driver, but Eric wasn't quite ready to become the kind of guy who had sex in the back of a taxi.

A soft moan from Kyle's side of the car drew Eric's attention. Kyle was sitting with his legs spread wide, turned slightly toward Eric, and was unabashedly massaging his cock through his jeans.

Eric watched him silently, hoping his eyes showed his approval. He idly thumbed his bottom lip as he took in the show. When had this become his life? He'd gone from very rare, extremely basic sex with his wife to no sex at all to . . . this. Being in the company of a gorgeous young man who was so hot for him that he couldn't even wait until they were home to touch himself.

"Save it," Eric heard himself whisper. "Wait until I can touch you properly."

Kyle bit his lip, then said, "You can touch me right now."

Eric shook his head. "Be patient. I'll give you whatever you want when we get home."

Kyle gave himself one more squeeze, then stretched his arm across the top of the backseat. His fingertips brushed the side of Eric's neck. "Anything?"

Eric's gaze was steady. "Yes."

He took Kyle's hand and kissed his palm. He flicked his tongue against the sensitive skin there, making Kyle suck in a breath. "I have a long wish list."

"Mm." Eric decided to be bold, and sucked Kyle's index finger into his mouth. He swirled his tongue around it, then sucked hard while Kyle made soft, whimpering noises. Eric's own cock was painfully hard, but he resisted touching it. As Kyle had taught him the last time they'd been together, sometimes it was better to wait.

Mercifully, the car reached their destination a minute later. Eric gave Kyle's hand a parting kiss, then exited the car. As soon as they were in the house, Eric threw his coat off, then pinned Kyle against a wall.

"Hi," Kyle said with a wicked grin.

"Hi." Eric dropped to his knees. He practically ripped Kyle's fly open, desperate to get his mouth on his cock.

"Whoa. Shit," Kyle said hoarsely.

"Can't wait." Eric yanked Kyle's jeans and underwear down to his knees.

"Fuck, I love how fired up you are. Did I make you mad, kissing that boy?"

"Let's stop talking about him," Eric growled before filling his mouth with Kyle's cock.

"I did, didn't I?" Kyle said, though his voice hitched in the middle. "You were jealous."

Eric answered by bobbing his head, sucking him hard and fast. Yeah, he was fucking jealous. He didn't like the idea of Kyle being with other men and he didn't want to examine that too closely. He just wanted to make Kyle scream.

"That's so fucking good. Holy fuck." Kyle gripped Eric's shoulder, and Eric could tell he was fighting to keep still. "Love your mouth, Eric."

Eric grunted, loving the sound of his name in Kyle's sex-ravaged voice. He wanted Kyle to say it when he came.

There was still a distant voice in Eric's head that was reminding him that this was a terrible idea. This was exactly what he'd promised himself he wouldn't do. But that part of his brain was being drowned out by Kyle's moans and whispered curses. He needed this.

"I wish you'd danced with me," Kyle panted. "You would have looked so fucking sexy."

Eric doubted it, but his mouth was too busy to argue. Maybe he should have danced with Kyle. Maybe he should have kissed him on the dance floor, in front of their friends and whoever else wanted to watch. Show everyone that this stunning man was his.

He isn't yours.

Eric pushed the thought away. For tonight at least, Kyle was his. He'd worry about the rest later.

He worked Kyle harder, sliding a hand up his thigh to play with his balls. His own cock strained against his jeans, rock hard and desperate for attention, but he ignored it, wanting only to pleasure Kyle. Wanting him to come in his mouth. Eric wanted it. Needed it.

"You trying to make me come already?" Kyle panted after another minute of Eric's efforts. Eric held his gaze, and nodded as best he could. He tried to relax his jaw so he could take him deeper. He was far from being able to deep throat, but he managed to work a little more of Kyle's shaft into his mouth.

"Oh, shit. That's incredible. Fuck. I wanna last, but it's too fucking much."

Eric could taste salty drops of precum on his tongue. Kyle's balls were heavy and tight between his fingers. He didn't want Kyle to last. He wanted him to shatter.

"I can't—Eric, fuck. I'm gonna—"

Eric stayed on him, and hoped he wasn't about to make a fool of himself.

The first burst of Kyle's release flooded his mouth, but Eric managed to swallow, even as Kyle kept spurting. Beyond the momentary panic of feeling like he couldn't breathe, Eric loved how powerful he felt.

When Kyle's orgasm subsided, he slumped against the wall as Eric released him from his mouth. "Wow," Kyle said breathlessly. "I am a very good teacher."

Eric chuckled, and stood up. He wiped his lips with the back of his hand. His mouth was still full of Kyle's lingering taste. "You are."

"Well," Kyle drawled, "how will I ever repay you?"

Eric planted a hand on the wall beside Kyle's head and leaned in. "Teach me how to fuck you."

Kyle's eyes went wide. "Holy shit. Really?"

"Really."

Kyle kissed him, and for a moment Eric thought he'd maybe forgotten that he'd very recently shot his load in Eric's mouth, but Kyle moaned happily when their tongues brushed each other. Eric was still painfully hard, but he lost himself in the kiss, pressing Kyle into the wall and grinding his cock against Kyle's hip. The bedroom suddenly seemed too far away.

When they broke apart, both men were panting. Eric moved in for another kiss, hating having the barest distance between their mouths, but Kyle licked his lips and said, "Upstairs, sexy. I promise it will be worth the trip."

Eric covered Kyle's naked body with his own as they made out like teenagers on the bed. Kyle could feel Eric's erection pressing against his hip, but despite his earlier urgency, Eric didn't seem to be in any hurry to do anything about it. He kept kissing Kyle's neck, and shoulders, and jaw before returning to his mouth for long, luxurious minutes that left Kyle breathless.

Between the late hour and the recent orgasm, Kyle's brain was a little foggy, but he was vaguely aware that they weren't supposed to be doing this, and that it was weird that Eric had suddenly changed his mind about not having sex. And that maybe this whole thing was a very bad idea.

But he couldn't bring himself to stop it. Not when Eric was kissing him like Kyle was something precious. Not when Eric was so eager to try something new with him.

Teach me how to fuck you. Jesus. Kyle would never forget the way Eric's voice had rumbled like thunder when he'd said that.

"Get the lube," Kyle said. "Gonna get myself ready to take that thick cock of yours."

Eric kissed him one more time before rolling off him and opening the nightstand drawer. Kyle took the lube from him and got on his knees on the mattress. He reached behind himself and got to work massaging and then stretching and opening his hole. As rarely as he bottomed these days, Kyle loved playing with his hole. He had an array of dildos and plugs in his bedroom and he was very well acquainted with all of them.

He wished he had one now. He could show Eric how well he could take one.

Eric seemed to be enjoying the show as it was. He watched Kyle with naked desire on his face, and possibly a bit of curiosity.

"Turn around," he said roughly. "Let me see."

Fuck. It was hot as hell when Eric was so overcome with lust that he forgot to be reserved and shy about sex. Kyle turned and planted one hand on the mattress, the other pressing a finger into his hole. The penetration was frustratingly shallow, but he knew he'd be rewarded soon with something much bigger.

"Can I help?" Eric asked. He palmed Kyle's ass cheeks with both hands, spreading them apart, which made Kyle groan his approval.

"Knock yourself out," he drawled. He heard the click of the lube bottle, and then felt one of Eric's fingers tracing around his entrance. Kyle removed his own finger, and Eric didn't hesitate to replace it. Kyle bucked happily as Eric's finger pushed in deeper than he'd been able to reach himself.

"Just like that," Kyle moaned. "Press down on—" He gasped as a jolt of familiar pleasure raced through him. "Right there. Fuck."

"Is that your prostate?" Eric sounded amazed that he'd been able to locate it.

"Fuck yeah it is. Keep stroking it."

Kyle's cock was fully hard again, and he gave it a few strokes while Eric probed him. He glanced over his shoulder and saw Eric concentrating on his task with a furrowed brow. Kyle bit his lip to keep from laughing. Eric could be kind of adorable.

"Can you get two fingers in there?" Kyle asked.

"Yeah," Eric said breathlessly. A second finger entered Kyle, and he moaned happily at the stretch.

"You think you'll be able to get that thick cock inside me?" Kyle panted. Between the way Eric was working his prostate, and the anticipation of being filled with Eric's cock, it was a struggle to keep things purely instructional.

"I think you can take it."

"I know I can. Fuck, I want it. You've got condoms, right?"

Eric moved like lightning and grabbed a strip of condoms out of the bedside drawer. He tore one wrapper open and quickly got himself suited up. Kyle watched him stroke lube over his sheathed cock, mouth watering. They were really going to do this.

"Lie down," Kyle commanded.

Eric stretched out on his back. "Like this?"

"Just like that. I'm gonna ride you so fucking hard."

Kyle straddled Eric's waist and reached behind to grab Eric's rigid cock. Both men groaned loudly when Kyle finally sank down on it, the stretch burning deliciously as Eric filled him completely.

"Wow," Eric rasped. "Fuck. Just give me a second."

Kyle smiled down at him. "I haven't even started yet."

"You feel amazing. And I've been worked up since we were at the club."

"Mm." Kyle moved slowly at first, giving his body time to adjust. He loved being on top—he liked sex in pretty much any position—but he was fucking *good* at riding cock. "How's this?"

Eric squeezed his eyes shut. "Fucking amazing."

"You ready for more?"

Eric opened his eyes and met Kyle's gaze. "I'm ready."

"Then buckle up, gorgeous."

Kyle went hard, bouncing on Eric's dick as he rolled his hips and took him deep. His own cock slapped against his stomach as he fucked himself.

"Holy shit," Eric gasped. "So fucking good, Kyle."

"Yeah? You like it? You like it when I do all the work?"

Eric grunted instead of answering. Kyle kept going. "You like having your dick in my ass, Eric? You like fucking a man?"

"Yes," he gritted out.

"Do you want to be fucked like this, beautiful?"

Eric's eyes were dark and wild. "Not like this."

"Show me. Show me how you want to be fucked."

With a growl, Eric rolled them over and captured one of Kyle's ankles in his hand. Then he pounded into Kyle, hard and fast, while Kyle howled shamelessly. This was beyond anything he'd been expecting. Eric, who had always been so happy to let Kyle take charge, reaching his breaking point and taking back his control was so fucking hot.

Kyle got a hand on his own dick, stroking himself quickly to bring himself to the edge. "This how you want it, baby?" he panted. "You want to be fucked hard like this?"

"Yes. Fuck. I'm so close."

"Me too, gorgeous. Oh, shit. I'm—" Kyle reached the edge and tumbled over it, his second orgasm in less than an hour hitting him hard as come jetted onto his stomach.

"Kyle." Eric breathed the word as he stilled and climaxed. His dark gaze locked on Kyle's as he shuddered through his release.

"So good, baby," Kyle murmured, rubbing Eric's flanks. Eric held himself on trembling arms above him, breathing hard with his head bowed. Then he came crashing down on him, kissing him passionately as Kyle tried to ignore the happy flutter in his stomach.

Eric pulled back and Kyle's heart ached at the sight of his bright eyes and wide, joyful smile. He leaned up to kiss Eric's smile so he wouldn't have to look at it anymore.

"You'll stay tonight, right?" Eric said in a low, scratchy voice.

Kyle's first instinct was to say no, but it was *very* late. "I can sleep in the guest room if you'd rather—"

"Stay," Eric interrupted. "Here. Please." He held Kyle's gaze, even though his eyes looked uneasy.

"Okay," Kyle said. It was a terrible idea. The worst idea. Tomorrow Eric would regret this lapse of discipline, and Kyle knew it would be harder to be rejected after he'd spent a night in Eric's arms.

They got cleaned up and Eric put underwear on, which seemed like an arbitrary bit of modesty, but Kyle did the same. For the first minute back in bed together, both men were silent and staring awkwardly up at the ceiling. Then Eric broke the silence by huffing out a laugh.

"What?" Kyle asked, grinning.

"Nothing. I don't know why this is so weird."

They both rolled on their sides, facing each other. "Does sex make you uncomfortable?"

Eric seemed to consider the question for a moment. "Maybe. Usually. I'm not used to—" He bit his lip, as if blocking the words from escaping.

"Not used to what?"

"I usually have more control over my . . . desires. Libido. I don't know what's been happening to me lately."

Kyle waggled his eyebrows. "*I've* been happening to you, sexy." Eric laughed, but it sounded forced. Kyle dialed it back. "Maybe it's just from, y'know, not having sex for so long."

"Maybe."

"And having sex with men is new and exciting."

Eric nodded. "That might be it."

Kyle swatted his chest playfully. "You're supposed to tell me it's totally because of me."

Eric's laugh sounded genuine this time. Then his face grew

serious, and Kyle realized he was about to say those exact words and possibly mean them, which couldn't happen if Kyle was going to maintain any control over his stupid heart.

So he cut him off by yawning. "That was incredible, but now I'm exhausted."

"It's late," Eric agreed, but neither man moved. They both kept gazing at each other until suddenly they were kissing again. Eric placed a palm on Kyle's cheek, and Kyle heard himself make a needy, breathy sound as Eric's tongue caressed his own.

Was there even a chance Eric felt the same way Kyle did? Not that Kyle even knew for sure how he felt himself, but was Eric also confused? Did his heart race when he saw Kyle? Did he think of him all the time? Was it possible Eric wanted more than whatever this was?

Kyle wanted to ask, but he also didn't want to ruin this moment. When they finally broke apart, Eric ducked his head shyly, but he couldn't hide his adorable smile.

"What?" Kyle asked.

Eric shook his head and gazed up at him through his dark lashes. "I don't know if I'll be able to sleep."

"Did I not do enough to wear you out?" Kyle teased.

"I can't stop looking at you." Eric's eyes widened, as if he couldn't believe he'd just said that.

Kyle froze. This was definitely leaving the no-strings sex zone, and he shouldn't encourage it. "You can look all you like."

Eric brushed a thumb over Kyle's cheek. "I'm glad you said yes. To staying."

Kyle closed his eyes, unable to bear the tenderness in Eric's expression. Eric was glad now, but what would the morning bring? Kyle could have saved himself a lot of trouble if he'd just gone home after the orgasms were over. Now he had to deal with his damn feelings.

"We should sleep," he murmured.

"Okay."

Kyle rolled on his side, his back to Eric's chest, and Eric wrapped an arm around him. His bicep was heavy and warm, and Kyle couldn't help snuggling back against Eric. He could pretend, for one night, that this was real.

CHAPTER EIGHTEEN

Eric did manage to sleep, but he'd kept drifting in and out. As far as he could tell, Kyle had fallen asleep immediately and hadn't woken all night. He was still asleep when Eric blinked awake for the final time, sunlight peeking around the edges of his window blinds.

He'd loved holding Kyle against him all night. Loved listening to him breathe as he slept. Most oddly, he'd loved the soft press of the sole of Kyle's foot against Eric's shin.

Kyle was still turned away from him, but Eric enjoyed the view of his bare, creamy shoulders, his smooth back, and the knobs of his spine. Every inch of Kyle was more interesting to Eric than it should be. He was dangerously infatuated with this man and knew it wasn't going to do him any good. When Kyle had been dancing with the young man with the blue hair, that should have made Eric see the difference between them. Kyle was young, and beautiful, and *fun*. Eric was not the horse that Kyle should hitch his wagon to.

He resisted the urge to wake Kyle with soft kisses along his shoulders and carefully left the bed, because he was sure that if he woke him, Kyle would leave. He took a shower, washing away any lingering traces of the fun they'd had the night before, and considered what he should say to Kyle when he did wake up. What did Eric *want*?

He liked Kyle far too much, he knew that much. And he'd never been this interested in sex in his life. He tried to remember what it had been like when he'd started dating Holly. He'd been attracted to her for sure, and they'd definitely had some hot, hormone-fueled sex in Eric's college dorm room.

And somewhere along the line, he'd fallen in love with her. It had been like sinking into a warm bath—comfortable, but not exciting.

What he felt for Kyle was different. There was an urgency to it, a gravitational pull that was getting harder to resist. And maybe he didn't need to resist it. Not yet, anyway.

When he returned to the bedroom, towel wrapped snugly around his waist, he found Kyle propped up on one elbow, blinking at the windows that were still covered by the blinds.

"Good morning," Eric said.

"Morning." Kyle's gaze raked over Eric's mostly naked body. "Damn. I like that outfit."

"You'd love the Admiral's locker room then."

"I'm sure I would."

Eric sat on the edge of the bed, facing him. "Sleep okay?"

"Yeah. You have great taste in beds."

"I have great taste in everything."

Kyle's lips curled up, and he touched his fingers to the bottom of Eric's towel. "You do. I wish you'd told me you were showering. I could have joined you."

"Another time."

"Or maybe," Kyle said silkily as he slipped his hand under the towel. "I can get you all dirty again right now."

Eric shuddered, but he trapped Kyle's hand with his own, stilling it. "I have a practice to get to soon. I'll go downstairs and make breakfast, and you can take your own shower, if you like." He stood up, adjusting his towel over his burgeoning erection.

Kyle fell back on the pillow, defeated. "Fine," he sighed. He grinned lazily up at him, and for a moment Eric could only stare, completely transfixed by this gorgeous creature in his bed.

"Breakfast," he said firmly, shaking off the desire to fall back into bed and let Kyle do whatever he wanted to him. He walked swiftly to his closet, eager to cover his body and clear his mind.

Eric had two omelets with sides of tomato slices and toast made by the time Kyle came downstairs, showered and wearing his clothes from last night.

"Hi," Eric said stiffly. "There's coffee made."

"Great. Thanks." Kyle figured this was the part when Eric told him that they couldn't do this anymore. Again.

His arm brushed against Eric as he reached for the coffee pot, and he didn't miss the way Eric jerked away from the contact. Jesus, this was going to be awful.

"Something wrong?" Kyle asked as he poured his coffee, wanting to get this over with.

Eric gripped the counter with both hands, and Kyle waited in miserable anticipation of the rejection to come.

But what Eric said was, "Can I tell you something? I'd need you to keep it a secret, but I need to tell someone."

What the hell? "Of course."

Eric hesitated, seeming to brace himself, then said, "I'm retiring. At the end of this season."

"Oh." So maybe Eric's mood had nothing to do with Kyle. And also, "Wow."

Eric's chin fell to his chest. "Yeah. It's, um, it's going to be hard."

"Are you unsure about it?"

"No. I know it's time. I just don't want to pull the trigger, y'know? Everyone is going to make a big *thing* about it."

Kyle placed a hand on Eric's forearm. His muscles were tense from gripping the counter.

"They'll miss you," Kyle said gently.

Eric sighed and rubbed his other hand over his face. "I'll miss them too. I'll miss everything. I don't know what I'm going to do after this season." He turned his head to look at Kyle, and found sadness in his eyes. "My whole life has been hockey. I'm not sure how I'm going to cope when that's taken away."

"Hey. Come here." Kyle pulled him into his arms. Eric pressed his face into the side of Kyle's neck, and they both just breathed for a minute.

Kyle was surprised to hear that Eric didn't know what he was going to do after hockey because Eric always seemed so capable and in control. He figured if Eric was retiring, it was because he had a solid plan for what comes next.

"You haven't told anyone yet?" he asked. "No hockey people?"

"No. No one."

Kyle tried to ignore the way his heart swelled with knowing Eric had confided in him with something this huge. Again.

Eric lifted his head, and Kyle released him. "I'm going to make an announcement soon," Eric said. "After Christmas, I think. Or maybe after the All-Star break. I don't want to do a press conference or anything. Just a written statement. But I'll have to tell my teammates first, and that won't be easy."

"You guys seem like a close bunch."

"We are. It's like walking away from your family, y'know?" Eric grimaced. "Sorry. I shouldn't have said that to you. I didn't mean—"

Kyle waved a hand. "Don't worry about it." He really didn't want the conversation to turn toward his issues with his parents. "And you'll still see those guys, right? You're staying in New York?"

"I plan to. But it won't be the same. And last night, at the club with Scott and Carter and Matti . . . it just got me thinking about it. I love those guys, especially Scott."

"Scott isn't going anywhere. And you *know* he's still going to hang out with you all the time."

"I know." Eric straightened his shoulders. "We should eat. It's probably cold now."

They sat at the kitchen island next to each other. As they ate, their legs kept brushing together, and Kyle kept stealing glances at Eric. Even when he was melancholy he was still so sexy.

"If you need someone to talk to, I'm here, okay? Anytime." Kyle grinned. "I mean it. I keep late hours."

Eric caught his gaze, and for a fleeting moment Kyle thought he saw the same longing he was trying to hide from his own expression. But then it faded, and Eric simply said, "Thank you."

"And if you need any . . . distractions, I'll be happy to help."

Eric laughed at that. "I'll let you know."

Kyle decided to take that as a good sign, and happily ate his omelet, already daydreaming about how he'd like to distract Eric.

"I'm going to be busy for a while," Eric said after a minute of quiet eating. "We hit the road tomorrow morning for a week, then I'm in Hamilton for a couple of days for Christmas, then gone again on the twenty-eighth for four more days."

Kyle wasn't sure if Eric was telling him this for a reason, or if he was just making conversation, but it almost sounded apologetic.

"Sounds hectic," Kyle said mildly. Truthfully, he did feel a pang of disappointment that Eric wouldn't be around. He had even been considering inviting him over to watch movies on Christmas Day. But of course Eric was spending Christmas with his family. Because that's what people whose parents weren't grossed out by them did on Christmas.

"It will be," Eric agreed. "But we have a week off at the end of January. I've been looking forward to it more than usual this year."

"Why's that?" Kyle didn't want to hope that *he* had anything to do with it.

Eric huffed. "Because I'm old. I've been feeling this season more than others. It's why I've decided it's definitely time to retire."

"Are you going anywhere for the break?"

"No, I'm just going to relax at home. I can't wait."

Kyle bit the inside of his cheek. Relaxing at home could include a whole lot of things. Things that he wouldn't mind participating in. If Eric asked.

There was also the very real possibility that two weeks or so on the road would be enough time for Eric to lose interest in whatever he and Kyle were doing. Maybe Eric would become reacquainted with an old high school crush back in his Canadian hometown. At Christmastime. Like a fucking Hallmark movie.

It was annoying how much Kyle wanted some assurance that Eric would want to continue to . . . spend time with him. Even if it wasn't sex, Kyle would love to go for another walk. Another meal. Visit another gallery. It was rare for Kyle to want to spend this much time with someone, but if he had his way, he'd stay for the rest of the day, and all night.

Eric had taken their dirty plates to the sink and started washing them by the time Kyle managed to stop his runaway thought train. He stood and awkwardly walked to sink, hovering next to Eric uselessly. "Can I help?"

"It's okay. I have to leave in a minute."

"Right. I'll get going then." He took a step toward the stairs, then hesitated.

"I'll walk you down," Eric said, drying his hands.

At the door, the two men stood facing each other for a tense, silent moment. Finally, Kyle gave Eric a quick hug. "Have a good road trip. Or two, I guess. And a merry Christmas."

"Thanks."

When Kyle pulled back, he found Eric gazing longingly at his mouth. It was an opportunity he couldn't ignore. He leaned in and murmured, "How about a farewell kiss?"

Eric answered by bringing their lips together. The kiss was soft and sweet, and Kyle regretted asking for it. It was too tender. Too heartbreaking.

"Thank you again," Eric said quietly. "Last night was incredible."

Kyle switched on his flirty, carefree shield. "Of course it was."

Eric's warm laughter was the last thing Kyle heard as he opened the door and made his escape from the man he was in danger of falling for.

CHAPTER NINETEEN

"If either of you fuckers opts out of the All-Star game I will personally kill you," Carter said. They were in the locker room, getting dressed for their first home game in two weeks.

"Why?" Scott asked.

"Because Gloria and I booked a week in Grand Cayman, and if one of you bails, they are going to replace you with me."

"Carter," Eric said calmly. "I'm a goalie."

"Right. Okay, well, Scotty has to go then."

"I *am* going," Scott said. "I love the All-Star game."

"You're the only one," Carter grumbled. "I have a long list of things I'd rather do during my week off than play a shitshow of a game in fucking Buffalo."

"Hey," Scott said. "I'm from near Buffalo."

"And I'm from North Dakota, but I don't want to spend my vacation time there either," Carter quipped.

Eric had no plans to skip the All-Star game. The line-up had been announced yesterday, and he'd been surprised and touched to be named to the team this year, since there were some really excellent younger goaltenders who deserved the spot as much as he did. He appreciated having one last opportunity to show off in the skills competition, and to secretly say goodbye to his colleagues.

Christmas had come and gone and Eric still hadn't told anyone that he was retiring at the end of this season. He just couldn't bring himself to say the words. Every week he'd have a new reason to justify waiting. He'd now decided to wait until February, after the All-Star game. He didn't want the attention that he'd get from the media, and the other players, if they knew it was definitely his last All-Star appearance.

He hadn't seen or spoken to Kyle in two weeks either. He'd taken the back-to-back road trips as an opportunity to clear his head and maybe allow himself to think reasonably about what he was doing with Kyle. He'd thought some distance would relieve his cravings for the man.

It hadn't worked.

Eric still felt heated every time he thought of their last time together. Which was often. In fact most of his thoughts had been dominated by Kyle. He'd thought about him when he was on the road—in planes, on buses, working out, and definitely in his hotel rooms. He'd thought about him while he'd been at home with his family. He'd thought about him a surprising amount on Christmas morning, even wishing that Kyle was there with him, meeting his parents and siblings, which was a little alarming.

Eric had wanted to text him yesterday when he'd gotten back into town. Maybe see if he wanted to come over. But he didn't want to seem too eager, and he also didn't like how unmanageable his feelings had become. Kyle was forcing his way into Eric's heart like a puck sailing into the top corner of the net while Eric was sprawled helplessly on the ice. He couldn't control what was happening, and he hated things he couldn't control.

Usually.

"You guys enjoy hanging out with Dallas Kent in the snow," Carter teased. "I'm going to be on a beach with the love of my life."

"Rum?" Scott asked dryly.

Carter threw a roll of tape at him.

ERIC:
What are you up to?

Kyle did not appreciate the way his heart lurched when he saw Eric's text. It was a completely inappropriate and disproportionate response.

KYLE:
Just leaving campus.

He watched the three dots blink on his screen for what felt like an eternity as Eric typed. Kyle couldn't imagine what this was going to be about. He hadn't heard from Eric in two weeks. He'd almost given up hope.

ERIC:
I was wondering if you might like to get coffee.

Well, that was adorable.

KYLE:
Sure. Where?

They agreed to meet at a café near Columbia that Kyle liked. He ducked into a bathroom before leaving campus. After a three hour seminar, he doubted he looked his freshest. He examined himself in the mirror and finger-combed the front of his hair so it wasn't falling into his face. He finally decided it was a lost cause and pulled a black winter hat out of his backpack. He had his favorite glasses on today, at least.

Maybe it was sad that he was so excited about a coffee with a friend, but he'd been having a hard time not obsessing over Eric Bennett lately. Every shift he worked at the Kingfisher he hoped Eric would walk through the doors, even when Kyle knew he was out of town. He'd watched most of the Admirals' road games, some on the televisions at work, and some at home. His heart had fluttered every time the broadcasts showed Eric's face, even if it was behind a mask.

Kyle could have texted him. He knew this, and had been tempted to do it several times. On Christmas morning he'd had a message all typed out—just a simple *Merry Christmas*—but he'd deleted it. For whatever reason, he'd made a deal with himself that he would let Eric make contact next. And if Eric never did, well. That was that, then. It wasn't like Kyle had never been ghosted before.

It wasn't like Eric had ever promised him anything.

So getting a text—an *invitation*—from Eric now, after a long and particularly tedious seminar class, was extremely welcome.

When Eric entered the café, Kyle's stomach flipped. Somehow he'd forgotten how gorgeous the man was in person: tall and elegantly dressed in a long wool coat that was dusted in snowflakes. When he spotted Kyle, he smiled warmly, and Kyle silently commanded himself to be cool.

"Hi," Eric said.

"Hi." They stood near the counter, facing each other. Kyle's hand twitched with the desire to touch him, but he didn't. From here he could see the snowflakes that were melting into Eric's hair, making it glisten.

"It's, um, nice to see you," Eric said. "It's been a while."

Had it seemed like a long time to Eric? Had he *missed* Kyle? "It has. Did you have a nice Christmas?"

"It was short, but good. It's always nice to go home." Eric's smile fell. "I mean—"

"It's fine," Kyle said quickly. "Mom called me on Christmas. We talked for ten whole minutes. It was very festive. Apparently my older brothers are both doing wonderful things and my parents are very proud of them."

God, why had he just said all of that? He saw unwanted sympathy in Eric's eyes, so he changed the subject, "Let's order. I need caffeine after that class."

A few minutes later they brought their coffees to a small table in one corner.

"I heard that you made the All-Star team. Congratulations."

"Thank you. It was a bit of a surprise, to be honest."

"Why? You've been playing well this season, haven't you?"

Eric gently removed the lid to his coffee cup and set it on the table. "Other goalies have been better. *Younger* goalies."

Ah. This.

"Eric," Kyle said carefully, "did you text me because you're feeling old?"

Eric's eyes went wide. "What? No, of course not." But his brow furrowed in a way that suggested he was considering the possibility.

"I've enjoyed everything we've done together, and, honestly, all of the time we've spent together. But if you're here because I make you feel young or something . . ."

"It's not that," Eric said quickly. "You *are* young, but when we're together I—" He cut himself off. Kyle *needed* him to finish that sentence.

"You what?"

"I don't think about our age difference. I think about it

when we're apart sometimes, but whenever I'm with you I just . . . forget."

There was definitely something romantic about that admission, but Kyle did his best to ignore it. It was probably unintentional. "I must not be doing as good a job moisturizing as I thought," he said dryly.

Eric chuckled. "That's not what I meant. And I'm not here to feed off your youth. I'm around plenty of young men when I'm at work."

"That makes two of us." Kyle sipped his latte. "Is something on your mind, though?"

Eric fiddled with his coffee cup. "I still haven't told anyone I'm retiring. And the road trips were . . . hard, I guess. Every arena we played in, I thought about how it might be the last time I ever play there. This might be the last time I'm flying from San Jose to Colorado with my teammates." He shook his head. "I don't know why those thoughts bothered me so much. It's silly."

"It's not. You're about to end an enormous chapter of your life."

"I know." Eric blew out a breath and said, "Anyway. I didn't invite you here to unload on you."

Kyle waggled his eyebrows suggestively. When Eric noticed, he ducked his head to hide his embarrassed smile.

"Why did you invite me?" Kyle asked.

Eric glanced up. "I found myself . . . missing you."

Kyle's mouth fell open, then curved up in a giddy smile that he tried, but failed, to get under control. "I may have missed you too." He lowered his voice. "I've thought a lot about our last night together."

Eric held his gaze, and Kyle saw the heat that ignited in them. "Me too."

He bit his lip, considering whether what he was about to propose was a good idea. It probably wasn't, but, "Maria just started her evening shift at Starbucks."

It took Eric a second. "So your apartment is empty, you're saying?"

"I have it all to myself. If you're not busy . . ."

"I'm not." Eric was already putting the lid back on his coffee, getting ready to leave. "Let's go."

Kyle laughed at his eagerness. "You know, if you wanted a booty call, you could have just said. You didn't have to meet me for coffee."

"I wanted to see you, not just . . . I mean, I like talking to you."

Ugh. Eric had to stop. Kyle was going to get all sorts of wrong ideas if he didn't stop. He decided to keep it sexy. "How about we talk *after* I show you what I've been dreaming of doing to you for two weeks?"

CHAPTER TWENTY

Eric was writhing on Kyle's bed, out of his mind with lust. Kyle had brought him to the edge three times already without letting him come, and Eric wasn't sure if he'd survive a fourth time.

"Please," he begged. *Begged*. And he wasn't even embarrassed about it.

Kyle grinned wickedly at him. Eric was completely naked and sprawled on his back. Kyle was looming over him, still fully dressed.

"Do you want to try something new?" Kyle asked.

"Is it you letting me come?"

Kyle laughed. "Eventually. One sec." He disappeared over the edge of the mattress, and Eric heard the scrape of something against the floor under the bed. Kyle stood again, holding a shoebox. He set it on the bed and opened it, then pulled out a set of black, Velcro cuffs that were linked together with metal clips.

"Yes or no?" Kyle asked, holding the cuffs up.

The answer left Eric's lips before he'd had a chance to think about it. "Yes."

"You trust me?" Kyle asked as he moved back onto the bed, straddling Eric's waist.

Again, no hesitation. "Yes."

Kyle inhaled sharply. "Fuck, Eric." He leaned down and kissed him, as slowly and commandingly as he'd been stroking Eric's cock a few minutes ago. Eric moaned softly into his mouth, not able to decide if he wanted this perfect kiss to last forever, or if he wanted more.

Kyle made the decision for him, pulling away and lifting one of Eric's wrists. That was when Eric realized he had subconsciously left his hands pinned to the mattress above his head during their kiss, already anticipating Kyle's restraints.

One wrist was wrapped in a cuff, and then the other. Kyle left the cuffs separated for now, and asked Eric if they were too tight. Eric shook his head, bewildered that they were really doing this, but too turned on to worry about it.

Kyle positioned Eric's hands on the pillow above his head, then used the hooks on the cuffs to bind them together. "I could attach these to my headboard," he said, "but I don't think I need to. Do I?"

"No." No, Eric would keep his hands right where Kyle wanted them. He could do that for him. He was nothing if not disciplined.

"One more thing," Kyle said. He went back to the shoebox and pulled out another piece of black fabric. It took Eric a moment to recognize it as a blindfold.

"Yes or no?" Kyle asked again.

Eric was less sure about this one. His eyes—his vision—were so important to him. He made his living watching, paying attention, and reacting quickly. Having that taken away from him, even for a minute, was terrifying. But also . . . thrilling.

"I want to try," Eric said. "Yes."

Kyle's smile was warmer this time, less mischief in it and more affection. "Tell me right away if you hate it. Promise?"

"I promise."

Eric took a long, slow breath and closed his eyes as Kyle slipped the mask over his head and fiddled with the elastic strap.

"Okay," Kyle said quietly. "How's that?"

Eric opened his eyes and saw . . . nothing. Blackness. His first instinct was to rip it off his face or tell Kyle to. But he gave himself a moment to adjust. "Talk to me," he said.

"I'm right here," Kyle said, then kissed Eric's jaw. "Is it okay?"

Eric took another steadying breath. "I think so. It's just . . . different."

"Any time you want to stop, tell me. But you look absolutely stunning right now. Fuck. You should see yourself."

"I'll have to take your word for it. Ah!" Eric's whole body jerked when Kyle captured one of his nipples with his teeth. The pain mixed with pleasure was so intense that he couldn't believe it had only been his nipple. His had never been particularly sensitive. He felt Kyle's hot breath brushing the burning flesh he had just bitten, and Eric wondered if he was going to do it again. The anticipation made his heart race, and he clenched his bound hands into fists.

He felt the wet warmth of Kyle's tongue as it lapped over the nipple, soothing it with gentle licks. Eric let out a long moan that was mixed with a sigh, melting into the mattress. Then Kyle bit him again, and Eric yelped.

"Good?" Kyle asked. He was struggling not to laugh, Eric could tell.

"It's weird. Intense. I've never done anything like this."

Kyle trailed featherlight fingertips across Eric's chest and down his stomach, and Eric thought for sure if he looked he'd see glowing lines of electricity on his skin in their wake. His body had already been overloaded with sensation from Kyle's edging efforts, and now he thought he might burst apart like a firework if Kyle touched his cock.

Then Kyle was gone. His weight was gone from Eric's waist. His heat was gone. His fingers, his tongue. His breathing. Eric searched for him with his ears. "Kyle?"

No reply. And then Eric heard a zipper, and a soft rustling somewhere to the side of the bed. He turned his head to follow it, and then felt something brush against his lips.

The head of Kyle's cock.

Eric could smell the now-familiar musk of it as Kyle teased his lips with gentle nudges and swipes. Eric opened his mouth in invitation, turning on his side and quickly swiping his tongue over his dry lips. He wanted it. Wanted to suck Kyle off blindly, with his hands trapped above his head. He wanted Kyle to feed it to him while Eric could only lay there and take it.

The spongy head of Kyle's cock slid past his lips and Eric hummed happily around it. Kyle planted one of his hands on Eric's head, fingers tangling into his hair as he adjusted Eric's angle.

"God, you look so fucking sexy right now," Kyle said huskily. "Absolutely gorgeous, baby."

Eric could only answer by sucking more of him into his mouth, straining his neck to reach. His fingers twitched with the need to touch him, but he obediently left them on the pillow.

"Fuck, this is better than I even pictured it. You love taking my dick like this, don't you? Love having nothing to do but suck me."

Eric moaned his agreement. He did love this. It should probably feel weird, or degrading, but it actually felt . . . peaceful. His brain was quiet. There were no pressures, no team depending on him, no scary life-changing decisions to make. There was just Kyle, and the need to please him.

He still had limited experience when it came to cock-sucking, but Eric had always been a quick study. He flicked his tongue over the head in a way that Kyle had seemed to love last time.

"That's good, baby. That's fucking incredible," Kyle babbled. His fingers tightened in Eric's hair, and then released him.

Eric was distantly aware of some noises, but he ignored them, too focused on his task to try to guess what they were. He could taste salty drops of precum, and he heard Kyle suck in a breath and swear softly. Then, Kyle pulled away, leaving him empty. Drool leaked out of the corner of Eric's mouth, but he couldn't wipe it away. He rolled to his back, frustrated.

A slick hand wrapped around his cock, unexpected and ruthless. Stroking him hard and fast, and Eric could only gasp and swear and jerk his hips. He knew Kyle would stop before he came. He knew there was no way Kyle would go to the trouble of restraining and blinding him if he was going to end things so quickly. But Eric's body didn't care. It optimistically thrust into Kyle's tight fist, seeking release. It was so close—right *there.* Eric could feel it pulsing inside him, huge and inevitable. Just a little more coaxing and it would surge out of him.

Kyle stopped, of course. Eric swore loudly as his cock twitched helplessly in the air above his stomach, seeking any kind of friction.

"Roll over," Kyle instructed, his tone not showing any sympathy. "On your knees."

Eric did as he was told immediately. He rested his forehead on the mattress between his forearms, his hands still linked together above his head, as if he was positioning himself in child's pose. He lifted his ass in the air, shivering at how exposed and vulnerable he felt.

"Your ass is a fucking masterpiece, Eric," Kyle said. He smoothed a palm over one cheek, then pressed his lips there. "And these thighs. Fuck."

Without warning, a slick finger glided over Eric's hole, and Eric hissed into the mattress.

"You want me to go deeper this time?" Kyle asked. "You ever had your prostate stroked?"

"Not—not by someone else." Eric had only attempted it himself a few times, and, flexible as he was, it had been difficult to apply the pressure he'd wanted there. He had a feeling Kyle would be able to give him exactly what he needed.

"Then this is going to be fun." Kyle massaged Eric's entrance with steady, circular swipes of the pad of this thumb, holding him still with a firm hand on Eric's ass cheek. Eric tried to maintain control of his breathing, but it alternated between holding it for too long, then gasping and panting as Kyle worked him open.

Without realizing what he was doing, he bucked back against Kyle's finger, wanting him deeper. The increased stretch burned, and Kyle swatted Eric's ass lightly with his other hand.

"Patience," he chided. "Just breathe and relax for me."

"Just like yoga."

"Exactly. Yoga where you get to come like a fountain at the end."

Eric laughed, and then moaned as Kyle pressed in deeper.

"Maybe you've done that before," Kyle mused. "Gotten yourself off right there in your yoga studio."

Eric grunted in response. He certainly hadn't.

"I'll bet you're flexible enough to suck your own dick. You ever tried that?"

"*No.*"

"There's something to work on during your retirement."

"Stop making me laugh," Eric said, his whole body shaking. He composed himself with a long, slow breath, then just enjoyed the waves of pleasure that rippled through his body as

Kyle made his nerve endings sing. It felt wonderful to be taken care of this way, to have everything removed so Eric could only focus on pleasure. He should feel helpless, but instead he felt . . . safe. Cared for. Loved.

A white-hot burst of pleasure rocketed through Eric when Kyle stroked his prostate. His body lurched forward, as if trying to escape the overwhelming sensation.

"Too much?" Kyle asked gently. He kissed Eric's shoulder, then his temple. Eric felt his warm breath against his ear. "Do you want me to stop?"

"No," Eric rasped. "Don't stop. Again. Please."

Kyle kissed the corner of his mouth, then disappeared. A moment later, he had a finger—possibly two—inside Eric again. Relief crashed over Eric, breaking over his skin and flooding his insides. Kyle was with him, inside him, right where Eric needed him. Giving him what Eric had craved for over two weeks. He worked Eric's prostate, sending jolt after jolt of sharp pleasure through Eric's trembling body.

Eric's cock—god, he had almost forgotten about his cock—felt like a kettlebell between his legs. It hung, huge and heavy as an anchor as Kyle devoted all of his attention to Eric's ass. Eric focused on it now, on how desperately it wanted to be touched. At how each press of Kyle's finger against his prostate forced drops of precum to weep out of Eric's slit. He could imagine a trail of silvery fluid connecting his swollen cock to the mattress. A pool of his arousal on the bedsheets.

Kyle gently squeezed his balls, and Eric cried out and clenched around the fingers that were still in his ass.

"God, they're like granite," Kyle said breathily. "I can't decide where I want you to come."

Eric wanted to tell him to make up his mind about that right fucking now, but instead he just whimpered and said, "Please."

Kyle chuckled behind him, then gently stroked Eric's cock a couple of times. Eric tried to hump his hand, but Kyle took it away as soon as his hips started moving.

"Need to come."

"I know. Fuck, me too. You've got me so fucking turned on. How do you want it? Do you want to see?"

Eric nodded against the mattress. "Yes."

Kyle guided him to his back and positioned Eric's hands above his head again. He straddled Eric's waist, and Eric relished the weight of him. Loved being trapped under him. Kyle's ass pressed against Eric's groin, and Eric realized Kyle had removed his clothes at some point. Kyle rolled his hips, and Eric's cock slid along his ass crack. Eric moaned loudly, torn between wanting to come like this, splashing his release against Kyle's bare ass, or stuffing his cock deep inside him.

"D-don't," he gritted out. "I'm too fucking close for that."

Kyle seemed to understand, and lifted his ass away from the landmine that was Eric's erection. Then his lips landed on Eric's, and Eric responded immediately, kissing him hungrily—wildly—loving the hot urgency of Kyle's mouth. Loving how intense the kiss felt with his eyes still covered. But god, he wanted to see. Wanted to gaze at Kyle and watch his face contort when he came.

"Kyle," Eric murmured against his lips. "Want to see you."

Two fingers slipped under the elastic that held the blindfold in place, and then it was gone. It took Eric a moment to realize he'd had his eyes closed under the cloth, and he blinked them open. Everything was bright and blurry, even though the overhead light in the room was off.

"Hi," Kyle said quietly.

Eric blinked again. His eyes were damp with tears, which he couldn't explain. "Hi."

Kyle was breathtaking. He was still wearing his glasses, but nothing else, and grinned when Eric noticed. His disheveled hair fell over his forehead, into his winter-blue eyes. His cheeks were pink with exertion and arousal, and Eric couldn't stop looking at him.

"You're so beautiful," Eric said. He sounded wrecked, his voice high and strained.

Kyle was slowly stroking his own cock, still straddling Eric's waist. The head was dark and shiny, and Eric wanted it in his mouth almost as badly as he wanted to watch Kyle jerk off. His gaze darted from Kyle's straining forearm to that tantalizing bulge in his bicep, to his wet, kiss-bruised mouth, then back to the glistening head of his cock.

"Tell me what you want," Kyle said shakily. "Tell me."

"Want you to come. Want it all over me." Eric hadn't let himself think before answering. He wasn't capable of thinking anymore.

Kyle stroked himself faster. His chest heaved as his breathing sped up, and he kept his eyes locked on Eric's. "Tell me to stop," he said. "Don't let me come yet."

Holy fuck. Eric was going to come without any contact on his dick if Kyle kept this up. He nodded because he couldn't find words. He would try to do this for Kyle. He would get this right.

He watched Kyle's face, observed every change in his eyes, in his breathing, in the tension in his neck as Kyle ruthlessly jerked himself. Eric watched him until Kyle's eyes kept snapping closed, then opening again. Until the flush in his cheeks spread down to his stomach. He didn't speak, didn't say he was close, but Eric knew.

"Stop." It was barely more than a whisper, but Kyle released his cock and threw his head back, groaning. He panted for a few breaths, then lowered his head to meet Eric's gaze.

"That was perfect, baby. I was right there. Holy shit."

Eric's chest was rising and falling rapidly too. He was exhilarated—full of pride and adrenaline and the constant pressing need to come. Kyle bent down, kissed him quickly, then slid down until he was kneeling between Eric's legs on the bed. Without ceremony, he gripped Eric's cock and stroked him hard.

"Fuck yes, Kyle. Make me come. Make me come. Make me—"

A finger slid back inside Eric's ass, seeking and finding his prostate immediately, and Eric arched off the bed and screamed as his release finally erupted from him. His come shot up like a fountain before splashing down on his stomach and chest, some painting Kyle's chest. Kyle kept pumping him, coaxing more jerks of his cock, more jets of cum from his balls until the last drop slipped out of his exhausted dick.

His finger stayed inside Eric for a moment after he released his cock. Kyle gently probed Eric's prostate, which sent a final tremor racing through his spent body. "Fucking stunning," Kyle said. "Fuck, it's like you save it all for me."

It was almost exactly what Eric did. He'd jerked off a few times over the past couple of weeks, but he'd thought only of Kyle each time. And he hadn't gotten himself off at all for the past several days, hopeful that the next time would be with Kyle.

"I wanted you," Eric said. "Wanted this."

"I know you did." Kyle was stroking himself again, still kneeling between Eric's legs.

"Come here. Closer. I want to do that."

Kyle huffed out a laugh as he moved to straddle Eric again. "Not gonna take long."

"Do you want it to?"

"No. Can't. Just make me come."

Eric made a tight tunnel of his bound hands and held it in front of Kyle's cock. "Will this work?"

Kyle pushed his cock into Eric's hands and groaned. "Fuck, Eric. That works just fine. So sexy with those cuffs on. *Fuck*."

He thrust eagerly, snapping his hips hard and fast, and Eric's mouth went dry as he imagined him thrusting into his ass. He was sure his hole had relaxed a bit, just thinking about it.

"Want you to fuck me, Kyle. Someday."

"Yeah, baby. Want that too. Fuck you just like this."

"I want—I want to do everything. With you."

Kyle's eyes went wide, and Eric worried that he'd admitted too much, but then Kyle gasped and said, "Oh fuck. Oh fuck, Eric. Here it comes. I'm gonna—" His announcement trailed off into a loud moan, and then he stilled and shot his load all over Eric's chest hair and even into Eric's beard.

He collapsed on Eric, and Eric looped his bound hands over his head and held them tight around Kyle's back. He held him close, nose pressed into Kyle's hair as he listened to his breathing settle.

"You might be ruining me," Kyle murmured finally. "Might not want anyone else after this."

Well, *that* was a dangerous admission, and the way Kyle tensed in his arms told Eric that he knew it.

"It was fun," Eric said lightly, ignoring the way his heart was expanding.

Kyle lifted his head and observed his face. "You have cum in your beard."

"I know."

"It's hot."

"I'm afraid I'll have to wash it out, though."

"Coward."

Eric chuckled and squeezed Kyle tighter.

"Feel better?" Kyle asked sleepily.

Eric couldn't recall why Kyle was asking the question. Had

he felt bad before? Had he ever felt bad in his life? "I feel amazing. Thank you."

"No more talk about being an old man." Kyle kissed his collarbone. "Not when you can come like a geyser."

"That had more to do with you than me, I think."

"You don't come like that when you're alone?"

Eric laughed. "I've never come like that in my life. You're magic."

"I'm *skilled*."

Eric kissed his hair. "You are."

Kyle ducked out from under Eric's hands and began to remove the cuffs. "You liked this, then?" he asked as he opened the Velcro. "The cuffs? The blindfold?"

"I did. I, um." Despite everything they had just done, Eric's cheeks heated. "I liked it a lot."

"Good to know." Kyle removed the second cuff and began massaging Eric's hands, which felt wonderful.

"Do you like it?" Eric asked. "Being tied up? Or do you just do it to other people?" A spark of jealousy flashed inside him at the thought of *other people*.

"I like it. Especially when I'm stressed or overwhelmed about something. It can be kind of . . ."

"Freeing?" Eric supplied.

"Yeah. Exactly. And peaceful, y'know?"

"Yes. That's how it felt. It was relaxing and exciting at the same time."

Kyle kissed Eric's palm. "I'm glad. That's what I was aiming for."

God, this man. Eric needed this man in his life more than was fair to Kyle.

Later, when they were both cleaned up, Kyle snuggled against Eric and idly played with his chest hair. Kyle's head was still spinning from everything they just did, and everything he still wanted to do with Eric.

He could admit to himself that he had feelings for Eric. Feelings that went well beyond friendship or base lust. Kyle wanted to be with him, but knew he shouldn't hope for that. Knew it would only lead to disappointment and heartbreak. Eric was still figuring himself out. He wasn't even really out yet, and he was a celebrity besides. And once he'd had his fun with Kyle, he'd move on to someone more *appropriate*.

Thirty years old and up.

Kyle was twenty-five, and what was five years, really? Hell, in a few months he'd be twenty-six. Would he really be that different when he was thirty? Did Eric really not see him as an adult now?

The thought annoyed Kyle, because it was probably true. Eric likely saw him as a good time, not as a man that he would consider having a mature and lasting relationship with.

Kyle was, once again, getting way ahead of himself. He and Eric had hooked up a handful of times over the past month or so. It certainly wasn't a great romance.

"I wanted to call you on Christmas," Eric said suddenly. "Or text you, at least."

"You did?"

"I was thinking about you that day. Well . . ." He squeezed the arm that was wrapped around Kyle. "I thought about you every day, to be honest. But on Christmas especially."

Kyle's mouth was suddenly very dry. "Why?"

"Because I knew you were alone." He exhaled loudly. "I should have called you."

Kyle lifted his head from where it had been resting on Eric's chest. "I was okay, but . . . I wouldn't have minded hearing from you." He smiled, and Eric smiled back, though it didn't reach his eyes.

"I didn't want to look eager." Eric shook his head. "It was stupid of me to worry about that. I'm sorry."

Kyle hadn't wanted to look eager either. He had deleted the text he'd planned to send to Eric on Christmas. But he didn't say that because it wouldn't help things. "I appreciate the thought."

Eric put a hand on Kyle's cheek, then leaned forward to kiss him. Another tender, adoring kiss that made Kyle want things he shouldn't.

"What time does Maria get home?" Eric asked.

"Usually around eleven. We've got time."

Eric chuckled. "Time for what? I've got nothing left if you're thinking—"

"Time for *food*. I'm starving."

"Me too."

"We should eat."

"Mm." Eric pounced on him, kissing his neck as Kyle dissolved into giggles.

Food could wait a little longer.

CHAPTER TWENTY-ONE

Two weeks later, Eric was in a rowdy locker room in Buffalo as the Eastern Conference All-Stars got ready for the skills competition. Old friends who were normally opponents were enjoying the rare opportunity to catch up. Other guys were loudly teasing each other. Eric quietly observed everyone.

It was an interesting exercise, bringing all of these rivals together in the middle of the season. Hockey was an emotional sport, and grudges ran deep, but they were all connected by this game that they loved. They were, in a way, all family.

Ilya Rozanov and Shane Hollander were sitting across from each other, and kept catching each other's eye and smiling. There was a mutual fondness there that Eric still couldn't quite believe. They were such famous rivals but, he supposed, they were also human beings who were more than their hockey skills. Obviously they had found things to like about each other and had become good friends.

Dallas Kent was in one corner, talking to another player who Eric didn't particularly like. Kent's teammate, Troy Barrett, was sitting in the stall next to Eric, but had been quiet the entire time he'd put his gear on. Now he was engrossed in his phone. Eric had no reason to like the kid, but he decided to attempt to be friendly.

"This is your first All-Star Game, isn't it?"

Troy looked up, startled. "Yeah. I was supposed to go last year, but I was hurt."

"I remember. What event are you doing?"

"Fastest skater."

Eric nodded. "Makes sense. You've got some tough competition, though."

"I don't think I'll win. But the other option was to do that fucking stupid obstacle course one and I don't want to embarrass myself in my first skills competition."

"Goalies definitely have it easy at these things."

Troy was only twenty-four years old. He wasn't a particularly big guy—probably five-nine or so, with minimal bulk. Like Kyle, he had a body built for speed. Unlike Kyle, he had black, glossy hair that kept falling into his piercing blue eyes. Those eyes didn't look happy right now, and Eric realized he'd never seen Troy look particularly happy. Not that he'd seen a whole lot of him.

"Usually after this thing we all meet up at the hotel bar, or sometimes there are room parties," Eric said.

"I figured. That would be fun, but . . ." He frowned at someone across the room, and Eric realized it was Dallas Kent. "Is Hunter going to be there, do you think?"

"Why?" Eric felt a flash of anger. Was Troy such a homophobic prick that he wouldn't socialize with Scott?

Troy looked at him with wide, sapphire eyes. "Not because—Jesus, I'm not like that, okay? I don't hate gay people. I just want to, I dunno, talk to him. But he might not want to talk to me. That's all."

Eric relaxed. "He'll talk to you," he said with certainty. "Scotty's the nicest guy in the world."

"Seems like it."

Eric decided, if he did nothing else useful with this final All-Star weekend, he could at least pass on some advice to this young man. "You know, I've been in this league a long time, and I've had to play on teams with people I didn't particularly like. Some of them were even star players. Fortunately, the locker rooms are big, and you can choose the people you want to keep close to you."

Troy's brow furrowed, then he looked at the floor. He tugged on his jersey and said, "I'm starting to figure that out."

Eric attempted a friendly shoulder clap—the kind Scott or Carter would do effortlessly. It landed a little awkwardly, but he hoped the sentiment came through.

Later that night, after the competition was over, a large group of players from both teams were gathered in the hotel bar. Eric was sitting at a small table with Wyatt Hayes—the goalie for Ottawa, and a very funny guy. They were approached by Ilya Rozanov.

"Move, Hazy," Rozanov ordered. "I need to talk to Bennett."

Wyatt shook his head but stood up. "No fucking respect for the guy who saves your ass forty times a game."

Rozanov handed him a ten-dollar bill. "Go buy yourself a beer."

Wyatt glared at him. "I can buy my own fucking beer. I'm an All-Star too, y'know."

Rozanov blinked at him, and Wyatt walked away, grumbling about Russian egomaniacs. Rozanov slid into Wyatt's chair. "You have not announced your retirement," he said, cutting to the chase.

"Your powers of observation never cease to amaze me."

"Why not?"

"I wanted to wait until after this weekend."

"You don't want a big deal?"

"No, I don't."

Rozanov grinned. "This is why we are different. I want a farewell season. A parade. Everyone crying at every game."

"I'm sure you'll get it."

He didn't miss the way Rozanov's gaze darted briefly to where Shane Hollander was standing. "Maybe."

"Scott told me you want him to help out at your camps this summer."

"Yes. But he is busy marrying that guy he likes to kiss."

"I think he'll help in the future. He's impressed with you. We all are."

Rozanov looked like he was almost embarrassed. He ducked his head, then glanced up shyly. "Yes?"

"Absolutely. If there's anything I can do to help, let me know."

"You could sell one of those expensive suits you like to wear and give us the money."

Eric chuckled. "I can give money without selling the suits."

"We could use more goalie help, at the camps."

"I could probably do that. I like that you've made an effort to be inclusive at your camps. I assume that's why you asked Scott."

"Yes. He is also not bad at hockey."

"That's the nicest thing you've ever said about him."

"Don't tell him."

Eric wasn't sure if he should share personal information with Rozanov or not, but something told him to trust him. "Not that it matters, really, but I'm bisexual. I mean, it seems like you already guessed that, but if you want that kind of rep at your camps . . ."

Rozanov's face lit up. "Bisexual! This is great. Did you fuck that blond teenager yet?"

"He's not a—" Eric bit his tongue. "He's twenty-five."

"Twenty-five was a long time ago for you. Do you remember twenty-five?"

"Where the hell is Wyatt?" Eric made a show of looking over Rozanov's shoulder.

"So you did? Fuck him?"

Eric should have been terrified by this conversation, but instead he just found himself wishing he could tell Rozanov that he hadn't just *fucked* Kyle. He wished he could say he was dating him. That Kyle was his boyfriend. "I'm not telling you anything."

"That is a yes."

At that moment, Shane Hollander approached their table. "Hi, Eric." Shane was basically the opposite of Rozanov: serious, polite, and quiet.

"Shane. Nice work in the obstacle course."

Shane smirked at Rozanov, who had not done nearly as well in the same event. "Thanks. It was pretty easy, honestly."

Rozanov glared back at him with eyes that burned with annoyance and something else. Before Eric could figure out what it was, Rozanov looked away.

Eric spotted Scott talking to Troy Barrett near the bar, which made him happy to see. Dallas Kent was nowhere to be found but, based on his reputation, he had probably found some female fans to keep him company.

"I'm going to head up to my room," Shane said. "I'll see you guys tomorrow."

"Goodnight, Shane," Eric said.

"I will probably head up soon too," Rozanov said.

Shane nodded, then turned quickly and left. Rozanov stayed at the table for about another minute, then told Eric he was going to the bathroom. He went, Eric noticed, in the direction of the elevators instead.

An hour later, Eric was alone in the elevator with Scott, heading for their side-by-side hotel rooms.

"What do you think you'll do?" Eric asked. "After you retire?"

Scott's brow furrowed. "Why?"

"Just curious."

"I haven't thought about it. I still have a lot of hockey left to play."

Eric nodded slowly. "I've been thinking about it a lot lately."

"Are you—" Scott dropped his voice to a horrified whisper. "Are you saying you're ready to retire?"

"I'm forty-one."

"Yeah, but. I mean. Look at you! You're in better shape than anyone else on this team."

"Have you been checking me out, Scott?"

"Sometimes! Can you blame me? Do you remember the height you got on your squat jumps at training camp this year?" Scott fanned himself theatrically.

Eric laughed. "Seriously, though. I can't play forever."

"You could *try*."

Eric smiled fondly at him as the elevator reached their floor. He really did love Scott, and it was time to be honest with him. He followed him down the hall and stopped when they reached Scott's room. Scott opened the door and gestured for Eric to follow him inside.

"Are you trying to tell me something, Benny?"

Eric steeled himself. This was it. "I'm going to be making the announcement soon. This is my last season."

Scott's mouth fell open.

"Don't tell anyone," Eric continued. "And don't try to change my mind. It's time."

Scott opened and closed his mouth a couple of times, then said, "You're sure."

"I'm sure."

"But I'll miss you," Scott said, as if that was all the argument Eric needed.

"I'll buy season tickets. I'll go to every game."

Scott sat down hard on his bed. "Not the same."

"I know. I'll miss you too. I'll miss everyone."

"Does Coach know?"

Eric sat next to him. "No. No one knows." It was a lie, but he didn't want to tell Scott that he'd confided in Kyle first *again*. That would open a whole new line of questioning. And he *definitely* didn't want to tell Scott that Rozanov knew. Scott would never recover. "I'm going to tell Carter as soon as we're all back together. I don't want him to hear it from someone else."

"Okay, well. Be sure, before you tell anyone else, all right?" Scott said.

Eric nudged him. "You make it sound like I'm rushing into this instead of finishing an eighteen-year career."

"It's too soon."

Eric patted Scott's thigh. "I'm retiring, not dying." He stood up, and Scott did the same, immediately wrapping him in a tight hug.

"You'd better be at every game," Scott said.

"I will." What else would Eric have to do? It's not like he'd be *busy*.

"I don't know if this TV is big enough," Maria quipped.

Kyle snorted. Kip had invited him and Maria over to watch the All-Star Game. He had moved into Scott's Manhattan penthouse a few months after they'd started dating, which had been a definite upgrade from living with his parents in Bay Ridge. Complete with a giant wall-mounted television.

"The players are basically life-size on this thing," Kyle said.

"Hey," Kip said, plunking a bowl of Doritos on the coffee table, "sometimes you need to see every drop of sweat during a hockey game, and every sequin during an episode of *Drag Race*."

Maria pointed at the television with her beer bottle. "Look. They're showing your ugly fiancé."

Scott's absurdly handsome face, with its square jaw and vivid blue eyes, filled the screen. He was talking to another player during a break in play, laughing at something the other man said. Eric hadn't played yet in this game, because as one of the three goalies on the Eastern team, he was only going to be playing the third period. The broadcast had only shown at the beginning of the game, when each player had been announced individually. He'd looked heart-stoppingly gorgeous under the dramatic lights with his mask off, waving at the crowd.

Kyle had seen quite a bit of Eric over the past couple of weeks. After their mind-blowing afternoon in his bedroom, he had craved Eric every minute they were apart. Given the number of times Eric had invited him over, it seemed the feeling was mutual.

But it was just sex. That was what Kyle reminded himself every time he left Eric's house, even though most of those times, he'd been leaving in the morning. Other than one afternoon hookup, he'd spent the night with Eric every time after, wrapped in his strong arms in that heavenly bed. They would always talk after sex, snuggled together and fighting sleep. The talking was almost Kyle's favorite part.

Almost.

"I had another customer last night who suggested we have a proper whiskey menu," Kip said during a commercial break.

"Yeah, I had two of those on Thursday," Kyle said, grateful for something to talk about that might cool his blood a bit. "I'll pass it along to Gus, but, you know."

"He's not going to do anything to change the place."

"Nope."

"What the hell is wrong with your boss?" Maria asked. "Why doesn't he want his bar to be good?"

"I don't know," Kyle said. "He's a nice enough guy, but his heart hasn't been in the place for a long time."

"I wish he'd at least consider new tables," Kip said. "Almost all of them wobble now, and they're kind of permanently sticky."

"He could at least refinish them," Kyle agreed.

"I wish you were in charge," Kip said. "You have great ideas for that place."

Kyle flushed a bit at Kip's praise. Secretly, he'd like nothing more than to be in charge of the Kingfisher. "Yeah, well. I guess it's popular enough the way it is."

"Only because people keep going there hoping to catch a glimpse of Scott," Maria said, standing up. "I'm hitting the bathroom and then getting more beer. Anyone need one?"

"Sure," Kip said.

"May as well," Kyle agreed.

After Maria was gone, Kip nudged Kyle and said, "Eric is there almost as much as Scott is now. For *some* reason."

"What are you implying?"

"That there's something going on with you two."

Kyle frowned. "We're friends. Remember how you said we should be friends? Well, now we are."

"Just friends?" Kip asked. "Because I've noticed the way he looks at you . . ."

The truth was, Kyle really did want to talk about this with someone, and this seemed like an invitation. "Okay. So I've been kind of . . . helping him out with the whole dating men thing. At first it was just talking. Like, we went to a gay bar together, just to get a drink."

"I thought Eric doesn't drink," Kip interrupted.

"He drinks *liquids.* We talked, and it was nice. And then we sort of . . . kissed."

Kip punched his arm. "I was *right*!"

"He kissed *me*! I swear. Like, I kissed his cheek, but then he totally went for it."

"Holy shit. Then what happened?"

"Nothing. We kissed. And then I offered to help him with any other . . . firsts."

"What did he say?" Kip asked eagerly.

"Nothing at first. We went our separate ways. Then a few days later, he invited me to his place for dinner. And . . . we had educational sex after."

"Educational sex?"

"Extremely *hot* educational sex. And then we did it a few more times."

"My mind is blown here," Kip said. "So are you two a thing, then?"

"No," Kyle said quickly. "Definitely not. It's just sex. Casual." He did not like the way Kip was grinning at him. "What?"

"You are so into him."

"Irrelevant."

"*Extremely* relevant!"

"What's extremely relevant?" Maria asked as she returned from the kitchen with three bottles of beer.

"Nothing," both men said at the same time.

Maria narrowed her eyes. "Well, that doesn't sound suspicious."

Kyle laughed nervously. "Just work stuff."

"And it has nothing to do with the fact that Kyle is clearly crushing hard on someone?" Maria accused.

"I'm—no, I'm not!" Kyle sputtered.

"Uh huh. I'm just saying, there might be more than one person in this room who's fucking a New York Admiral."

Kyle's mouth fell open. He would honestly love to tell Maria all about Eric, but Eric wasn't fully out yet. And besides, it wasn't like it was a real relationship. He decided to deflect attention away from himself.

"Why? Are you fucking Matti Jalo?"

"I *wish*," Maria sighed as she dropped onto the sofa. "We got food together once after that drag show in December and I never heard from him again."

"Aw," Kip said. "Was he nice to you, at least?"

"He laughed at my jokes and asked me questions. Guys! He asked me questions! About *myself*!" She grabbed a throw pillow and hugged it to herself.

"Wait. And listened to your answers?" Kyle asked.

"He asked *follow-up questions*. It was legit the best date I've ever been on. Except for the part where it wasn't really a date."

Kip hugged her. "Sorry, buddy."

"Like, I know that I don't have a shot with Matti Jalo, but still. Damn."

Kip gasped. "Of course you have a shot with him! I'm engaged to a hockey superstar! Me! We used to work together, remember?"

Kyle nodded. "If anything, it's weird that you're *not* dating an NHL star, Maria."

They all laughed, and then were distracted from their conversation when Scott scored a goal on the television.

"That's my guy," Kip said happily, then leaned against Kyle and rested his head on his shoulder. The warmth Kyle felt from this casual touch was welcome, and didn't contain any of the anguish or guilt he may have suffered before. He leaned into the arm of the sofa so his friend could relax more solidly against him.

It seemed to take forever for the third period to happen, but finally Eric was in the net and Kyle was watching the game a lot more closely. Maria's mom had called her, so she'd taken her phone to the kitchen, leaving Kip and Kyle alone again.

"You should talk to him," Kip said sleepily.

"Who?" Kyle asked, as if he didn't know.

"Eric. If you have feelings for him, you should find out if he shares them."

"And what if he doesn't?" Kyle asked, instead of denying the feelings he knew he had for Eric.

"Then at least you tried. Because what if he *does*?"

The idea was overwhelming. Kyle hadn't allowed himself to truly imagine a life where he was Eric's boyfriend. Where he was allowed to fall in love with him.

He watched Eric make a save on the television, and quietly contemplated Kip's question.

What if he does?

CHAPTER TWENTY-TWO

"What do you think?"

Eric cringed inwardly at his own impatience, but waiting and watching while Scott read the statement Eric had written to announce his retirement was torture. It was the day of their first game after the All-Star break, and Eric had decided to make his retirement official, starting with his teammates tonight.

"It's good." Scott smiled sadly as he handed Eric's phone back to him across the restaurant table. "So you're really doing this?"

"I'm really doing it. Tomorrow morning that gets posted on the Admirals website and social media accounts. I'll tell the team tonight after the game."

Scott's cheeks puffed as he blew out a breath. "Are you going to have your phone turned off all day tomorrow?"

"Definitely."

"Do you have anything planned to distract you?"

Eric poked at his vegan paella. "No."

"I'd offer to hang out with you tomorrow," Scott said, "but Kip and I are meeting with our wedding planner."

"I'll be fine. Maybe I'll watch that show Carter keeps telling me to watch."

"You mean the one that his girlfriend is the star of?"

Oh. "Uh, yeah. I guess so."

"Maybe retirement will give you a chance to finally catch up on pop culture, Benny."

"Sounds exhausting."

"Is there no one . . . else . . . you might like to spend tomorrow with?" Scott asked casually.

"Are you asking if I'm seeing someone?"

"Well . . ."

Eric wished he could say yes. The time he'd spent with Kyle over the past few weeks had been incredible, but he always felt guilty afterwards. He had no right to be taking up so much of Kyle's time, and he was starting to worry that he was leading Kyle on. Sometimes—okay, a *lot* of times—Eric could envision a future where he and Kyle were a real couple. But it wasn't a fair thing for him to want. As much as Kyle didn't seem to think their age difference mattered, Eric knew better. Kyle was too fun—too full of life—to be attached to an old goalie who very likely would need reconstructive shoulder surgery soon. Who would have the body of a man much older than Eric even was. The fifteen-year difference between them would feel like forty.

"No. No one," he told Scott now.

"What about—?"

"No." Eric set his fork down. As much as he knew the situation was hopeless, he'd been desperate to talk to someone about this for weeks, and here was his chance. "Kyle and I . . . we've been . . . doing stuff."

Scott's eyebrows shot up. "Stuff?"

"Hooking up. That sort of thing. It's casual, but . . . I like him. A lot."

"Oh. Wow. Okay." Scott's cheeks pinked the way they always did when a conversation turned to sex.

"I need to put a stop to it. The sex part, I mean. I don't think I'm the sort of person who can do that without it meaning more. I wouldn't have slept with him in the first place if I hadn't had deeper feelings for him." The words rushed out of him, now that he'd removed the barrier. "It's not fair of me to pretend these hookups don't mean anything to me when they mean a lot."

There was silence, and Scott said, "Wow. You've been really going through something, haven't you? Jeez, I had no idea."

"I know. And I can handle it myself, mostly, but . . ."

"Are you sure he doesn't feel the same way about you?"

"I don't know. We get along well, and he told me he's attracted to older men, but being attracted to older men and having sex with them isn't the same as being in a relationship with a busted old goalie with an unreliable libido."

"Um."

"Sorry. That was probably too much information."

"No! No, it's fine." Scott's cheeks were flaming. "That's, uh, do you mean you don't usually like sex?"

"I like it a lot, when I find someone I want to have sex with. It's just not very often that I'm drawn to someone in that way. I know it's weird."

"It's not weird," Scott said quickly. "I went most of my life without sex, although that was more out of fear than a lack of, um, interest." He laughed nervously. "Anyway. You like Kyle and you like having sex with him, right?"

"Yes."

"And he presumably likes you and likes having sex with you."

Eric bit his cheek to stop a smile as he thought of their last time together. Kyle had tied down Eric's wrists and ankles, and had him spread eagle on the bed using some gear that Kyle had brought over. They'd sucked each other off at the same time,

Kyle's lean body stretched on top of Eric, until they both reached the edge. Then Kyle had turned and ridden Eric hard until they both came.

And after, Kyle had stayed the night. Eric had held him close while they'd slept, and in the morning they'd had sex again. That time there had been no cuffs or toys. Just toe-curling kisses and lots of smiles and laughter.

That might have been when Eric had realized he was damn close to being in love with Kyle.

"I'm in over my head here, I think," Eric admitted.

Scott's eyes were sympathetic, which only made Eric feel more pathetic. "As I've said, I'm probably not the best person to give advice on dating, but it sounds like you should probably talk to him."

Eric considered Scott's sensible suggestion, then shook his head. "I can't. Even if he wants a relationship with me, it isn't fair to him."

Scott took a sip of water, then said, "You know, I thought the same thing about Kip once. At first because of the sneaking around, and then because of the attention I knew we'd get as a couple. But eventually I realized it wasn't my decision to make. Kip deserved a say, and so does Kyle. He's young, but he's not a kid."

"I know. I just—" Eric sighed. He knew everything Scott was saying made sense, but he still wasn't convinced that asking Kyle for more than what they had now was fair. "I'll figure it out. Let's talk about hockey instead. Are the guys going to be shocked tonight, do you think?"

Scott chewed his mouthful of rice thoughtfully. After he swallowed, he said, "Maybe not shocked, but I think it will still hit them hard. We take you for granted, y'know?"

"Tommy's ready for the job."

Scott nodded. "I'm sure of it. He'll be great." He smiled sadly. "But he's not you."

"I'll be staying in Manhattan. You'll still see me. I've put way too much work into that house to leave it."

"When I first moved to the city, I didn't think I'd ever get used to it. But now I can't imagine living anywhere else."

"Same. I think I'm here for life." Even as he said it, the thought entered his brain that he *could* imagine leaving if he were in a real relationship with Kyle, and he wanted to leave New York. It was an absolutely ridiculous thought.

"Well then," Scott said with a grin, "we can grow old together."

"I've got a bit of a head start on you, Scotty."

Scott laughed, but Eric hated that it was true. He hated that he was so much older than nearly all of his friends. So much older than the man he couldn't seem to stop thinking about.

For the millionth time, Eric shut all of his thoughts and feelings about Kyle into a box and locked it. He needed to focus on the game that night against Toronto. Between the retirement announcement and the fact that his team really needed a win tonight, his love life should really be the least of his concerns.

The mood in the locker room was somber after the game. The Admirals had played hard, but they'd been unable to hold their lead until the end. Toronto had tied the game with just over a minute to go in the third, and then had scored again in overtime. Eric felt terrible about letting that one in.

And now he needed to announce to his teammates that he was retiring. Hell, maybe they'd be relieved after that performance.

"Hey," Scott said loudly. He walked to the middle of the room, still dressed in gear from the waist down, and shirtless from the waist up. "That was a tough one. But we fought really fucking hard and we don't have to hang our heads about that, all right?" He pointed at one of the rookies. "Woody, that play you made in the second period to get us our third goal? Fucking incredible. One of the best I've ever seen."

There were murmurs of agreement around the room, and even a few claps.

"Benny, I know you're beating yourself up about those last two goals, but forty-eight saves? And there were at least five that were basically impossible. You stood on your head for us tonight."

"Yeah, Benny!" Carter called. Other guys repeated it and clapped.

"Breezy," Scott turned to Brisebois. "You blocked that shot from Kent." That got some whistles and cheers from the guys. "Fearless, man. Fucking fearless. Love to see it. How's your leg?"

"Bruised. But I'd tear my whole leg off and throw it if it stopped Kent from scoring."

Laughter erupted, and even Eric was smiling.

Scott sat beside Eric and said in a low voice, "There. I warmed them up for you."

Eric smiled gratefully at him. Scott and Carter were the only ones in the room who knew Eric was retiring. He'd told the coaches and management a week ago, but this part would be the hardest.

Eric stood up and waved, which made everyone go silent immediately. He rarely took the floor so this was unusual enough to get some attention. "Hi. I'll keep this short, but I have something to tell you guys."

The room was so quiet that Eric thought his teammates could probably hear his racing heart. He took a steadying breath. "This is going to be my last season."

Shocked exclamations started, and Eric held up a hand to silence them. "Playing in the NHL, and especially playing here in New York, with all of you, has been such an honor. I never dreamed, growing up, that—" He had to pause to clear his throat, because it had gotten tight in a hurry. He tried again. "It's been incredible. I wouldn't trade a second of it. But it's time to walk away." He paused, and managed a wry smile. "While I can still walk."

There was some quiet laughter, but he could see the shocked confusion on his teammates' faces. Did they really think he would play forever? "Come on, boys," he joked. "I'm forty-one. You had to see this coming."

There was silence, and then someone—Prentice, it sounded like—said, "You're only forty-one?"

Everyone laughed, and that opened the floodgates.

"I thought you were at least sixty."

"Goalies didn't even wear masks when you were a rookie."

"My grandpa grew up watching you."

Eric shook his head. "Fuck all of you. I can't wait to never see you again."

He sat back down, smiling, and Scott wrapped an arm around him. "They love you."

"I know." Eric watched the action in the room through damp eyes. "I'm really going to miss this."

He removed the rest of his gear in the exact same order he'd been taking it off since high school. He laughed with his teammates when someone made a joke, and smiled when Carter teased him. He was still a part of this team. He wasn't done yet.

Kyle hadn't been expecting to see Eric at the Kingfisher that night. Especially not without Scott. The game against Toronto had been on the television at the bar, so Kyle had seen the brutal overtime loss. He hadn't even had a chance to text Eric in an attempt to cheer him up.

But here he was. Tall and handsome in his wool coat and cashmere scarf, but his face was showing signs of exhaustion and misery. He spotted Kyle behind the bar and walked toward him.

"Hi," Kyle said with a sympathetic smile.

"Hi."

"I watched the game. Sorry about that."

Eric nodded. "Yeah, it sucks."

"I'd offer you a whiskey or something, but . . ."

Eric huffed. "Tonight, I'd almost take it."

Those words were heartbreaking. "Have a seat." Kyle gestured at the barstool next to Eric. "I'll keep you plied with soda water and juice."

"Thanks." Eric removed his coat and scarf and hung them neatly on the back of the seat. When he sat down, he immediately slumped forward with his forearms on the bar. "What a fucking night."

Kyle placed a soda water with lime in front of him. "Tell me all about it."

"You don't want to hear about it."

"I'm a bartender. It's my job to listen to sob stories." He playfully tossed a bar towel on his shoulder and leaned in. "Lay it on me."

"I told my teammates that I'm retiring. I told them after the game."

Kyle's mouth fell open in mock astonishment. "You didn't play *that* badly."

Eric laughed. "The public announcement will be tomorrow morning. The team is sending out a statement."

"How'd they take it? Your teammates?"

"They seemed shocked. And then, y'know, they joked about how old I am. So they're coping in their own ways." He tapped his fingers against the soda glass. "I guess this is really happening."

He looked so lost. Kyle wanted to take him to the back room and kiss him happy. "Tomorrow will be a shitshow, I'm guessing."

"Yeah," Eric sighed. "I'm not looking forward to it. I'm going to turn my phone off and just, I dunno. Avoid it."

"You don't have a practice tomorrow?"

"No. I wanted to make the announcement on a day off, so I could at least avoid reporters."

Kyle suddenly had a wonderful, terrible idea. "Spend the day with me."

Eric's eyebrows shot up. "Really?"

"Yeah." Kyle shrugged. "I've got a day off tomorrow too. We could, I dunno, watch movies or . . . leave town." He laughed at that, but then thought of an even better idea. "Hey, we could go hiking! I know some great spots outside the city. Have you been to Blue Mountain?"

"I haven't." Eric seemed to be perking up. "That would be great, being outside all day."

Kyle was practically bouncing with excitement now. He'd been in desperate need of some quality outdoors time. "Let's do it! Do you have a car?"

"I do."

"This is going to be awesome. You'll feel like a new man after this."

"Okay." Eric was smiling at him, looking almost as excited as Kyle felt. He also looked like he needed something else from Kyle.

"I'm working until two at least tonight," Kyle said. He stopped there, knowing that Eric would understand what he was saying.

"Right. I figured."

"You should go home," Kyle said gently. "Rest up for our big adventure."

Eric nodded. "Yeah. Okay. Text me when you're awake tomorrow."

"I will." Kyle really wanted to hoist himself up on the bar and kiss him, but he resisted. Frantic kisses on the street aside, they'd never kissed in front of other people. "Bright and early, handsome."

CHAPTER TWENTY-THREE

Eric had been second-guessing his decision to spend the day hiking with Kyle right up until the moment he'd spotted Kyle waiting for him on the sidewalk outside his building. Eric knew it had been irresponsible of him to agree to this outing; he was either leading Kyle on, or letting his own heart be misled. Either way, it was only going to further complicate the way he felt about Kyle. But the way Kyle smiled as Eric pulled the car up in front of him, excitement all over his face, made him not particularly care about bad decisions.

"Yay! Hiking!" Kyle sang.

He'd had his glasses on, and a warm knit hat. He'd looked adorable, and Eric's heart had fluttered uselessly in his chest.

He's not for you, Eric had reminded himself. *Not like that.*

Now they were completely alone, standing together at the top of Blue Mountain and taking in the spectacular view of the Hudson River and the snowy mountains beyond. It had been a perfect day so far. Kyle was an expert hiker, completely in his element on the trails, and Eric felt like he was meeting him for the first time. There was flirty bartender Kyle, and brilliant grad student Kyle, but then there was this man: flushed and happy from a day spent outdoors in the cold.

Eric was falling hard for all sides of Kyle, and he didn't know how to stop it.

"Did you get some good pictures today?" Kyle asked.

"Hm? Oh. Yes, I think so." He thought of the image he'd captured of Kyle, cheeks pink and smiling up at a squirrel he'd spotted in a tree, and was glad he'd lugged his camera along on this hike. "Some really nice ones, actually."

"Good. Maybe that's what you should do after you retire: travel and take photos."

"It might be lonely," Eric said without meaning to. He'd considered doing exactly what Kyle had proposed—it was how Eric had spent a few of his summers. He'd enjoyed traveling alone, but he'd hoped his retirement would be shared with another person. Someone who loved being outdoors and was knowledgeable about history and art. Someone with a gift for languages, and a passion for learning. Someone who made Eric laugh and relax and . . . *want*. When was the last time Eric had wanted anything as much as he wanted Kyle?

This was bad. This was really fucking bad.

"Where would you go?" Eric asked, hoping to derail this dangerous line of thinking. "If you could travel anywhere?"

"Anywhere. Everywhere. I want to see it all, but I've been looking at Greece lately. Maybe do a language course there."

"Sounds nice."

"I want to hike on the Pelion Peninsula."

"And follow in the footsteps of Achilles?"

Kyle grinned. "Exactly. Maybe find a handsome centaur who wants to teach me a few things."

"Is that what you're into? Horses?"

"Nope. Just intelligent older men with thick cocks."

Eric was sure the hike down the mountain wouldn't be improved by having an erection. "Behave," he scolded.

Eric silently told himself to behave too. Last night, when he'd gone to the Kingfisher, he hadn't wanted to make plans for an outing today. He'd wanted Kyle to go home with him, but this unexpected day together was worth so much more than sex.

"Should we keep going?" Kyle asked.

"Sure."

They didn't speak for a while. Kyle walked in front of Eric and kept glancing up at the trees. It was wonderfully quiet on the trail, the silence only interrupted by birds, squirrels, and the occasional gust of wind rattling the tree branches. It was perfect and peaceful and made it far too easy for Eric to think as they walked.

Even just walking behind him, Eric's heart would swell every time Kyle turned his head to look at something, giving him a view of his profile. His pink cheeks, his glasses, his content half smile. He could imagine walking behind him like this in Greece, in Italy. Anywhere Kyle wanted to go.

Or he could imagine quiet nights at home in Manhattan. Maybe reading together on a couch, Kyle's toes tucked under Eric's thighs. Then falling into bed together, laughing and kissing and—

Eric nearly crashed into Kyle, who had stopped abruptly.

"Wh—?"

"Shh," Kyle whispered. "Look."

Eric looked where he was pointing and saw two deer standing in a clearing. He went perfectly still, not wanting to do anything to spook them. The deer stayed for a while, calmly eating something that grew close to the ground. When they finally disappeared into the forest, Eric let out a whoosh of breath. "Wow."

Kyle beamed at him, eyes bright under his glasses. "You don't see that in the city."

"No." Eric's heart was thudding against his ribs. He was filled with a strange adrenaline after being so close to wild animals, even ones as serene as those deer had been. In that moment, Kyle looked achingly beautiful.

Kyle eyed him curiously. "What?"

Eric shook his head. "Nothing."

Kyle stared at him for another beat, then grinned and said, "You know what I could go for after this? Pancakes."

Eric laughed, partly with relief that the tension had been diffused. "I can't remember the last time I ate pancakes."

"Well, that's depressing. There's a diner nearby that serves them all day. I checked."

"You checked out pancake options before our hike?"

Kyle shrugged, still smiling. "I'm from Vermont. We take our pancakes seriously."

Oh god. This version of Kyle was dangerously enchanting. When he was cheerful and flirty and playful, it took down all of Eric's defenses. He wanted nothing more than to press Kyle against a tree and kiss him breathless.

But Kyle had already resumed his trek down the mountain, leaving Eric to trail, spellbound, after him.

An hour later they were sitting in a cozy booth at a classic New Jersey diner. Their server had just dropped off two large plates of pancakes. Eric tended to eat nutrient-packed, high protein meals, and pancakes were mostly empty calories, but he could indulge this once. They smelled amazing.

Eric watched as Kyle poured an ungodly amount of maple syrup on his pancakes.

"Vermont," Kyle reminded him again when he caught him staring. He slid the bottle over to Eric, who poured a modest drizzle on his own plate.

Eric moaned when he had his first bite of pancake. "Oh my god. These are so good."

"Right? You shouldn't deprive yourself of pancakes."

"I don't know if you're a good influence or a bad one."

"Clearly good. Before you met me it was a dark existence of no pancakes and weak orgasms."

Eric nearly spit out his next bite of pancake. He managed to swallow. "That's true." It *was* true. His life had been far from terrible before, but Kyle had made it *fun*.

Kyle was smiling at him now. His cheeks were still rosy from their hike, and his hair was a mess from being stuffed under a hat.

God, he was cute.

Eric tried not to imagine a life with Kyle based on their incredible day together. This day was a special one, and he shouldn't let it mislead him into thinking they could have this every day. That they could be more.

What he hadn't thought about all day was his retirement. The statement had, he assumed, been posted on social media and on the Admirals website that morning, but his phone was turned off and he was blissfully unaware of the reaction to the announcement.

"How are things at work?" he asked.

Kyle seemed surprised by the question. "At work? Fine, I guess. Gus has been even more absent than usual. I wish he cared more about the place. He only shows up often enough to make sure we haven't changed anything. God forbid we improve the place."

Eric had heard Kyle complain about Gus many times. He didn't seem to hate the man—he had actually described him as a sweetheart—but he was frustrated by Gus's apathy toward his business.

"What would you do with the place?" Eric asked. "If you were in charge?"

Kyle blew out a breath. "Well, for one thing we'd have a great cocktail menu. Including zero proof cocktails," he added with a wink. "The décor could use some work. Probably an overhaul, really. I like the cozy tavern vibe, but it shouldn't feel worn out and dirty, y'know?"

"It could use a bit of fixing up," Eric agreed. He'd had the same thoughts about the bar himself. A bit of money and effort could make a world of difference to the place.

"Aram has mentioned wanting to organize more events there. Build more of a Kingfisher community."

"That's a good idea."

"And we actually have a really good chef, but you wouldn't know it. Lucy is way too talented for that place. If she had free rein in that kitchen, we'd have an incredible menu."

Eric took all of this in, considering it. "Sounds like you guys have been thinking a lot about this."

"For *years*. Oh my god. I love the place, seriously, but it needs help. I don't know why Gus doesn't just sell it. Although the new owners might just gut the place and fire us all."

That would be a shame. The Kingfisher had really grown on Eric.

They ate in silence for a few minutes, Kyle devouring his pancakes with gusto, and Eric slowly savoring each maple-sweet, buttery mouthful.

"Thanks for suggesting this today," Eric said when he had finished. "It was exactly what I needed."

"Don't thank me. I'm having a great day."

"Well, I appreciate it, anyway. I know I'm not the most fun person on earth."

"Oh my god. Can you please stop acting like you're my old uncle Eric who I am forced to spend time with? You're my friend, and I don't mind looking at you, so this is all a win for me."

Eric studied him for a minute. Kyle stared right back at him.

"Okay," Eric said finally.

Kyle's brain was a mess for the entire drive back to the city. He liked Eric so much. He wanted to tell him. He wanted to spend the rest of the day and night with him. He wanted to fall in love with him because he knew it wouldn't take much. Just permission.

"Do you have to work tonight?" Eric asked.

"No, thank god. I'm way too tired for that."

He glanced over and noticed that Eric's jaw looked tense. "You're not ready to face it, are you?" Kyle asked gently.

"Nope."

When they reached Chelsea, Kyle said, "Why don't you come up for a bit? We can avoid the real world a little longer."

Eric seemed to consider the offer, and Kyle could sense the rejection coming.

"We both know what will happen if I go upstairs with you," Eric said.

"Yeah. I thought—don't you *want* that to happen?"

Eric's knuckles were tight on the steering wheel, and his jaw was clenched as he stared straight ahead, avoiding Kyle's gaze. "It doesn't matter what I want. We can't keep doing this."

Kyle's heart clenched. "Why?"

"Because I'm not the kind of person who can have sex with a friend and just be cool about it." He dropped his hands into his lap and looked down at them. "I'm confusing what we're doing with something . . . else. Something impossible."

Kyle swallowed around the lump in his throat. "Impossible?"

Eric finally met his gaze, and Kyle could see tears in his eyes. "If things were different, Kyle—"

"No," Kyle interrupted, fury welling inside him. "If you're telling me that you have real feelings for me—that you want *more*—but you think the age difference is too much, then you can stop right now."

"It's true, though."

"I'm not a *kid*."

"And I'm not right for you, Kyle."

Kyle shook his head, tears burning his eyes. "You *are*." He may as well admit it. Nothing to lose now. "You're *perfect* for me. Haven't you noticed how good we are together? It can't just be me who feels it."

Eric smiled sadly back at him. "It's not just you."

"Well then?" Kyle's voice broke on the second word.

"I'll never forgive myself if I let you waste your time on me. Your *youth*."

"Fuck my youth!" It tore out of Kyle, louder than he'd meant it to. "And fuck you for thinking I can't make my own decisions."

Eric lowered his head. "I was twenty-four when I married Holly. And sixteen years later we realized we weren't right for each other."

"So what? So you shouldn't try in case one day you change your mind? You think falling in love isn't worth the risk?"

Eric's eyes went wide, and a tear spilled out, trailing down his cheek into his beard. "I know you think—"

"I *know*. I don't *think*. I know how I feel about you. I want to be with you Eric. I—"

"You said it would be casual," Eric said, a tremor of anger in his voice. "You said sex didn't have to be a big deal. No strings attached, right?"

Kyle sniffed and looked away. "Right. Guess I fucked up." He put his hand on the door handle. "*Again*."

"Kyle . . ."

"Nope. I get it. This isn't what you signed up for. I'm just a kid with a weakness for men who only see me as a fun time."

He opened the door, then turned back and said, bitterly, "You graduated, by the way. Top marks. Thank you for attending Kyle's gay sex school."

"Kyle—"

But Kyle was already out of the car, and slamming the door behind him.

Tears streamed down his face as he walked quickly to the elevator. Why did he keep doing this? Why couldn't he fall for a man who actually wanted to be with him? The worst part was that he wasn't sure Eric didn't want to be with him. If Kyle were a few years older, they'd probably be celebrating their monthiversary for real now. Or maybe Eric had never even considered lowering himself to being in a relationship with a twenty-five-year-old homewrecker.

He finally made it to his apartment, which was mercifully empty, and locked the door firmly behind him. He slumped to the floor, his back to the door, and buried his face in his hands, miserable and frustrated.

CHAPTER TWENTY-FOUR

The thing about the playoffs was that Eric was never sure when his last game would actually be. It was even harder to know when his last *home* game would be.

The last game ended up being an away game in Washington at the end of the first round of the playoffs. The score wasn't even close, so Eric stood alone with his goal posts—his constant companions—and quietly counted down the last ten seconds.

When it was over, he gave the crossbar behind him a pat. "Thanks for everything, fellas. Treat the next generation well, okay?"

It was devastating to not even make it out of the first round, but Eric was touched by the D.C. crowd's standing ovation for him after the game. The arena had put his picture on the big screens as the announcer reminded the crowd that this was Eric's final game. There had been plenty of Admirals fans in the building, but all of the Washington fans were applauding too. Between the crushing blow of elimination and that touching display of affection from the fans, Eric was a blubbering mess when he finally made it to the locker room.

"I'm sorry," he said to Scott, whose eyes were as red and wet as Eric's. "I wanted to take us further."

"We lost together," Scott said firmly, even through his tears. "I'm just sorry your last game wasn't at home."

He hugged him, and then Carter piled on, and soon the entire team was hugging each other with Eric in the very center. He loved these guys so much.

The room was somber for a while, but it wasn't long before Carter had picked the mood back up. "My last game," he said, "is going to be legendary. I'm going to score five goals, and the last one is going to bust a hole right through Dallas Kent."

Everyone laughed and cheered. Eric was grateful for Carter. He didn't think he'd be able to stand it if his last time sharing a locker room with these guys was quiet and miserable.

Eric had had a quiet celebration of his own during their last regular season home game. His family—parents, siblings, nieces and nephews—had all come down from Hamilton to watch the game, and they'd gone out afterward and had spent the next day together. It had been nice, but Eric hadn't been in a celebratory mood for a long time. Not since Kyle had slammed that car door in his face.

It had been two months since that day they'd gone hiking. Two months since he'd seen Kyle, or spoken to him. He'd thought about texting. He'd thought about just showing up at the Kingfisher. He thought about Kyle every single day. But Eric had had the playoffs to focus on, and he still believed that he'd done Kyle a favor by separating himself from him. Being away from him hurt like he'd broken every bone in his body, but it was for the best. Just like a broken bone, this would heal in time.

But god, if only he could have introduced Kyle to his family. He knew it would be a shock whenever he told his family that he was attracted to men. It would be a bigger shock if he introduced Kyle as his boyfriend, but he was starting to not care about shocking people. The truth was that he couldn't stop thinking about Kyle's fierce declaration: *You're perfect for me.*

And despite Eric's hopelessly practical brain telling him otherwise, Eric knew it was true. His *heart* knew it was true.

Kyle had been the brightest thing in Eric's life, and Eric was having a hard time finding joy in anything since he'd lost him. His spare time had mostly been filled with having his living room redecorated to best complement his new painting. Now he spent his nights staring at that painting, alone, and wishing he hadn't gone through so much trouble to accommodate something so bleak. Wondering if he should have instead made room in his life for something warmer.

Eric's thoughts were consumed by Kyle during the team's short flight home that night. Maybe it was the emotional roller coaster of the playoffs, or maybe it was the cliff dive of officially ending his hockey career, but Eric found himself wondering if it wasn't too late to try again with him. Kyle could be with someone else now. He could have forgotten all about Eric. And wasn't that what Eric wanted?

No. God. Even thinking about the possibility of that was agony. Eric didn't want Kyle to be with anyone else. And Eric didn't want to be with anyone but Kyle.

He stared out the window, watching the lights of New York City twinkle up through the darkness. Hockey was over. That chapter of his life was officially done. When he walked off this plane, he would be saying goodbye to his teammates, to his career. And when he thought about the rest of his life, all he knew was that he wanted Kyle in it.

He needed to be fearless, one more time. This time with no masks, and no armor. He needed to go to Kyle with his heart in his hands and apologize for not giving him a chance. For not giving *them* a chance.

And god, he hoped he wasn't too late.

* * *

Kyle froze when Eric walked into the Kingfisher. Hadn't he just played his final game *tonight*? In *Washington*?

Kyle looked for Scott, but he wasn't there. It made sense because Kip wasn't working tonight. This was Eric, alone, and he was striding purposely toward Kyle.

What the hell was this? Was Eric sad about his career being over and was hoping for some distracting, no-strings sex with Kyle? There was no way Kyle was going to agree to that.

Probably.

He steeled himself as Eric approached and said, as blandly as possible, "Hey."

"Hi." Eric's eyes were wide and uncertain. If he had more to say, he didn't seem to be in any hurry to say it.

"What?" Kyle asked finally, patience wearing thin.

"I—" Eric glanced around the bar. "Is there somewhere we could talk? Just for a moment?"

"Why? You looking for some pick-me-up sex? Pass." Kyle made a show of drying a perfectly dry beer stein, hoping to appear uninterested in Eric's presence.

"No, that's not why I'm here at all. I promise. I just . . . I'd really like to talk to you."

"Again, why?"

"Because I need to apologize."

Kyle scoffed. "Took you two months to figure that out, huh?"

"Yes," Eric said earnestly. "It did. But that doesn't mean I wasn't thinking about you every day."

Fuck. Kyle couldn't help the way his heart raced at that. He'd thought about Eric constantly over the past two months with a mixture of anger, sadness, and regret. Looking at him now, so handsome in the suit he must have left the arena in, Kyle couldn't deny that he still wanted him.

He spotted Aram lingering at the table of three very handsome men. "One sec," he told Eric. He walked over to Aram and gently tapped his arm to get his attention.

"What's up?" Aram asked.

"Can you watch the bar for a few minutes? Eric wants to talk to me about something in private." Kyle knew how intriguing this sounded, but it was the best he could come up with.

"Sure," Aram said, though he eyed him curiously.

Kyle walked away before there could be follow-up questions. He led Eric to the storeroom behind the bar. He closed the door firmly behind them, then stood facing Eric, unsure of what to expect.

Kyle folded his arms across his chest defensively. "I've only got a few minutes."

"I'm sorry," Eric said immediately. "I was wrong, and I'm so sorry. I ruined everything, and I wish I'd gone upstairs with you after that hike."

Kyle frowned at him. "You regret not having sex two months ago?"

"No. I regret everything that could have come after having sex two months ago."

Kyle's heart stopped beating. Was this really happening? "What could have happened?"

Eric took a step toward him. "I could have told you how I really feel. That I have loved every moment we've spent together, whether it's having sex or just talking. That I want to have more of those moments. Years of them."

Kyle swallowed, his eyes burning. "Oh." He let those words sink in, then recalled the opposite words Eric had said months ago. "What happened to *people should only date people their own age*? Because I haven't magically aged fifteen years in the past two months."

"I'm sorry I said that. I'm sorry for so many things." Eric gazed imploringly at Kyle. "Do you hate me?"

Kyle relaxed his arms, and sighed. "I've *tried* to hate you."

Eric's lips curved up slightly. "Did it work?"

"No. Fuck, Eric. I can't hate you. I want everything you just said. I've wanted it for months."

Eric was so close now. His gaze kept darting away from Kyle, and he was making a meal of his bottom lip. Kyle would prefer to be the one doing that.

"I want to be with you, Kyle. I want to be your boyfriend. Partner. For as long as you'll have me."

Tears were flowing freely from Kyle's eyes now. He didn't care. He smiled wetly and said, "How dare you tell me this in the backroom at work."

Eric chuckled and stepped toward him. "It wasn't how I planned it."

Kyle wrapped his arms around his neck. "You know I have to go back out there and serve customers after this, right?"

And then Eric's lips were on his, and they were kissing wildly. Kyle's body sang with relief after too many weeks of not having this. Eric gripped Kyle's head, his fingers tangled in his hair, making a mess of it.

"We shouldn't—" Kyle panted, breaking the kiss.

"I know," Eric said, then kissed him again. His hand slipped under the hem of Kyle's T-shirt, pushing it up to expose his stomach.

"Oh, fuck," Kyle gasped. He thrust his hips forward so his crotch could make contact with Eric's, and then went back to devouring him. He couldn't believe this was really happening, and he was so overcome with desire that he was considering fucking Eric in this storeroom.

Eric suddenly stepped away. "Sorry," he said, wiping his mouth with his forearm. His face was flush with arousal, and probably some embarrassment. "I shouldn't have—I didn't mean to—"

"It's okay. I *really* don't mind."

Eric smiled at him like he couldn't believe he was real. Kyle was sure he had the same expression on his own face.

"I want to go to Greece with you," Eric blurted out.

"You do?"

"Yes. Soon. When can you go?"

"I—"

"And I was thinking . . . do you think Gus would sell this place? To me, I mean? And maybe to Scott too. I don't know. I haven't talked to him about it. But I think he'd love to co-own it with me, and you could be the manager and—"

Kyle cut him off with another kiss, but it was sloppy because he was laughing at Eric's uncharacteristic babbling. "That all sounds incredible, but I need to finish my shift right now."

"Okay. Right." Eric kissed him again. "We should talk. After."

"After," Kyle agreed. "I'll be done in an hour."

"Come to my place?"

"It's way past your bedtime. Are you sure?"

Eric leaned in and kissed him again. "Fuck bedtime. I'm retired."

EPILOGUE

"I now pronounce you married," the wedding officiant proclaimed. "You may kiss the heck out of each other."

Everyone laughed and cheered as Scott and Kip did exactly that. Eric's heart swelled, watching them. He caught Kyle's gaze where he stood opposite him, next to Kip. Kyle's eyes were wet, and he smiled at Eric.

It had been a perfect July day that had turned into a perfect evening, with a cool breeze coming off the ocean. The ceremony was happening outside, just as the sun was setting, on a grassy hill that overlooked the Great South Bay. Scott had done a good job making sure the wedding would be a very private event. He had booked the entire resort, and there was no press allowed. This day was just for friends and family.

There were a lot of friends and family, though; over two hundred guests were in attendance, but Eric only had eyes for Kyle. He was unbearably handsome in his tuxedo. Especially with his glasses on.

Scott turned and hugged Eric. "Thank you for being here."

"Wouldn't have missed it. I'm happy for you." Eric meant that wholeheartedly. He was thrilled for his closest friend. And it was nice to be at the wedding of two people who were truly in love with each other. He hoped to have one of those weddings himself someday.

"I'm happy for you too," Scott said. He nodded in Kyle's direction. "He's good for you. You should keep him."

"I hope to."

Scott gave him a final squeeze, then turned to grab his new husband's hand. The guests had all been standing for the short ceremony, and the large crowd swallowed the newlyweds up in a sea of hugs and backslaps.

Kyle stepped toward Eric. "That wasn't too disgusting."

"Not bad at all," Eric agreed.

Kyle leaned in and kissed him, which was a relief after looking at him for so long without being able to touch him. His lips were soft, and a bit cold from standing outside by the ocean, and Eric melted against him.

"Walk with me a bit?" Kyle asked.

Eric took his hand and squeezed it. "Of course."

The inn had a path that led down to the beach. When they reached the sand, Eric slipped his shoes off, then bent to remove his socks. Kyle grinned and did the same. Being with Kyle had made Eric looser. He still liked routine—still exercised, still kept to a healthy diet—but he was more impulsive, and less concerned with what other people thought of him. He didn't feel the need to be perfect, and obviously the weight of having to perform on the ice had been lifted.

Retirement, so far, had been pretty excellent.

He and Scott had officially become the new owners of the Kingfisher a month ago. The renovations were still a work in progress, but they were planning a grand re-opening party for when Scott and Kip returned in August from their month-long European honeymoon. Eric had recommended some spots in Greece that he and Kyle had particularly loved during their own trip at the end of May.

"It's not Crete, but it's not bad," Kyle said now, as they gazed at the Bay together, toes buried in the sand.

On the beach in Crete, Kyle had been exquisite. His damp skin had glistened in the sun, exposed other than where it had been covered by his short swimsuit. Eric had snapped a photo of him peeking back over his shoulder, his long bare legs outstretched on the sand. That photo was now in a frame in Eric's bedroom. He thought, if he'd had his camera with him now, he could take an equally stunning photo of Kyle in his tuxedo in the purple early evening light.

They still lived apart, but Kyle spent most nights at Eric's. Eric hoped he would move in with him eventually, but he knew moving out would complicate things for Maria, unless Kyle just never bothered telling his parents he wasn't living there anymore. It was a very real option Kyle had been considering. Why not let his shitty, rich parents pay for an apartment for his friend?

"We should go back to Greece," Eric said. "Soon."

"We just got back!"

"I know, but . . ." Kyle was always a delight, but in Greece he had truly come alive. Besides enjoying how great he'd looked in a bathing suit, Eric had been constantly impressed by Kyle's knowledge when they'd toured historic sites and museums, and by how easily he had translated Greek for him. He'd loved hearing him speak the language to the locals. After full days of being turned on by Kyle's brain, Eric had been eager to ravish his body at night.

"We should go somewhere else. Italy, maybe." Kyle clapped his hands together. "Sicily!"

"Anywhere you like," Eric said. It was true. Kyle could suggest the city dump and Eric would follow him happily.

"For now we should probably go back inside. The important part of the reception is probably about to start."

"Probably." Eric stole another kiss, and then they walked back up to the inn to celebrate the marriage of the friends who had inadvertently brought them together.

"What if I just asked him to dance?"

Kyle grinned at Maria, who was staring at Matti Jalo's back across the room. "Then he'd be the luckiest man in the world."

Maria straightened her shoulders, which made her breasts look even more incredible. "I'm going to do it."

"Maybe wait for a slow song?" Kyle gestured toward the DJ, who was, at the moment, playing a Pitbull party anthem.

"Right. Okay. Good. Time for another glass of wine then."

Kyle laughed as she marched toward a server with a tray of full wineglasses. A moment later, strong, familiar arms wrapped around him from behind.

"Having fun?" Eric asked.

"So much fun." Kyle turned to face him. "Where were you?"

"Talking to some of the guys. You know."

"Miss them already?"

Eric scrunched his nose. "Almost."

"You want to dance to Pitbull?"

"No."

Kyle kissed him. The music changed to a slow song, and Eric said, "I could maybe handle this one."

They held hands as they walked together onto the dance floor. The song was a wedding staple—Elvis Presley's "Can't Help Falling in Love"—but wrapped in the arms of the man he loved, Kyle felt like the first time he had ever heard it.

He brushed his lips against Eric's ear and murmured, "Do you remember when this song came out?"

Eric snorted. "Fuck you."

Kyle laughed against Eric's neck. He'd made a lot of jokes

about Eric's age when they'd been in Greece, exploring ancient temples.

"Hey," Eric whispered. "Maria is dancing with Matti."

Kyle whipped his head around in a completely nonsubtle way. He quickly spotted Matti, since he was the tallest one in the room, and sure enough, Maria had her arms stretched all the way out to circle his neck. They were gazing at each other and smiling, and Kyle *really* hoped tonight would be the night they hooked up because it had become increasingly clear that Matti was into her.

"Look at how hard he's crushing on her," Kyle said, grinning. "He'd be a fool not to make his move tonight."

"Well, some people just need a little time, y'know?"

"Not everyone is as sexually confident as I am," Eric agreed.

The road to becoming a real couple had been a strange one for Eric and Kyle, but Kyle couldn't be happier with where it had led them. He loved that they were building a business together at the same time as they were deepening their relationship. Everything in Kyle's life was so perfect right now that he was worried about the other shoe dropping.

But there was no reason to think about that now. Not while he was dancing with his wonderful boyfriend in a room full of their friends.

"I love you," he said. They said it to each other all the time, but it hadn't gotten old yet.

Eric kissed him, pausing their rotations on the dance floor. Kyle melted into it, lightheaded despite only having drunk one glass of wine.

"I love you too," Eric said when they finally broke the kiss. And then he yawned.

"Past your bedtime?" Kyle teased.

"I *have* been looking forward to being in a bed with you for a few hours now." Eric's eyes sparkled with mischief.

"God, I've created a monster."

"*Your* monster," Eric growled. Then he nipped Kyle's earlobe.

The song ended, and Eric squeezed Kyle tight against him. "I'm so glad you're in my life. I'm sorry it wasn't sooner."

Kyle placed a hand on Eric's cheek and gazed at the man who had finally been worthy of his heart. "You saved your best years for me, gorgeous."

Don't miss Role Model, *the next book in Rachel Reid's Game Changers series, available wherever books are sold.*

GAME CHANGERS
HOCKEY UNIVERSE

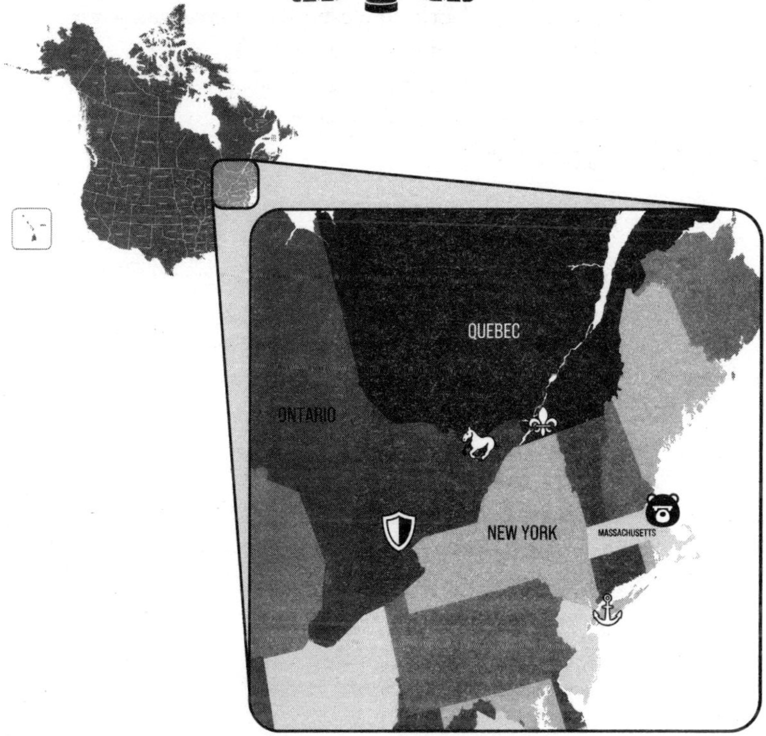

LEGEND:

1	**Toronto Guardians**	Ryan Price (*Tough Guy*), Troy Barrett (*Role Model*)
2	**Ottawa Centaurs**	Shane & Ilya (*Heated Rivalry/The Long Game*), Troy Barrett (*Role Model*)
3	**New York Admirals**	Scott Hunter (*Game Changer*), Eric Bennett (*Common Goal*)
4	**Montreal Voyageurs**	Shane Hollander (*Heated Rivalry*)
5	**Boston Bears**	Ilya Rozanov (*Heated Rivalry*)

ACKNOWLEDGMENTS

As always, a huge thank-you to my amazing editor, Mackenzie Walton, who makes everything I write so much better. To my husband, Matt, and my kids for their support and patience. To my agent, Deidre Knight, for believing in me. To everyone who has told me they like my books, because it truly does mean a lot and your encouragement pushes me to keep writing when I'm frustrated and tired. And to the app that allows me to watch live NHL games on my iPad while I'm writing so I can multitask.

NEW YORK TIMES BESTSELLING AUTHOR

RACHEL REID

GAME CHANGERS

Don't miss the rest of *New York Times* bestselling author Rachel Reid's Game Changers series—the inspiration for the #1 hit streaming show *Heated Rivalry*!

Be the first to find out about promotions, news and exclusive content by following our socials **@HarlequinBooks** or visiting **Harlequin.com/GameChangers**

TikTok